GOODBYE, LARK LOVEJOY

GOODBYE, LARK LOVEJOY

A NOVEL

KRIS CLINK

The Enchanted Rock Series, Book 1

Published by SparkPress, a BookSparks imprint,
A division of SparkPoint Studio, LLC
Phoenix, Arizona, USA, 85007
www.gosparkpress.com

Published 2021
Printed in the United States of America
Print-ISBN: 978-1-68463-073-8
E-ISBN: 978-1-68463-074-5

Library of Congress Control Number: 2020917550

Interior design by Tabitha Lahr

To Marissa and Sharla—
you know all my secrets and still love me.

My Summit Sisters, Julie, Amy, & Jamie—
you never left me (or the purse) behind.

Lindsey, Jamie, Brad, & Kenzie—you're always in my heart.

And,
to Mike—
you always knew.

Contents

One

Would the neighbors notice if I set fire to their hedge? Lark tightened her grip on the jogging stroller. *Just one match, maybe two would do it.* She held her breath and increased her pace until the border of yellow roses was behind her. *A rose by any other name still smells like a funeral spray.*

She drained her lungs and glanced over her shoulder at five-year-old Jamie. Despite Houston's Jell-O-thick humidity, the boy pedaled wildly. *Ding. Ding. Ding.* Jamie thumbed the bell on his "big-kid bike" and slowed at a grassy space residents had nick-named "Doggy-Doo Boulevard."

"Mom, what's that mean?" he asked, pointing to a sign staked below a belt of loblolly pines.

"Means I'm paying too darn much in HOA dues."

"Says *that*?" His forehead crinkled.

"It says, THERE IS NO POOP FAIRY." She shook her head at the latest on the subdivision's common grounds and Jamie's mouth bent into a half-smile, suggesting she'd piqued his interest.

Braking, he shot her a thoughtful look, like he was rolling the words around in his mind. "A *poop* fairy? What's a *poop* fairy?" he asked. "Like a tooth fairy?"

Lark's gaze caught on the boy's dark eyes—so much like his father's. But Jamie didn't just share his father's name and dark features. The pair were cut from the same squeaky clean, impeccably folded fabric.

"It's a funny way to ask people to clean up after their dogs," she explained. Jamie seemed satisfied by that, and they continued their trek through Bayou Cove, a neighborhood shoehorned between Memorial and River Oaks where, in recent years, affluent young professionals like Lark and her late husband had breathed new life into houses built during the Nixon era. This Saturday morning was especially quiet; many families had sneaked off to Galveston and Lake LBJ for a long weekend before their children returned to school.

A cloying bitterness gripped Lark's throat as they passed an idle T-ball tee awaiting Daddy's return and a wooden placard boasting a family's loyalty to the All Saints football team. Wherever she looked, stately homes brandished the trappings of domestic life like trophies.

The hollow *whomp* of a basketball hitting a backboard drew Jamie's attention, and he stopped pedaling to gape at a man and his teenage son shooting baskets in their driveway. The man waved to Lark as the teen stood still to watch the basketball arc and drop into the basket.

"Did you see that?" Jamie asked, his eyes wide.

Like children staring into a toy store, Lark and Jamie watched with envy.

"Sure did." She swallowed and turned away to peek over the top of the stroller.

Charlie was unusually quiet. His cheeks were rosy from the heat, and a hand covered his eyes as he dozed—a rarity for the toddler, who'd jettisoned naps before his third birthday. The pint-size force of nature, who had his mother's wavy blond hair and clear blue eyes, had remained in constant motion since he screamed his way into this world.

Stillness is overrated.

For three years, their house had been a hub of activity—relentless visits from friends, family, and nursing staff. A brief season of sympathy and casseroles had ended abruptly, after which point Lark felt like their home had been relocated to another planet.

People hadn't trickled back into their lives as she had expected. Spontaneous run-ins tended to fall on the side of a distant wave, the other parties careful not to get too close in case widowhood, like a virus, was catching. Most couldn't mask their pity with a paper sack, and if Lark heard "bless your heart" one more time, she'd scream.

The ones who knew Lark and James least intimately were boldest. They'd stare at Lark and her boys like a family of homeless refugees, or nose around like gossip reporters.

"Are you keeping the house?"

"Are you staying in Houston?"

"Are you dating?"

"Is it hard doing it all by yourself now that he's gone?"

She glazed over these queries with polite smiles, repaying their sympathy with her own. As her father said, "It takes a certain breed of stupid not to know when you're being offensive."

Women in James's former law practice sent text messages— "How are the boys?" and "Praying for you" and "Anything we can do for you?" But they didn't invite her to their homes, and they didn't say, "Let's do lunch." Their texts were like one-and-done greeting cards—once sent, forgotten.

In part, her loneliness was her creation. The same wall she'd erected to keep prying eyes from witnessing her husband's rapid decline had remained standing, formidably tall, after his death. Recognizing her part in this, she'd taken charge and reached out to old friends after the memorial, only to find that while she cared for her husband, life had gone right on by for everyone else. New jobs. Fresh hobbies. People were busy—so, so busy. Tennis. Junior League. Church. Yoga. Pilates.

Whatever.

She was beginning to wonder if she'd outgrown her old life—or, perhaps, it had outgrown her? Either way, something had to give.

Even Lark's parents had stopped coming to town, not that she blamed them. They'd put their lives on hold, making the five-hour drive whenever they could, during James's illness. Following the memorial, they'd begun remodeling their home and staying in touch via phone.

While her mother debated the merits of soapstone versus granite and discussed paint finishes and textiles, Lark listened and responded appropriately, hungry for adult interaction. She missed her family and had offered to pack up her boys for a weekend in Fredericksburg more than once, but her mother wasn't having it, citing concerns about the boy's safety. "It's a full-on construction zone," Millie maintained.

Had the fortress of Lark's childhood memories fallen victim to the latest trends?

Turning onto their block, Jamie slowed, as he always did at that point in their route, watching for his mother's signal.

Finally, Lark said, "Race you home."

"Vroom, vroom!" he revved.

She followed his red bike helmet like a beacon. When a white Mercedes sedan slowed in front of their home, she directed him to move to the sidewalk and tossed a nonchalant wave at the car's occupant.

Lark pulled the house key from the tiny pocket on the back of her running shorts and met Jamie on the porch. No sooner had she pushed the stroller over the threshold, she heard a car door snap closed.

"Somebody's here, Mom," Jamie said quietly, careful not to rouse his brother.

"Stay here. I'll be right back." She stepped back outside and pulled the door shut behind her.

"Mrs. Mead?" Auburn hair swept the shoulders of the woman's Lilly Pulitzer shift dress, and her heels clacked against the brick pavers like tap shoes.

"Yes," Lark said, not recognizing her.

"Sorry to bother you. Taffy Teegan—I'm a realtor. I have a client who looked at your house, back before you bought it?"

The hairs stood up on Lark's neck, and she straightened her posture. *Here comes another vulture, looking to pick over the leftovers.* Houston's market was tight, and since James died, the frequency of unsolicited real estate offers had increased.

"My clients are expecting. Three boys already, so they're hoping this one's a girl."

"How nice."

"They're looking for a larger home and wondered if you were interested in selling?"

"No, thank you," the words flew from Lark's mouth like a song she knew by heart.

A tense smile remained on Taffy's face but her feet didn't budge.

"Taffy?" Lark asked in a near-whisper. "Is that your name?" She angled her head to one side and peered through the woman. Taffy was a name fit for a cat or a stripper, not for a seemingly professional woman.

"Yes." She laughed. "When it came to naming me, my parents weren't particularly kind."

"Here's the deal, Taffy." Lark didn't amend her expression. "Just because a woman's husband dies, she doesn't have to pull up stakes and run away. My sons and I are alive and well, and no matter how many times *you people* come by uninvited, I'm not changing my mind—we are not leaving."

"I understand, and I'm sorry." Taffy fidgeted with her key fob. "I've walked in your shoes."

Like a lioness might play with a taffy-flavored gazelle before slicing into it with her teeth, Lark tossed out, "My shoes?"

Taffy lifted the pair of black sunglasses holding her hair back and gestured with them. "My twins were eight. Glioblastoma." Her mouth clicked. "He went quick—I'll give him that."

A wave of guilt slammed Lark's senses. "I'm so sorry."

"For your loss?" Taffy grinned. "If I had a nickel."

"Right." Lark pumped her head and smiled. "How are your twins?"

"Thanks for asking. They're good, in college, so I'm pounding the pavement to pay tuition." She waved the solemnity away, gesturing to the other homes. "Anyway, I'm not sure if you're aware, but some of these have doubled in value since you bought."

Lark gave a skeptical tip of the head. "Doubled?"

"Last month, that colonial behind you sold for one point eight. Supply is slim and demand is high in Bayou Cove."

The front door creaked open and a barefoot Charlie sneaked out and ran to Lark's side.

"Charlie!" An exasperated Jamie chased behind. "We're s'posed to wait inside."

"He's fine." Lark ran a hand over Charlie's head, teasing a curl with her fingertip. She cleared her throat, redirecting her gaze to the woman. "I'm sorry. I can't help you."

"If you want to talk—about houses, or . . ." She arched her brows. "Anything else, call or text me." Short, nude fingernails held a business card. Lark took it, and Taffy's mouth bent into an understanding smile. "Take care."

"Thank you." Lark lingered a second more. "Know what? Big guy's starting kindergarten soon." Lark winked at Jamie. "But . . ." she lifted the card and gave it a confident shake. "If I change my mind, I'll call you."

"I'd appreciate that. Until then, I'll let you get back to your boys." Taffy clacked back to her car.

After the front door snapped closed behind her, Lark stood in the foyer and fanned herself with the card. A second later, a mechanical *whirr* blasted a chill over her skin. "Thank you, baby Jesus, for air conditioning." She dropped the card on a chest guarding the entrance.

"Yeah," Jamie agreed, and fanned himself. "Are we getting a new house?"

"No, honey."

"She said somebody wants ours."

"Don't miss a thing, do you?"

"No." He gave her a shy smile.

"It's not for sale, so they'll have to find another house."

"Oh." He pulled at the shorts drooping below his narrow hips. "Wish we *were*." His eyes widened. "What if we could live at Grammy and Poppy's? That would be cool."

"We're good right here, sport."

Jamie's shoulder nudged up and he lifted Taffy's business card. He turned it over in his hands and his lips twisted as he tried to read. "Two . . . I don't know that one."

"What's it mean?" he asked, pointing to the writing on the back of the card.

She bent over his shoulder, and read, *$2M*, soundlessly.

"Means your mom might need to make a phone call. Can I have that?"

AFTER LUNCH, LARK PEELED BACK the drapes flanking the windows of her formal dining room and smiled at the pair of palm trees bordering the front walk.

Those trees had caught their attention when they'd first looked at the house ten years earlier. Closer investigation had revealed flaking white paint, sagging gutters, and cracked concrete. But despite that—and despite the past owner's attachment to avocado green and harvest gold finishes—Lark had seen a heart that she'd known would carry them through anything. James hadn't been sure about a heart, but he'd agreed the house had good bones.

Emboldened by HGTV remodels, they'd taken a leap of faith—committed to sanding battered woodwork, stripping orange wallpaper and gold shag carpet, tearing out gold tile, and banishing every gaudy speck of the 1960s. A year later, they'd transformed it into a haven where they'd started their family and where James had spent his last days.

It had been a passion project and staying there now felt like a way to remain connected to the life she'd shared with James. In her heart, though, she knew he wasn't there anymore. Little by little, that life they'd shared seemed farther and farther away, leaving Lark feeling like Miss Havisham, living in the past as she forced herself to relocate her identity.

Their home wasn't going to bring James back to her and it wasn't going to make the pain disappear, yet she wasn't willing to move so another family could live the life she and James were supposed to enjoy.

She could hear Dr. Phil asking, "How's that working for you, Lark?"

When she realized it wasn't Dr. Phil's voice but that of her brother Harlan, a forest ranger on Idaho's Snake River, she picked up the phone.

"How's life on the Snake?" she asked when Harlan answered.

"Quiet." Harlan's voice was as deep as Sam Elliott's and smooth as if he gargled with single-malt scotch. "What's up?"

"I can't believe I'm going to say this, but I might sell our house."

"Can't blame you. It's a lot of house for you guys. Heck, it's a lot of house for the Brady Bunch, but whatever floats your boat."

"Yeah, well, this morning while we were outside, a realtor showed up and said some of these houses have doubled in value since we bought."

"Wouldn't be surprised—you guys practically rebuilt the thing. Think you'll stay in Houston?"

"Haven't really given it any thought."

"What's keeping you there?"

"Kindergarten in a month."

"Newsflash—they have schools outside of Houston. Look, moving there was about James. Now, it's your turn to choose."

"Where would I go?"

"Wherever you want. Now's the time, before he starts school. I know it's a fun city, but, man. That place stresses me out."

"It can stress me out too."

"Don't want to end up like Dad."

"Old and grumpy?"

"Rushing to the hospital with chest pain."

"Come again?" she asked.

"His heart trouble."

"What heart trouble?" An icy prickle flew up her spine.

"You didn't know?"

"Does it sound like I knew? Spill it, Harlan."

"I don't know. I guess it was last month, Mom took him in with chest pain. They put him in for the night and inserted a stent the next day. Mom said he's good to go now."

"Mom and I must've spoken a hundred times about their frigging remodel. Not one word about Dad's heart." Anger seeped into her words. "Are you telling me everything? He's really alright?"

"As far as I know. I didn't know they hadn't told you. I'll bet they didn't want you to worry."

"I could've been there with them. What else haven't they told me?"

"That's all I've got."

"Hey, I've got to go," she said, her mind already forming her next conversation. "Love you."

"Love you, too. Give 'em hell." Harlan laughed.

"You can bet I will."

Two

"Damsel in distress, I am not," Lark spat into the bathroom mirror. "When they call back, I'm going to give them *hell, all right.*" She tugged the elastic band holding her hair. Her curls shook loose and she leaned in for a tighter examination. "What the . . ."

She gave a cynical laugh at a new sprinkling of white hairs playing at her hairline. "Well, you certainly earned them."

Her phone rang and MOM flashed on the screen beneath her mother's face.

It's go-time.

"What's wrong?" Unease stippled Millie Lovejoy's voice.

"Why do you ask?" Lark would make her mother work for it.

"Your message on the machine. You sounded upset. Are the boys okay?"

"If something happened with the boys, wouldn't I call you?" *Reel her in slowly. Then give her all you've got.*

"I'd hope so. What's this all about?"

"Hypothetically, let's say you or Dad had a cardiac event. One of you'd call me, wouldn't you?" There was a long pause. "Right, Mom? You'd call?"

"Yes."

"Interesting, because Harlan and I were shooting the breeze earlier and he mentioned a trip Dad made to the hospital. Apparently, I was the only one in the family who didn't know about it."

"I'm sorry, honey. We didn't want you to worry. They put in a stent. That's all. He's fine."

"Now . . ." Lark infused a pound of sarcasm into that tiny word. "Tell you this much. If Harlan or I ever kept something like that from you, there'd be hell to pay."

"We didn't want to add to your—"

"Cut it out, Mom. I'm an adult."

"Okay. Fine. Next time one of us goes to the doctor, you can haul the boys across half of Texas and see for yourself that we're fine."

"Dad didn't just 'go to the doctor.' I would've wanted to be there for him. Things happen to people your age."

"Thank you for the reminder." Millie huffed a breath. "If the doctor said your dad was in trouble, I would've called you."

"I wish I believed you, Mom. You have to stop treating me like I'm broken."

"You're not broken, but—"

"But *what*? You think I'm going to roll into the fetal position when life goes south? I'd say I've proven I can manage."

"Honey, you've managed beautifully."

"Don't patronize me. What if every time you called to check in on us when James was sick, you heard, 'Nothing to see here? Go back to your embroidery.' Trust works both ways."

"We do trust you, but you've been through so much—"

"Mom."

"Fine. We should've called."

"Next time, let *me* decide if I'm going to worry."

"I'm sorry, and, yes. I will."

"Thank you. How's he doing?"

"Your dad? He'd be doing better if he'd finish the yardwork."

"Not too concerned with the lawn, Mom. How's his heart?"

"He's fine. Tell you what, the house is almost finished. Why don't you and the boys come for a visit so you can see for yourself?" Millie's voice turned cheerful. "Can you manage a weekend before school begins?"

"Maybe more than a weekend."

"How's that?"

"Time to make some changes."

"I don't understand."

True on so many levels.

"There's really nothing for me here anymore."

"What do you mean nothing for you there? All those friends? I never saw so many people at one funeral."

"Those were James's friends and coworkers, not mine."

"You can go back to the domestic violence shelter."

Fresh pain welled up at the mention. "I thought so." Lark sighed. "But since they got a grant, they don't need a pro bono attorney anymore. The new director said she'd call if they get into a bind. That was two months ago."

She was walking through the house as she talked, and she peeked in on the boys on the sofa in the den. They were unaware of her presence, eyes glued to a *PAW Patrol* cartoon. She strolled into the ridiculously unused dining room.

"Oh, honey. I'm sorry to hear that," Millie said.

"I'm not surprised. I canceled more than I showed up during James's last year. Last time I went in, I felt like I didn't belong. The staff didn't know who I was."

Most days, I don't recognize myself either.

"Maybe James's firm has something?"

Lark cringed. The firm was as cutthroat as law firms got. "They're not interested in a fair-weather attorney."

"What are you trying to say?"

Lark pulled back one of the twelve smoky-blue velvet chairs surrounding the dining room table and sat down. Chosen by a decorator, the chairs were attractive but as comfy as a metal bench. She set a hand on the table and ran a finger over the inlay—a line of silver embedded seamlessly within the wood. A lovely accent but cold, so very cold.

She jerked her hand back and pulled it to her chest. Deep in her bones, she knew what she had to do, but she wasn't sure how to form the words; once she spoke them, she might not be able to turn back. She tamped down her hesitation and breathed out, "I guess . . . well, what if I came home?"

"Here, home? To visit or live?"

"To live." Saying it was like coming up for air and being met by a warm spring rain.

"How can you leave that magnificent home?" Millie asked.

Is she kidding? There were days Lark felt like the house might swallow her whole. She closed her eyes and her mind was flooded with images of her childhood home—her old bedroom, the line of grapevines she and her father had planted, the live oaks, the scent of her mother's lemony-clean kitchen.

"The schools *are* excellent here." As a fourth-grade teacher at Gillespie Primary, Millie knew the lay of the land. "We don't want Jamie's bright mind to go unnoticed by a teacher overwhelmed with less prepared students." Her voice rose with excitement. "Plus, there's a fine nursery school for Charlie at the Methodist church. And your dad can ask his attorney friends about jobs for you. You'll be back to work in no time. Oh, honey, I'm so excited!"

The next thing Lark knew, her father had been passed the phone.

"Your mom's crying and smiling. Can't tell if she's happy or sad. What'd you say to her, kid?"

Lark filled him in while Millie chattered on in the background. Miraculously, Frank seemed to absorb both conversations.

"New Braunfels is close enough for James's parents to see the boys whenever they want," Lark said.

"That good or bad?" Frank asked.

"Be nice."

"I am nice." He chuckled. "Seriously, though, leaving Houston doesn't sound like you."

"Think I should stay?"

"Nah. Houston's a madhouse. Wouldn't raise a cat there. But you're an adult. Doesn't mean a hill of beans what I think."

"Not true, Dad. I trust your opinion."

"Hmm. Well, what can I do to help?"

"We'll need a place to live."

"Prepare to fork over big bucks—since the high rollers discovered the Hill Country, home prices have gone nuts. Why don't you and the boys stay here for a while? Your mom has fixed it up nice. Then you can take your time. See how it works for you. If it doesn't, you can pack up and try somewhere else while the boys are still young."

"Counting my summer internship in Calistoga, I've lived four places in my life. Wandering isn't my style. If I'm coming home, it's to stay."

"Music to my shell-shocked ears," he said.

"Dad, I called earlier to talk about your heart."

"My heart's fine."

"I heard that much . . . from Harlan," she said flatly.

"SNAFUs happen to a body as old as mine. Doc's got me all fixed up now."

"I'm glad, but I sure wish you would've told me."

"Didn't want to bother you."

"You're never bothering me. Hearing about you from Harlan, weeks after it happened . . ." Tears pricked her eyelids. "You hurt my feelings."

"Aw, kid. We weren't trying to keep secrets, just didn't want you to worry. I'm sorry we hurt you."

"Just like you guys wanted to be there for me, it's important for me to support you. Next time, promise you or Mom will call?"

"I hear you, kid. Here's hoping, there won't be a next time. But I promise."

"Dad?"

"Yeah?"

"I love you."

THE NEXT AFTERNOON, LARK MADE a pitcher of iced tea and invited Taffy Teagan to join her on the rear patio. They enjoyed pleasant conversation while the boys chased invisible bad guys around the wooden play set in the yard.

Lark shook her head. "'Everything happens for a reason' is the one that just kills me."

"That one has to be the worst," Taffy said.

"What reason? I didn't drop enough change into the Salvation Army bell-ringer's bucket while I was rushing into Target for a pack of diapers?"

"A reason? How about this one? God needed another angel up there."

"Holy Mary, mother of Jesus, if I never hear that one again it'll be too soon."

"Can I get an amen?" Taffy cocked her head to one side. "I loved him, but my husband was not angel material. And try explaining to two teary girls why their daddy got called up to the army in the sky."

Lark set a hand on Taffy's arm. "How about, 'He's in a better place'?"

Taffy eyed Lark's house dramatically. "Must've been a hell of a place to make him want to leave this one." She took a sip of her tea.

"Look, Mom!" Charlie screamed across the yard, waving from the top of the fort.

"Nice job, little man," Lark shouted back. When he disappeared inside the wooden structure, she turned to Taffy. "Oh, what about 'God only gives us as much as we can handle'?"

Taffy shuddered. "Most of the time, I tune out and remind myself they mean well. They don't know what to say, so they just say whatever absurd line pops into their heads, and we're so numb it flies right past us."

"Isn't that the truth?" For the first time since James died, Lark felt understood. "The one that really stuck in my craw was 'In time, you'll move on.' Like, after a designated time, a buzzer will go off, and a voice from beyond will say, 'Excuse me, Mrs. Mead. You've grieved enough. Now you can forget your husband and move along to the next one.' Moving on, the myth of widowhood."

"My niece forwarded a TED Talk about these Indonesians who keep their deceased loved ones around the house for months, even years." At Lark's shocked expression, Taffy added, "They're preserved, and the family dresses them, moves them around, sets a place for them at dinner like their dead grandma's still alive."

"Are you still speaking to this niece?" Lark asked.

"Yes, she's a sweetheart. Turns out she was on to something. See, that particular Indonesian community has grieving down to a fine art. They don't throw together a memorial service when they're in shock; they take their time adjusting to the loss. Out of sight doesn't mean out of mind."

"Amen."

"They believe in honoring the relationships, and they don't get into a rush or worry about other people's expectations. It takes as long as it takes. When they find closure—whatever that means to them—they plan a lavish funeral and the whole town celebrates the person's life. At the end, they sacrifice a water buffalo."

"Ick." Lark winced.

"The buffalo's like a transport vehicle to the afterlife."

"Interesting," Lark said. *And disturbing.*

Taffy waved her hands. "I'm not telling you about it because I endorse the storing of dead bodies or the killing of innocent animals—I'm just saying that our emotional attachments don't dissolve into thin air when someone dies. We can't toss those feelings into a big box and hope a day will come when we can open it up and not feel anything. We can keep the love we feel for our husbands, carry it with us wherever we go, even into the next relationship."

"Not sure there's going to be a next relationship—ever." Lark stared at the play fort, at Jamie and Charlie, and considered what she'd just heard. *Can it be so simple? Can I carry my love for James wherever I go?* "But I like that idea."

Taffy raised her tea glass. "So, here's to loving them, wherever they are."

"And here's to those poor water buffaloes," Lark said, clinking her glass against Taffy's.

"You're funny," Taffy said.

"I used to be. Not anymore. Not since . . ." Realizing her forehead was locked in a frown, Lark forced it to relax. "Speaking of moving on, tell me about these clients of yours."

"No pressure, if you're not ready."

"Doesn't commit me to anything to hear you out. If the price is right, I might become a disciple of the 'things happen for a reason' concept."

"They're willing to offer two." Taffy added a wincing smile. "I don't think they'll go much higher."

"Two?" Lark swallowed. "Million? Sight unseen?"

Taffy nodded. "I told you—they really want it."

Lark could practically hear James screaming, "Get packing," from the heavens.

IN THE NEXT WEEKS, LARK deployed a burst of energy like never before in her life. She might as well have strapped a rocket pack to her thin frame. She buzzed through closets with abandon, donating clothing and toys and selling all but a few select pieces of furniture. She sent Charlie's crib and a dozen or so boxes to her parents' home, and movers carted the rest to a storage facility in Fredericksburg for safekeeping.

After the moving truck pulled away that afternoon, the neighbors commandeered Lark and her boys for a last-minute sendoff, complete with hot dogs, cupcakes, and bottomless margaritas for the adults.

The next morning—Lark's thirty-eighth birthday—she woke in no mood to celebrate. Aside from having slept next to two whirligig boys on an air mattress, the previous day's margaritas were now supplying a pulsing bass inside her head, leaving little room for normal thoughts.

Damn if that car refuses to pack itself.

The boys darted through the vacant house, caught up in their own superhero adventure, while Lark deflated their temporary bed. With the press of a button, the mattress crinkled into a dispirited, unwieldy pancake.

But then came the hard part. Lark worked herself into a sweat trying to cram the mattress back into its bag. Whoever had packaged the mattress had failed to include a warning label: RETURNING MATTRESS TO *EASY CARRY BAG* MAY INDUCE THE DROPPING OF F-BOMBS.

"Easy carry bag, my ass. This is like cramming a baby elephant back into his mother's womb."

After a considerable amount of time, she managed to stuff most of the thing into the bag and decided that was good enough. She heaved it to the attached garage and dropped it into the already overfilled way back of her Toyota Sequoia.

Mother trucker, this isn't my day for Tetris. Lark willed the mess to reorder itself. "Fit. C'mon. Fit. Fit. Fit. Dammit." To make space for the bag, she shifted items, knocking loose a lidded plastic box and sending it crashing to the garage floor in a clicking, thwacking, clunking LEGO tsunami of epic proportions.

"Mooommmm," Jamie called from the house. "Mommm." His voice dampened as he appeared beside her with her phone in his hand. His shoulders wilted forlornly when he saw his precious blocks scattered across the floor.

"Don't worry," she said. "I'll get them before we leave."

"Okay." He pushed some blocks to the side with his foot, then blinked a few times and pushed the phone at her. "You got a picture."

After squinting at the screen for a few seconds, Lark felt herself blush. "Happy birthday to Mommy," she murmured at a GIF containing a half-naked Chippendales dancer jiggling his happy-birthday-wishing hips.

"Yeah," Jamie said, unaware his mother was enjoying Hottie McChippendales's slippery six-pack. He rubbernecked into the crook of her arm. "Why's he wearing his swimsuit?"

The question jerked Lark from Beefcake Station and reawakened her mom brain. "Um, well." Lark rummaged for a child-friendly explanation for the man's shimmery gold . . . what were those? Pants?

Sure, pants.

"Well, he's at a party, like the one you went to for Nate?" After a long blink, she swiped the image away and shoved the phone into the waistband of her yoga pants.

"Nate had a *clown* at his party, Mom." His mouth pinched to one side.

"Yes. Yes, Nate *did* have a . . . clown." She swallowed on the last word and cut her chin to the side, glancing at the ceiling. "An interesting choice." She shrugged. "To each his own. Can you help me pick these up?" She slid to her knees, and her kneecap met the knife edge of a LEGO figure. "Holy shhhh—"

"You okay, Mom?" Jamie patted her arm.

She bent down and picked up the offending gray toy, teeth clenched.

"You found my Aquaman Black Manta shark!" His eyes sparkled with elation.

"Make you a deal—you keep an eye on your brother, I'll finish up here?"

He nodded, and she set the toy in his hand.

"Charlie, Mom found Aquaman," he shouted as he ran into the house.

Lark removed the phone from her waistband and relaxed against the bumper for a second assessment of the baby-oiled, bedroom-eyed, buff-beyond-words gentleman. It *was* her birthday, after all.

Her ringer cut the moment short, however, and her brother's photo replaced the GIF.

"Harlan," she said in a lackluster voice.

"Happy birthday," he said.

"You remembered?" She laughed. "How's your day going?"

"Not bad." Harlan Lovejoy was a man of few words. "You're really doing this?"

"Yep."

"Hope Mom doesn't make you crazy."

"Why would she make me crazy?" Lark affected her mother's voice: "Sashay your pretty little self into the ladies' room, wipe the raccoon from your eyes, brush your hair, and swipe a touch of color on your lips—not too much or you'll look like you're trying too hard. *Voilà*. You've got life handled."

"Scary how much you can sound like her."

"Years of practice."

"CHARLIE," Jamie growled from the house.

"Duty calls. I'd better run."

"Drive safe. Love you."

"Love you too," she said.

AFTER SHE CONFIRMED THAT HER boys weren't killing each other, Lark sneaked up to the master closet and dragged James's ashes from the shelf. She carried him protectively down to the garage, placed him in the passenger seat, and padded the surrounding space with a baby quilt. "You'll ride shotgun, right here beside me."

She returned to inspect the house. In the emptiness, earlier days came into view—romantic dinners, crawling babies, their best memories—and she was determined to take those with her when she left.

When she'd finished her final walk-through, she and her boys climbed into their crowded car.

She turned the key and then hesitated, her hand hovering over the gearshift. She turned to look at her boys; their eyes sparkled with hope and excitement about their next adventure.

"Here we go," she said with a confidence she didn't quite feel. "On our way to our bright and shiny future."

Three

With the big-city skyline in her rearview mirror and nervous energy pulsing through her body, Lark drove toward Fredericksburg. The road unraveled before her with possibility, and that possibility scared the hell clean out of her.

With shaky hands, she held it together, and the ride went as smoothly as any cross-country drive with two young children could go. By the time her Sequoia crossed Austin's city limits, her boys had consumed every morsel she had packed, and had watched the same movie twice.

When the whines and stomach growls intensified, she pulled off the interstate. Her mouth watered at the sight of In-N-Out Burger, but she yielded to the majority. As much as she loathed clowns, if she ever met Ronald McDonald, she'd lay a big wet smooch on him for the joy his tasty meals left on her children's faces.

Two Happy Meals and a Diet Coke later, three satiated Meads left Travis County and coasted toward the Hill Country on a sodium high.

Lark imagined their life in Fredericksburg. A cute bungalow off Main Street came to mind—a place the boys could ride their bikes to the malt shop and Lark could jog to the Pioneer Museum without stopping for traffic. They'd attend community festivals, and Lark would show her boys the peaceful beauty of the Enchanted Rock. Going home made all the sense in the world.

The backseat went silent when the post–French fry carb crash set in, leaving her free to marvel at the growth of the Hill Country wine industry, as evidenced by the breathtaking landscapes. From Dripping Springs to Johnson City, grapevines marched like disciplined armies over former ranchlands. The sight poked at bruises Lark believed had healed sixteen years ago.

Memories of a summer in Calistoga flooded her mind—the cool air, the vines, the taste of an oaky chard, and her fellow interns, nine good old boys who'd edged her out of prime learning opportunities.

She'd earned high marks in the viticulture program at Texas Tech, and she'd been desperate to apply her bookwork to the vineyard. But when she'd complained about how the other interns were treating her, the vineyard manager had shrugged and reassigned her to the tasting room, limiting her exposure to the vineyard, grape presses, and bottling rooms. At summer's end, she'd returned to college jaded by her internship.

In viticulture, there's a theory about growing grapes. Struggling Plant Theory suggests that giving plants everything they want—ample growing space, water, and optimal soil conditions—results in fatty, bland fruit. Make them work for it, on the other hand, and the plants take on a mind of their own. They fight for water, sun, and space. The strongest plants wind their tendrils onto the trellises. They push past the others. They learn to do with less water, and they press their roots deeper into the soil to find moisture and skim nutrients from their leafy vines, allocating nutrients to the fruit and creating succulent winemaking grapes.

All her big talk about becoming the next Kathryn Hall or Heidi Peterson Barrett had been just that—big talk from a girl who didn't have what it took. *Those winemaking dreams sailed with the Nina, Pinta, and GD Santa Maria. Olé!*

With these two boys, she couldn't afford a wound-licking recalibration. "Time to wipe that raccoon from your eyes and get on with it," she muttered to herself.

"What?" Jamie asked.

"We're almost there." Not a moment too soon after that last Diet Coke.

THE LAND ON THE EDGE of town bustled with construction activity. At its center, a limestone tower advertised HARTMANN-HAAS CELLARS in gold script. From the size of the buildings, Lark assumed one was a tasting room and the other was an event center. A masterful blend of metal, distressed brick, limestone, and stucco created the illusion of an estate deserving of a historical marker.

A mile farther along, a metal sign read WILLKOMMEN TO FREDERICKSBURG.

"That's German for 'Welcome to Fredericksburg,'" Lark said.

"Why's it in German?" Jamie asked.

"The first people to live here came from Germany."

"Huh."

She wanted to take her time pointing out other landmarks, but that Diet Coke was sending a merciless pulse to her bladder. If she'd stopped twenty miles sooner, at the Buc-ee's mega-station, they could've used the bathrooms, filled the fuel tank, bought a week's worth of groceries, and posed for pictures in front of the giant beaver statue. But the convenience store up ahead would have to do.

"What's this?" Jamie asked as she turned into the parking lot.

"Mom's going to the potty."

"Can we get a snack?" Jamie asked.

With a resigned, "Sure," Lark parked beside the gas tanks.

"Shy-nee." Charlie waved at the window, and Lark pulled him from the car and ushered both boys inside the store.

Before leaving them alone, she bent down and tapped Charlie's nose. "Stay with your brother."

"I'll watch him, Mom." Jamie threw in a poorly executed two-eyed wink and used one of his father's favorite sayings: "We've got this."

Lark rushed toward the glowing RESTROOM sign, claimed a vacant stall, and slid the barrel-lock closed. A second later, a pair of red flats appeared outside.

"Tweety Bird?" the woman's twangy whisper delivered a wave of déjà-vu, and Lark shot a death stare at the silver door. Never would be too soon to hear that horrible nickname. And how about some manners?

"Lark Lovejoy?" the woman said.

Oy! My name is Lark Mead.

Lark sat in silence, wondering what Emily Post might recommend regarding bathroom etiquette. Lark decided to improvise. Holding it was impossible, and the acoustics made every drop sound like a gulley washer.

At last, the woman cleared her throat. "Sorry, I must've been mistaken."

The bathroom door whooshed closed and Lark finished her business and washed her hands in front of the water-spotted mirror. She peeled a hair tie from her wrist and twisted her curls into a lopsided bun. "Good as it's gonna get." She gave a wry laugh and narrowed her eyes. "Goodbye, Lark Lovejoy, whoever you *used* to be."

She pushed the door open and scanned the store for her boys, only to have her view blocked by a woman with long, sable hair and hopeful eyes.

"Why, Lark Lovejoy, it *is* you." Southern warmth cuddled her words. "It's me—Bianca." Like a child reuniting with her long-lost puppy, she wrapped her arms around Lark. After a few seconds, she let go and stepped back.

"Hi." Lark squinted, trying to place a child she'd last seen in sixth grade.

"I know, right? I told my girls I thought Lark Lovejoy was here. Lo and behold."

"Oh, I'm here." Lark lifted up on her toes. "My boys are here, too . . . somewhere."

"My girls have to meet you." Bianca's commanding gaze drew a girl closer. "This is Riley." She pivoted the girl by her shoulders, displaying her like an entry in the Gillespie County stock show.

Seeing Riley helped Lark visualize her childhood friend. At the girl's age, Bianca and her daughter could've been twins, assuming

Bianca traded her pink-foam-rolled curls for a fuchsia-striped pixie cut.

Riley gave an unenthusiastic wave and a tinsel-tracked smile. From skinny jeans, her meager calves poured into black high-top Chuck Taylors. A Ramone's T-shirt suggested a teenage rebellion on the horizon. This one was going to give her momma a run for her last dollar.

"Annnd . . ." Bianca pointed to a younger girl. "This is Sydney."

Sydney smiled around her red plastic straw. Chestnut braids fell upon her shoulders, and she wore pastel leggings and shimmery pink Mary Janes. She was all girl.

"Got one more at home. Dale insisted we try for a boy—Garth's three." Bianca lowered her voice and tilted her head. "He's a little pisser, but he's *my* little pisser." She let out a hoot. "Xerox copy of my husband. Can't wait to introduce you to Dale—just the sweetest man. He'll be tickled pink to meet Tweety after hearing me talk about you all these years."

"You live here?" Lark asked.

"Last year, that husband of mine plucked us out of Austin and dropped us smack in the middle of Green Freakin' Acres." She mocked his voice, "'Better place to raise kids.' Man's content so long as he can run around the corner and find a big ole hardware store."

"Men and their tools."

"Mm-hmm." There was a pause, and Bianca gave a maternal smile. "Scoot around. Let me have a look at you." She made a circle with a finger. "Can't believe Tweety's a . . ." She mouthed, "*Grown-ass woman.*"

A quarter-turn later, the absurdity of the request hit home and Lark righted her stance. As she did, her eyes caught a flash of Jamie's yellow shirt.

"Bianca, I've enjoyed catching up, but my parents are expecting us." She gave a gratuitous wave and Bianca's smile fell.

An aisle away, Jamie stood in front of a novelty toy display, driving a tiny truck through the air.

Lark tapped his shoulder. "Where is your brother?"

"Jamie . . . will . . . find . . . Charlie." Jamie's robot voice was no match for his mother's fiery gaze. Without breaking eye contact, he returned the truck to its display shelf.

Shame churned in Lark's belly. *Why did I waste time chatting with someone I hardly remember?* On her tiptoes, she took a panoramic view of the store, but she couldn't locate Charlie.

Terror beat at her chest like a Morse code operator. Grainy pictures on milk cartons . . . dot, dash, dot . . . *America's Most Wanted* . . . dash, dot, dash. An AMBER Alert . . . dash, dot, dot . . . John Walsh showing Charlie's face on TV . . . dash, dot, dash . . .

Charlie was gone.

Her feet zigzagged through the store; her heart pounded. She performed a mental inventory of Charlie's clothes—denim shorts, a blue shirt, white socks with a yellow stripe, and red Adidas sneakers.

"Charlie-baby, where are you?"

At once, a tiny voice crept into her senses. Desperate to hear it again, she stilled herself and stared ahead at a shelf filled to the brim with incompatible groceries—Wonder Bread, dusty cans of green beans, and toilet paper.

Nothing made sense. Nothing but . . .

"Shy-neeeeeee." Charlie's voice sliced through the clatter in her head.

In front of a beer display, her eyes fell on the red sneakers she'd fastened that morning, and anxiety drained from her body. "Charlie, you don't need a beer . . . although Mommy might," she muttered.

"Charlie." Jamie stood behind Lark, his arms crossed indignantly.

"Ma'am?" A tall, tanned man with warm eyes, a generous smile, and a strong chin stepped forward, impeding access to those red sneakers.

"Mommy?" Charlie popped out on the man's right, looking as delighted as if he'd just awakened to snow on Christmas morning.

The man ran a hand over his toast-brown military-grade haircut and he bent to one side so he was tilted at a peculiar angle; it reminded Lark of the metal cowboy in front of a roadside diner they'd passed earlier on their drive.

Lark stepped toward Charlie.

Charlie gazed up at the man. Then his hand fell to the metal leg like he might memorize it by touch. "See ta-shy-nee leg."

Lark curled down on one knee and swiped his hand away like the leg was on fire. "I'm sorry he bothered you," she said without looking up.

"Don't worry," the man said. "I don't bite."

"No, I'm sure you don't, but kids need to learn how to act around strangers."

"We can fix that stranger problem, ma'am. My name is Wyatt Gifford."

"Okay, not the point here," Lark shot back.

With a stare, she directed Charlie toward his brother. Then she pushed back up to her feet—too hard. She tilted back and, and she lost her footing, her hand flew backward and caught the grip of a refrigerated case, only to have the door swing open and catapult her toward Wyatt's chest with an inelegant grunt.

"Whoa." Wyatt curled an arm around her waist. "I've got you."

What is that? Cedar? Vanilla? Maybe oranges? Stop smelling the man, and step away, woman!

Lips pursed and brows dipped, she slipped away from him. "Thanks," she said in a "no thanks" tone and shot a wary look at him.

"Wait." He narrowed his eyes and crooked his head in a sideways stretch. "I didn't lure your kid over here, if that's what you think."

"You didn't walk away." She lifted a shoulder.

His jaw grew tight and he turned to the beer cooler.

"I'm just trying to protect my kids." She spoke to his backside. "Sir?"

"I heard you." He pulled a twelve-pack of Shiner Bock beer from the case and walked away, ending their conversation.

In the next aisle, Jamie held a bag of Sour Patch Kids candies and flashed a hopeful face. To his left, Charlie pointed to a package of yellow cakes. "Twinksies?"

"Go ahead." She waved her permission.

Charlie grabbed the package like a starving orphan but had already lost interest by the time they reached the checkout.

Wyatt paid for his items in front of them.

"Stop it, Charlie. It's rude to stare at people who aren't normal," Jamie's voice was loud and clear. All eyes fell on him, including Wyatt's.

"Wuz you do, Jay-mie?" Charlie angled his palms forward.

Lark tugged them aside as Wyatt silently made his exit.

"Jesus," she breathed out as the door jingled shut, "take the wheel."

Four

Wyatt

Wyatt Gifford, war hero, electrical engineer, and part-time carnival side show freak, was bone tired. Since eight that morning, he had dressed and redressed himself four times and shared secret after secret with the fine nurses, therapists, surgeons, and physiatrists at the Brook Medical Base and the Center for the Intrepid.

The staff were as nice as they could be, but Wyatt couldn't breathe right until he slipped back into his civvies, clambered into his truck, and slammed the door shut. At least for the next forty miles, he could be just another guy driving down the highway.

All those appointments didn't leave time for lunch. When he reached Fredericksburg, he pulled into the convenience store by his house. He wasn't looking for company, just the necessities: beer, chips, and a tin of salsa.

He picked up a bag of Tostitos and his gaze fell to a set of the bluest eyes he'd ever seen. They belonged to a boy with curly blond hair who pointed at Wyatt's prosthetic leg, which was protruding from his khaki shorts.

The kid mumbled as he pointed, though it was beyond Wyatt what the hell his garbled words meant.

Then, his mother found him—and man, she was a tough nut to crack. Or, maybe, just a nut? Either way, it wasn't Wyatt's problem.

Happy to escape the whole scene, he paid for his items and tossed the receipt in the bag. While the automated doors dragged open, he glanced behind him and his eyes snagged on a familiar darkness shrouding the older boy's eyes.

Wyatt had seen that look before, in war-torn areas where tragedies had marred childhood innocence. Even when Wyatt and his buddies had worked to coax smiles, they hadn't come easily. That was Afghanistan, where kids couldn't tell if the camo-clad strangers were friendlies or junkyard dogs barking English.

Unease threaded through him—that look didn't belong on a kid in a Texas convenience store. He tried to shake it off and trained his eyes on the door.

Walk away, or you'll regret it.

A woman's voice crept into his ears. "That wasn't very kind, Jamie."

With a sigh, Wyatt set his bag on an empty newspaper stand and wandered toward the family, but the mother didn't notice him until he spoke.

"Hey," he said. "Ma'am?"

"Lark," she said through her teeth.

"Okay, Lark. Your boy didn't mean any harm."

Lark's head tipped to her chest in a gesture Wyatt read as defeat. After an awkward pause, she glanced up and her mouth quirked into an apologetic half-smile. "We're so sorry."

Wyatt nodded and his eyes snapped to Jamie.

Through tears, Jamie hiccupped, "I'm . . . sor . . . ry." The boy's embarrassment was evident but a deeper sadness lingered underneath it, waiting to claw its way out.

"Hey, buddy." Wyatt took a step closer and his mouth edged into a sympathetic grin. "I didn't think you were being mean about my leg. I knew what you meant."

"You're not mad?" Jamie asked.

"No way."

Lark stepped over to the snack bar and returned with a handful of paper napkins. She pushed one over Jamie's nose.

"I'll do it." A shamed frown crossed Jamie's face and he took the napkin.

Wyatt looked away and Charlie offered a grin that had Wyatt's name all over it.

With a sigh, Lark put out her hand. "I'm Lark Mead. Thanks for being so understanding."

Wyatt met her hand. "It's really okay—"

"We should get going." Lark put an arm around Jamie and tried to turn him toward the door, but he resisted and squinted.

"What happened to your—?" He pointed to Wyatt's prosthesis.

"Well, I'm a soldier in the Army." He scratched his neck. "I mean, I was."

"Where is your—"

"Jamie." Lark's cranky face returned.

"He's okay, ma'am." Wyatt turned to Jamie. "There were bombs hidden under the road—not here, but on the other side of the world. Anyway, one exploded and hurt my friends and me."

Jamie's head shot back like the IED had just detonated right there in the store. "Why'd they put bombs in the road?"

Wyatt huffed. "They weren't getting along with the folks we were helping."

"That wasn't nice."

"No, sir, it wasn't."

"Is that your . . . body?" Jamie stared at the prosthetic.

"Might say that. I've got a metal leg."

"Shy-nee." Charlie's mouth dropped open.

"Like a Transformer," Jamie said.

Wyatt knocked his chin to one side. "I played with those when I was a kid, too."

"You did?" Jamie gave a quivering smile.

"Sure I did. They were awesome."

"Yeah, I like 'em too. Do you still fight bad guys?"

"No." Wyatt cringed as the word left his lips. "I'm all through with the Army."

The Army's through with me.

"Was there lots of blood when that happened?" Jamie asked.

"Jamie," Lark warned.

"He's fine." Wyatt waved her off. "Truth is, I don't remember." *Don't even want to try.*

"A good thing, right?" Lark said.

"Oh, yeah." He arched his brows and held her gaze, drinking up the welcome change in her expression.

"Where's your old leg?" Jamie asked.

Wyatt brushed a hand over his hair. "God's honest truth? Not sure where it went."

"Where do you get those legs?"

"Sweetie, we should let Mr.—I'm sorry, I've forgotten your last name."

"Gifford. Call me Wyatt." He raised a finger and pointed it at the boy. "I've got a minute, Jamie. This part's super cool. These smart doctors at the Army hospital make arms and legs for people like me."

Jamie's eyes dropped for a pause and his expression curdled. "Mom? How come Dad didn't go to that hospital?"

Lark bent toward him. "Baby, your dad wasn't . . ." She gave Wyatt a helpless expression. "Only Army people go to those hospitals."

"But he could'a gone there and *that* doctor could'a made him new arms, and he wouldn't have died."

Wyatt's smile deflated like a pin-stuck balloon. *No wonder the kid carries so much pain. Explains the mother's pissed-off-with-the-world attitude, too. This family is covered in bad luck, just like another family I can't stop thinking about.* A lump hit his throat. *Keep it together, man.*

"Baby, we'll talk about your dad at Grammy's." She bit her lip, and her expression told Wyatt this wasn't a conversation for the Mini Mart.

Wyatt set a hand on a grocery shelf for balance and took a knee. "Losing your dad's a tough one. I'm sorry, buddy."

The nod Jamie gave him was an uncertain one, but even as he wiped a tear from his face with the back of his hand, he looked straight into Wyatt's eyes.

Got to give it to this lady—she's raising him right.

"Bet your dad's watching over you, and I'll bet he's real proud. You're brave, taking care of your brother and your mom." Wyatt exchanged a grin with Charlie and shot a quick glance at Lark. "Sorry about your loss, ma'am."

"Sorry about your injury."

Wyatt nodded and pushed himself back to his feet. "You've got two fine young men here." Wyatt winked at Jamie.

"Thank you." Lark smiled, and the scar on her chin twisted into a dimple.

Lark
....

HOW DID A QUICK TRIP TO THE *convenience store turn into a scene from a Lifetime movie?* What little fight she'd had after the impromptu reunion with Bianca was toast after Wyatt's eyes became glassy. It was high time she and the boys got on their way. To lighten the mood, she made a silly face at Charlie.

Wyatt ran a finger under his eyes but didn't walk away.

"Well." Lark sighed. "My parents are probably wondering if we got lost."

"Don't want to worry your grandparents." Wyatt tapped Jamie's shoulder. "Right, man?"

"Right, *man.*" A gleam of pride lit Jamie's expression.

"Bye, shy-nee," Charlie said.

"His name's not Shiny." Jamie exhaled a dramatic sigh. "It's Wyatt."

"Bye, Wy-tat." Charlie waved.

Wyatt waved back and walked away, smiling. Heaving another sigh, Lark removed a credit card from her pocket, paid for their items, and passed the bag to Jamie.

At the car, she had just fastened Charlie into his seat and flung the door closed when she heard her name being called.

"Lark." Bianca raced toward her faster than a prairie fire with a tail wind.

"Son of a bi—" Lark's voice skidded to a stop. "Bianca."

"You're a speedy little one." Bianca wiped her brow and pushed a lock of hair from her face. "Can't leave until I get your number." She pulled a phone from the bedazzled pocket of her denim jacket.

As they exchanged numbers, Bianca gestured for her girls to wait in their car and lowered her sinfully long eyelashes in a contrite expression. "I overheard your conversation back there with the Army man."

Was it too much to ask for a few days to unpack before sharing my story with everyone in Gillespie County?

"Even though a heck of a long time has passed, I'll be here for you." Bianca's hand rose and her glittery, French-tipped fingernails caught the afternoon light. "Hand to God."

"We're gonna be alright."

"Mmm-mmm. Of course, you'll be." Bianca's whiskey-colored eyes locked on Lark's face. "Sweetie, I can see it, clear as day. That heart of yours is scraped raw as a skinned knee."

Lark forced a smile.

"Well, your positive attitude will help." Bianca poked Lark in the ribs and grasped one of her upper arms. "You could take down some roller-derby queens with those guns. Working out?"

"Lifting kids, I guess." *And, until recently, a grown man.*

When it seemed impossible to move any closer, Bianca narrowed the space between them even further. "You may not remember all that mess with my family, but you and your parents were there, picking up the pieces and loving on me when no one else knew I existed."

"I . . . uh . . ." Lark couldn't assemble the crumbs of Bianca's past.

"Well, no matter."

"You're sweet. Thanks." Lark edged toward her car door but Bianca didn't move.

"We just made town, and my youngest . . ." She sighed. "Not sure how much you caught."

"The whole kit and caboodle." Bianca snorted. "Kids can make a momma drink."

"Well, we'd better get on our way or *my* mom will be dispatching the Texas Rangers." Lark turned to open the car door.

"Things happen for a reason." Bianca's words pulled her apart.

Lark sucked in a breath. She had heard all the silver linings bullshit she could stand.

As if Bianca had read her mind, she raised a hand. "Not talking about your loss, honey—there's no rhyme or reason to losing someone you love. But you coming home? Us running into each other? Years don't keep people from caring."

"No, I guess they don't."

"These are the times you find out who your friends are. Like it or not, I'm gonna be at the front of the line for you."

They hugged and Bianca flounced away. Lark watched her ascend into a limousine-long black Suburban before opening her own car door and climbing behind the wheel. "Bianca Romero, the Tweety you knew was swallowed by a vicious putty tat," she said in a cartoonish voice.

"Huh?" Jamie asked, poking his head between the front seats.

"Nothing."

"Why does she call you Tweety?"

"It was a name she gave me when we were little girls. Put on your seatbelt."

A few minutes later, Lark turned into the cul-de-sac at Treaty Oak Circle. When she saw the Austin stone of the Lovejoys' ranch home, she knew her little family would be just fine.

Her gaze flew to the tree directly in front of her, and she pointed. "I practically lived up there when I was a kid." The live oak had a trunk as wide as a Volkswagen, and in the crook of its fork, a weathered tree fort floated, cradled by branches that spanned the horizon like the undulating arms of a Hindu goddess.

"Kinda scary," Jamie muttered.

"Look who's waiting for you," Lark said.

From the side of the house, Frank Lovejoy appeared in his trademark blue jeans, a plaid button-down shirt, and cowboy boots. The beard, mustache, and hair grown past his collar made him almost as unrecognizable as the animal running at his side.

"What's that?" Jamie unsnapped his seatbelt and leaned over the center console.

"Um . . . a dog?" Lark pushed her sunglasses on top of her head. "Probably."

A foot tall, the dog resembled a stubby hyena with pointy ears and a ratty tail—the sort that might be cute in an animated movie but was downright creepy in the flesh.

"Will it bite?" Jamie asked, watching his grandfather wave the animal away.

"Maybe. Stay here." Lark climbed out of the car. "Hi, Dad." She wrapped her arms around Frank. Gratitude flooded her senses, and her eyes became foggy. "So glad you're okay."

"I'm fine." She felt him studying her face, but she avoided his eyes and focused on the gray hair on his neck.

"Willie Nelson?" She made a ponytail with her hand.

"Not yet." A smile appeared behind all that facial hair. "Missed my chance in the sixties, better late than never."

"Poppy!" Jamie cracked open his door, and Frank waved.

"Hold on, kid." Frank put a hand on her arm. "Don't worry about me. Doc said I can go another 50,000 miles." He winked one of his hooded blue eyes. "Enough about your old man. Today's your day, hmm?"

Pumping her head up and down, she pulled on a smile to hide the emotional stew brewing inside. Not wishing to upset him, she agreed with a limp shrug and a wobbly chin.

"Come here." He folded her into his chest. "Happy birthday." After a beat, he released her. "Should we get them out?" He gestured to the boys.

"Eh," she said, laughing, and squeezed her father's hand. "Love you."

"You too, kid." They moved toward the Sequoia, and his eyes shifted to the stuffed cargo area. "Better get you unloaded."

"I can unload my stuff," she said.

"Don't do that to me. I'm not an invalid." He opened the rear passenger door and the mutt reappeared, barking and rotating like it was nailed to a Sit-and-Spin toy.

Frank told Jamie to stay put and closed the door. "Hush!" he barked at the dog, and the dog quieted.

"What *is* that?" Lark asked.

"You know your mother—thinks it's her job to save every lost soul."

"Sister Millie, hard at work. Let us pray for her." Lark folded her hands together.

"Pray for *me* is more like it. She went to a meeting at the school last week and found this fleabag. Nobody else was taking the ugly bastard, so she dragged him home. I call him 'Walter Cronkite.'"

"Walter *what*?"

"Told her we weren't keeping him, but that stubborn woman put her foot down and said, 'We're keeping him, and that's the way it is,' like Walter Cronkite used to say at the end of the evening news, so . . ." He shrugged.

"Can we come out now?" Jamie asked. His voice ignited another barking tirade.

"Enough." Frank stomped his foot, sending the furball scampering toward the house. He opened the door and helped both boys out of the car.

"Poppy." Jamie patted Frank's arm. "We saw a man with a robot leg."

"Robot legs, huh?" Frank's jaw slackened.

"No. A robot *leg*. Only one." He pointed one finger and dropped his voice to a whisper. "The other one was real. Kind of scary at first, but then we talked to him, and he was kinda cool."

"Tell me about it while we unload. C'mon."

"Leave what's in the front seat, please," Lark said.

"I'll carry my LEGOs. They're real important. Where's Grammy?" Jamie asked.

"At the store. She'll be along in a bit." Frank pulled out a suitcase.

Lark led Charlie to the house; she slowed when she reached the row of trellises. "Poppy and I planted those." A hand fell to the vines, tangled as a pile of wire hangers and heavy enough to bow the wooden frames. "Charlie-man, they might not look like it, but these were something once."

Five

Lark

From the outside, the house hadn't changed since Lark last visited. A few steps inside told another story.

Her breath caught, and she felt like she had walked into the Hill Country version of *Twilight Zone*.

New paint and décor neutralized the homey scent she was craving, and the interior had become a cold iteration of the house where Lark's fondest memories resided. Icy white cabinets had taken the place of oak ones. One side of a milky quartz island opened to the kitchen with a prep sink. Across from it, an eat-in bar and six chrome barstools backed up to the family room.

"What have they done . . ." Lark turned silent when her father walked in behind her. "See Grammy's new, *shiny* oven?" She said to Charlie, feigning interest.

Charlie returned an unimpressed whimper.

She shook him playfully. "Come on, Charlie-man. Thought you'd be all over *shiny* things."

"Let's get another load, son," Frank prodded Jamie outside.

Lark moved to the living room and made a silent O with her mouth. "Sweet baby Jesus, this could be trouble."

"Twubble?" Charlie frowned at her.

"When Grammy and Poppy chose this setup, they didn't know we were coming to stay. We'll need to cover this place in plastic and bubble wrap before we let you run around, Charlie-man."

Battered dark wood floors made way for tile. Shaded in steely grays and cream, it supplied a chilly vibe beneath sleek furniture in similar hues. Chic steel lamps floated on glass tables. Beneath it all, a dyed blue cowhide rug provided a surprise accent of softness.

Limestone rose from the fireplace to the twenty-five-foot ceiling. Three cedar trusses spanned the width of the room. At the top of the exterior wall, triangulated windows followed the roofline on each side of the fireplace, inviting natural light to pour into the house.

Frank set a box on the island. "What do you think about the place?"

"Reminds me of the lobby at the Four Seasons Hotel in Austin." Lark swept a hand across the room. "Where do I check in?"

Frank's mouth twisted into a wry smile.

"Wouldn't guess this was your style."

"Married to your mom long enough to know if it makes *her* happy, she'll make *me* happy."

"I think I understand why you had heart trouble." She inspected a glass orb displayed on an etagere. "Mom didn't spare a dime."

"Ah." He waved off her comment. "It was time for an update."

Jamie schlepped the plastic LEGO box into the room and set it in a corner as he scanned the room like an emperor deciding how to divide a continent.

"Not so fast, buddy. These go back there." Lark pointed to a hallway.

"We set them up in Harlan's old room," Frank said.

Lark beckoned to Jamie and started down the hall. When she reached her brother's room, her mouth fell open. "Harlan's going to freak when he sees this."

Once bathed in hunter green and Waverly plaid, the room now featured stark white woodwork, obnoxiously bright canary yellow walls, and minimalist teak furniture. Devoid of knickknacks, it was a blank canvas but for the Spiderman comforter on the bed and the white crib in the corner of the room.

"Where's your room, Mom?" Jamie asked.

"This way." Lark moved toward the end of the T-shaped hall. When she reached the door, she closed her eyes and turned the knob.

Regret and awe churned as she opened her eyes. Her eighties-era pine dresser, desk, and four-poster bed were gone, replaced with a cottage-style gray chest with brushed nickel hardware, mirrored nightstands, a bed with a blue upholstered headboard, and a crisp white duvet. *Lovely, but it doesn't feel like home.* "Wow. Grammy went all out, didn't she?"

Hope surfaced at the sight of a crocheted lavender afghan draped over the arm of a club chair. She pulled it to her face. "Jamie, your great-grandmother Larkan made this for my twelfth birthday. You would have loved her."

"Did she die?"

"Yes, baby."

"Is she in heaven with Dad?"

"I suppose so." She ran a finger over the crocheted weave and shifted her gaze to a floral painting that hung where her wedding portrait once had.

"What's wrong, Mom?"

"Nothing, baby." Her throat clicked, and she swallowed the lump of prickly emotions sticking there.

"Sad about your dead grandma?"

"Uh-huh. Hey, did you ask Poppy to show you his tractor?"

"Not yet." Jamie rushed out of the room, and Charlie wiggled out of her arms to follow his brother.

Lark returned to her car to remove the precious cargo from the front passenger seat. She carried James to her bedroom, placed him in the nightstand drawer, and rested a hand on the top of the white box. "Welcome home." She paused for a moment before she closed the drawer.

LARK HAD HOPED TO CAJOLE Charlie into a nap. She hadn't expected to fall asleep with him. But she woke to her father's voice in the kitchen and her sleeping toddler beside her.

She remained still, soaking up every snuggly second, while her parents chatted quietly with Jamie. Until—

"You awake, Mom?" Jamie asked, rousing them.

All good things must come to an end. An odor bit at Lark's nostrils. *Sweaty feet? Fritos? Roadside skunk carcass?* One reluctant eye peeled open. "What is that smell?"

Jamie shrugged and opened his hand, "Poppy gave me Corn Nuts. Want some?"

"No, thank you."

Jamie tossed the last fragments into his mouth.

"Wash your hands before you touch Grammy's new furniture."

He nodded and turned toward the hallway. Before he cleared the room, his brother had crawled off the chair and started toddling after him.

Lark slipped into the kitchen, where her father sat at the island.

"Get a good nap?" Frank held a cabernet glass in a weathered hand.

Nodding, she stretched her arms over her head and blinked steadily.

Her mother whirred about the kitchen in a denim shirt and black leggings. She wore her ginger hair in a shoulder-grazing, shaggy bob—a new look for her.

"Hi, honey," Millie said over her shoulder.

Lark turned to her dad and mouthed, "She cut her hair."

Millie balanced a spoon on the side of a saucepan and crossed the kitchen to submerge Lark in a welcoming embrace.

"Love this look." Lark touched her mother's hair. "You guys are full of surprises."

"Time for a change, don't you agree?" Millie's hazel eyes sparkled beneath her choppy bangs and her hands trailed over Lark's arms. "And to think, thirty-eight years ago, you and I were just getting to know each other." Her hands moved to Lark's face, and she kissed her on the forehead. "Happy birthday, honey."

"I'm so glad to be home," Lark said.

Millie pushed back and examined her daughter. Her high cheekbones rose in a tight smile. "So thin. We need to fatten you up."

"Mil, she's fine," Frank warned.

Millie's face relaxed. "Ignore me, honey. I'm just a worrier."

Lark winked at her father.

Millie heaved a great sigh and clenched her fists. "I don't want you to stress. I have Jamie's school worries under control."

"Mom, I can care of my boys."

"Registration paperwork only needs your signature." Millie waved her arms as she returned to the stove.

"Oy." Lark helped herself to her father's glass. The cabernet was jammy, with delightful hints of chocolate.

He peeled back a layer of foil to reveal a succulent tenderloin trickling with juices.

"When do we eat?" she asked.

"Give me a few more minutes." Millie gestured with a hot pad.

"Dad, want to help me attack that mess of grapevines this weekend?"

Millie interrupted with a sarcastic chuckle. "We're ripping them out. Tell her, Frank." Her face brightened. "We're replacing them with knockout rose bushes."

Enter my inner arsonist, stage right.

"She's kidding, right?" Lark asked Frank.

Millie removed a pan of roasted carrots from the oven. "With Jamie starting school and a job search, you don't have time to help your father with yardwork."

Lark and her father exchanged knowing glances and Frank smoothed his beard. "Ah, Millie, it might be fun."

"Neither of you have the time." Millie whirled around with fresh eagerness. "I almost forgot to tell you, I picked up information on this single mom's group that meets at the library."

"Ugh."

"You would do well to make a few like-minded friends." Her lip hooked on the last word as she transferred a wet head of romaine lettuce to a salad bowl.

"Mom?" Lark approached her at the island's prep sink. "Can we tap the brakes? I just got here."

"I'm just trying to help." Millie tipped her head to one side.

In order for them to live together in peace, Lark needed to engage a coping mechanism that balanced respect for her parents with self-preservation. She touched her mother's shoulder and waited for Millie to meet her eyes.

"I appreciate all you've done, but school doesn't start for two more weeks."

After a few silent seconds, Millie's frown dissipated. "Jamie and I brainstormed foods he could take in his school lunches, and we made a list."

Lark shook her head and Frank gestured for her to follow him into the dining room.

"She's excited you're home. She'll settle down," he said in a subdued voice.

"Hope so," Lark muttered. "I take it Charlie's table manners aren't ready for prime time?" She gestured to a high chair parked between a pair of light-colored dining chairs. "Come here, Charlie-man." She heaved him toward the chair, wiggling in defiance.

This ought to be fun.

"Here. Let me." Frank pressed the tray in place before the toddler could escape.

"Here comes dinner," Millie announced like a pied piper, with Jamie following her. "Special salad for our younger guests."

"Not sure how much salad Charlie will eat," Lark said.

"He'll eat this salad. It contains Grammy's magic." Millie set a red plastic plate on Charlie's tray and another in front of Jamie.

In addition to petite portions of steak, mashed potatoes, and green beans, the boys' plates included skewered vegetables—artfully folded butter lettuce leaves, cucumber moons, red and yellow grape tomatoes, blueberries, pineapple—finished with stripes of ranch dressing.

God bless Pinterest.

"Magic salad's cool, Grammy," Jamie said.

With that vote of confidence, Millie took her seat.

Seconds after Frank offered a toast to Lark, Millie jumped on her meddlesome horse again. "I left the information on nursery schools on top of the chest in your room."

Lark stuck a forkful of vegetables in her mouth.

"Classes fill up—especially at Charlie's age."

Frank winked—a silent reminder.

She's excited. She'll settle down.

Lark nodded.

"Dawdle, and he won't get a spot."

Another nod and a bite.

"He needs the socialization."

She's excited. She'll settle down.

A tight smile.

"You know what I mean? Missing out on those opportunities during all that . . ." she waggled her eyebrows.

She's excited. She'll settle down.

"Uh-huh," Lark said.

"Dad and I can help you with the tuition."

Your "help" sounds a lot like control.

"Mom, I've got money, and I'll cover it."

"We're trying to help," Millie sang, inviting guilt to take a seat at the table. The air thickened with unspoken words.

"You *are* helping," Lark said. "You've always been there when I needed you most, and I get it. You guys put your life on hold for me. I'm sorry."

"Nothing to say 'sorry' about," Frank said.

Millie shot her a maternal smile and took a sip of her water.

"Coming home wasn't about me needing your help. I came home because it was best for my family, and because I want to be around for you two. If, God forbid, one of you were to get sick, I want to be here like you were there for me."

"We understand," Frank said.

"And *while* we're staying here, we don't expect you to take care of us—but have no doubt, I will be eternally grateful for everything you and Dad did for us when we needed you most."

"No need to thank us, honey." One side of Millie's mouth quirked up—a recognizable tell that sent an alarming tickle down Lark's spine. "Having you in our lives is a gift unto itself. You carry a burst of sunshine wherever you go."

"Burst of sunshine, my rear," Lark mumbled, earning a laugh from her father and a disapproving scowl from her mother. Years of witnessing her mother's wishful-thinking compliments had seasoned Lark's spidey senses. She knew when she was being played.

"Ahem." Millie rolled her eyes between Jamie and Charlie.

"Rear isn't a bad word, Grammy," Jamie said.

Millie smiled and moved the food around on her plate.

"Do you remember Bianca?" Lark asked.

"Of course I do," Millie said.

Lark swallowed a bite. "Ran into her at the Mini Mart. She lives here now."

Millie cocked her head to one side. "Lark, honey, you've had so much on your mind." She closed her eyes for a beat. "You don't remember? I told you last spring." She rose from her chair and tapped Jamie's shoulder.

Jamie responded with his awkward two-eyed wink and followed her into the kitchen.

A few minutes later, they returned, dragging out the words to "Happy Birthday to You," and Millie placed a candle-lit, buttercream-frosted cake in front of Lark. "Make a wish, honey."

Lark closed her eyes and blew out the candles. As ribbons of smoke drifted from the cake, Millie pushed two bags across the table.

Lark untied the expertly entwined gold ribbons and removed a selection of gift cards from the pink bag—one each for Nordstrom, Amazon, a local boutique, a bookstore on Main Street, and Home Depot. Lark pursed her lips at the last one.

"For when you buy a house," Millie explained.

"You think of everything, Mom."

Absolutely everything.

The larger bag contained a supple, leather-bound notebook with LARKAN LOVEJOY MEAD, JD embossed on its red cover. Inside, a calendar and blank pages promised to organize Lark's life, Millie style. *Not-so-subtle nudges—Mom's specialty.*

Lark received the message, loud and clear: if she failed to take action, her mother would take the reins and lead the way.

Six

Lark

Over the next few days, Lark burned through six reels of P-touch labeling tape and derived an embarrassing level of satisfaction as she unpacked and organized the mundane into plastic bins.

Millie had returned to work to prepare for the upcoming school year. Her absence from the house provided the physical and mental space for Lark to establish a comfort zone within the new version of her old digs.

Everything about Fredericksburg excited Jamie and Charlie. A town overflowing with bakeries, boutiques, and peach orchards, it was about as Norman Rockwell as a Texas city could be.

Bianca delivered on her promise, converting her eagerness into helpful support for Lark and playdates for the boys. The Jarboe's backyard pool treated Jamie and Charlie to a splashtastic time full of giant inflatable dragons, flamingos, and unicorns. All the while, Lark and Bianca revived a long-neglected childhood friendship with ease. The stories had changed, but at an imperceptible level their "Best Friends 4-ever" connection had endured. Bianca provided a listening ear, inviting Lark to vent. Seemingly without trying, she infused their conversations with humor and settled Lark's nerves about Jamie's transition into kindergarten.

WHEN THE FIRST DAY OF school came, Jamie woke and dressed himself in the clothes he'd set out the night before. With frenetic determination, he slurped his last Cheerio, strapped on his backpack, and waited by the door.

Refusing to be coaxed into his clothes, Charlie kept him waiting. The toddler wasn't interested in pajamas, and he didn't want to wear the T-shirt and shorts Lark pulled out, either. Charlie Mead was at peace in nothing more than a Pull-Ups diaper.

"Nakey jaybird," Charlie said, squirming on the floor.

"Not today, Charlie-man," Lark said, wrestling his wiggly body into his clothes. "Jamie needs to get to school."

Once dressed, Charlie resisted when Jamie prodded him toward the car. He fussed as Lark buckled his car seat. He whined as Jamie bantered cheerfully during the drive. And when they reached Gillespie and Lark peeled him from the car, he became tearful.

A family walked by, and the mother offered a pitying expression.

"Charlie, stop," Jamie said. "You're making people look at you."

With a deep breath, Lark gripped Charlie's hand, lifted her head high, and shepherded her boys into the school. *Not exactly the first day-of-school Instagram pic I envisioned.*

HOORAY FOR SCHOOL was posted above the blackboard, but the room felt pressurized with high expectations. The students looked like they were waiting to learn their fates. Their parents loomed over them in awkward two- and three-parent groupings, taking up entirely too much space amidst the tiny desks, chairs, and tables.

With forced cheer, adults directed their pint-size prodigies to sit, stand, and smile as they snapped post-worthy pics on their smartphones.

"Let's get a picture in front of your desk," Lark said.

Jamie provided a helpless smile as Charlie shouted, "Poppy!"

Frank meandered through the room and put a hand on Jamie's shoulder. "Didn't want to miss your first day."

"I didn't know you were coming," Lark said.

"Can't stay. I was in the neighborhood. Thought I'd wish him luck."

"Hi, Poppy," Jamie said with a nervous grin.

A woman with a gray ponytail and welcoming eyes cut in and bent to Jamie's eye-level. "I'm Mrs. Rhodes." She shook his hand, then stood and reached for Lark's hand.

"I'll leave you to it," Frank said. He gave Lark a quick hug and slouched away.

Her father couldn't take James's place, but he could at least give Jamie and Charlie a father figure—a loving, involved one. Lark smiled with relief at that thought.

Jamie unpacked his supplies at his desk, and a girl with frizzy red hair pointed to the next desk. "My name'th Thadie."

Is that Katie? Sadie? Lark couldn't be sure—until she glanced at the desk and saw the laminated name taped there. *Thank you, baby Jesus. The child's name is Zadie.*

"Wanna go thee the hamsther with me?" Zadie asked.

"Uh-huh." Without looking at Lark, Jamie muttered, "You can go, Mom."

"Grammy's not far away if you need her and—"

"I'm okay." He gave her that terrible excuse for a wink.

"Okay, sweetheart. Love you." Lark took her time leaving the classroom, clinging to hope that he might lean in for an embrace, or at least give her a smile.

Instead, he tossed a "bye" over his shoulder and followed his new friend to the hamster cage.

AT HOME, LARK PULLED OUT her timeworn jogging stroller. "Hey, grumpy man. What do you say we get some fresh air?"

Charlie knew just what to do. "Ready," he hollered.

At the corner of the cul-de-sac, Lark plugged in one of her earbuds and hit play. When the music didn't start immediately, she waited, recognizing the silence. In seconds, chirping crickets and peaceful night sounds shot through the tiny speaker.

Her feet reprised their familiar rhythm in time to the *whop*, *whop*, *whop* of helicopter blades. At last, Billy Joel's smoky voice crooned the first line of "Goodnight Saigon."

Following years of avoiding the subject of her father's time in Vietnam, teenage Lark discovered "Goodnight Saigon" on an old cassette tape in the family's basement. When she was older, she acquired the CD. In recent years, she'd added the digital version to her smartphone, and she included it on every running playlist she created. The steady tempo matched her pace, and she clung to each lyric as a speculative glimpse into her father's past and a period of history her family had locked away. She clung to the song as a palatable accounting of her father's journey. It provided mental pictures of an eighteen-year-old Frank Lovejoy leaving his wife and baby to fight a war so gruesome he refused to speak of it when he returned.

The song ended too soon, as it always did. The screws in Lark's mind loosened as sunlight warmed her skin. She couldn't say how long she ran; she only knew that Charlie was out like a light when they came home.

A FEW HOURS LATER, LARK made herself comfortable in the kitchen, using the island as her desk. Poised with a pen, her laptop, and a weathered spiral notebook she'd once used to document James's medications. She'd ripped out the pages since then. She thumbed the spiral's metal rings and noticed a curled paper strand lodged within them—a solemn reminder of the notebook's former use.

Her screen flickered to life and she started navigating through job websites. She located only one position for an attorney . . . in a city an hour and a half away.

Cold calls to firms in Fredericksburg, Comfort, and Boerne produced similar results: "We're not hiring"; "Thank you for your interest"; "Best of luck."

The chamber of commerce website offered links to various local businesses, but the wineries were what held Lark's attention. Lush grapevines teased her into adding words like "tasting room," "fieldwork," and "winery" to the job search engine. *What can it hurt to check out my options?*

Soon, the prospect of a career change shot her into a quagmire, and she picked up the phone. Harlan would do what was needed—either reinforce her confidence or set her straight.

For reasons unknown, their parents had waited a full eleven years before having their second child. Lark finished first grade the year Harlan graduated high school. And though Lark sometimes wished they weren't quite so many years apart, their age difference wasn't all bad. They never fought over who would drive Dad's car, who was hogging the bathroom, or who had eaten all the ice cream.

When Lark reached adulthood, she and Harlan found common ground. By the time she began law school, Harlan, who was going through a particularly dark period in his life, had turned to her as his sounding board, and they were speaking daily by phone.

Harlan's tech start-up had appeared in magazines and captured the spotlight at Austin's South by Southwest festival. He was making seven figures a year and living in a high-rise condo in Austin with the woman he'd dated since high school.

And he was absolutely miserable.

Ultimately, he sold his business, ended his relationship, and returned to college. A year later, he put on a Parks and Wildlife uniform and never looked back.

How I wish I could harness as much courage.

"I made a big mistake moving here," she said when her brother answered the phone.

"Mom cramping your style already?" he asked.

"Fredericksburg's job market's cramping my style. There's nothing. Get this—I called the domestic violence shelter to offer pro bono services like I did in Houston. They told me they'd 'add me to the list.' With 12,000 residents in town, they don't require many legal aid volunteers."

"You'll find something."

"Don't tell Mom, but I looked at some winery jobs, too . . . manual labor and tasting room positions. Could be fun."

"If you don't need the money, why not?"

"You know why not. Her name starts with an 'M' and ends with 'illie.'"

"She doesn't get a vote. You're almost forty, Lark."

Lark slapped her forehead. "I came dangerously close to forgetting my own age."

"With age comes wisdom. You get to make the calls now. If making wine's your jam, do it. Heck, you went to school. Start your own winery."

She gave a sarcastic laugh. "Apparently, school doesn't matter. I've read these winery owners' and managers' bios. Most don't have degrees or special training—just 'a passion for growing and pressing grapes.'"

"So?"

"So, I wasted four years studying, and the best I can do is work as a server in a tasting room?"

"*Is* that the best you can do?"

Lark didn't respond.

"Look, I'm about to say something. Hear me out."

"Go on."

"You can sit in that house till you're eighty, making Mom or the boys your excuses, but that's bull and you know it. You have resources most people don't."

"What?"

"Freedom, money, schooling—"

"Wine isn't that grape-stomping scene from *I Love Lucy*. Technology's changed. They're cloning plants now. Even if I tried, I'd spend years just figuring out the regulations and licensing." She huffed. "Who knows if I can even remember anything I learned in college?"

"You're smart. What you don't remember, you'll learn again. Quit making excuses. If you want it bad enough, you'll do it."

Lark rolled her eyes. "Thanks a lot."

"Look, I want to be supportive, but I'm not a fan of your excuses. I'm many things, but I'm not an enabler."

"This is why you're not married."

"Maybe." He laughed, and then his voice flattened. "I'm serious. I've been where you are, career-wise. You think Mom celebrated when I told her I was selling my company? She was grumpy for months. It sucked, but we got through it."

"You had a plan."

"So make a plan, Lark. If I'd bitched and moaned to people about why I wanted to be a forest ranger but never done anything about it, I'd have worn out my welcome real fast. Besides all that, what you do isn't anyone's business. All due respect, that includes Mom and Dad."

"I don't know."

"I'm saying this out of love. It's like you're sitting in one of those big movie theaters with twenty movies going on at the same time and you're complaining about the one you're watching. If you don't like what you see, get off your ass and check out another one. No one's holding you down."

"With the boys, I can't hide in the forest like you."

"You gonna make them your next excuse?"

There was a long silence, and it was probably a good thing he couldn't see her face.

"Right. You've heard enough." Another pause. "A bear's breaking into one of our trucks. Got to run."

"That bear got a name?"

"Why?"

"Figure you two must be old friends by now, considering how he shows up whenever you don't want to talk anymore."

"It's the damndest thing."

"I'll bet."

"Lark, I'm serious. Figure out what you want and man up."

"Man . . . what?"

"Sorry. Mostly men up here."

"Another reason you're not married?"

"Maybe. Listen, decide what you want and call your shot. Say it. You want to work in the fields trimming grapevines—"

"Pruning," she corrected.

"Fine. You want to prune? Prune the hell out of those vines. Mom can get happy in the same pants she wore when you pissed her off."

"There's a colorful image."

"C'mon."

She held her breath for a second. "I'll think about it."

"Seriously, I've got to run. I love you."

"Love you too."

The call ended, and she returned to her computer. With a click, plants clinging to trellises like vined menorahs appeared on the screen. She increased the focus to amplify the oxygen-supplying lobes of the kiwi-colored grape leaves.

Possibilities glided into her consciousness. *Do I have what it takes to step away from the safest choices?*

Before she could fully weigh her courage, the door squeaked open and Frank appeared in the kitchen. "Hey, kid."

"You're home early." She snapped her computer closed like a child hiding a secret.

"Thought I'd hang out with Charlie while you go after Jamie."

Lark smiled. "Thank you. That's a great idea."

❧

A HALF HOUR LATER, LARK joined the throng of other parents outside the school's entrance.

"Who rattled your bird cage, Tweety?" Bianca tapped her shoulder.

"Hi." Lark took in Bianca's flowery scent and relaxed at the sight of her blessedly familiar face. "Kindergarten's going to take some getting used to."

"He'll do great. Don't worry."

He might do great. His mother's future is another story.

Bianca's smile grew and she squeezed Lark's arm. "Having you here's the best."

The best, huh? Lark wouldn't consider a dead husband and moving home to live with her parents at the ripe age of thirty-eight as the best of anything. Dolly Parton would be challenged to infuse as much woe into her songs.

"Raising our babies together is going to be so much fun." Bianca glanced behind Lark. "Where is Charlie?"

"With my dad. Yours?"

"Garth stays with a sitter on Mondays so I can help Dale with invoices."

A guy adjusted his ball cap as he joined the waiting parents. His mouth bent into a half smile and fine lines knitted around his smoldering eyes.

"There you go." Bianca slapped her on the arm. "Cute daddy. No ring."

"Too soon." Lark played it off with a shrug, but she couldn't argue against his attractiveness. The guy was hot.

"Okey-dokey. Noted. Not to worry—you've got time to sample that cutie pie when you're ready."

Lark laughed. "Don't hold your breath."

While they waited for their children to be dismissed, Bianca pointed out a few parents—a banker named Cathy and a realtor named Della. Granola-mom Hannah wore long braids, didn't vaccinate any of her five children, and was a known germaphobe. Superdad Jeffrey stayed home with the kids, made cupcakes, and coached soccer while his wife ran the hospital.

But what's the story on the cutie-pie in the Ranger's cap?

"And *her. . .* " Bianca's face soured as she gave a slight nod toward a petite woman with a matronly black ponytail and a serious case of resting bitch face. "Before she decided to stay home with her kids, Francie Varga was a VP, or, I don't know, something important." Bianca blinked a few times. "She gets things done around here," she whispered, "but . . ." She sighed. "You'd think she's running the United freaking Nations."

Lark twisted her mouth. "Well, I want to get involved. Would you mind?"

"Here goes nothing." Bianca steered Lark across the courtyard. "Francie?"

"Ohhh." Francie dragged out her words and her eyes conveyed a judgmental glint. "Hello, Bian-cah-h-h."

When she had made the necessary introductions, Bianca stepped back and busied herself with her phone. Apparently, her work was done.

Francie quizzed Lark about her recent move and became downright friendly when she learned Lark was Millie's daughter. As luck would have it, Millie had one of her twins in her class.

Lark mentioned her interest in volunteering and Francie raised one artfully sculpted brow. "Your child will bring a form home. There's a whole process."

"In the meantime, if you need help, I can give you my number," Lark offered.

"Someone will call you once you clear the background check. Remind your husband—daddies help, too. We can always use more worker bees."

"Oh, I'm—"

"Just return the form to the office." Francie gestured to the school. "Newbies start on cafeteria duty."

"At some point, I'll be working during the day, but—"

"The bulk of PTO work is done by those of us who are homemakers and house-daddies." Francie might as well have worn a sandwich board reading, WE'RE CLOSED.

Uninterested in more one-sided banter, Lark separated herself. "Well, I told Jamie I'd meet him in Mom's classroom. Nice meeting you, Francie."

"Mind if I come with?" Bianca asked, stepping back in.

Lark nodded, and they walked into the school.

End-of-the-day lunchbox aroma and fatigue hung in the air, ending the new-school-year freshness all too quickly. Hair had become sweaty. Shoes had gotten scuffed. Young bodies were wilted with exhaustion.

Bianca lobbed her head backward. "Don't take Francie personal. She's like that with everyone." Blowing a strand from her face, she whispered, "Even Mr. Rogers would've called her an asshole." She looked at the ceiling and crossed herself. "God rest his sweater-clad soul."

Seven

Lark

On the other side of a door marked Mrs. Lovejoy, Fourth Grade, a cluster of students whirred in anticipation of the ringing end-of-the-day bell. Emboldened by her Class Leader lanyard, a black-haired girl held a finger to her lips, shushing her peers into a line of tiny soldiers.

"Mrs. Lovejoy's back there," the girl said. "She left me in charge."

"Big responsibility," Bianca said before following Lark to the rear of the classroom, where Millie was pushing a bin of markers into a cabinet.

"What a nice surprise," Millie said to Bianca.

"Needed a Millie hug," Bianca said.

Millie indulged her in an embrace.

"How was your first day?" Bianca asked.

"You are not my teacher," a boy growled loudly at the class leader.

"Hold on," Millie said, already strutting away to upend certain mutiny.

"Gotta run after my crew," Bianca told Lark as she scooted toward the door. "Catch up with you later."

The bell rang and Millie guided her students from the room.

"Hi, Mom." Jamie appeared, looking somewhat weathered. "Guess what?"

He sidled into her. "I got to hold the hamster. His name's Goober."

"Cool," Lark said, leading Jamie into Millie's classroom.

Millie walked to her desk. "Heard you did great today, Jamie." She turned to Lark. "He made some new friends."

"Did you?"

"Uh-huh." Jamie yawned.

"Mom, this guy needs a snack." Lark ruffled his hair. "We're going to head home."

"See you back there," Millie said with a nod, and Lark led Jamie to a corridor, where they joined an indecisive herd of students migrating toward the exit.

"Mom." Jamie pulled Lark's hand and lobbed his head toward a boy. "Kingsley's my friend."

Lark pulled Jamie to the side as the boy approached, excited to meet her son's first friend in his new school.

Kingsley's flaxen-haired bent upward on one side and his white button-down oxford was crumpled. Behind him, a woman looped a rather mature-looking North Face backpack over her arm.

Lark could practically see an aura of old money circling Kingsley's mom. Hot off the pages of *Town and Country Magazine*, she was flawlessly coiffed, golden skinned, and dressed to the nines in that way women do when they're trying not to look like they're trying hard. As if she needed the height, she wore four-inch hemp espadrilles with an embroidered white cotton tunic, slim-cut jeans, and a commotion of bracelets in every metallic denomination.

"Is this your new friend?" the woman seemingly asked her son, keeping her gaze pinned on Lark. "Kingsley told me about his new pal; he wants to know if they can have a playdate."

"I'm Lark."

"Elke." She waved. "Can we get these two together?"

"Please, Mom?" Jamie asked in an urgent tone.

"After school tomorrow?" The woman's lips stretched into a wide, welcoming smile that said, "Come on in, the water's fine."

"Um, sure." The words didn't come easily, but the sight of Jamie enjoying being a kid eased Lark's tension.

"I'll take him home with us tomorrow. Can you pick him up around five thirty?" Elke said.

Lark gave her a blank look.

Elke frowned a question.

"I'm sorry." Lark smiled nervously. "School and playdates are all so new."

"Sure, sure," Elke said and handed a business card to Lark. "My cell phone."

Lark ran a fingertip over its raised gold ink.

"Our house is behind the other buildings." Elke glanced at her watch, one of those high-tech telephonic pieces attached to a gold watchband—an actual piece of jewelry. Her mouth gave a regretful twist. "Kingsley's about to be late to piano."

"Oh, okay. Enjoyed meeting you," Lark said.

Elke and Kingsley hurried away.

"I really get to go?" Jamie asked.

"You bet," Lark answered mindlessly while she inspected the card. Below two interlocked Hs, it read, HARTMANN-HAAS CELLARS, WOLF AND ELKE HARTMANN-HAAS, PROPRIETORS.

THE NEXT DAY, LARK WRESTLED Jamie's backpack from him, troubled him for a quick hug, and reassured him she'd meet him in a few hours.

"Okay, Mom. Bye." Jamie ran off with Kingsley and crawled into Elke's white Mercedes road warrior–edition SUV.

At five twenty, Lark pulled through the gates of the Hartman-Haas's place, slowing on the rough-cut road to observe a crew hauling shrink-wrapped stacks of acrylic ghost chairs and Chiavari seating into what looked like an event building. She drove farther and braked beside a barn-like structure where men unloaded massive stainless-steel tanks from a semi-trailer. What she'd give to get out of her car and snoop around.

Around a corner and down in a valley, the big show unfurled itself: acres of grapevines traipsed over hills as far as she could see.

She squinted at the trunks to estimate their age. Since they were as wide as her hand, she guessed they had to be at least thirty or forty years old. Compact grapes dangled beneath emerald leaves, signaling the upcoming harvest.

At the prospect of returning to winemaking, excitement filled Lark's chest. Would Elke invite her to participate in the crush season? Could it be this easy?

"Mommy?" Charlie said. "Where's Jamie?"

Ah, the reason we came here. Move along, Lark.

A windmill and cistern sat at the edge of a homestead that blended German farm building design with half-timbered Anglo settlements, typical of 1880s South Texas Hill Country architecture. Established by pioneers in the area, the style was characterized by hand-cut limestone, rough mortar chinking, and a metal roof.

The odor of fresh paint drew Lark's eye to the bright red cedar overhang projecting over the wide porch. She rang the doorbell and detonated a barking tirade inside the house; in short order, two caramel-coated doodles leapt up at the door's bubbly Pulegoso glass.

Elke cracked the door. "Hold on." She closed it. "Down," she yelled, and then opened it again. Behind her, the dogs disappeared into the house. She shook her head. "I'm sorry."

"Don't worry about it. We're dog people," Lark said.

"They're *Wolf's* animals." Elke bristled. "He's never home to take care of them, and they're horrible."

If she thinks they're horrible, she should see Walter Cronkite.

"Come in." Elke waved them into a foyer.

A staircase hugged one side of the living room; a formal area was arranged on the other. Weather-beaten logs framed the windows. White candles filled the fireplace. A pair of cream sofas flanked a petrified wood coffee table. Left of the foyer, a grand piano swallowed a room its former occupants might have used as a home office or a dining room.

"Kingsley," Elke called up the empty staircase.

Pounding feet struck the floor overhead, and then her son appeared at the landing with Jamie in tow.

"Take Jamie's little brother upstairs so his mom and I can visit."

"C'mon, Charlie. Kingsley's got the coolest stuff up here." Jamie threw a wave from the top of the staircase.

Charlie eagerly climbed toward his brother.

"Let's go in here." Elke gestured toward a narrow hall covered with black-framed photos of Kingsley. They passed through it and entered an *Architectural Digest*–inspired kitchen that didn't seem to fit at all with the home's original architecture.

"Have a seat." Elke gestured to tufted leather bar stools on the eating side of a massive white marble island. Expansive windows flooded the space with light. Reclaimed wood accents balanced white cabinetry to deliver tasteful elegance. "Want a drink?"

"Ice water would be great," Lark said.

Elke disappeared around the corner and returned with two ice-loaded glasses. She filled them with water and passed one to Lark.

"Love this ice," Lark said, noting the nugget-shaped ice, the kind she'd only had at fast-food restaurants.

"Can't stand the chunky refrigerator-made ice, so we bought a commercial dispenser." Elke picked up a chef's knife and diced celery while they talked. Suddenly, her face darkened, and she pointed the knife toward an overhead speaker playing Gwen Stefani's "Hollaback Girl." "Sorry about the language." With her other hand, she swiped at her phone to change the song and Michael Bublé's "Quando, Quando, Quando" filled the room. At the chorus, she swayed and wiped the butcher-block cutting board.

"Your home's lovely." Lark admired the fluid marriage of old and new, including glass cabinets showcasing artsy pieces and collectibles—a celadon vase, a serving platter adorned with Kingsley's handprints, and a two-foot-tall Jan Barboglio metal angel.

"I prefer to build new," Elke said. "Old houses have their problems. Ancient plumbing, low ceilings, closets like suitcases. Wolf had a guy draw plans for a whole house remodel, but he said the winery comes first."

Of course, it would.

"The house sat empty for years after my grandparents moved to San Antonio. It was so outdated. No space to park our vehicles." She gestured with the knife. "I refused to move in until he fixed this kitchen. I would've bulldozed the place and started over, but my grandparents are still alive, so we have to, at least, pretend like we're keeping up the historical designation." She rolled her eyes.

"Do you and your husband tend the vines?" Lark asked, hoping the question might lead to an expanded discussion.

"Grandad leased the land to other wineries after they moved." Elke's feeble shrug spoke volumes about her involvement in the winery. "He offered it to us when we got married, but who wants to live in Fredericksburg when you have Seattle? Right?"

"What changed your mind?"

"Wolf traveled constantly between Seattle and Chicago, finally got tired of the rat race."

"Does he like it here?"

"He hasn't been around long enough to know yet. Still wrapping up our businesses." Elke's smile couldn't hide her irritation.

"Oh." Lark pointed to the window. "What varietals do you raise?"

"Can't say for sure. Chenin blanc and Syrah?" She squinted at the ceiling. "Wolf has a guy for all that. Honestly, I never understood the appeal. More of a vodka girl."

Looks like any hope of finding work here will require an introduction to Wolf's Grapevine Guy . . . not to be confused with Wolf's Architect Guy or Construction Guy.

Lark's eyes flitted to the double-sided stainless refrigerator, covered in a conglomeration of Kingsley's artwork and photos of the family looking effortlessly happy. A snapshot of Elke, tanned as a coconut in an itty-bitty bikini, included a man with crow-black hair and a too-white smile, strikingly similar to the slick fiancé in *Titanic*. In another, the family grinned with red faces in Aspen. The photos reminded Lark of a family in a store-bought frame. Bitterness gripped her stomach but she refused it the attention it needed to survive. With an uncomfortable swallow, she said, "You're blessed."

"We are. So very blessed." Elke turned to look at the vibrating phone on the island. "Excuse me." She disappeared into the laundry room and Lark's hand drifted to her sternum—balm on a wound she couldn't heal.

"Mommy, look!" Jamie's raspy voice paused the highlight reel in Lark's mind.

He waved a plastic robotic toy at her. "Kingsley's got *Quickshadow*."

"Cool." She pulled on an amused expression.

"Kingsley said it's rad. Rad means cool, I guess." He gave an inquisitive shrug.

In addition to being named Kingsley in a class of Austins, Dillons, and Noahs, the kid's kindergarten coolness was off the charts.

That apple didn't fall far from the tall blond tree chopping celery in this kitchen.

"Jamie," Kingsley called, and Jamie turned on his heel.

"Wait for me!" Charlie padded behind the other boys.

"They're having fun together." Elke came around the corner. "We should do this more often." Her artfully highlighted bangs fell forward and she pushed them away from her eyes. "Do you work?" She put a hand over her face. "I know you work, but out of the house?"

"I'm an attorney, but I haven't found work here yet. I'm not too jazzed about working in a law office."

"I hear you. I worked for a high-end hotel chain until we had Kingsley. Wolf's travel schedule made it impossible to stick with it."

"What did he do before you moved here?"

"Stockbroker. Later, he managed a hedge fund, but one day he comes home and says he's burned out. 'Pack your bags, Elke. We're leaving.' All that toxic energy finally got to him." She waved her hands over her head. "So, Grandad's offer finally made sense."

Elke leaned across the island and dropped her voice. "Hope I'm not stepping where I'm not welcome, but Jamie told us about his father in the car on the way home—as much as a kid his age knows to tell."

"I'm curious—what did he say?"

"Kingsley's been on this kick—trying to get Wolf to take him camping. Jamie said his dad would've taken him camping, but 'he's in heaven now.'" Elke took a drink from her water bottle and nodded. "Your boy's a sweet kid."

"He is—so much like his dad."

Elke pursed her lips and tilted her head. "If I can help . . . picking up from school or whatever you need, text me."

"Thank you."

"Hey, you guys want to stick around for dinner? Wolf's actually going to be in town tonight."

As tempted as she was to talk to Wolf about the winery, Lark didn't want to deny her new friends their family time—especially after hearing about Wolf's travel schedule.

"Maybe another time. Mom's expecting us right now."

Lark urged her boys to put away Kingsley's toys before they jumped into the car. As she drove away, she caught sight of fresh lumber framing an addition on the rear of the house. She shook her head at the sight. *What more could they need?*

THE FOLLOWING WEDNESDAY MARKED JAMIE'S first kindergarten field trip. Lark assumed her criminal background check had turned up clear, because she was invited to chaperone.

She and Charlie waited in the hall outside of Mrs. Rhodes's classroom with a few other parents, including the handsome daddy from Jamie's first day. Lark tried not to gawk at him, but she couldn't restrain her runaway imagination. *Hello, Mr. Salt and Pepper Waves. I'm Lark, and you're gorgeous.*

"Hey." The guy nodded at Lark.

"Hi. I'm Lark, Jamie Mead's mom."

He glanced up at her for a second—long enough for her to take in his eyes, blue like the pilot light on a stove.

"Levi Gallaher. Mitchell's my son." He crossed his arms over his chest and they waited in silence.

Lark pretended to examine her cuticles.

"Parents!" Mrs. Rhodes interrupted Lark's preoccupation. "We'll load the students on the buses. You can follow in your cars."

Mr. Handsome met Lark's gaze. "Want to ride together?"

She pointed to Charlie. "He needs a car seat. Want to ride with us?"

Levi pursed his lips thoughtfully and gave a brisk nod. "Sure." He followed them to the car without another word.

❧

IT TOOK LARK A FEW BLOCKS to gather up the nerve to break the silence. "We just moved here."

"Oh. What's your husband do?"

I'm not wearing a ring, Mr. Oblivious.

"He *was* an attorney." Lark paused, considering Charlie sitting behind her. "He isn't with us anymore. ALS? Lou Gehrig's disease."

"Oh, man. I feel you. A drunk driver took my Melissa two years ago."

Handsome and heartbroken. Should I offer him a hug?

"I'm sorry." And she was sorry. There was little relief knowing you weren't the only parent who had lost a spouse.

He fidgeted with a keyring. "Thankfully, our kids weren't in the car." A hand tapped the armrest. "Moved from Kerrville to be closer to her parents. She grew up here."

"What was her maiden name?"

"Ryan."

"Melissa Ryan? *Walker* Ryan's baby sister?"

"You knew Walker?"

"We dated in high school." Lark blushed. "What a nice guy."

"Agree."

They arrived at the alpaca farm, and she unstrapped Charlie from his seat.

"Say, Lark?" Levi walked behind her. "Want to meet for dinner one of these days? Talk about the single parent gig? No pressure. Not like a date or anything." He shrugged and rearranged his ball cap.

"Yeah, sure."

Not like a date? He sure didn't linger in the gray area for long.

Levi wandered away, and out of nowhere, Bianca appeared. She tossed a glance at Charlie. "Had I known, I would've brought Garth to play with Charlie. Anyhow, *you've* been busy."

"Huh?"

"You and the cutie pie?" She turned her lips in and made big eyes.

"Oh, he rode with us."

"What's he like?"

"Quiet."

"Mom!" Jamie waved at her and pointed to the animals.

A breeze spread a bitter smell of damp hay. The alpacas bobbed and ducked, clucked and hummed—not so different from the children clustered together with their mouths agape.

The farmer showed the kids where the animals ate, slept, and pooped—the last part ignited giggles when the kids learned alpacas did their business in a communal space.

Elke waved from the opposite side of the alpaca corral.

"Friends?" Bianca asked.

"Jamie and Kingsley had a playdate."

"And?"

"She's nice."

"Meh. Jury's out." Bianca flicked her hair from her face, swatting it back like a bothersome insect.

"What'd she do to you?"

"Can't put my finger on it. Maybe the way she carries that Louis bag like an infant while her kid runs around like Lucifer on speed."

"Come on."

"Learned a long time ago to trust my instincts. That one sets off all sorts of alarms in my gut."

"Eat a hamburger."

The farmer paraded out a gingerbread-colored alpaca named El Jefé. He told the kids they could pet him. Eager hands rose, and he pointed at Jamie.

Jamie's eyes went wide with excitement and he stepped forward.

At the sight of her older son's euphoric face, Lark put to rest all doubt about their move to Fredericksburg. Jamie was home, sweet home.

Jamie's interest in animals didn't stop at the farmyard. Later that day, while riding home from school, he spied a ten-foot-long plastic crab dangling from a building.

"Can we go there, Mom?" he asked, pointing to the restaurant, which was covered in fishing nets and Godzilla-size plastic sea creatures. The name on the sign read, Marco Polo, A Culinary Experience.

"One of these days," she said.

"One of these days is what you say when you don't want to do something." Skepticism occupied Jamie's voice.

"You know how much Grammy loves making dinner for us."

"Doesn't she get tired of cooking all the time?" He let out a long sigh.

"Never."

Back at the house, Lark opened the refrigerator and found a foil-covered casserole with a note attached:

Bunco game night at Judy's house. Dad's meeting with his beer team. Bake lasagna at 350° F for twenty minutes. Love you, Mom

"What's that?" Jamie leaned into her and spied the note.

"Poppy's got a meeting tonight and Grammy has bunco."

"What's bunco?" He said the word like it was a disease.

"A game—Grammy's playdate with friends."

"Huh." He lost interest.

"Want to go to that restaurant with all the crabs on it?"

"Really?"

Lark nodded and Jamie punched the air.

"We're getting crabs, Charlie!"

Eight

Lark

The hostess at Marco Polo led Lark and her boys through the tin-walled dive past memorabilia and photos of Marco Regalado, the restaurant's octogenarian owner, who proudly displayed his prize fish mounts alongside bumper stickers proclaiming GOD BLESS JOHN WAYNE and WILLIE NELSON FOR PRESIDENT.

She guided them to a red leatherette booth and set menus on the table.

"Where's the fish tank?" Jamie asked.

The hostess shrugged and stepped away.

"I thought dolphins and sharks would be here, Mom," he whispered across the booth. His eyes slid to the side, then bloomed. "What is *he* eating?" He crooked his head toward a man sliding oysters into his mouth.

"Raw oysters."

Jamie's head snapped back. "Don't they have a oven to cook the food, Mom?"

"You can order cooked food, too." She nodded at the menu in front of him.

"Good." Relief hit his face.

The simple menu consisted of oysters, jumbo shrimp, popcorn shrimp, crab balls, and crawfish, each served with an order of French fries and coleslaw. The boys had baskets of popcorn shrimp, fries, and hush puppies—not the most nutritious spread, but they didn't leave a crumb behind. Lark made a mental note to return with her dad. With the trophy mounts, lobster traps, and nets strewn from the rafters, this was his kind of place. *On second thought, never mind. One fried meal from this place might land Frank back in the ER.*

THE SEQUOIA HAD ALMOST CLEARED the parking lot when Charlie whined, "Dino-raur, Mommy?"

"What's that?"

"He left his dinosaur." Jamie's words triggered alarm bells.

Lark drove to the front of Marco Polo and locked the car. "Stay in your seats. I'll be right back."

Wyatt

UNFAZED BY HIS SISTER'S TARDINESS, Wyatt arrived at the crowded restaurant and ordered a couple beers, two dozen raw oysters, and all the fixings—just what the doctor ordered for him and Kelli to relax after a long day.

He wasn't surprised she hadn't arrived on time. Her hands were full. She worked full time as a nurse, and her husband spent every other month on an offshore oil rig. When he was gone, all parental responsibilities for their daughter fell on Kelli's shoulders.

Wyatt scanned the news on his phone while he waited.

"Hey, stranger," a woman with smiling, clear blue eyes said.

"Howdy, Miss Mead."

"Lark," she corrected him.

"Howdy, Lark. Where are the guys?"

"In the car." She gestured with the toy. "Charlie left this. Wish we would've known. We would've asked you to join us."

"I'm meeting someone, my—"

"Of course. Well, I'd better run. Good to see you."

"You too."

Wyatt found it funny how speaking to her for just a few seconds could lighten his spirits, especially when he considered the way Lark had received him the first time they met.

Her mention of a dinner invitation sparked a fire in him. Maybe it was the way her hair was always in a mess—kind of a sexy mess—or the tiny scar on her chin. Would have been easy enough to dislike her that day in the store until Jamie asked about the leg. But the picture got clearer when the kid started talking about his dad.

He reasoned why the kid's mother might be furious with the world—probably in the same shape as Vince Blazek's widow. Wyatt could only guess. He hadn't gathered his nerve enough to face her.

The bell over the restaurant's front door clanged and he waved to his sister.

"Sorry I'm so late." Kelli slid into the booth. "Got home from speech therapy and Zadie had this birthday party, but I hadn't gotten a chance to buy a gift yet, so we had pop into Toyland, and . . ."

Wyatt knew the drill; he buckled up for one of Kelli's vent sessions.

"Feels like I never get to come up for air." Her lip curved into a snarl. "I wake at Satan's butt-crack of dawn, make Zadie's lunch, and drop her to the babysitter. I'm throwing this kid out of bed at five, dumping her at this woman's house to feed her breakfast and take her to school. When I get there to pick her up, she's already told someone about her day. When I ask about it, she acts like I'm asking her to remember being born."

"Sorry."

"Hoped I'd get time to change clothes." She looked down at her scrub top.

"You look fine. I ordered beers for us."

"How about—"

"Oysters are on their way," he said.

"Oh, I almost forgot this one . . ." She ran a hand over her long, sandy brown ponytail. "Red wants another baby."

Buckle up. The ride's about to take off again.

"Sure, he's Mr. Mom when he's not on the Gulf, but how does that help me when I'm pulling shifts at the hospital and raising Zadie by myself? If he was home all the time, I'd be all-in. I mean it. Red's a kick-ass father. I'd have a litter if I could."

The server delivered the icy tray of oysters and a tin bucket of crackers.

Kelli suspended her vent session to doctor the metal cup of cocktail sauce with an extra glob of horseradish. "Who-all's coming to Mom and Dad's this weekend?"

"Just TJ and Kermit." Wyatt tilted the Tabasco bottle, adding the fiery sauce into the mix.

"Not so much." As Kelli leveled his hand over the cup, she glanced to the side and dropped an irritated brow. "In-com-ing," she sang under her breath.

"Long time, no see." A woman approached and leaned into Kelli for a side hug.

"How are you?" Kelli asked.

"Hi." The woman wasn't just cute; she had curves in all the right places and a breathy voice. This one had a lock on the best kind of sin, no doubt about it.

"Howdy," Wyatt said, soaking up the attention.

"So, this is your brother?" She shot a knowing glance at Kelli.

Kelli dismissed it with a nod. "Wyatt—Carmen Loera. Carmen—Wyatt," she said, gesturing with her tiny fork. "Carmen and I worked together at the hospital."

"Until one of us got a promotion." Carmen wiped the edge of her glossed lips. "How's that new job going?"

"It's going." Kelli opened a package of saltines with the grace of a longshoreman.

"She didn't tell me you were so handsome," Carmen purred.

She didn't tell me she had a friend like you, either. Wyatt pointed two fingers and pivoted them from his eyes to Kelli's. It was their stink-eye sign.

"He's alright." Kelli motioned toward him with a saltine.

"Bet Kelli's glad to have you around." Carmen tilted her head and her long, dark waves floated over one shoulder. "I sure would be."

Kelli slapped a runny oyster on her saltine.

"How long's he been in town?" Carmen asked, as if Wyatt were invisible.

Kelli shoved the oyster-topped cracker into her mouth, lifting a finger to pause the conversation as she swallowed.

"Six months," Wyatt answered.

"Well, then." Carmen gave a sultry half smile. "Before I spill a big bunch of embarrassment all over my pretty shirt." She swung seduction like Obi-Wan's light saber. "Anybody special in your life?"

"Um." Wyatt licked his lips. "No, ma'am."

"Ma'am?" Carmen giggled. "I'm barely thirty."

A theatrical cough exploded from Kelli's mouth.

"Well." Carmen locked her gaze on Wyatt and gave a small shrug. "If you want to get together . . ."

Kelli coughed again, this time with a deadpan stare.

Carmen took a step back. "Kelli has my number."

"Oh, yeah, I've got your number," Kelli said.

"Okeydokey," Carmen said. "I'll look forward to hearing from you."

And I'll look forward to calling.

A hot rush raced over his skin. The doctors had warned he might suffer in the sex department, but Carmen had just confirmed that when presented with the right stimulation, all systems were a-go. Of course, she had no idea about the carnage beneath his shirt.

"Bye, Kelli. Wonderful meeting you, Wyatt." Carmen sauntered away.

When the coast cleared, Kelli dropped her fork and jabbed her finger across the table. "That one's a *no*. You hear me?"

"She was sweet, and friendly." Wyatt cocked his chin to one side. "Plenty friendly."

"Is she your type now?" Kelli stirred another clump of horseradish into the seafood sauce.

"She's cute, and she smells like flowers."

"Listen to me, brother." Kelli clenched her jaw and spoke through her teeth. "That one could suck the chrome off a trailer hitch."

"Whoa, sister. You kiss our mother with that mouth?"

"Calling it as I see it." She gestured with her beer bottle.

"Jesus, Kel, you're being pretty harsh on a woman you've only worked around at the hospital."

"I know *enough*. She won't be so cute when she sinks in those claws and bags you with a baby."

"A baby?" he muttered and looked away.

"Wyatt," Kelli said.

His gaze remained pinned on a blue marlin's bayonet of a nose.

"Wyatt, c'mon." She nudged his hand and they locked eyes. "You haven't met women like her. I'm serious."

"Sure you are."

They ate in silence until Kelli pushed herself out of the booth. She pointed to the tray of oysters. "I'm running to the ladies' room. Don't eat all of those."

Wyatt gave a slight nod and slathered a cracker with cocktail sauce. He plopped an oyster on top and crammed the entire thing into his mouth.

A minute later, Carmen slid into Kelli's seat. "Thought I'd catch you alone for a sec."

Wyatt raised a finger, nodding and pointing to his overstuffed mouth.

"Let's take Kelli out of the middle." Carmen waved a piece of paper in front of his face, teasing him to grab it.

With a painful swallow and a cautious glance at the ladies' room door, he accepted the paper and shoved it into his shirt pocket.

"All that time in the desert, you probably have some catching up to do, hmm?" Carmen's lip curved into a flirtatious grin.

Wyatt felt his face turn red. Turning to the oysters for a diversion, he slid the mini fork into the gritty corner of an oyster shell, but the meat wouldn't separate from the shell.

"I'd be happy to show you around." Carmen cocked her head to one side.

That oyster wasn't giving in easily. Wyatt slid the fork into the stubborn adductor muscle.

"Call me any time." She set a hand on his arm, and he stole a look.

The fork broke through the muscle and shot the clammy orb from its shell. It left the table, sailed into the air, arced down . . . and slapped the tile in front of Kelli's feet.

With a glare that could've dropped a deer at 500 yards, Kelli's gaze flickered from Wyatt—fork still in hand—to the oyster on the floor to, finally, Wyatt's arm, where Carmen dared to place a hand.

"I hated seeing your brother sitting over here all alone," Carmen said in a babyish voice. "Keeping him company until—"

"I'm back now." Kelli turned to her brother. "Better not have been the last oyster."

Wyatt shrugged and pointed to the two remaining ones.

Carmen shimmied out of the booth and past Kelli, mouthing, "Call me," behind Kelli's back.

The siblings didn't speak for a long moment.

"Wyatt." Kelli ground out. "See what I mean? Leave you alone for two minutes and she's jumping on you like a dog on a meat wagon."

"Nobody's . . ." He lowered his voice. "Nobody's jumping on anyone. I'm a grown man. If I wanted to jump, or whatever, it'd be *my* business."

"Fine." She inverted her palms. "Just don't come to me when you're riddled with some nasty disease."

"I wouldn't dare."

Lark
....

THE FOLLOWING AFTERNOON, A CURIOUS George cartoon and a handful of Thomas the Tank Engine toys entertained Charlie while Lark resumed her job search.

She was unsurprised by the lack of prospects—and not entirely disappointed, either. The idea of hanging out in a law office all day didn't light her on fire. Becoming a lawyer had never been her dream.

After that summer in Calistoga, she returned to Texas Tech to begin her senior year. Jaded from her internship experience, she began to question the wisdom of pursuing a job in a male-dominated business.

Then, 1,800 miles away, the Towers fell. Though far from the Big Apple, a seismic shift occurred in the Lone Star State—for Lark, anyway. Winemaking became trivial, and California lost its shimmer.

Millie latched on to Lark's sentimentality and uncertainty and started arguing the practicality of a legal career over winemaking. Her arguments took hold, and Lark reconsidered. Perhaps her mother should've studied law?

Lark took the LSAT and earned a seat in the following year's class at Tech's law school, where she met her husband. Meeting him had made going to law school worth it, even if it wasn't doing much for her now that he was gone.

The prospect of hanging a shingle in a rented office remained viable, but damn it all, she wasn't feeling it. She'd rather open an interpretive dance studio.

The jobs she was finding that did look promising were too far from Fredericksburg. And she didn't meet the qualifications for the corporate law gigs close to home.

With nothing but time on her hands, she made virtual visits to Hill Country wineries via their websites. Ultimately, she landed on the Gruene Wine Festival's website.

Made up of twenty-five acres between San Antonio and Austin, the town with a funny spelling of a common color had gotten its start in cotton, but its famous dance hall was what had put it on the map. Nightly concerts at Gruene Hall featured impromptu performances by Garth Brooks, Willie Nelson, and Little Richard and gave up-and-comers like George Strait and The Chicks a place to cut their teeth. The Gruene Music and Wine Fest, meanwhile, invited tourists to sample Hill Country beers and wines at a park within throwing distance of the hall each year.

Years earlier, she and James had attended the festival, drawn to the concerts and tubing down the Guadalupe River with friends. Unimpressed with regional wines, Lark had skipped the tastings. Now, however, at thirty-eight, Lark couldn't deny the success surrounding her. She saw the error of her former ways, and she hungered to be a part of Hill Country winemaking. With each click through the festival website, she pictured herself strolling from booth to booth, sampling, studying, and becoming acquainted with regional wine producers. She'd call it "research" for her next career.

Who am I kidding? My viticulture acumen is as stale as the hot-rolled hairstyle I wore in college.

She couldn't expect to jump into winemaking on a dream she'd rejected years ago. Creating wine wasn't as simple as growing healthy fruit. It took work and money and a sense of timing, not to mention an understanding of physics and chemistry, to create a delicious pour.

Shake those cobwebs loose, Lark.

She opened that worn spiral notebook and tapped her pen against her temple. Soon, formulas for flow rates, gases, and temperatures landed on the page.

Keep stirring.

"One vine produces around 3,000 grapes," she said aloud, narrating as she wrote. "Seventy-five grapes per cluster . . ." She opened her smartphone's calculator and tapped the screen. "Need four clusters for a bottle. That's 3,600 grapes. Say I start with 2,000 cases?" More tapping and writing. "I only need . . ." More tapping. "Six acres and 7.2 million grapes. Mother trucker."

She returned to the notepad and listed the basics—land, trellises, fences, bottling equipment, irrigation, pest management, marketing, and labor.

Simmer.

The internet put information at her fingertips, providing estimates for holding tanks, glass, filters, and foil spinners. With each detail, her dream began to shape into an actionable vision. A business plan came to life with a template she found on the Texas A&M Agricultural department website.

Stir.

An initial investment might get her started. But with ongoing expenses, assuming her winery avoided floods, fires, and pestilence, her little idea would operate for three to five years with zero profit. Zero.

Did I stir too hastily?

Unwilling to kill the dream, she switched gears and clicked through real estate websites, searching for a property befitting a winery.

"Fredericksburg real estate is some of the most expensive in Texas," one website read.

"Well, screw me."

"Huh, Mommy?" Charlie, who was playing quietly with his wooden trains on the floor below her, said.

"Nothing, baby."

After toggling filters and refreshing her browser, the O'Keeffe Ranch came into view. Hope bloomed in Lark's chest. She'd fallen in love with the house when she attended a party there in high school. Living in that three-story Queen Anne with a wraparound porch would be a dream come true.

More clicking led to photos of the land but none of the home's interior. External views proved the years had not been kind. But it wouldn't be the first time Lark had turned an eyesore into a show-place. A positive charge filled the air as she imagined painting the weathered siding and refinishing the wood floors.

"160 acres with commercial development potential," the sales copy said. "Access to highways and the Wine Trail."

Winner, winner, chicken dinner.

When her eyes locked onto the asking price, her smile flattened. Not ready to give up, however, she sketched a crude map on the lined pages and carved the land into segments. Assuming the well hadn't run dry and the irrigation system was functional, both could feed the drip lines to nurse trellises.

Leasing another segment to ranchers for use as grazing land would provide revenue. Distant wooded portions along the back of the property might serve as hunting leases.

She drew a line down the middle of a clean page, then designated one column as Source and the other Expenses. James had invested well and purchased life insurance, enough to incite a debate. Lark had contended he had purchased too much. He'd said she'd thank him one day. Between that, the cash from the sale of their house, and the payout from James's 401(k), her portfolio was impressive. "Damn," she mumbled.

She couldn't bring her husband back. But for the sake of their sons, she could create a healthy future from what he'd left behind.

That afternoon, when she reached Gillespie Primary to pick up Jamie, self-doubt had begun to abrade her optimism. Her wine-making ideas now felt more like whimsical daydreams. *Who am I kidding? I have two boys to raise; I don't have the luxury of risking the financial legacy James provided for our family.*

On the drive home, she received a call from Jim Mead, her former father-in-law.

"How are you?" Jim's voice played over the Bluetooth hands-free player.

"We're doing well. How are y'all?" she asked.

"As good as could be, considering. Am I bothering you?"

"Nope. I'm in the car with the boys. You're on speakerphone."

"Oh, tell them 'hello' for me."

"They can hear you, Jim."

"Oh, alright. How does Jamie like his school?" His question exposed his confusion about the workings of a hands-free system.

"I'll let him tell you. Jamie?"

"Grandpa, it's me," Jamie said.

"Hi, son. Are you enjoying Fredericksburg?"

"Uh-huh. Guess what?"

"What?"

"I got to play on the monkey bars in our physical educlation class today, and I crossed the bars faster than other kids."

"Physical educlation, huh? Your dad was athletic, too." Jim's voice quavered at the end, and he cleared his throat. "Are you helping your mom take care of Charlie?"

"Uh . . . yes, sir."

"Hi, Gamm-pah." Charlie waved to no one, searching for Jim's voice.

"He's waving at you," Jamie narrated.

"Hi, Charlie. We miss you." Jim paused. "Lark, do you have a minute?"

"Sure," she said, disguising her reluctance.

"Nadine and I hoped to give you some time to settle in."

"We're settled. What's up?"

"Before Jamie and Charlie forget who we are, we'd like to take them for a weekend."

"They'd never forget you."

"A chance we'd rather not take. They're all we have now."

"Jim, they're energetic guys—a weekend may be more than you want. Maybe I could bring them to you for an afternoon?"

"We'll be good. Please, Mom?" Jamie shout-whispered.

Jim's laugh indicated he'd heard. "Sounds like Jamie's on board."

Lark envisioned Charlie lifting Nadine's prized Home Shopping Network knickknacks and throwing Hummel figurines like plastic Army men.

"Are you still there?" he asked.

"Sorry. I'm driving and I don't have a calendar close." She doubted her nonexistent social schedule would interfere with their plans.

"Please, Mom?" Jamie's tone grew urgent.

"We can pick them up next weekend, or the next?"

She thought about the wine festival in Gruene, a stone's throw from New Braunfels. A few days on her own might do her some good, and she'd be down the road from her boys if something went south.

"I could bring them to you this weekend while I putter around in Gruene," she offered.

"You're welcome to stay here if you'd like."

"A friend invited me to meet her for the weekend, so I'll stay with her." The little white lie flew off her tongue too easily. "Still firming up plans, but I'll bet we can make it work."

"Nadine will be elated. She didn't want to pull them away from you while you were still grieving, but—"

"Jim, I think we're all missing him."

"We didn't see James enough when he was here, and we're not willing to make the same mistake again."

Lark's chest ached at Jim's remorse. "One of the perks of our moving is being closer to y'all."

"How sweet. So, how's the house hunting going?"

"We're hanging tight at Mom and Dad's for a while."

"You'll start searching for work, too?"

"That's my plan."

"I imagine staying with your parents must be a help, saving money."

"We're doing alright."

"If you'd like to go through your bills and statements together, I can explain any of the financial terms you might not understand."

"What a generous offer." Lucky thing Jim couldn't see her eyes rolling. "I'll call you to talk about the weekend after I get everyone down for the night. Around nine, okay?"

"Of course. Speak to you later, dear."

"You bet." Lark pressed the red box on the screen to end the call. "So many questions. Ay-ay-ay."

"Ay-ay-ay," Charlie repeated.

"Mom, if we see Grandma Nadine and Grandpa Jim, can we sleep over there all by ourselves?" Jamie asked.

"Will you help with Charlie, keeping him out of trouble?" Lark's stomach twisted. Asking him to be responsible for his brother seemed wrong, but the Meads hadn't exactly been hands-on grandparents. They couldn't know what they were getting themselves into when they agreed to keep the two boys—especially Charlie. The boy lived full tilt. His curiosity took him in every direction. *What could go wrong?*

Nine

Lark

"What's brown and stout and sure to knock your lederhosen off?" Lark's father asked, walking into the house with a paper sack under one arm.

"No telling," Lark said.

"Lovejoy Ale." Pride blossomed on his face. "Your mom and I haven't had this much fun preparing for Oktoberfest since you lived at home."

"Aw. That's nice."

She'd all but forgotten the event before moving back to Fredericksburg. All over town, posters advertised FUN FOR ALL AGES with animated pictures of polka dancing revelers and younger attendees waving from kiddy-scaled amusement rides in the Kinderpark.

Frank wiped at his beard. "Lovejoy Ale. The guys let me put our name on it. Lovejoy's a lot easier on the tongue than Beukelman or Tiefenthaler. Besides, Lovejoy Ale says, 'Drink this beer and you'll find love and joy.' Hmm?"

"Won't hear me argue, Dad."

Frank put a finger over his mouth. "You're getting an early sample." He removed an amber bottle from the sack and pulled a juice glass from the cabinet. "Ready or not."

When he handed her the glass, an aromatic fusion of pastureland and molasses hit her lungs. If "ready" or "not" were her choices, "not" would be the ringer.

"Don't sniff it, drink it," he said.

At his hopeful expression, she tipped the glass and endured a palate-punishing sip. "Ooh," she pulled the cup away from her mouth. "Too stout for me."

Hope fell from Frank's face, and she adjusted her expression. "Sorry, Dad. I'm a light-weight."

"Right. Right. But if you were into those stouter ales, would you like it?"

The eagerness in his eyes was almost enough to take a second sip. *Almost.*

"I'd beg for more," she said.

"Good enough for me." He nodded, capped the bottle, and placed it inside the refrigerator. "I'll see what your mom thinks. She's been sewing up a storm for you and your guys."

"How's that?"

"Lederhosen for the boys and Fraülein costumes for you and her—matching ones."

Wearing a matching Fraülein costume with my mother? "Fun" isn't quite the word for it.

"What a surprise. That's so . . . thoughtful of her," she said through her teeth.

It was no secret that Millie lived for those annual Oktoberfest cooking contests. To hear her tell it, everyone raved when she added clever twists to traditional German potato salads, strudels, and schnitzels. When she came home that day, she changed out of her teacher clothes, eager to tweak that year's entry—Millie's Rolls of Love and Joy, à la cabbage. Wearing a "Mom"-embroidered apron, she was in her element in the kitchen. She boiled cabbage leaves and sautéed ground beef, caraway seed, and marjoram before mixing it all together, rolling the meaty goodness inside the leaves, and finishing the rolls in a braise of seasoned broth.

A half-hour later, she removed a pan from the oven, sending a savory mist into the air.

"Smells delicious, Mom." Lark's gaze returned to her notebook.

"What are you working on?" Millie set the hot pan on the counter and peered over her shoulder.

"Just playing around with an idea for a winery."

"Around here? In Fredericksburg?"

"Would you prefer I explore options elsewhere?"

"Not what I meant." Millie set a hand on her hip. "You may love the stuff, but working for a law firm will provide a more dependable livelihood than any winery could."

"Seeing as how I can't find a legal job with both hands and feet . . ." Lark gave a resigned sigh. "Just a thought. Who knows? Maybe when Jamie and Charlie are both in school, I'll be ready."

"You'll be a partner in a firm by then."

"Or I could work at a winery to learn more."

"You need benefits and eight-to-five workdays. No weekends. You have to be two parents." Millie's eyes rolled toward the great room, where Jamie and Charlie were playing.

"I'm sure wineries offer benefits. There are so many around here."

"Too many, if you ask my opinion."

Good thing I didn't ask.

Millie shook her head. "I can't believe these graperies generate enough business to stay in the black."

"Graperies? There was a time you were excited for me to pursue winemaking."

"I'm always excited about anything you do. I trust you'll make responsible choices for your boys."

Stealth manipulation mode is engaged. Check.

"You guys loved it when I talked about becoming the next Heidi Peterson Barrett while I was at Texas Tech." Before she went to college, Lark threw the famous female winemaker's name around when her mother argued that winemaking wasn't a "girl's job." She popped her head to one side. "Now wine's evil?"

"It's not *evil*. If it's good enough for Jesus, it's good enough for me. But Jesus didn't scrap his dependable carpenter job to become a full-time winemaker."

"I can't cure the sick and I'm not qualified to save the world—"

"Drama won't get you a job, either."

"WOOOOO!" Charlie zipped through the kitchen and crashed into the back of Lark's chair.

"Seen any evil dudes?" Jamie coasted to a sweaty stop behind his brother, panting.

"Not around these parts. Better run along before Grammy slaps you down for thinking outside the box."

Millie pulled on her wise-guy face.

"Huh?" Jamie asked.

"Fancy bath towel . . . er . . . cape," Lark said.

"Yeah. And Mom?" His voice fell to a whisper. "Works to clean up melted brains, too."

"No bad guys or melted brains here," she said.

"They went over there," Jamie announced before zigzagging out of the room, cape flying in the air behind him.

Charlie growled and followed hot on his brother's heels.

Lark's phone whooshed with a text from Bianca: *Are you coming?*

"Fudge." Lark slapped her leg.

"What's wrong?" Millie asked.

"I forgot about a PTO meeting tonight."

"Need me to keep Jamie and Charlie?"

"Would you mind?"

"No." Millie's face changed, and she started pacing around the kitchen. "Lark?" She paused at the corner of the island. "Your dad and I make plans." She cocked her head. "Not as often now, but every once in a while."

"Not so often . . . with us here?"

"It's not about you. But we do like to go out once in a while. Provide more notice the next time, please."

"I can skip it. I haven't even showered today."

Charlie rushed to Lark's side. "Jay-mie's metting my brain."

Millie's stony face slackened as she eyed the Spiderman training pants on Charlie's head. "Get on with that shower if you're going," she said in her teacher voice. "If you have time, try on the dirndl, and I'll finish the alterations while you're gone."

Ah, the dirndl.

Lark wasn't going to wear the Fraülein costume. With neither the heart to tell her mother nor the figure to fill out the blouse, she retreated to her bedroom.

After the door snapped closed behind her, an uncomfortable tightness surrounded her, like she'd wedged her feet into shoes a half-size too tight.

She leaned into the bathroom and twisted the dial to warm the water while she scrutinized her closet. The clothes she brought from Houston hung on the left. Relics from her younger days dangled on the right. Drawn to the old stuff, she pushed the items along the metal rod, uncovering a bewildering collection of faded homecoming mums strewn across a single padded hanger.

"Can't believe she saved these," Lark said aloud as she touched one of the dinner plate–size corsages. "Who decided these ridiculous things boosted school spirit?"

Below the silk flowers, her name shone in glittery letters glued to yard-long ribbons. Depending on the year, the boy's name on the tacky mishmash of tiny cowbells, teddy bears, and miniature mascots dangling from the yard-long ribbons changed. Four homecoming mums with four names—RICKY, CALEB, ADAM, and WALKER.

She lingered on the last one.

That stupid, crushed homecoming mum from 1997 was worthless. What she'd considered serious at eighteen was trifling now. She hesitated to look at a plastic dry-cleaning bag that held waterfalls of ivory tulle hostage.

"Not today, Satan." In one swift motion, she returned the hangers to their previous positions. Then she turned to her dresser and fished out a black T-shirt, yellow cardigan, and pair of cropped jeans, which she carried into the bathroom and dumped next to the sink before undressing.

The shower provided a safe place to release all the emotion she'd been keeping under the pressure of her "Happy Mommy Show." Dense air pressed on her lungs and she leaned against the white subway tiles in an expectant position as grief rose to the surface. Fat tears mingled with the water.

A sudden knocking indicated she wasn't alone.

"YOU ALRIGHT, LARK?" her mother asked, her voice muffled like it was coming through a paper towel tube.

"Jesus," Lark mumbled. "I'M FINE."

"YOU'VE BEEN IN THERE A LONG TIME."

"GIVE ME A FEW MINUTES," she said in her patient-mommy voice. She rushed through the rest of her usual showering business, turned off the water, and stepped out to towel off.

As cool cucumber-aloe lotion turned her warm skin to gooseflesh, the knocking resumed.

"Just a minute," she said, plucking her tangled strands of hair into manageable waves.

"Can I come in, Mom?" Jamie pleaded.

As she turned the knob, he pushed the door open and rushed past her into the bathroom.

She moved into the hallway to give him privacy—and stepped directly into her mother's path. "What's wrong with the boys' bathroom?"

Millie shot her a puzzled expression. "He heard you cry, and he's worried about you," she whispered. "He's not the only one."

"I'll be fine, Mom. Have a little faith in me."

A NERVOUS TRICKLE RAN DOWN Lark's spine as she turned into Bianca's neighborhood. The line of cars indicated the meeting was heavily attended, and she perked up at the promise of making new friends.

A short blond woman answered Bianca's door. "Here for the meeting?"

"I'm Lark Mead."

"Eva Zavala. Everyone's in there." Eva motioned in the direction of a Tuscan-inspired dining room. Past the table, where guests filled their plates with cut veggies and crackers, Bianca's voice poured from the kitchen. Lark followed it.

Glazed gold walls mingled with the ambient lighting to warm the faces of the women.

"There's my girl," Bianca trilled.

Over the next half hour, Lark met PTO members who offered invitations for playdates and made small talk about their children.

One pair of women didn't mingle; they were seemingly engaged in a serious discussion. Of the two, she'd met the brunette in the T-shirt, jeans, and heeled boots. *What was her name? Missy-something. Or, was it Bitsy? Teensy?* Whatever her name was, the poor lamb couldn't seem to get a word in edgewise.

The chatty one whipped around. "Lark Lovejoy?" The woman's straight dark hair met her shoulders, and she wore a cropped cream blazer and loose-fitting copper-tweed slacks.

Smiling in response, Lark tried to place her.

"I'm Sissie," the other woman interjected.

Sissie, that was it. But who's the other one?

Cooler than iced tea, Sissie and her friend exchanged glances.

"We've heard about the elusive Lark for years," the friend said in a raspy voice.

"Elusive?" Lark chuckled. "Sounds so dramatic, like something on a nature video. The hunter has finally located the—"

"Cougar?" the chatty one said. Her mouth turned up on one side, accentuating a beauty mark.

"Hardly." Lark's laugh became a snort, and, she covered her mouth. "Sorry."

"You're missing the point. This is Sissie *Dietrich*." The woman quirked a sculpted brow as if she expected Lark to recognize the name.

A warning prickle ran down Lark's spine and she shifted her gaze to the agitator. "Excuse me. You seem to know who I am, but I don't think we've been introduced."

"Della Betancourt, I'm Sissie's best friend. About time you met, don't you think?" If arrogance were a sport, this chick's body would fold in half with gold medals.

"Nice to meet you." Lark gave a little nod. "What am I missing?"

"Dietrich?" Della repeated it an octave higher. Her head sloped with indignation. "Ring a bell from high school?"

"Caleb Dietrich? You're his wife?"

Sissie nodded.

"Small world. How is he?"

"They're separated." Della lobbed the words like grenades.

"Oh." Lark leveled her smile and swallowed. "Sorry to hear that." She had mixed feelings about Caleb. They'd only dated for a few weeks. After she broke it off, he'd continued an overt flirtation—nothing that fell into stalker territory, but it had left Lark wondering if she should be flattered or creeped out.

Della stared, unblinking. "You and Caleb reconnect yet?"

"Last time we spoke was . . . when? Our ten-year reunion?"

Della huffed and shot a glance at Sissie.

"What's going on?" Lark asked.

"Caleb's been giddy as a schoolgirl since he heard you were coming home."

"This is the first time I've left the house during an evening since I moved here," Lark said.

Sissie's face drew closed, like she'd given up, but Della had her back.

"How would you feel if *your* husband couldn't keep from wetting his pants every time someone mentioned his ex-girlfriend?" Della asked.

"My husband passed away." Lark hazarded a look to the right and left. *Where is Bianca when I need backup?*

"I'm sorry for your loss," Sissie said.

"Thank you. I—"

"Do you know how many times poor Sissie heard him go on about the perfect Lark Lovejoy?" Like a stage mother, Della rolled her hand in a circle, prompting Sissie to perform on demand. "'Lark was the one . . .'"

"'The one all the guys remember,'" Sissie murmured.

"My personal favorite is, 'Any of the guys would've married Lark if she would've come home to Fredericksburg after college. She was our fantasy girl.'"

"What the . . ." Lark's voice fell away, and she tightened her posture, preparing to cartwheel this nonsense into next week. "We barely dated in high school—it was hardly serious."

"He was serious about you." Della made a sucking noise through her teeth.

"I can't even . . ." Lark stumbled over her words and moved closer. In a boiling mix of empathy for Sissie and anger for Caleb, her heart threatened to vault from her chest. She took a breath to steady herself. "Do you and Caleb have children?"

"One." Sissie nodded. "A daughter starting high school. But I still volunteer at Gillespie, it's something Della and I do together."

"That's generous of you." Lark didn't loosen her gaze. "Look, I'm sorry you're going through this."

"I'll get through it," Sissie said.

"Yeah, she will," Della's glass of wine had apparently provided enough smugness to keep competition in the air. "Sissie's daddy is Thomas Klein. The divorce lawyer? When he's done ripping a new one through Caleb, the jerk won't have two crumbs left to spend on the next woman." Her expression left no doubt who she meant when she said "the next woman."

Sissie's lips tightened and she gave an almost undetectable head shake.

Lark took an uncomfortable step toward Della. "I'll bet Sissie's grateful you have her back. Friends are important during a separation—especially when you can't tell who or what she might be up against."

"No doubt," Della said.

"Don't waste all that fire on me. I have no intention of dating him, or anyone, for that matter." She turned to Sissie. "I'm sorry Caleb spoke about me like that to you."

"I'm sorry about . . ." Sissie's face was grim.

"You don't need to apologize for me," Della said.

Sissie's expression hardened. "Della."

"Okay," Della mumbled. "Can't be too careful."

"Right. Well, it was nice meeting both of you." Lark walked away from them and toward Bianca.

"What, honey?" Bianca said, decoding Lark's frown. "Was someone catty to you?" she whispered. "Point 'em out and I'll pour a fiery can of whoop-ass on them."

"Keep a lid on that can. I can handle myself."

Bianca shot her an "if you say so" shrug and clapped her hands. "Ladies, I hope by now you've met my bestie. Lark has two darling boys. Jamie's in kindergarten and Charlie's three. Her mom's Millie Lovejoy. She teaches fourth grade."

"We love her," a woman said.

"My son's in Mrs. Lovejoy's class," another remarked.

"They recently moved here from Houston," Bianca said.

A woman said something about a husband and Bianca propelled a lemme-at-'em scowl in the direction of the voice.

"It's alright," Lark said in a low voice. She turned to the woman. "He died last year. We're doing okay." Bianca squeezed her shoulders. "Enough about me. I'm excited to hear what's planned for the Thanksgiving event!"

Twenty-some sets of eyes stared at her. Lark became uncomfortably self-aware. Moisture beaded on her forehead and her hands turned cold. *What has come over me?* She felt like a frightened bird slamming itself against a closed window.

Ten

Lark

....

"Honey?" Bianca whispered, bending toward her. "Your face is milky white. You okay?"

Lark couldn't explain what she didn't understand. "I need to run. I forgot I was supposed to help Mom."

"You sure?" Bianca asked.

With Lark's nod, Bianca created the space for her to pass and she returned to her car. When her body normalized, she drove home.

She parked in the driveway and the line of trellises threw shame on her as she passed. All the weeks she'd been in Fredericksburg, and she hadn't lifted a finger to release them from their torment. So much for all the possibility she thought she'd find when she returned home.

The house was empty, but her parents' voices seeped inside through an open window over the kitchen sink. Lark stole a peek and saw the boys playing around the old tree fort.

"You don't have to *do* anything," her dad was saying. "Just be there for her."

"Crying like a baby in the shower? It broke my heart when Jamie asked me to help her. Poor kid just planted himself outside that door worrying about her. I fudged and told him she'd stubbed her toe, but he knew better."

"*Rrrr.*" Walter Cronkite announced his presence with a growl.

"Shush," she whispered.

"*Grrr.*" Walter had other ideas.

"It's just me, you dumb dog."

She set a hand on the top of the mutt's kennel. He shoved his nose against the wires and snuffled her fingertips.

"Sometimes I wonder if I should shake her and tell her to get her act together for the boys' sake," Millie's words pulled Lark to the window. "Or should I hold her like a baby? Tell her she can cry as long as she wants?"

"*Rrrr,*" Walter rumbled again. The clock was ticking. The needy little bastard wouldn't stay quiet long.

She reached into the refrigerator, grabbed a piece of American cheese, rolled it into a ball, and tossed it at the dog kennel. When the ball landed squarely between the metal tines of his jail cell, Lark rewarded herself with a fist pump and Walter rewarded himself with the cheese.

"Charlie—both hands," Frank hollered. His voice dropped. "Takes time, Millie. Hold on." He stood. "Charlie, BOTH HANDS. Show him, Jamie."

"Okay, Poppy," Jamie yelled.

"I don't like seeing her struggle, either," Frank muttered.

Lark leaned against the cabinets and flattened a hand over her chest.

Walter reminded her of his presence with a single yap.

A bowl of grapes sat on the counter. She couldn't remember if they were safe for dogs to eat. After another whine, she stopped debating. Eyes still fixed on the window, she pulled one from its cluster and tossed it. The grape bounced off the wire, and the dog gave a whine.

"She doesn't have a choice," Millie said. "The boys need her. She needs to wrap that pretty little head around her responsibilities. Time to lock in a job and take care of her family. We raised our kids. It's her turn."

"I see you, Charlie," Frank said.

"Stop frowning at me," Millie said.

"Way to go, Jamie!" His voice quieted. "James hasn't been gone long. Give her enough time to get her bearings."

"She's not healthy. What's with all this running? Miles and miles she goes, and what does she have to show for it? She's a string bean."

"With your cooking, you'll be calling her a pumpkin soon."

"Maybe so." She tsked. "She doesn't handle challenges like the girl we raised."

"She's not a girl, Millie. She's a woman who's had her life on hold taking care of a dying husband. Give her some credit."

Lark's stomach clenched. *Dad said she'd settle down. From the sounds of it, she's just getting started.*

"The boys run around her, waiting for her to see them . . . really see them." Millie gasped. "Are you ready for this? She's talking about opening a winery. She said it was in the idea stage, but I could see those wheels turning."

"She's always wanted to make wine. To tell you the truth, I don't think she ever had her heart set on the law."

"Maybe, but this isn't the time."

"You never thought it was the time—even when she was in college, you tried to talk her into being a teacher. She's not you, and you have to support her."

"I support her just fine. She needs stability now. A winery, Frank?" Millie's words didn't bother Lark as much as her sarcastic tone did.

"Mil, he left her with plenty of money. If she never worked again, she'd live a more comfortable life than the one we're living. Besides, you said she's only thinking about it. Isn't it better for her to think about the future instead of the past? She's always had a head for business. We paid for her to go to college to learn the wine game."

"We paid for a law degree, too."

An angry heat rose inside Lark's chest and she slipped out of the house and back into her car. Taking advantage of the remaining light, she aimed for the O'Keeffe Ranch.

A FEW MINUTES LATER, SHE parked in the driveway at the ranch. The dipping sun offered enough light to appreciate the land's sharp variations, which suggested it might be less hospitable for grapevines and more suited for an orchard or grazing animals.

The house hadn't been especially attractive in the online photos, but up close it gave off an eerie vibe. Milky paint covered the basement windows. Years of neglect had stripped the clapboard siding of its color, exposing rotten wood. Weathered shingles curled on their ends and sections of the delicate fretwork had broken away, making it look like a second grader's gap-toothed smile.

Lark approached the porch with caution, and her knees shook when wood planks pitched with squeaky warnings.

Within minutes of her arrival, the bloated orange sun teetered on the horizon, threatening to sink and flood the land with darkness. An owl hooted. A floorboard wobbled, and her knees buckled. She grasped the slanted railing and scurried away from the haunted house.

"No thanks." She jerked the door closed behind her. "What was I thinking?"

Still not ready to face her parents after what she'd overheard, she locked the doors and swiped at her phone until she retrieved a specific playlist.

A horn section filled her car with pleasant noise. A few seconds later, Otis Redding reminded her to try a little tenderness. She closed her eyes and sang, the lyrics thundering from her belly. She smacked the dashboard as Otis brought the song to a high point and it ended, leaving Lark feeling like she'd just walked out of a holy roller's salvation show.

Her mother was right about one thing: she needed to get her act together. But first she had to decide where that act would take her.

She had no doubt Fredericksburg was good for her boys, but she had to find a way to make it work for her, too. The Meads wanted to spend time with Jamie and Charlie; it was a perfect time for Lark to rediscover herself.

She opened her phone's browser to search for a hotel room in Gruene.

FRANK HAD INSTALLED MOTION-ACTIVATED security floodlights. They lit in succession, spotlighting Lark like an escapee from a maximum-security prison, when she returned. Fearing an audible alarm would follow, she hurried inside.

"How was PTO?" Millie sat on the sofa beside her napping husband before a muted television playing a news program. She dropped an embroidery ring in her lap and looked over pearl-encrusted half glasses.

"Interesting." Lark considered her words.

"Hey, kid." Frank roused himself and picked up the magazine tipped on its side in his lap. "Did she show you the video?"

"Haven't had the chance," Millie said. "She just walked through the front door."

"Here." He stood, dug his phone out of his pocket, and pushed it into Lark's hand. "Your mother turned on the Carly Simon music she likes—"

"Carole King," Millie corrected.

"Whatever. First, she was unloading the dishwasher. Next time I looked up, she and Jamie were dancing. Pretty soon, Charlie joined in. God, they were cute."

Watching her mother dancing with the boys threw her off her game. How was she supposed to unleash the Kraken on a woman after looking at this video?

"Better download 'Sweet Seasons' to your iPhone," Millie said. "Jamie said he wants to listen to it on the way to school tomorrow."

Lark nodded.

"You've raised the kindest boys." Millie said. Perhaps she was regretting her earlier comments. She lifted the embroidery ring and turned it around to show Lark. "I'm adding a Spiderman symbol to Jamie's Oktoberfest costume."

"They ran around outside until they were as worn out as Walter." Chuckling, Frank gestured at the dog crumpled at his feet. "Then your mother threw them in the bathtub. Lights out in no time."

"Sounds like they put you to work?" Lark said.

Frank adjusted his glasses. "We enjoyed 'em. The only work we had around here was a bit of cleanup from someone's irritable bowel syndrome."

"Oh no." A mix of guilt and worry washed over Lark. "Which one?"

"The little twerp," Frank said matter-of-factly.

"Excuse me? Did you just call your grandson a—"

"Walter. He must have gotten into the trash or found something outside, because he messed in his cage, in the kitchen, you name it. Lucky for us, we installed the tile."

"Definitely."

Note to self—grapes and Walter don't mix.

"Did you meet other moms?" Millie asked.

Lark sighed. "Do you guys remember Caleb Dietrich? We went out sophomore year?"

"As I recall, you had quite the time shaking him. They don't even have a child at Gillespie anymore, but his wife still volunteers with her friend, Della."

"Oh, I met Della. She's a hoot." Lark bristled. "Operates on a whole other level."

"Hmm. Did you meet Caleb's wife too?" Millie asked.

"Soon-to-be ex-wife." She yawned. "I'm beat. See you in the morning."

"Goodnight," Frank and Millie said together.

MORNING CAME AND LARK STIRRED in a pre-awakened state, pulling the sheet over her shoulders, as her bed shook.

"Mom, your digit-clock says 9:52 a.m." Jamie jumped on her bed. "Are we going to school today?"

"Mother trucker." She bolted upright, pushing curls from her eyes.

"Mrs. Rhodes says we're s'posed to be there by 8:05 and if the second bell rings, we're late."

"Get dressed. Brush your teeth."

"Okay, but, the second bell already rang, so we're gonna be super-duper late."

"Pronto."

Lark hurried to the boys' room. Charlie lay in his crib, talking to the stuffed wolf he held in one hand and the toy train car he held in the other. He turned toward her, full of fresh energy.

"Hi, Mommy," he said in a croaky morning voice.

Her phone rang and she darted back to her room to pick it up.

"Hello, Mom," Lark answered, cringing.

"Lark, they told me Jamie isn't here. If he's sick, you have to call the office before nine."

"He's not sick. I overslept." She clenched her jaw.

"Do you need me to wake you up in the mornings before I leave for work?"

"No, I can handle it."

"Is Charlie missing preschool too?"

"No, Mom. He doesn't go on Wednesdays."

"Thank heaven."

"We'll be there in a few minutes."

"Don't forget to pack his lunch."

"I can feed my children, Mom."

"Fine. We'll talk later."

Jamie pulled on a shirt he'd outgrown a year earlier, but today wasn't the day for a style lesson.

"Mom, what about my lunch?" Jamie asked when they were halfway to school.

On top of not wanting her child to starve, Lark wasn't giving her mom the satisfaction of being right.

"Jamie, because you were so responsible and woke us this morning, we're going to do something different. You'll get to choose what you eat for lunch today."

"Cool . . . I mean, *rad*."

"You don't have to use the same words Kingsley uses. There's nothing wrong with *cool*, Jamie."

"I like rad. It's cool, you know?"

Lark pulled into the Mini Mart parking lot and led the boys inside the store, past a basket of apples, bananas, and oranges. They stopped in front of a refrigerated case filled with pre-packaged meal kits.

"Which would you like?" she asked.

Jamie pointed to one of the brightly colored boxes filled with crackers, cheese, and some form of processed meat.

Indecision weighed on Lark's shoulders; she imagined a she-devil of mommy shame wagging her red, dagger-like fingernails. She bit her lip. *It's not like I'm drowning the kid in the bathtub. He'll survive one Lunchable.* She grabbed it from the case before she changed her mind.

"What about breakfast?" he asked.

She screwed up her face and grabbed two juice boxes and a package of cinnamon-sugar donut holes.

"Breakfast of champions," a man's voice said from behind her.

Lark whipped around and caught a delightful sniff of Wyatt Gifford's freshly showered body, handsomely covered in dark jeans, a black button-down oxford, and cowboy boots. Remembering she hadn't brushed her teeth, she tilted away rapidly.

"Wy-tat." Charlie waved his arm back and forth like a castaway flagging a rescue plane.

"How are you guys?" Wyatt eyed Lark and her brood.

"Late to school." Jamie scowled. "Hope I'm not in trouble."

"You're fine." Lark ran her fingertips over Jamie's wayward hairs. "We overslept."

Wyatt winced in empathy. "Oops."

"We'll get through it." Man, she said that a lot these days. "We better run along. Have a good day."

"You too." Wyatt's smile sent a warm flush up her neck.

Lark tossed a pack of gum on the counter. Who knew when she might be doing this fire drill again?

THE BOYS SUCKED DOWN THE donut holes, not making a peep between the store and Gillespie. When they arrived at the school, Lark hoisted Charlie to her bony hip and escorted her tardy student to the office, expecting the Spanish Inquisition after her mother's phone call.

To her surprise, checking him in was relatively painless. The secretary sent Jamie on his way to the kindergarten hall with a slip of paper to pass to his teacher.

Lark pushed the door open to leave and Levi Gallaher's heavenly blue eyes met her on the other side.

"Hi." Levi held up two lunchboxes—Hello Kitty and Captain America.

"Bringing lunch?" She repositioned Charlie on her hip.

"Hazel had dance last night and I never got to the grocery store. You?"

"Overslept."

"It happens." Soft waves fringed the edges of his Texas Rangers baseball cap. "Call me if you ever need a hand. My number is on the class list."

"Thanks."

"Hope your day gets better," he said.

It just did.

Eleven

Wyatt

....

Seeing Lark put a nice shine on Wyatt's day. Back at his office, he waded through a backlog of paperwork until his phone pinged with a text from his ex-girlfriend. It wasn't the first message he'd gotten from Ashlen Paine in recent months, and it was unlikely to be the last.

Almost a year after she broke his heart, Ashlen's text messages renewed the sour taste of resentment in his mouth. Not ready to make nice, he tossed the phone on his desk. He had weightier issues to consider, like keeping this job.

Since his company had changed ownership, nothing had been the same. The TXEnergy staff understood that Foudre Unifie translated to "Unified Lightning," but everyone read the acronym the same way—FU. If the constant reframing of policies and time-wasting conference calls were any indication of things to come, employees were in for more changes.

"Don't forget your ten o'clock call with HR," Barbara, his secretary, reminded him.

"Not HR. What is it now?" Wyatt asked.

"Heck if I can remember." She stepped out.

A few seconds later, she called from the hall, "Principal Workforce Officer."

Wyatt shook his head.

In the world of Foudre Unifie, colorful leadership titles reigned supreme. Instead of a VP of Technology, it had a Chief Innovation Officer. The term "Marketing Director" was so last year. The new company employed a Global Trend Officer.

As the clock ticked closer to his conference call, scenarios spun through Wyatt's mind like debris in a dust storm. If the rumors of downsizing were true, his six-month tenure placed him at the front of the lay-off line.

He enjoyed the work and gave it his all, but some variables were out of his hands—like when the company tasked him with convincing community leaders to approve the use of wind turbines. The Hill Country prided itself on being "energy neutral," at least in terms of keeping the landscape free of energy-producing equipment. He'd been unable to deliver on this last assignment, and he had a bad feeling about this call.

He closed his office door and dropped into his chair. "Here goes nothing." He punched numbers on his phone's keypad and waited for a computer to connect him to a woman in New York City.

"Good morning," an effervescent voice answered. "This is Song Chu, Foudre Unifie's Principal Workforce Officer. Am I speaking to Mr. Gifford?"

"Yes, ma'am. You can call me Wyatt."

"Hi, Wyatt. You're probably wondering why I scheduled this call. Well, we've begun a new evaluation process. It will help us assess existing roles and efficiencies to create and implement ECCs, Efficient Collaboration Circles."

"Okay." *More ABCs—great.*

"Before we can discuss your role in the ECC, we need to update information on acquired staff. Did you finish the updates I requested last week?"

"Um . . . no. Not yet. I spent the last few days overseeing an equipment upgrade in Llano. I'm driving out there after this call to inspect the site before I sign off. When I finish—"

"You'll complete the updates?"

"Sure."

"I'll make a note in the system, so you won't be flagged as a DR."

"DR?"

"Delayed Response."

He made a note of the term on his desk pad.

"The managers will use the updates in the next steps."

"Next steps?"

"Our SET, or Strategic Exploration Team, will examine staff skill sets and performance records to find the best fit within our business models. Adjustments will be made to address efficiency gaps."

"I'm not sure I understand."

"It's simple—we want to place the right people in the right seats on the bus to best serve the organization."

Sounds like people are about to reach their stops whether they pull the cord or not.

"The new system will be a win-win for all of us." Song went on to explain other administrative processes unrelated to Wyatt's responsibilities.

When she finally took a breath minutes later, he jumped in. "Alright. Hate to rush you, but I'm supposed to be at a site visit in a few minutes."

"Your willingness to participate in this process is appreciated. Not everyone shares your enthusiasm."

"I'll bet," he said.

There was a pause.

"I'll schedule a call with you next week to talk through your updates. Include any changes in responsibilities or accomplishments that have taken place between your date of hire to the present."

"I've only worked for TXEnergy for six months. Not sure I have any updates."

"Have you attended continuing education classes or received a certification?"

"I got commendations from the Army."

"Include those and add a note if you're interested in relocating or cross-training for other positions."

Is she trying to yank my chain?

"Okay," he said.

"Any questions?"

He had questions, alright. Unfortunately, he didn't have time to extend their conversation—he had a job site to inspect in Llano. With the conference calls and two complicated installations, this week felt more like a month, but he was keeping his eye on the prize. In a few short days, he and two other members of Viking Platoon would be reuniting in Gruene.

He didn't care either way about the Gruene Wine Festival, but one of his buddies was excited about it, and Wyatt was just excited to get together.

Ding. An email dismantled his focus. Along with a list of documents she wanted him to complete, Ms. Chu was requesting a comprehensive market analysis that included current and prospective customers in each of the five counties he covered.

Ding.

A subsequent email instructed Wyatt to "update the status of any and all negotiations for the delivery and implementation of wind turbines using the attached template." Unconcerned with Wyatt's weekend plans, Song expected to see them in her inbox on Monday morning.

Lark

LARK'S INBOX DELIVERED DISAPPOINTMENT on a daily basis. Occasionally, while sorting through the blitz of premature holiday ads, she'd discover a law firm had reviewed her resume—standard form letters in the vein of "We've chosen another candidate" and "We wish you well in your future endeavors." They hadn't even offered her an interview.

Her mother wouldn't stop talking about her father's attorney friends. She pushed and pushed—"Mention your dad's name when you call; I'm sure he'll hire you in a heartbeat"—and finally, Lark agreed to email her resume. If it was meant to be, she wouldn't scrap a viable option.

And she'd jump at the chance to provide pro bono legal assistance to victims of domestic abuse like she had in Houston before James became sick. The work had been satisfying.

The shelter had changed the way she observed people. No matter how well a person projected confidence, abuse revealed itself in sneaky ways. Shoulders slumped. Voices softened. The gaze dropped too easily. But when those clients saw a way out, a glimmer of hope showed on their faces, telling Lark she had made a difference.

Her laptop came to life and she opened her resume.

"Way too much white space. Don't think caring for my kids or an ailing husband are what anyone's looking for." She shrugged and typed out a new cover letter—one she'd send to her father's friend.

Charlie ran past her, donning his protective head-shorts to prepare for his next round of what he dubbed Hypoman—chasing today's furry villain, Eve-will Wapper-Cronkite.

After several rounds, Walter dropped to the floor and exhaled a breathy *oof*. His perky ears drooped over his eyes like nightshades. The ratty fellow was growing on Lark.

"Mommy, I want to hold you." Charlie's energy faded and he crawled into the chair.

Lark set the laptop aside and wrapped her arms around him.

"Mommy, where Daddy go?" He spoke into her neck.

"Baby." She kissed his head as he pulled away to look at her, then tapped his chest. "Daddy's in here."

"Here?" Charlie pointed to his chubby white belly.

"Daddy's in heaven, but part of him is inside you, in your heart."

Charlie frowned at his chest and eyed the room.

"I know, baby."

He buried his head in her shoulder. In minutes, his snores tickled her neck. She closed her eyes and, without meaning to, joined him in a nap.

LARK WOKE TO A SOLITARY BARK, then a fusillade of them. She moved Charlie from her lap and he curled into himself like a warm cinnamon roll.

Bianca waved through the window adjacent to the front door.

"Hi," Lark said as she opened the door.

"Can we talk?" Bianca asked, marching ahead into the living room and taking in the remodel. "Pretty spiffy! Not what I remembered."

"Still getting acclimated myself."

Bianca nodded, letting the words glide away as her attention landed on Charlie. "Aww, sweet boy," she whispered. "You're a lucky momma."

"I am."

"Lucky, but stressed?"

Lark gave a slight shrug.

"Blessed with these beautiful boys and buckets of responsibility. Lark, I don't want to pry—"

"About leaving PTO early? I told you, I needed to help Mom. She's doing all these crafts for Oktoberfest."

Bianca nodded, took a seat on the sofa, and patted the space beside her until Lark joined her. "Well, here we are." Her voice was lamb's wool soft. "Just you and me." She sat up straight and patted her thighs. "Your mom's a sweetheart."

Lark nodded.

"You know, this morning at the school, she thanked me for including you in last night's meeting. She knew you must've enjoyed yourself because you came home so late."

Lark's breath caught and emotion threatened to burst from her veins. She stood and waved for Bianca to follow her to her bedroom. Once inside, she closed the door.

"Fine, here's the deal. I took a drive to clear my head."

"I'm worried about you." Bianca set a soft hand on Lark's forearm.

"Don't be. I'm just working through some things . . . trying to figure out where I fit here."

"With your parents?"

"Yes, plus finding a job, trying not to screw up my kids so badly they grow up to hate me . . ." She slapped a hand over her mouth to prevent more self-pity from leaking out. "You don't need me to dump all this on you. Jesus, you're like my only friend."

"I am?" Bianca laid a hand on her chest. "I'm your only friend?"

"Yes." Lark frowned at Bianca's apparent joy at her admission. "At some point, I'm hoping to make a few more."

"I can't believe I'm the one you chose to be your only friend." Bianca sounded a little emotional.

Lark turned to look at her old friend—someone who had carried their bond through years of hardships. Someone who celebrated every time they saw each other. Someone she could trust.

"Don't be so surprised. You're pretty damn special," she said. "Your friendship took me by surprise—just what I needed. Not sure I'll ever be able to thank you."

A seltzer of tears sprang from Bianca's eyes and her mouth twisted into an ugly, grimacing smile. "These . . . are . . . happy . . . tears." She put her arms around Lark and spoke into her hair. "I just love you, Tweety."

Bianca was right. Years and geography couldn't fracture a friendship forged by second grade innocence.

Lark bit her lip. "Love you too."

When they finally pulled apart, Bianca studied Lark's bedroom. "Did your mom do all this because you were coming home?"

"Before. Basically, they packed up all of our old stuff and converted our bedrooms to guest rooms."

"Pretty."

"I miss my tattered quilt on my battered old bed."

"We can pretend. Turn on that Thompson Twins cassette and pull out that stash of Twizzlers in your closet."

"How do you remember?"

"Best times of my life—until college and meeting Dale."

"He's pretty great?"

"He helped me work through some dark times."

"I'm sorry for whining to you about my problems."

"Stop saying that. Just tell me what I can do for you, Tweety."

"Um . . . do you think we could stick a fork in Tweety?"

Bianca jerked back her head.

"It makes me feel small," Lark said.

Bianca closed her mouth and nodded, understanding. "Well then." She slapped her hands together. "Poof! Tweety's gone. Now, you're the magnificent, grown-ass Lark Mead."

AFTER BIANCA LEFT, LARK RECEIVED a call from the Airbnb host in Gruene she'd contacted telling her the room she'd requested was available. She confirmed the room and then, realizing she had forgotten to call the previous evening, dialed the Meads.

"Hello," Jim answered in his froggy voice.

"Jim, I'm so sorry. I totally forgot to call you guys."

He coughed. "We worried when we didn't hear from you. Is everyone alright?"

"Oh, yes. I forgot I had to attend a PTO meeting. Good news—I worked out our plans for the weekend. What if I bring Jamie and Charlie to you Friday afternoon? Then pick them up Sunday morning?"

"Oh, I thought you were calling to say they couldn't come—this is outstanding! Nadine's not going to be able to sit still when I tell her the boys are coming to stay with us."

Nadine sitting still was the least of Lark's worries. With Charlie underfoot, his grandmother would be lucky if she got to sit down at all that weekend.

Twelve

Lark

Excluding the occasional greeting card or gift for the boys, James's parents had fallen off the face of the earth after the memorial service. Since then, time had thickened the polite tension that had always existed between Lark and the Meads.

The Meads' interest in connecting with their grandsons gave her pause. A firm believer in "when you know better, do better," Lark hoped this visit marked a change in their relationship.

Worry coiled around her middle when she flipped on her blinker to turn into the Mission Oaks subdivision of New Braunfels, however.

"We're here," Lark said as cheerfully as she could as they pulled into the driveway.

"Let's go, Charlie." Jamie released his brother from his car seat and, before Lark could say anything, the two of them scurried toward the house.

Lark caught up to Jamie and Charlie as they took turns leaning on the doorbell.

A shadowy figure with dark hair appeared behind the etched-glass doors.

"Grandma!" Jamie said with reassuring enthusiasm

"Who's there?" Nadine asked through a crack in the door.

"Me. Jamie."

"Meeee too," parroted Charlie.

Nadine flung the door wide open—revealing clothes better suited to an over-fifty beauty pageant contestant than a grandma hosting two rowdy boys for the weekend. She wore a matching violet cardigan set, pencil skirt, and kitten heels. Black hair cupped her face, and she was made up with her usual fresh application of Estee Lauder Poppy lipstick, the shade she'd worn since Reagan was still in office.

The four of them trickled into the kitchen, where Nadine had set out Ritz crackers and grapes. While the boys shoved crackers into their mouths, Lark walked out to the car to retrieve the boys' bags. Just as she stepped back through the front door, she ran into Jim.

"Here. You should've let me get those." Jim took the bags from her and his booming voice quieted. "This weekend means a lot to us." His expression was cloaked in sadness. "We hope to be there for Jamie and Charlie."

"I'm so glad to hear that. James would be pleased."

He cleared his throat and looked around the room. "I'll take these to . . ." He paused. "The boys will stay in James's room." He ducked his head and disappeared down the hallway leading to the bedrooms.

They had planned ahead. Toys in unopened packages waited along one wall of the living room. Nadine's fragile figurines had been lifted to high shelves in incompatible clusters.

But Nadine hadn't packed away her real treasure: the collection of photos on the kitchen counter.

"Thought I'd pull these out in case the boys want to look at them . . . so they can learn about their daddy." Nadine was pensive, almost apologetic.

"Great idea." Lark lifted one from the stack and ran a delicate finger over the shiny photo. "Hello, stranger."

"I wanna see." Jamie's head popped up, whack-a-mole style, through the crook of her arm. "That's Dad."

"Daddeeee," Charlie echoed from across the room, a word that should've been met with the welcoming arms of a father.

Please keep remembering him, Charlie-man.

"What are your plans?" Nadine asked.

"Nothing exciting. I'll probably just read one of the novels I brought along."

The man in the photo felt farther away than he ever had before, and Lark realized that her memories of him were growing fuzzy. She returned the picture to the stack, her heart aching with heaviness. Her gaze shifted to Nadine, who was studying her from across the kitchen.

Returning to her regularly scheduled Happy Mommy Show, Lark painted on a too-bright smile. "If you need me, I'll be close. Don't be afraid to call."

"We'll be fine, dear." Nadine said. "Thanks for letting us have them. Just yesterday, James was his age." She bent her head toward Jamie. "We're looking forward to making new memories with them."

AFTER SOAKING UP BIG CUDDLES from some small people and a reserved side-hug from Jim, Lark motored toward Gruene with her new friend, Siri, as navigator.

It was a short drive to the Airbnb, a hydrangea-blue cottage with flowers pouring from window-mounted flower boxes. *And, thank you, baby Jesus, not a rose to be seen or sniffed.* Attractive as the photo on the website, its white picket fence and clapboard siding were straight out of a Hallmark movie.

Well, almost. A sign hanging on the porch read, THE BABE CAVE: LEAVE YOUR WORRIES AND YOUR SHOES AT THE DOOR.

"Perfect," Lark said and toed out of her shoes. Balancing her belongings, she rang the bell.

"Lark?" A sprite of a woman cracked open the door.

"Yes, ma'am."

"I'm Annabelle Granger." Her voice was as soft as velvet, and she wore her hair in a graceful, silvery bob. "Call me Belle." She frowned at Lark's bare feet.

"Your sign said . . ." Lark pointed to the porch.

Belle exhaled a sweet little laugh and peeled Lark's bag from her shoulder. "Get your shoes and come inside."

A moment later, Lark found herself standing barefoot on a braided rug.

"Sit down." Belle gestured to an overstuffed loveseat and Lark fell into a hug of floral chintz. A second later, Belle placed a glass of iced tea on a crocheted coaster beside Lark. "Here, honey."

"Thank you."

"You are cute as a bug, and I'm pleased as punch to have company this weekend." Belle sat beside Lark. "So . . ." She dropped her hands on her knees. "A pretty lady like you? Here all by your lonesome?"

The only room in Gruene comes at a cost. Privacy.

But Belle's eyes were warm, so Lark indulged her with the Cliffs Notes version.

When Lark finished, Belle gave a slight nod and looked down. "Five years ago, I lost my Samuel. Lord—I still love the dickens out of the man." Her bony shoulders trembled. "Fifty-one magnificent years together. No matter how many, they're never enough." She took Lark's hand and patted it with each word. "But losing a husband when you're so young, with kids?" She gave Lark's hand a squeeze.

"You're sweet." Lark took a sip of the tea. *About time to lift this gloomy vibe.* "Are you going to the wine festival, Belle?"

"Heavens, no. Samuel and I bought this place to get away from San Antonio. It was our sanctuary. So peaceful—except when tourists block our sidewalks and weave around town like they just learned how to operate an automobile. This place is just awful this weekend."

"Oh, yeah." Lark squeezed her eyes at the ceiling. "Pretty sure that's exactly the way they describe it on the Chamber of Commerce's website." She looked at Belle without moving her head.

Belle gave a small chuckle. "Oh, don't mind me, I'm an old poop. Can't tell you much about wine, except I know what I like. You?"

"I studied wine in college but didn't do anything with it. Ended up in law school."

"Were you satisfied with your choice?" Belle asked.

"I'll let you know. I've considered revisiting winemaking. Never too late, right?"

"Never too late—take it from a seventy-eight-year-old. The clock ticks too blasted fast."

A car door snapped closed outside. "That's probably Theo, my man-friend."

A minute later, Belle introduced Lark to that man-friend, a retired gastroenterologist with a full head of white hair.

"I'll check on that faucet." Theo's head dipped in a nod and he strode into the kitchen.

"Shall we?" Belle gestured at a hallway and Lark followed her to a guest room covered in floor-to-ceiling, soft-hued cabbage roses. *Roses! Just what I need.* She sniffed the air. At least the wallpaper was odorless.

"Wi-fi code is on your nightstand. Let me know if you need extra towels."

Lark dropped her bag on the iron bed and poked her head into the en-suite bathroom, which was complete with a claw-foot tub. *For that tub, I can forgive the wallpaper.*

"Make yourself at home. Oh, you should know—restaurants stay packed on festival weekends. I don't usually include meals, but I'm happy to cook if you'd like."

Lark thanked her and closed the door to unpack. She powered up her laptop and retrieved the wine festival schedule. Friday events were restricted to premium ticket holders. Those tickets were sold out.

"When in Rome—or, in my case, Gruene." She brushed out her hair and left the house on foot.

Beneath the massive live oaks, she inhaled the relaxed buzz in the air. Quaint businesses were scattered between Victorian houses and historical sites—a fudge shop, a fly-fishing outfitter, and a half-dozen cafés and bars—every one of them humming with tourists. In the town's center was the landmark water tower and The Grist Mill restaurant. Listed as a "Must-Visit" on Yelp, the place had an hour-long wait. The hostess suggested the first-come, first-served bar.

Lark found the watering hole packed butt-to-champion-rodeo-belt-buckled-butt. Toe-tapping music played overhead, and she snagged a prime people-watching spot at a high-top table. On the server's recommendation, she ordered a jalapeño margarita and onion rings. The margarita was rimmed in tajín—a blend of chile, lime, and sea salt—to balance the sweetness of the drink.

The bar's atmosphere was unique, with a potbelly stove squarely in the middle of the space. Tin and rough-hewn lumber covered the walls and ceilings. A wild boar hung on one wall beside a trio of irreverently preserved jackrabbit heads mounted to wooden plaques. *What the . . . ?* Her eyes snagged on what looked like a ferret resting over a man's mouth. She blinked a few times and forced her gaze to her margarita while she reconciled her surroundings. *This requires confirmation. Just pretend you're looking at the dead animals on the walls.*

She turned and squinted, putting on a show of paying interest to her surroundings. Her eyes landed on the man's face again. *Yes, indeedy-do. I've stumbled on the mother of all 'staches.*

Then he caught her staring and, beer in hand, sauntered to her table. His gait begged for the musical accompaniment of *High Noon*. *Buh-dum-ba-da.*

"Anyone ever told you your smile's so bright, it could put out a man's eyes?"

"You'd be the first." Lark couldn't help but smile.

"Want a drink?" he asked.

She raised her margarita, and his nod acknowledged he'd received the message.

"Here for the festival?" he asked.

"Yep."

"Not much of a wine guy." He set his beer on the table. "I've tried that gin-fan-dell."

Does he mean Zinfandel?

"It was alright, but I'm pretty much a beer guy—Crown and Coke when I'm feeling wild." He offered his hand. "Grady Paxton. They call me Pax."

"Nice to meet you, um, Pax."

Make you a deal: you stop staring at me, I'll stop staring at that 'stache.

"Where you from?"

"Houston." She wasn't lying.

"Didn't catch your name."

Didn't offer it.

"Lark."

"That's a pretty one." He rocked back on his heels, lifted his beer, and took a drink. "Been next door? One of the oldest in the whole damn country." He cocked a thumb behind him.

"Not in years."

"Heckuva band playing tonight."

"No tickets." She shrugged.

"You're in luck. Got an extra ticket right here." He tapped the breast pocket of his shirt. "Might cost you a dance."

"Tempting, but I'm on my way out."

Suddenly, fear took hold of his face and he took a step backward.

"Uh!" Lark flinched as a hand hit the small of her back.

"Wyatt?" came out of Pornstache Pax's mouth. "Didn't know you and she—"

Wyatt? I only know one man by that name.

"Dammit girl," a voice said from over her shoulder. "You were supposed to meet me a half hour ago."

She turned 180 degrees and her eyes landed on a familiar face. *Of all the beer joints in all the world, Wyatt Gifford shows up in this one?*

"You ready?" Wyatt tossed her a wink. "They're gonna be waiting on us." He threw a nod in the direction of the restaurant's deck.

Ready for what? What is he doing here? "I, um, you, and . . ." Her words wouldn't fall into a logical order. "I haven't paid."

Wyatt swirled a finger over her table and the bartender nodded.

"Sorry." Pax upended his palms defensively.

"Think I'd let this one get away?"

Lark felt her brows slam together and she puzzled out her options. *Better off with the devil I know than the hairy varmint I don't,* she

decided. As Wyatt guided her toward the deck she said, "I had it handled, but you certainly expedited my getaway. Do you know him?"

He nodded. "Not a bad guy. Can't blame him for rolling the
dice with a pretty young lady on a Friday night."

"I'm old enough to take care of myself."

"Well aware." He choked out a laugh. "I've seen you in action.
If I hadn't stepped in, who knows what you might've done to the
poor bastard?"

"Whatever. How'd you know I was here?"

"I didn't. Meeting friends who should be here by now." He
scanned the crowd. "Went into the bar to check for them. There
you were."

"Huh."

He gestured to a table set for four overlooking the river—prime
real estate, judging by the line at the hostess stand. An icy bucket
of Shiner beers rested beside a basket of chips and queso.

She raised her eyebrows. "How'd you score this?"

"Got my sources."

"Plan on drinking this bucket by yourself?"

"I told you. I'm meeting friends."

She shifted her eyes around the table. "I should get going."

"Where you headed?"

"Honestly?" Her mouth quirked to one side. "Nowhere in particular. Hanging out while my boys visit my in-laws in New Braunfels."

"Then here you are." Wyatt offered a beer from the bucket.

Lark set her phone on the table and breathed out a sigh. "Here
I am." She took the beer.

After small talk about the festival and the weather, it was time
to get to know him a little better.

"You were really great with Jamie that day at the Mini Mart
. . . so willing to share your story with him," she said. "Marines,
was it?"

"Marines?" His brows flew up. "Try Army." He wiped his
forehead and blew out a breath. "Well . . . we were in Kabul. Heard
of it? Beach resort, jet skis, tiki torches?"

"I remember sand on the evening news. Missed the tiki torches."

"About right. Not much water where I hung out." Wyatt humored her with a chuckle. "Our deployment was supposed to end in a few days before . . ." His gaze dipped below the table.

"Did you have any warning before it happened?"

"You're never really not expecting something like that." He gave a slight head shake. "It was just another day at the office. In my case, on patrol with a buddy of mine, scanning the road for anything suspicious." Wyatt's mouth pitched up on one side. "He wouldn't shut up, going on about the Nebraska football team." The skin around his eyes squeezed tight as he trained them on a stain on the wood table. "Other than Daniel, his kid, that team was all the guy ever talked about."

"Excuse me," a young man interrupted.

He was delivering Lark's bar bill; Wyatt reached for it, but Lark quickly passed her credit card to the waiter. "I've got it," she said. "Thank you."

Wyatt nodded. "Where were we?"

"Your buddy . . . talking about football?"

"Not just football—University of Nebraska football. My friend, TJ, said something over my shoulder radio and I think I responded. Not completely sure. It all happened so fast. He must have stepped on it." A few seconds passed before he continued. "Shot my eardrums to hell. Only way I know I flew into the air is because it hurt like hell when I came down. After that, everything went black." He traced a water ring in the wooden tabletop for a few noiseless seconds. Then the tension left his face and made room for a vacant grin.

"Woke in sunny Germany. Hearing returned, but it was like being underwater for the longest time. It came back. Not so easy for the leg."

An update about the football fan was noticeably absent.

"So, that's the story," he said, pulling a drag off his beer.

"I'm sorry. Must be tough."

"The worst is when folks see my leg and then look at me like I'm a feral dog about to turn on them. Kinda like you did the day we met in the Mini Mart."

"I didn't look at you like that," Lark's eyes narrowed suspiciously.

"All due respect, but the hell if you didn't." Wyatt's deep-set eyes shot sparkles.

"I wasn't worried you might turn on us. I thought you were kidnapping my kid."

"What a relief." He waved to someone behind Lark.

"Lieutenant Gifford," a man brayed.

"Excuse me." Wyatt stood and walked toward a pasty-looking man.

Apparently, Wyatt's company was in high demand. Behind the man, a woman tossed a weave of bronze braids over her shoulder while she waited her turn.

"Look at you," the man said, and Wyatt held out his arms in a ta-da gesture. "You could suit up and hop on a C-5 to the motherland."

"Kerm, this *is* the motherland."

"I know." The guy looked at Wyatt like Jamie might consider an action hero. "Bet you could do it, though."

"Army disagrees with your assessment."

"Excuse me." The woman shoved the man out of the way and wrapped Wyatt in a teddy bear hug.

They walked to the table and Wyatt gestured to the woman. "Lark, I'd like you to meet TJ Reynolds, or Viking Romeo—that's what we called her. She was our radio specialist, and that voice went everywhere with us."

Dimples appeared on TJ's full cheeks as she smiled at him.

"And this crazy guy is Kermit Corrigan. Kerm and I patrolled together."

"Kermit? Like the frog?"

"Kermit like the town in west Texas."

"Way west," TJ said.

"Three hours further, you're in Juarez, baby—ay-ay-ay!" Kermit squealed.

"Head hurts picturing you chasing those poor señoritas." TJ pushed him toward the table.

"Kermit," Lark repeated.

He leaned across the table. "I was born Elliott Corrigan, but the Army wasn't too concerned with my given name. S'pose they could've called me worse?" He shrugged.

"Oh, you can depend on it," TJ said. "Shoulda seen these two on patrol. Like watching Foghorn Leghorn and a scrawnier, uglier version of Elmer Fudd."

"Hey, now." Kermit argued, but his narrow eyes, thin frame, and pallid skin illustrated TJ's point.

Lark tried not to be too obvious, but as she studied Kermit's face and gap-toothed smile, she saw not Elmer Fudd but an entirely different cartoon character—Alfred E. Neuman from the covers of *MAD Magazine*.

"Heads up," TJ said in a confidential tone. "Kerm has a way of . . . well, let's just say his mouth forgets to check in with his brain." She briefly closed her eyes. "He's not mean-spirited, but when his mouth gets going . . ." Another pause. "The man could tick off Mother Teresa."

Lark gave a polite laugh and TJ picked up her menu.

"Are you still in the Army?" Lark asked TJ.

"Sort of. I'm a recruiter in Durant, Oklahoma. Not far from Dallas. I work with eighteen-year-old babies. Truth is, every one of them thinks he or she will finish boot camp as a Ranger." She snickered. "I was the same way."

"We all were," Wyatt said.

"How do you know each other?" TJ pointed a finger between Wyatt and Lark.

"Well . . ." Lark cracked a smile at Wyatt. "I was about to be picked up by a mysterious stranger until Wyatt derailed him."

"You were really interested in him?" Wyatt said.

"Maybe." Her smile reappeared, and she directed her words at TJ. "He was what you'd call an overly ambitious admirer. Not my type." *As if you have a type. Where is all this bravado coming from?*

Lark's phone buzzed and she opened a message from her in-laws reassuring her of the boys' welfare.

Nothing on fire. No one hurt. All good in the Meads' hood.

TJ stole a look at Lark's screen. "Your kids?"

Lark touched the screen and her phone lit up with a photo of Jamie and Charlie on each side of James.

Kermit squeezed one beady eye. "They with their dad?"

Wyatt shot an icy stare across the table.

"I'm just saying, there's a dude in the pic—"

"Kerm." Wyatt sliced a finger across his throat.

"I'm widowed."

Apologies came. Then, the worst of it—all three faces bent with pity and the table went silent with fear, like they didn't know what to do with Lark now that they knew her story. After thanking them for their kind words, she gave a slight smile. *Translation: Please stop looking at me like I'm the last surviving member of the Donner party.*

"Looks like you're doing alright," TJ said.

"We're on the mend." The words seemed accurate, although she wasn't completely convinced. It must have satisfied their curiosity, because Wyatt changed the subject.

"It was the funniest thing—her little guy introduced us," Wyatt said with a half-smile, like he wasn't quite sure how she'd handle his description of their first meeting.

"It was wild—our first day back in Fredericksburg." She pointed to the photo, "That's Charlie. He thought Wyatt was a toy Transformer because of his leg."

"Cute," TJ said.

"Might've been cute if his mother didn't think I was a kidnapper," Wyatt said.

TJ's expression shifted. "You didn't."

"I did . . . er, at least, I didn't know why he was hanging around my kid."

"I wasn't hanging around him. The kid, Charlie, wouldn't leave me alone, and when she found him with me, whew." Wyatt made a show of wiping his forehead.

"Uh-oh. Looks like someone tore Wyatt a new one." Kermit laughed. "Made you her be-yotch?"

"Here he goes," TJ said.

"Wasn't my finest moment." Lark turned to Wyatt. "I'd like to think we're friends now."

"Oh yeah," Wyatt said. "We're friends."

Kerm tossed his head back and slapped his hands together. "Must've kissed and made up if you're here with us tonight?"

Thirteen

Lark

The phrase "kissed and made up" lit up bright as neon in front of Lark, and she felt the blood drain from her face.

"What's that for?" Kerm clutched his arm like he'd been injured.

"What the hell?" Wyatt raised a finger to pause Kerm's next word. "Don't."

"Don't . . . what?" Kermit licked his lips. "I was going to say—"

"Kerm." Wyatt's jaw tightened.

"I was sorry," Kerm finished.

Wyatt met Lark's eyes and mouthed, "Sorry," shaking his head. She pushed back her chair. "I should probably get going."

"Don't leave," TJ said, making an I-told-you-so face at Kermit. She shifted closer to Lark and whispered, "Please don't let him run you off. We pretty much ignore 99 percent of what comes out of his mouth. Learned a long time ago, the man's got more quirks than Gary Busey on acid."

A snort escaped. Lark covered her mouth too late to muffle it, and the table erupted in laughter.

"What was that?" Kermit asked.

Kermit, the twerpy judge of fine manners?

TJ winked at her. "Can't choose your family *or* the people you serve with. Either way, you're linked for life, no matter what dumbass garbage falls of their mouths."

"I said I was sorry." Kerm kept trying to dig himself out of that hole.

TJ wasn't through with him. "Driving to Gruene, he whined to me how he can't meet *the one*. But look at him. He can't even get through dinner without making a mess of things."

"I'm a different sort of man, right?" For some bizarre reason, Kermit turned to Lark when he spoke. "Not easy finding someone who digs a guy like me, and I can't wrap my head around the way women operate."

A tall order.

"What do you want?" She had to ask.

"I wanna look across a crowded room and see her looking back at me like I'm the one she's waited for her entire life," he said thoughtfully, staring across the deck like Kate Upton might be there, blowing a kiss meant just for him.

"Oh, sweet boy," Lark said. "Love isn't so simple."

"Hmm?" Wyatt murmured.

"I'm not saying it's impossible, but the love at first sight stuff only goes so far. Take it from a woman who lived through the best and worst. Love at first sight takes you to the dance. Commitment keeps you there."

"Sorry," Wyatt said, and Lark offered an appreciative smile.

"Thought love meant never having to say you're sorry?" Kerm blurted.

"Love means you damn well better say you're sorry when you screw up," TJ said.

"Not just when you screw up. Every day, you have to hold on tight and drill into the muck together." Lark sipped her beer. "Relationships require work."

"Well, I stand corrected, folks." Kermit smacked the table as if his fist were a judge's gavel. "The reason I'm not married is I'm a selfish, unpredictable prick."

For the first time all night, everyone agreed with Kermit Corrigan.

The quesadilla and onion rings weren't just delicious, they kept Kermit's trap occupied long enough to appreciate the sparkly lights swaying from the trees and the music drifting from the neighboring dance hall.

But all good things must come to an end.

Kerm turned to Lark. "I may be a lost cause, but . . ."

Wyatt threw a hand over his face and TJ mumbled a swear word.

Kerm ignored them. "Tell me this. Why can't Wyatt find a good woman?"

"And, cut." TJ said. "Anybody else need to run to the ladies' room?"

Latching onto TJ's offer like an eject button, Lark followed her to the crowded restroom. When she exited, Lark found her waiting in the corridor.

"I need a cigarette. Join me?" TJ tilted her head to the side.

"Sure. I don't smoke, but I'll sit with you."

They made their way to a picnic table in the courtyard separating the Grist Mill from the Gruene Dance Hall.

"Wyatt's a good man—been through more nastiness than a man deserves in a lifetime."

"Surprised he's not dating anyone."

"Yeah, he fell for a real stunner. Talked like they'd have the house, babies, all that. After the IED, she bailed. Pretty is as pretty does."

"She broke up with him because of . . ." Lark stopped herself. *What am I doing? Wyatt isn't my business.*

"No," TJ shook her head. "She was screwing around with her boss in San Antone." She tapped a finger on the edge of the table. "Never told him, but they weren't a match. Everyone saw it coming except him."

"Poor guy."

"Yeah, and she won't leave him alone now. Texts him all the time."

"Wants to get back with him?"

"Hell no. Says she wants to talk, say she's sorry. Doesn't matter, because he won't answer."

"Good." *Shut up, Lark. You don't know these people.*

"You two live in the same town. You're friends. He'd trust your advice. You could tell him to get back out there? Maybe show him the ropes?"

I can't even find the ropes, much less show them to anyone else.

"I'm probably not the right person. I'm not an expert on . . . on anything."

TJ shrugged, dropped her cigarette on the ground, and snuffed it out with her foot. "Just sayin', he could use a good friend."

Lark didn't answer as they walked back to the table.

"You guys ready?" TJ asked as they approached the men, appraising a table cleared of plates.

"Not quite." Wyatt pointed to a server delivering fresh batch of beers to the table.

TJ nodded in understanding and returned to her seat, but Lark couldn't make sense of ordering another bucket when they were about to leave.

"No thanks," Lark said when TJ set a beer in front of her.

"Don't have to drink it." TJ pitched her head toward Wyatt.

What else am I supposed to do with it?

TJ nodded at the bottle.

Unable to read the subtext, Lark took it.

"Last, we toast to the fallen." Wyatt raised a beer in each hand, and bottles went up, chasing all humor from the table. Even Kermit's face turned solemn as Wyatt spoke.

"He didn't make it back to enjoy the life he fought for. To Blazek."

Everyone tipped the bottles to their lips. Wyatt took a drink from one, while he tipped the other over the railing. The table remained silent until all the beer had fallen into the Guadalupe.

"Anybody talk to Jana?" Kerm asked.

"I called her a few weeks ago." TJ pursed her lips. "She's struggling. Her parents are pushing her to move home. But she's got friends . . . a job . . . her son's doing well in school." She turned to Lark and whispered, "Blazek's widow. She lives in Omaha, but her parents—and Blazek's—live in the middle of nowhere: Broken

Bone, Nebraska. They want her to bring Daniel there so they can help raise him now that—"

"Broken Bow," Wyatt corrected.

"Wherever. She's got her own life. Her kid likes his school. Can't blame her for wanting to stay put." TJ lifted a shoulder. "She asked about you, Wyatt. Thought you were going to call her?"

"Yeah, I will," he said, staring at the table.

"Did she say anything about me?" Kermit asked.

"It was a short conversation," TJ said.

After a few minutes, Kermit started to stir in his seat like a kid in church. They paid out and crossed the courtyard to The Gruene Dance Hall.

Lark followed along, more interested in the building's antiquity than dancing. Covered in whitewashed paneling and misaligned windows, the hall had been around since the 1870s. Its claim to fame was that it was Texas's oldest continually operating dance hall.

Wyatt held the wood-screened door open and Lark walked inside.

The wood planks bent underfoot. Unlike the creaky planks at the O'Keeffe Ranch, Lark found these soft and welcoming, seasoned by dance hall guests through the years. Rough timber rafters crossed the ceiling. Above the bar, a massive oval LONE STAR BEER sign hung. Her eyes caught on the photos—hundreds of them covered the wood cladding, signed by the entertainers over the years. Everyone from Ernest Tubb to George Strait.

An old-fashioned pull-lever machine dispensed packages of cigarettes adjacent to a NO SMOKING sign. Apparently, the place didn't mind supplying the goods so long as smokers took their habit outside.

Wooden picnic-style tables were scattered around. Chicken-wire mesh windows invited the night air to flow into the hall. Above the windows, antique metal signs advertised products like the NEW FORD V-8 and the RINGLETTE PERMANENT WAVE SHOP. At the far end, a Texas flag hung over a stage. Drapes had been painted on each side of the stage with a Hill Country landscape in the middle, serving as the backdrop for performers.

Every atom of the structure vibrated with the music—like the old dance hall had a heartbeat. People drifted on and off the dance floor in waves, depending on the liveliness of the music. All the while, Lark and Wyatt remained seated at one of the long tables.

Wyatt's hand crossed Lark's vision. "You in there?"

"Sorry. Caught me."

"Zoning out?"

"People-watching." The music grew louder and Lark leaned into his side to speak over the din. "I imagine who they are and what brought them here."

"Interesting." He ran a hand over his chin. "Can I play?"

She gave a mock salute with her beer. "Point out a pair."

Wyatt nodded to an elderly couple—a bald man sitting on the edge of the dance floor, slapping his knees to the music, beside his blue-haired, sparkly-eyed mate.

"Those sweethearts?" Lark smiled. "I'd say they've been married sixty years. Her knees are spent, but he wouldn't dare dance with another."

"Got all that from looking at 'em?" he asked.

"Yep."

Wyatt rolled his head toward a man wearing a rope-thick gold necklace and dipping one hand into the hind pocket of his date's jeans. The woman was stuck in the seventies, her frosted hair styled in Farrah Fawcett feathers.

"You don't want to know." Lark shielded her mouth. "I'm guessing those two hooked up tonight for the first time, probably in the parking lot."

Wyatt cringed.

"Tonight's the beginning, middle, and end," she said.

"How about them?" He pointed to a couple in their thirties.

"Ohhh. Good choice. Had a fight about taking out the trash. He's felt guilty all week, promised her a night out—even arranged the sitter for their babies. Look at them."

The couple laughed as they two-stepped.

"He did right by her. They're going to be just fine," she said. The man dipped the woman and Lark flashed a sly grin. "See?"

"I guess." Wyatt snickered. "They make it look fun. Wanna go out there?"

She hesitated, shifting her gaze to his bum leg. "Tell me if I'm getting too personal, but with your leg?"

"Losing a leg doesn't make it hard to dance."

"What does make it hard?" She asked innocently enough, but the words echoed inside her head shamefully. *What the hell, Lark? Get it together.*

When Wyatt's face matched the red stripe on the Texas flag, she dropped her head toward the table.

"It's alright." Wyatt tapped her arm—the second time he had touched her. This time, it sent an alarming warmth through her body.

"Shake it off," Wyatt said. "Hard part's finding a decent partner. You up for it?"

Trying to erase her embarrassment, she rose from the table. "Been a long time, but I'll give it shot."

Wyatt

BEFORE THE IED TOOK HIS right leg and his confidence, he'd known his way around the two-step, swing, and Cotton-Eyed Joe. Now that opportunity was staring at him head-on, however, he worried he might have bitten off more than he could chew.

Have I outkicked my coverage?

With a look into Lark's twinkling eyes, Wyatt's cautious approach to the dance floor relaxed into one of guarded optimism. He took her hand as the band played a cover of Jon Pardi's "Head over Boots," a song that offered Wyatt just enough of the confidence-building mojo he needed to get back on that horse.

Dancing required more effort than he remembered. His body didn't move as fluidly as it had before. Like fresh air in the wintertime, the experience hit his senses with a pleasant discomfort.

As they spun around the floor, the old moves came back to

him. Except for the tender spot where his new limb met his body, he might have forgotten about his loss.

Don't think so hard. Let your body lead.

Perhaps he had underestimated the agility required? His left leg carried the work of both. It shook, throwing off his concentration. The folks at the Center for the Intrepid said he was a quick learner, that he made progress faster than anybody they'd seen in his predicament. *Maybe they say that to everybody?* Anyway, dancing wasn't an activity he'd cared much about when he was in rehab.

She must have read something on his face, because she asked, "You okay?" But it was compassion, not pity, reflecting from her face, and he felt safe with her. So, though it wasn't easy, he kept dancing, ignoring the shakiness of his left leg.

With deft balance, he bent to wrap an arm around Lark's waist and—as if that IED had never even touched him—he swung her into a dip. She threw her head back. Tiny to look at, but Lark felt like lead balanced over his arm. *Holy hell, what have I done? Don't drop her, man.* His feet felt like they were stuck in cement. *This was a terrible idea. Abort mission.*

A few seconds felt like a lifetime. The shaking intensified. He tilted to the side, but his prosthetic didn't bend like his old leg. He closed his eyes, mustered a power that could've been sent only from the big man Himself, and, in one jerky, too-close-for-comfort motion, shocked Lark back to her feet.

"Whoa. That was awesome," she said, looking back at him with those clear blue eyes.

Wyatt smiled with relief. He'd stuck the win.

Nearby, TJ spun Kermit around like a rag doll. She could've mopped those wood planks with his head and rung him out, and Kermit would've begged for another round.

Dimming lights signaled a slow one, and Wyatt took Lark's right hand and pulled her close. Her hair grazed his chin. Chills traveled down his spine. Something woke inside him. He hadn't felt like this in—he couldn't say.

When the song ended, he gave her hand a squeeze, unsure if she'd noticed.

"Care if we take a break?" he asked. "I could use a Coke."

Lark nodded. "Sure." They walked toward the table. "I'm curious," she said. "How old are you?"

"Twenty-seven," he said. At her wide eyes, he added, "C'mon. You can't be much older."

"I'm thirty-eight, young man."

"Whooee, you *are* ancient." He laced her arm over his. "I'll help you to your table, Granny."

Lark gave him a playful punch. "Watch out, Sonny, or I'll hit you with my cane."

Fourteen

Lark

....

She loved to dance, AND it had been years since she'd pulled James on the dance floor at a friend's wedding. Until tonight, remembering was all she'd been able to do.

In the arms of this kind man, she let herself go. Guilt and grief fell to the background, and a semblance of her old identity emerged. The crisp night air hit her lungs and the music vibrated under her toes. Wyatt was gentle and strong at the same time, guiding her through steps she had long forgotten, spinning her in dizzying circles and dipping her like she was weightless—he made her feel more alive than she had in years.

While TJ took Wyatt for a spin, Lark relaxed at the table. The beer trickled down her throat, cold and bubbly. A waft of cool air quenched her skin. Even the picnic benches were comfortable. *A perfect night.*

"Hey, you." Kermit plopped his red neck in the seat beside her. *Scratch that. Almost perfect.*

"What's the dealio with you and Wyatt?"

"There isn't a *dealio*. We're friends." Irritation fizzed in her chest. She wished she could just erase Kermit from the planet.

"You two were having a heckuva time out there." Colorless eyebrows bounced over his unblinking eyes.

"Just two grown-ups having a pleasant evening."

"Whatever. You see them out there?" He pointed to Wyatt and TJ. "That's not how you looked. You guys were more like those folks." He pointed to a man fishing his tongue down a woman's throat. "Minus the smoochy-smooch." He added a bucking snort.

"You must've been pretty bored to watch us all night."

Lark, you hypocrite. You speculated about those couples. Doesn't feel so hot being on the other side of that creepy microscope, does it?

Kerm gazed at her while he took a long gulp from his bottle, a look that translated to, *I'm right and you know it.*

Jesus, take the wheel.

She couldn't exactly keep watching Wyatt in Kermit's presence, so she directed her gaze to her phone. While she was having all that fun, she'd received four voice mail messages.

"I need to take a call," she said.

"I'll be right here," Kerm yelled as she stepped outside.

"Lark, this is Belle, Annabelle Granger, at the house where you're staying? We had a gas leak, so we can't sleep at my house tonight. Theo, the man you met, said we can stay at his place. Call me and I'll give directions."

Lark didn't call; she sent a text instead: *No problem. Staying with family. I'll check in tomorrow. Good night.* She stared at her phone, not excited about her next call—especially at this hour.

Nadine, I hope you were serious about having me sleep over.

"Everything alright?" Wyatt appeared in the courtyard. Sweat beaded on his forehead and pain bent his features as he stepped toward her.

"Yeah." She described the problem with her accommodations. "I'm going to call my in-laws." Lark flinched inwardly but managed a smile.

"It's after one. Think they'll be awake?"

"No." *Odds are good they've been asleep since eight.*

"Stay at our place. My parents won't mind."

"With your parents?"

"Yeah. We have tons of room, and I can drive you back to your car in the morning."

Stay with a random guy's parents? Or wake the Meads and tell them you're at a bar at 1:00 a.m.?

"You sure your parents won't mind?"

"Absolutely. And park your worries about me driving. I've been tanking up on Cokes for the past two hours."

Who have I become?

He called his parents while they walked to his truck. From what Lark could hear, his mother would've welcomed the entire dance hall full of people if they needed lodging.

From the passenger seat, she picked up on the adaptive controls Wyatt clicked around the steering wheel. "I think we lost TJ and Kermit," she said, glancing back.

"They know the way," he said.

About ten minutes outside of Gruene, he flipped on his signal and tabbed on his high beams.

"Looks like the kind of place they hide bodies in horror movies," Lark remarked.

"No one's hiding any bodies. You're safe." The lights swung up a gravel road and he parked along a driveway separating a red brick 1970s rambler-style home and barn.

As they entered the house, Lark stuck close to Wyatt, taking in the lodge décor—a mix of traditional furnishings, upholstered chairs, and antiques. Dead animals leered from the walls: deer, elk, and one dead moose with a taxidermized grin.

A woman with a gray ponytail looked up from her crossword puzzle to offer a smile as bright as the long day had allowed as they entered the living room. "I'm Suzie." She stood and gestured to her husband, an older, slightly haggard version of Wyatt who was slumped in a chair. "He's Owen."

"Hello." Owen waved a sleepy hand.

Not bothering to ring the bell or knock first, Kermit squawked, "We're baaaack," and walked right inside.

Suzie welcomed them warmly. She started a pot of coffee and set out a plate of oatmeal raisin cookies. "Lark, I put a new toothbrush on the bathroom counter and one of my sleep shirts on the bed so you'll have pajamas. You get Wyatt's room, TJ's set up in our daughter's room, and the boys are in the basement."

"The boys." Cute.

"Ready for a round of Trivial Pursuit?" Suzie asked, gesturing to the game on the coffee table.

"On that note, I'm going to bed. Y'all have fun." Owen disappeared down the hall.

After a few rounds, the game yielded more yawns than pie pieces. Kermit crawled onto the sofa and rested his head in TJ's lap like a sleepy puppy.

"Lark, I'll show you to your room." Suzie led her to Wyatt's bedroom and closed the door.

Lark kicked off her shoes, switched off the lamp, and crawled into the twin bed. It smelled of spice, like Wyatt, and comforted her to sleep.

A STREAK OF SUNLIGHT WARMED her face. She stretched an arm and sliced through a line of dancing particles streaming from the wood blinds covering an eastern-facing window. She tossed back the maroon comforter and rose to inspect pictures on the walls. One wall documented a gawky teenager's journey through high school—in football, track, and basketball uniforms. Huge feet anchored his thin body like he was a great Dane halfway through puppyhood.

Another wall featured a fuller-faced Wyatt, a military cadet at Texas A&M University standing fiercely straight with a prominent Adam's apple. There were shots of him alone, with young women, and one kneeling beside the Aggie mascot—Reveille, a rough-coated collie, the highest-ranking member of the A&M Corps of Cadets.

Lark's brother, an A&M alum, had told her about Aggie Corps boots like the ones displayed on the pine dresser. Customized for upperclassmen, they were crafted of British tan leather and accented with blunted brass spurs. A photo showed Wyatt wearing them in a starched khaki uniform with a military-grade saber slung on his belt.

She picked up a silver frame and a striking Army lieutenant met her eyes. With his strong chin and the severe pitch to his hair, Wyatt's ambitions were unmistakable.

Her stomach clenched like a fist, holding her to examine what he lost.

You're not the only one who'd had to reset your expectations, Lark.

Quickly, she replaced the frame and threw her purse over her shoulder, then slinked from the darkened hall to the white-tiled bathroom. Her clothes were wrinkled and her hair was a mess. *I have walk of shame written all over me.*

The toothbrush Suzie had set out for her seemed like a good idea. Then again, if the woman in the mirror was any indication, Lark wasn't an expert on good ideas. *Do I really have time to brush my teeth? Call an Uber and disappear, woman!*

She breathed into her hand. That vile mouth couldn't be ignored.

A few minutes later, teeth brushed and hair restrained, she aimed for the front door.

"Morning," Suzie said in her soft-spoken twang.

Busted.

"I made coffee. Pour you a mug?"

"I should really get . . ." Lark tried.

"No one's ever complained about my coffee." Suzie dangled the carafe like a dealer to a junkie, and it practically called Lark's name.

"Have a seat." Suzie pointed to a chair.

Lark set her phone on the table, eyeing its diminishing power status.

"Over there." Suzie nodded at a charger. "Recharge while we visit."

Holy hell. I'm about to get reamed by Wyatt's mother. Should I just tell her right from the start, no hanky-panky, just friends?

"Sleep alright?"

"I did." She lifted the mug of warm coffee to her nose. "You're so nice. I'm not sure how I'd react if one of my boys brought a strange woman home. They're only three and five, but if they were grown . . ."

"Mmm-mmm . . ." Subtle crow's feet framed Suzie's eyes. "I didn't realize you were a *strange* woman."

"Doesn't begin to scratch the surface." Lark snickered. "Is Wyatt around?"

"Outside, helping Owen unload a pallet of deer corn. The others galloped off to town." Delicate fingers stroked the handle of her mug. "With so much commotion, we didn't get a chance to visit last night. Tell me about yourself."

"Not much to tell."

"Surely a woman who considers herself strange has a story to tell. Hum a few bars."

In one long breath, Lark hit the highlights. When she was done, she laughed. "Sorry, I feel like just I spewed up three years of history in one minute."

"Feel better? That's how spewing usually works."

"I don't get out much. I guess, I'm figuring out how to do this single parent thing."

"Good luck with that—I'm still figuring out how to parent, and mine are grown." Suzie took a sip. "I like to think I have an eye for these things, and from my view, you've got this."

A tear slid past Lark's lashes.

"Oh, no. I didn't mean to make you cry, sweetheart."

"My husband used to say that—'You've got this.' Sorry, I'm working through it." She swiped at her eyes.

"Sometimes, all you can do is say, 'Lord, do what you will with me.' While you're waiting, pay attention to what's left." Suzie swished her hands over the table. "Those broken pieces? Just sweep them out of sight. No matter how you shove them into place, they won't stick. So focus on what's around you now. The rest only gets in your way."

Lark nodded, holding her elbows in her hands.

Suzie rose to her feet. "I'll keep you and your boys in my prayers."

"Thank you."

Suzie held her arms out toward Lark. "Giffords are huggers. Bring it in." Her brown eyes disappeared over her smile.

As if the last twenty-four hours could get any weirder. Lark leaned into this woman she barely knew, soaking up her comfort like a child with a skinned knee.

"You *do* have this, sweetie."

The warmth of Suzie's arms scared her and she started to pull away, but the rustling door drew her attention. Together, she and Suzie turned to face Wyatt and his father.

Awkward stares bounced around the kitchen. Lark pulled at her blouse in a feeble attempt to straighten the wrinkles.

"Did we interrupt?" Owen pitched a face at Suzie.

"Nope. We solved all the world's problems." Suzie tossed a wink at Lark.

Lark's phone pinged and she pulled it from the charger.

"Everything alright?" Suzie asked.

"The lady I'm staying with. The gas line's fixed, so I can come back."

"I can take you whenever you're ready," Wyatt said.

"This must be it." Wyatt pointed to the plumbing truck in Belle's driveway. He parked on the street, climbed out of the truck, crossed to the other side, and opened her door.

"Thanks for everything—the company, your friends, dancing, letting me stay at your parents' house."

"Think we can meet up in Fredericksburg? Maybe grab a cup of coffee or a beer?" he asked.

Be cool, Lark. Nothing wrong with two friends having coffee or a beer.

"Sure. I should treat—maybe take you to dinner to thank you."

"That'd be great. Mind punching in your number?" He handed her his phone.

"Sure." She typed in her number and passed it back.

"If you like steak, I've been dying to break in this new grill," he said.

Dinner has the terrifying potential of being construed as a date.

"Oh, Wyatt. You don't need to cook—"

"No worries. It'll be fun for me. Just a casual dinner—nothing fancy, okay?"

The warmth of his eyes disarmed her and she nodded. "Alright."

"Well, I'd better take off." He leaned toward her for a hug, and their clumsy platonic embrace sent surprising warmth through her body.

AFTER SHE SHOWERED AT BELLE'S, Lark called the Meads. Nadine seemed no worse for the wear. "We took the boys to the Fork & Spoon for a French toast breakfast," Nadine said. "All that sugar went over like gangbusters. They're having a grand time, and we're loving every minute."

It sounded too good to be true, but maybe Lark had become more cynical in recent days. She made her way to the living room.

Belle dropped her newspaper. "Breakfast?"

"Sure," Lark said, anticipating a breakfast of store-bought donuts.

"Let me get my pocketbook." Belle grabbed a pink leather wallet and Lark joined her for an unhurried walk to a café off the main street.

"This place is famous for their Benedicts and crepes." Belle tapped at the menu.

Lark ordered a green chile Benedict covered in a sunny Hollandaise sauce. Combined with a trio of ibuprofen tablets and a bacon-garnished Bloody Mary, it completed a healing trifecta that dulled the after-effects of the prior night.

"The young man who drove you home . . . friend of yours?" The edges of Belle's tulip-pink lips lifted.

"He *is* a friend." Lark touched on the high points as Belle ate up every detail with a spoon.

"Wyatt's a war hero, recovering after an IED ended his career. He has this amazing attitude. Listening to his story puts me to shame. I've whined enough."

"Did he say something to upset you, dear?"

"No. He was sweet. I imagine he has his low points. He and his friends faced scary times over there. Members of his platoon died."

"Sounds like that young man is lucky to have made it home."

Lark nodded. "Hearing his story, I couldn't help thinking of what I was doing while he was marching in the desert, trying to make the world a safer place. Probably sorting through sale racks at Lululemon?" She chuffed.

"From what you told me last night, you were doing something far more important, like caring for your boys and your husband."

"Wyatt and his friends knew the risks and volunteered, I suppose. I didn't get married knowing I'd be taking care of a husband with ALS or raising children by myself."

Belle pursed her mouth for a second. She seemed to measure her words like a chemist pouring a test tube of this into a beaker of that—a little too much, and *boom!* After a long moment, seemingly finally satisfied with her creation, she swallowed and opened her mouth. "If someone had told you, would you have walked away from your James?"

"Of course not." Lark's words flew from her mouth.

Belle cupped her thin fingers around Lark's hand. Her sparkling eyes drilled into Lark's soul and exposed vulnerable places. "You did all you could."

Lark gave a slow nod.

"He's not coming back, sweetie."

"He's not a switch I can turn off."

"No one would expect you to forget him." Belle waved a hand around them. "You're here with a life just waiting for you to climb aboard. But before that can happen, you have to give yourself permission to uncover spectacular happiness."

Fifteen

Lark

M iles away from Belle's house, "spectacular happiness" echoed in Lark consciousness like an annoying advertisement that plays over and over during reruns of your favorite program. She just couldn't shut it out, and it ticked her off. *Spectacular happiness, my foot.*

An attendant scanned her wristband and waved her into the wine festival. Once inside, she skimmed the list of vendors twice, but there wasn't a Hartmann or Haas to be found.

Disappointment didn't stop her from exploring. She sampled wines from recognizable wineries as well as hobbyists, many of whom had concocted quite palatable experiments.

From table to table, winemakers shared their stories. Some had humble beginnings: a pair of retired teachers from Dallas had opened Valentine Ranch, which specialized in dessert wines.

Others had reinvented themselves after finding success in other careers—including an ear, nose, and throat doctor from Kansas selling something called Pinna Pinot. When Lark didn't understand, the good doctor explained that "pinna" pertained to the outer ear.

She didn't need an anatomy lesson to identify the disquiet in her soul. Like a jealous anchor, it dragged behind her through the succession of booths. Most provided spit buckets for serious connoisseurs, but they went unused.

At the N'Otis Winery booth, Lark tipped her glass to her lips, inviting the crisp golden fluid to shake hands with each bud on her tongue. Hill Country winemakers knew their way around a Chenin Blanc. A touch of pear combined with a hint of grassiness delivered sunshine in a glass but this label raised the bar even further, teasing elderflower and grapefruit flavors to enhance the white wine's crisp finish.

"How about a red?" the woman behind the table suggested.

With Lark's nod, she poured a sample.

Lark shut her eyes and angled the glass, inviting the wine's aroma to prime her palate for adventure. A soft sweetness hit the tip of her tongue, delivering surprising hints of dark chocolate across the middle. The wine unpacked a symphonic cassis of currant and tangy blackberry, finishing with a blossoming crescendo at the base of her throat.

"Iron fist in a velvet glove," the woman said. "Big fruit, low grip on the tongue."

Lark nodded. "Mourvedre?"

"Yes."

Lark took a second taste. "Spanish? Rhone?"

"Well, well, well. You know your varietals."

"This is delicious." Lark closed her eyes and nodded. "I need to take some of this home."

As Lark paid for two bottles, the woman said, "This one's my baby."

"You're the winemaker?"

"Natasha Otis." She offered her hand.

"Lark Mead."

"Well, Lark, we're a small winery outside of Comfort, and we produced 3,000 cases last year."

"How many hands does it take to run your operation?"

Natasha's mouth fell open. "Haven't had that question today." She squinted. "Eight regulars, including me."

"During crush?" Lark asked.

"We pick up seasonal help. Do you make wine?"

"I wish." Lark exhaled, releasing the words in one long breath, "Studied viticulture in undergrad, spent a summer in Calistoga, and forgot all about it to go to law school."

"Viticulture's not a cinch major. Neither is law school."

"Yet I'm not using either. I just moved back to Fredericksburg."

Natasha waved a hand around the park. "Center of the wine trail is the right spot."

"Timing's not great for a career change. I have two little boys."

"Their father can't help?"

"Not from where he is." Lark frowned, deliberating an explanation. Natasha stared, bewildered.

"Um . . ." Lark stalled. *Prison? Bermuda?* Finally, she said, "Heaven."

"Sorry."

Unwilling to acknowledge Natasha's concern, she offered a simple, "Thanks," and lifted an empty bottle to inspect the label. "Starting now is overwhelming."

"You've got the education, and you live along the wine trail. Plenty of experienced help around. Don't let the money scare you off. Winemaking, at its essence, is growing grapes, and ag banks are here to help."

"How'd you get into it?"

"Ack, long story." She laughed. "Needed a distraction after my divorce. Basket weaving and knitting weren't doing it for me, so I played around with a half-acre." She nodded to a couple as they passed. "A few years in, I bought more land. Took six years for the stock to deliver fruit worthy of my brand. The rest, as they say—"

"Is awesome."

"I like your style," Natasha said.

"N'Otis a family name?"

"Otis is my maiden name. I added my first initial and created N'Otis. You could say it was me putting everyone on notice—making it clear I wasn't playing around anymore."

"Clever. Wish I had your courage."

"You've got more than you know. Misfortunes yield strength. Hey, when you're ready to explore, look me up. I'll show you around." Natasha winked and pushed a business card across the table.

"Maybe after my kids are both in school full time." Lark stuck the card in her pocket.

"What are you afraid of?"

Natasha's question hit Lark like a slap. *Who the heck does Miss Put-Them-on-Notice think she is?*

"You don't have to answer to me, but you'd better figure it out for yourself. Speaking from experience, once you answer that question, your future will roll out in front of you like a red carpet." She turned her hand in this sweeping motion, and Lark could almost see the image. "The very things that scare us hold us back from our potential."

"If that were true, my potential would be spread around the state like pollen in the spring." Lark chuckled.

"Keep joking. Makes it easier to ignore the work begging to be done in here," Natasha tapped her chest.

Lark's smile fell away from her face and she took the wine she'd purchased without another word. With a brain slushy from wine, she walked back to Belle's house, hungry for a nap.

WHEN SHE WOKE A FEW hours later, Lark looked at the clock and picked up her phone. She didn't want to interfere with Jim and Nadine's time with the boys, but it seemed like days since she'd spoken to them.

Nadine answered the phone in an unusually cheery voice. She rattled on about what the boys had worn and how they'd brushed their teeth so well, but she said she didn't want to interrupt "movie time with Grandpa" so she didn't pass them the phone.

Fair enough.

It sounded too good to be true, like Jim and Nadine had grown into the patient grandparents they'd never been before. Then, Nadine explained why their dinner plans had changed.

"We decided not to go out tonight. Jim thought it would be best to eat at home. Less sugar to level out all that energy. Other than the sugar, we're having a grand time."

A grand time, huh? They probably have Charlie duct taped to a chair.

THE NEXT MORNING, LARK WOKE to the smell of fresh coffee and bird sounds just outside her window. Her weekend of play at its end, she packed her car, eager to wrap her arms around Jamie and Charlie.

"When you go back home, you might forget what we talked about. You don't have chapters in front of you but whole books. Live while you can." Belle hugged her good-bye.

The forty-mile drive to New Braunfels felt like a thousand. Lark missed her boys, and a part of her wished she could rewind the clock, forget all that meddlesome advice from practical strangers. *Don't people have boundaries anymore? The wine lady asking what I'm afraid of? All that spectacular happiness? Who needs all this unsolicited hippy-dippie advice? Not me.*

Jim and Nadine's house appeared normal from the outside, and she had no reason not to think her boys had enjoyed staying there until she reached the front door.

Nadine's calling card was her prim and proper appearance. At dawn or in the dark of night, the woman had her signature style down to a science. Full makeup and hair went without saying. "Casual dress" meant a starched blouse tucked around her lithe middle and shoes, purse, and belt matched to Jackie-O perfection. She couldn't so much as weed her flowerbeds without color-coordinated gloves.

"Come in." An anesthetized Nadine wore pink house slippers and a rumpled white blouse. Her silky bob was jumbled like a black Brillo pad. Thin purple lines traversed her cheekbones where fractured blood vessels had been left un-foundationed. Years of Estee Lauder Wild Poppy lipstick stained her lips like a faded tattoo.

Without eyeshadow, kohl liner, and mascara, her face looked blank, like a featureless Mrs. Potato Head.

Charlie Mead has left his mark.

"Jamie's reading to himself," Nadine led her into the living room, where Jamie held his favorite book, *The Can Man*. He couldn't read all the words, but he knew them from memory. Across the room, Charlie sat on a footstool, clutching his dino-raur like a security blanket.

"Mom?" Jamie dropped the book and climbed out of the chair.

"Mommy?" Charlie asked in a whisper of his normal tone.

"Come here, baby." Lark waved to him.

Charlie didn't move, and his gaze locked on Nadine's face. When Nadine nodded, he zoomed from the chair. "Mommmeee!" he squealed.

"Did you have fun with Grandma and Grandpa Jim?"

"Uh-huh," Charlie said, clinging to Lark's shirt.

"Were they good for you?" Lark asked, nervous for the answer.

"Oh, yes." Nadine released a little chuckle. "They sure are active—especially that Charlie!"

The words seemed innocent enough, but Nadine's tone made Lark's momma bear instincts rise to attention. Her eyes narrowed and her mouth opened—but then she paused.

Lark stood there, perplexed, unable to process her hesitancy. Had James performed a cross-universe intervention? Assuming his abilities had been restored in heaven, had he yelled, "Nooooo, Laaaarrrrrrkkkkk?" from the heavens?

Her mouth snapped shut, the noise in her head fell silent, and her eyes landed on Nadine—crumpled with exhaustion but still looking over Jamie and Charlie with unambiguous affection.

The realization hit. What Nadine had expected from the weekend hadn't been only to reconnect with her grandsons. She'd needed to connect with her son—by way of the boys. As Nadine touched Jamie's shoulder, she must have pictured James. In rocking Charlie, she'd held her baby boy again.

Nadine had lost her near-perfect boy. This weekend had been her attempt to recover but also to grow past those memories—to play house with two near-perfect boys, a semblance of the son she lost.

And she'd gotten Jamie and Charlie instead.

Nostalgia overtook Lark's anger as she watched Charlie grip the tail of Nadine's shirt like a baby elephant hanging on to its mother. "Nama," he called.

Nadine's face filled with love and she pulled him close, a shaky hand tousling his irrepressible curls. He grabbed her face and planted a sloppy, wet kiss on her cheek before dropping his head on her shoulder. "Lub you, Nama."

Jim appeared, and his uncompromising gait slowed at the sight of Charlie in Nadine's arms. For a moment, they were the only ones in the room. He and Nadine exchanged a look—their connection irrefutable. Time stood still as James's absence and presence filled the room.

"Grandpa." Jamie's tiny voice broke their intimacy. He patted Jim's arm. "Want me to help you water your plants?" Jamie turned to Lark. "Grandpa Jim has a cool plant that eats flies. It's rad."

"Sure, Jamie," Jim said, but his eyes were still locked on Nadine.

Lark humored Jamie, oohing and aahing over Jim's Venus fly-trap plant, before they all climbed into the car. Soon, she and her boys were rolling out of the Meads' driveway—until Lark saw Jim rush out of the house, waving like a man batting at a swarm of bees, and braked sharply.

She rolled down the window. "What did we leave behind?"

Jim's bottom lip trembled and he put a hand on the door. "James asked me to give this to you after things settled down." He pressed an envelope into her hand.

"How?" The writing on the envelope was foreign, yet familiar.

"He . . . he told his friend, Mark, what to type for him."

Among James's take-no-prisoners law partners, Mark had stood out. He'd visited often, and had advocated for James when his speech became compromised by ALS.

"What's in it?" Lark asked.

"Can't say. I assume he wanted you to pass along his thoughts to the boys." He shrugged. "He said you'd want to wait to read it in private."

Giving a slow nod, she stared at the envelope. "Thank you."

Jim patted the car door a few times before turning back to the house.

Lark pushed the envelope into her car's center hutch compartment, saving it for a more private reading.

As they pulled away, Jamie tapped the back of her seat. "Mom? What did Grandpa Jim give you?"

"Some boring papers. So, did you and Grandma read *The Can Man* together?"

"Yeah. She likes the story too. She said it's hard for people to get what they want all by themselves, and they can help each other even when they don't mean to."

Lark nodded, amazed by his awareness.

"Mom, I wish I could help Grandma. She cries sometimes."

"Because of your dad?"

"Yeah. Maybe she shouldn't look at pictures of him anymore." Jamie spoke with a weariness in his voice.

"Oh, sweetie, did those pictures make you sad too?"

"Yeah. Mostly for Grandma. I wish Dad would come back for a minute, so she could hug him one more time. She said she had a lot to tell him, but she ran out of time. She told me she wished she could hold him again the way she holds Charlie and me."

"Jamie, you're sweet to worry about her. We all miss Daddy, don't we?"

"Yeah, but I don't feel so sad anymore."

Lark searched for the right words. "Dad wouldn't want you to be unhappy."

"I don't like crying. Sometimes I pretend Dad's not in heaven, just at work . . . like the other kids' dads. I'm not so sad then."

"Your dad's watching, and he's so proud of you." Lark took a sip from her water bottle.

"He's proud of Charlie, too," Jamie said. "Even if he pooped on the carpet in Papa Jim's office."

"He what?" Lark choked on her water.

"He needed to go to the bathroom, and he didn't know where. He had to go BAD. I told Grandma we needed to go with him. She didn't believe me because Charlie said, 'I do it. I do it.' But I kept telling her we should help him, so finally, she went, 'Okay,' but when I ran after him, he wasn't in the bathroom. I looked all over and found him in front of Papa Jim's desk."

"What did Grandma do?"

"She helped Charlie. Then she cleaned Grandpa Jim's office." He let out a long breath. "And then she told Grandpa he could come back in the house."

"Oh, Lord."

Jamie sighed. "Yeah, oh, Lord."

Sixteen

Lark

......

When Jamie laid eyes on the streak of exhaust rising from the cab of his grandfather's green tractor, the car filled with noise. "Charlie, look! Mom, hurry," he yelled, about to spring from his seat.

"Huh?" Charlie rolled his sleepy head toward the window.

"Poppy said we could ride with him the next time he tractors, and he's tractoring now." Jamie slipped off his seat belt and hunched over the car's console. "Hurry, Mom."

"Don't you worry—he'll be out there for hours, especially if your Grandma's in a mood."

"Where's *Amood*?" he asked, like it was a place instead of a condition.

"Nowhere." She parked the car. "Go inside and say hi to Grammy first."

He ran toward the house and she removed the letter from the console. With the envelope safely folded in her sweatshirt pocket, she carried Charlie into the house.

"Hi, honey." Millie folded towels into a stack on the kitchen island.

"Grammy's here, Mom." Jamie swiped his forehead.

"Where else would I be?" Millie asked.

"Mom said you might be in *Amood*."

"Where's that?" Millie's puzzled face begged for an explanation.

He lifted a shoulder. "Mom said Poppy tractors more when you're in *Amood*?"

"Interesting." Millie contemplated the towel she had been folding.

Lark carried Charlie to the sofa, laid him down, and covered him with a throw, then returned to the kitchen.

"How was your weekend?" Millie asked.

"Relaxing. As for Jim and Nadine . . ." She sighed. "Well, they'll recover."

Millie grimaced. "What happened?"

"It'll be more entertaining if I let Jamie tell you." Lark bit her lip and retreated to her bathroom.

Behind the locked door, she removed the envelope from her pocket and traced her name in James's deteriorated handwriting.

With a deep breath, she sliced the seam of the envelope with a pair of cuticle scissors and unfolded the papers. At the first type-written line, she slid to the floor.

Dear Lark,

I thought long and hard about what I wanted to say to you before I left this world.

Business first—you're reading this because I'm gone. I can tell you not to be sad, but I know better. This body betrayed us, but I'm not a slave to it anymore. I wish I could tell you what happens next. Just know that I tried to live an honest life. I hope that takes me to a place of peace where I can watch our boys grow into the fine young men I know they'll become.

My parents love you, even if they don't always show it. Since I quit working, Dad and I have talked more than we ever did before. Learned a lot about him. Suffice it to say, hurt people hurt people. We're good now. Keep in mind, I'm all they ever had. I hope our boys can fill the space I leave in their lives. I trust you'll do your best to make that happen.

Thank your parents for making me a part of the Lovejoy clan. Tell Harlan to keep giving your dad hell for all his jokes about my Red Raiders. Tell 'em I'll be there in spirit every fall, so keep Dos Equis on hand—the lager, not that amber stuff. Salt and lime, por favor.

You gave me a lifetime of beautiful memories. You care for your family with all your heart. This morning, I watched you marvel as Jamie showed you his latest LEGO creation. When you helped Charlie with his socks, you folded each cuff and squeezed his chubby ankles before he toddled away. When you feed and dress me, you look at me with so much respect. Thank you for loving me more when I had less to give.

Forgive me for not telling you about the ALS right away. I didn't want to put a cloud over the pregnancy. Timing was crazy, but, once Charlie got here, life made sense. We needed another reason to hope. I'm afraid he won't remember me. Please tell him that even though I wasn't around very long, I loved him. Tell him how I watched him sleep in his crib, praying I'd be around long enough for him to recall my face when I was gone. Tell him what an absolute blessing he was, how his belly laughs threw light on all the darkness. Tell him how he made my last few years better for us.

Jamie's an old soul. He understands more than he lets on. Thank him for his compassion—how he placed blocks in my hands when I was too weak to play, how he invited me to watch DVDs because sitting was all I could do. Please tell him how much I respect his thoughtful side.

And please describe me as I was before—how much we played and laughed. I couldn't help him learn to ride his bike, but my chest swelled with pride watching him that day he took off from our driveway. Tell him how he impressed me with his maturity and willingness to step up and help with Charlie while you cared for me.

When Jamie turns twenty-one, pull out my scotch glasses and pour him an Oban over ice. One finger—not too much. It's strong. Do the same for Charlie when it's his turn. Ask our boys to toast their old dad. God willing, I'll be up there watching, celebrating every milestone.

I know you'll teach them responsibility and how to be gentlemen. While you're at it, teach them how to live and love. Please discourage them from defining their lives by my absence.

I'll ask you to do the same. Please regret nothing about the life we shared. You have been my best friend and my greatest love. Before ALS struck, I was having the time of my life with you. Hang on to those memories—God, we had so many! New Year's Eve 2008. Jamie's first steps. The way the water hit our skin in Maui (man alive, I'll never forget the way you filled out that black bikini—wow). Bringing home the boys for the first time. Weekends we didn't get out of bed. My thirtieth birthday. Your thirtieth birthday. Date nights. Watching It's a Wonderful Life on Christmas Eve. That Valentine's Day you surprised me with tickets to U2. Saturdays on the sofa, reading and snuggling.

After I got sick, you gave me every opportunity to lead our family, to be the man of the house. When you had to grind up my dinner, you never made me feel pathetic. You weren't afraid to laugh with me, cry with me, and love me through the worst of it. Even though we won't grow old together, know that my best memories included you.

When you know time's short, everything looks different—like when you get glasses for the first time and see all the tiny leaves on the trees you never noticed before. What bugged you before no longer matters. You forgive *easier, and you don't waste time. You see the best in people. Knowledge is power, right?*

A day will come when the darkness will lift. Let our love fuel the next chapter of your life. Challenge yourself. Explore. Rebuild your life in your own way. Do your pro bono work or make wine like you always wanted. Do what scares you. Make it epic.

While you build your new life, show Jamie and Charlie how to love again. I trust you'll find someone worthy of your love. Ask him to be a father to Jamie and Charlie and thank him for finishing what I started. Be happy again. Know I'll leave this world a better man because of the love we shared.

I love you.

James

TEARS WELLED IN LARK'S EYES and she held the pages to her chest.

"Mooooommmm!" Jamie shouted, banging on the door.

"Hold on." Lark rose from the floor and turned the knob.

"Poppy said I could drive with him." Jamie burst in, breathless. "But only if you say okay."

Charlie appeared behind him, pointing. "Less go."

Jamie arched his neck to look at her and his face changed. "You okay, Mom?"

"I'm fine." She put on a smile. "Give me a second." Blinking away her tears, she walked into her bedroom and slid the letter into the nightstand drawer beside James's ashes.

THE TRACTOR IDLED AND DIESEL smoke poured a line of gray exhaust from a pipe over the cab. Frank pushed the door open. "Alright with you if I take them for a spin?" he yelled over the engine noise.

Lark nodded and guided the boys into the tractor's cab.

With a boy on each knee, Frank put the tractor in gear.

Lark pulled out her phone and snapped a picture. A second glance showed she had a voice mail notification. She pressed the phone to her ear.

"Lark, it's Wyatt. I'm back in town. Thought you might come over one night so I can grill those steaks. I'm available any night this week. Okay, well . . . that's all. Take care."

Emotions careened from every angle—her boys waving happily from the tractor, Wyatt's message, and that gut-wrenching letter—likely the last words she'd ever receive from James. *Why in the hell would he do that to me?*

Anger percolated in her chest and a temptation rose to call Jim, to ask how long he had planned to hoard his son's final words. Had he been holding on to it in case he needed it as leverage to see Jamie and Charlie?

Her chest heaved. Her teeth ground until the muscles in her head and neck ached. She walked to the old tree fort and took a seat on the bench below it. Her phone pinged with a text message from Nadine: *We enjoyed having the boys visit. You're a great mother, and they're lucky to have you.*

Lark responded simply: *Thank you.*

A second later, the phone pinged again. *Mother trucker.*

This one was longer: *James was lucky to have you, too. We miss him so much. We didn't come to Houston often enough when we had the chance. Now that you live closer to us, we want to be present for their school events, if you don't mind. We want to do better.*

Lark stared up at the winding branches of the live oak. "James, I see what you're doing up there." She heaved herself up and headed for her bedroom.

A NAP HAD SOUNDED SO GOOD, but sleep didn't come readily. Finally, Lark gave up and picked up her phone. After checking some emails and reading the news for a while, she listened to Wyatt's message again. *What would it hurt to call and thank him? No harm, no foul.*

With each ring, energy coiled tighter under her skin; she felt like a racehorse ready to bound from a starting gate, and she questioned her resolve. *What was I planning to say to him?* She couldn't remember.

"Hey," he answered.

"Wyatt." His name left a pleasantly peculiar taste on her tongue. *Get it together, Lark. Thank you. I'm busy this week. Have a nice life. Click. Move on. Now, go!* "I got your message."

"Yeah, I have these steaks. What about dinner tomorrow?"

Politely unfasten the hook. "Might be a stretch for me." *Atta girl.* "My parents are consumed with Oktoberfest this week. Not sure what to do with my boys."

"They're welcome to come. Bring them."

Jesus H. Christ, he isn't going to make this easy. "They go to bed pretty early."

"No worries. I'm flexible. If it won't work, maybe another time?"

"Alright. Thanks for asking." *That's a no, right?*

"So, you'll let me know if you can swing it?" he asked.

Argh. What would it hurt to eat dinner with him? Get in. Eat. Get out.

"I'll see if my parents can cover the boys," the words left her mouth seconds before her brain caught up with them. Asking her parents for help required providing them with details she wasn't ready to share. She'd think of something.

FRANK WAS STILL ENTERTAINING THE boys, so Lark decided to take advantage of her free time: she plugged in her headphones, turned on her running soundtrack, and inspected the tools in the small barn behind the house.

Thomas Rhett serenaded her as she perused the pegboard wall where her father stored tools. With a pair of red-handled pruning shears in hand, she started pulling and trimming the twisted vines she'd been eyeing for weeks. *Why did I ever think it was a good idea to plant different varietals side by side?* After so many years, isolating them was impossible.

Discovering potential required clearing away the broken pieces, not just the superficial ones. "Prune ruthlessly," one of her professors had once said.

After another trip to the barn to retrieve a set of sturdy loppers, she squatted before the plants repentantly. "Ladies, it's time to clear away the broken pieces holding us back. I'll be quick."

With that, she pulled the clippers apart and fixed them a few feet above the base of one of the plants. She pulled the handles together, and cringed, almost expecting blood to leak from the trunk.

With a snap, the trunk was free, and she moved on to the next— one snap after another until she released every plant.

She cut the debris away from the wires. In a few cases, she cut the wires, too. It wasn't an easy sight to take in—stubby, branchless trunks parallel to the warped posts. Pride and regret swirled with hope in a strange emotional stew, but there was no going back now.

Frank directed the tractor to the front of the house. He killed the engine and helped the Jamie and Charlie out of the cab. While the boys ran toward the house, Frank lingered by his daughter's side.

"Hmm." He pulled off his sunglasses and squinted at what was left in the ground. "I'd ask what they said to tick you off, but even I know they don't talk."

"I heard them screaming for help, loud and clear."

"Why do I think you're not talking about the vines?"

Before she could answer, her mother appeared from the open

garage with eyes like she'd caught a toddler-aged Lark cutting her own hair—shaken with a twist of *what-did-we-do-here*?

Frank put up a hand and Millie turned on her heel.

"Nothing to say? That's a first," Lark said.

"You trying to kill the woman?" He snickered.

"She told me she was planning to pull them out. Figured we all deserve a chance to redeem ourselves."

AFTER A SHOWER, LARK THREW the boys in the bathtub and helped her mother prepare dinner, avoiding the elephant sitting squarely in the middle of her brain—what to do about Wyatt's invitation.

The boys ran circles around Walter, injecting the house with their usual brand of chaos, while their mother blended butter and sour cream into a potato mash.

"I take it we're not tearing down the fence beside your grapevines?" Millie asked.

"If by 'fence' you mean the trellis, then, I hope not."

"Mmph." Millie checked the pork chops in the oven, pushing the disappointment from her features. "Are you excited about Oktoberfest?"

"Oktoberfest?" Lark yawned, too tired to muster pretend enthusiasm. "Mhmm."

Charlie ran into the kitchen and struck Lark's leg. "Mommy, Jay-mie calls me dumb."

"Jamie," Lark said.

"I didn't call him dumb. I said hooking LEGOs to Thomas the Tank Engine is dumb."

"That's not how he heard it. Careful with your words."

"Sorry." He touched Charlie's arm, and Charlie growled and spun away from him.

"I'll go talk to him." Jamie dragged himself out of the room.

"Thank you," Lark called after him.

"Anything else going on with you this week?" Millie stirred gravy.

"Met some people in Gruene who live here. We might meet for dinner tomorrow night. Still working out the details."

"Would we have met?"

"I doubt—"

"Mom!" Jamie called, running in the kitchen. "I had my cars just the way I wanted them, and now Charlie's messing them up."

"Jamie, he wants to play with you," Lark pleaded.

He nodded and disappeared.

"Would you like us to keep the boys during your dinner?" Millie offered.

"I'll ask Bianca for the name of a sitter."

"Not necessary. We'll be home tomorrow night. Enjoy your new friends."

"Awesome. Thank you." *That was too dang easy.*

"A few more girlfriends will do you good." Leave it up to Millie to assume she knew exactly what Lark needed.

Seventeen

Wyatt

WYATT DROVE TO FREDERICKSBURG ON Sunday, but he didn't go straight home. Instead, he spent several hours at his office completing all those assignments Song had thrown at him the previous week.

It wasn't all bad. While he was there, Lark sent him a text, agreeing to join him for dinner the next night.

Nervous energy shot through his body. Dinner with Lark required preparation, but damn it all if he didn't have to contend with Song Chu's busywork first.

ON MONDAY MORNING, THE CORPORATE office emailed Wyatt, commending him for completing his updates. *Whoop-ti-do.* He didn't have the mental fortitude to tackle anything new, so he cut his day short. He'd worked on Sunday; who could blame him?

Before he drove home, he popped into a gift shop on Main to purchase a simple glass vase and candles. Finally, he hit the liquor store for wine, and then the grocery store for flowers.

Back at home, he stared into his closet. *What to wear?* He flipped through his button-downs until he faced his Army dress uniform at the back of the closet.

"Focus on today, man." He laid a light blue oxford shirt and a pair of jeans on the bed and walked into his bathroom.

He pulled back his black-and-white shower curtain to start the hot water and grunted at the sight of the "old man bench" behind it. Showering with one leg required the balance of a tightrope walker. Sitting on that bench kept him safe, but it reminded him of his brokenness, too.

When he was done showering, he hauled himself from his bench to the tile floor in an ungainly dance, and he shoved the curtain closed with an angry *whoosh*.

Perched on his bed, he wrapped his thigh with gauzy white cotton, aligned it with the socket, and inserted his leg. The immediate pressure on his stump rattled him to his core.

Back in the bathroom, the fog on the mirror had dissolved, making for a clear reflection the scores of scars on his chest, a view no one besides his family and the nurses and doctors who had cared for him at the hospitals and clinics had ever seen.

From the bathroom counter, his phone rang. He propped it by the sink and answered by speakerphone.

"You busy?" Kelli asked.

"Getting ready for company."

"Kermit again?"

"No, a friend."

"Man, woman, or animal?"

"Woman."

"About time you moved on."

"Just a friendly dinner at the house. No biggie." He shook cologne on one hand and splashed it under his chin.

"What's her name?"

"Lark."

"That's a name?"

"Yes. Why?"

"Just wondering."

Wyatt angled his body sideways in the mirror, raking his hair. "Would longer hair suit me?" He pushed it to the left and then to the right, but it made no difference. "Like, if I let my hair grow out like Bradley Cooper's?"

"Bradley Cooper's yummy."

"Do you think mine would curl like his?"

"What's wrong with your hair?"

"The bristles on my toothbrush are longer. Look like I'm still in the Army."

"Don't start changing for some stupid girl."

"She's not . . . I'm not . . . Kelli, my haircut draws attention like I'm advertising PTSD."

"Your hair's fine."

Wyatt squinted one eye, shrugged at himself, and lifted the phone from the counter before tabbing off the light.

"You sound nervous. What's the deal?" she asked.

"Um . . ." He scanned his modest house.

"Just a friend? Do you like her? I mean, like her, like her?"

"She's sweet and funny. Was widowed last year and has these two boys. They're so damn cute—"

"Go slow. You don't need to be her rebound guy."

"Give me a break."

"I don't want to see you get hurt."

"Should I set the plates on the table ahead of time or just silverware?"

"You're not dining with the queen."

"Not helping."

"Pull out the paper plates as you go."

"Still not helping. Forget the plates. What side does the knife go on?" He checked out his dining room table from different angles to confirm that he hadn't missed a dusty spot.

"Ask Mom," she asked.

"Leave Mom out of this, okay?"

"Fine."

"What's Zadie doing?" he asked.

"In her room, probably changing clothes fifty times." She groaned. "Okay, here's some advice."

"Yeah?"

"Don't make your bed. Makes you look like you're planning to take her back there and sleep with her."

"Jesus, Kelli. I'm not a monk."

"Just saying, if your bed's company ready, you may be tempted."

"I made it this morning, like always."

"Showering before she comes over?"

"Already did."

"What are you wearing?"

"Jesus, Kel." He fidgeted with the silverware. "I'm gonna set the knife on the right. Easier to reach."

"You got candles on the table?"

"Too much?"

"She *is* a woman."

"I got that."

"If you put candles on the table, she's gonna think you have feelings for her."

"She'll get that from candles?"

"Dinner with candles means something totally different from without."

"Alright. I've got to run."

"Let me know how it plays out." The concern in her voice was hard to miss.

Wyatt hung up. "Right," he said to the empty dining room. "I'll get right on that."

Lark
·············

OKAY, GOOGLE, RIDDLE ME THIS: *How should a woman prepare for dinner with a younger man?* X-rated results flashed on the screen and she closed her laptop. *You're a nasty little trick, Googleman.*

At that, she turned her attention to the dinner itself. She'd offered to bring something to go with the steak. *Oh, the options—a bottle of Geritol? A walker with tennis balls attached to the feet? A copy of Dad's* AARP *Magazine?*

She opened the freezer and three pans of Millie's German potato casserole stared back at her. *Ask and you shall receive.* The casserole, a decadent fusion of potatoes, bacon, cheese, butter, and mayonnaise, would be the perfect side dish for Wyatt's steaks.

In the twenty-four hours since she'd accepted his invitation, her intentions had morphed from purely platonic to "Let's just see what happens." With the boys at school and daycare, respectively, she'd spent the day pampering herself—taken a luxurious bath, shaved her legs, and painted her toenails. Whether tonight was about dinner or more, she would be ready.

Time to get dressed. She breathed a silent thank-you for the fact that her parents had taken the boys to a restaurant for dinner, affording her time to primp without her mother's probing.

Simple black cotton T-shirt dress, above-the-knee short. She pulled off her shirt and jeans. Her eyes flew to the woman in the mirror wearing a purple sports bra—she hadn't even gone running today—and white granny panties that could've been sold as birth control.

Her dresser was thin on date-appropriate underwear, but she managed to fish out a dinner-with-a-friend black bra and cotton panties with a lace trim. When she finished dressing, she ran a brush through that wild hair and thumbed off the light.

WYATT'S HOUSE WASN'T FAR FROM Main Street, although she wasn't familiar with his specific block. She flipped on her turn signal at East Creek and scanned the faded numbers on the curb.

"Where are you? 206 . . . 201 . . . 203 . . . wrong side of the street, dummy." She twisted to the other side. "204 . . . And there's his truck. 202 East Creek."

Light glowed from a gas-lighted pole in front of his post-war brick bungalow. A weathered porch swing shifted in the breeze from the white porch.

She slung her purse over her shoulder and took the grocery sack from the backseat. The heavy front door was left open. Through the mesh of the wood-framed screen door, Wyatt sang along with a Tim McGraw song.

Her hand rose to knock, but it fell to her side as a surge of guilt or shame or *whatever* torpedoed her confidence. For a dizzying second, she considered retreating. *It's not too late to bail.*

"Howdy." Wyatt's silhouette materialized behind the screen and he pushed the door open.

Frayed nerves sent words flying from her mouth. "My boys love that song. Jamie sings that line as, 'You've given me the most beautiful set of rings.'"

Wyatt grinned and took the grocery bag from her. While he carried it to the kitchen, she inspected his living arrangements.

Simplistic was an understatement; it was more like the setup a man might have after his wife kicked him out of the house. Two navy blue leather recliners floated like icebergs over an ocean of darkened oak planks. Between the chairs, a metal-framed end table stored about six months of *Sports Illustrated* magazines. A flat-screen television rested on a TV stand—the sort you'd buy at Walmart—and a cast-iron stove loomed in a corner of the living room like a watchdog.

"Do you use the stove?" She dropped her purse in a corner.

"Would if it ever cooled off enough."

She followed his voice into the kitchen and found him peeking in the sack.

"Brought Mom's potato casserole, a cobbler, and ice cream." She opened the freezer and rearranged the TV dinners to make room. "I should pop the casserole in your oven."

"Sounds good." His wide, flirty grin sent a rush across her skin. "How hot?"

There's a loaded question if I've ever heard one. She caught herself staring at his forehead, which was beading with sweat like it had the night they danced. She blinked at the memory of his warm hands on her waist.

"Like, broil or bake?" Wyatt studied his oven like he'd never seen it before.

"Bake, 350 degrees."

He turned the dial and placed the pan inside.

"White wine?" he asked, clearly prepared as two empty glasses sat at the ready.

With her nod, he opened the fridge, setting off the faint click of bottles.

To the left of the kitchen was the dining room. Spindle-back chairs encircled an antique wooden table set for two—a noble effort, even if the silverware placement was slightly off, with a knife on the left and fork on the right.

"Lark?"

She backed up.

Wyatt handed her a glass. "Here's to your boys' fascination with my robot leg."

Lark met his glass. "Cheers."

"You know, my niece is in kindergarten at Gillespie. I've been wondering if Jamie knows her. Zadie Isbell? She's got red hair and—"

"Zadie's your niece? Small world. She's a sweetheart. Introduced herself on the first day of school. That girl's large and in charge."

"No kidding. She can be a handful."

"Can't they all?"

"Not sure if Jamie mentioned, but she's been dealing with speech troubles. She's got a lisp. It frustrates the hell out of her." He gestured with his wine glass. The embossed Aggie seal on his class ring caught the light.

"My brother's an Aggie too." She tilted her head toward his hand.

"Your brother's an Aggie, and you're not? What went wrong in your family?"

She gave him a jaw-achingly fake smile. "Very funny. I went to Tech—in Lubbock."

"Hmm. Different strokes, I guess."

"I liked it. Got two degrees from the place."

"Pretty *and* smart."

They stared at each other for a few long seconds, then Wyatt threw a thumb back. "Gonna step out to the patio and check my grill."

She examined the kitchen. Wyatt had exactly four of everything . . . four white bowls, four white plates, four white coffee cups . . . four, four, four. The simple life of a single man.

Dave Matthews screamed lyrics over robust acoustical accompaniment. Normally, she liked Dave, but right now the music added to the static filling her ears. "What am I doing here?" she mumbled at the oven. Her pulse beat faster, reprising the physical reaction she'd suffered at the PTO meeting at Bianca's house. *Why was this happening?*

"Ahem." Wyatt appeared behind her. "Sorry to interrupt." He lifted his grilling tongs. "Forgot these."

Her ears were buzzing so loudly now she could barely hear his voice. She wrapped her arms in front of her body.

"You don't look so good." He touched her elbow.

She exhaled loudly. "Whatever *this* is . . . I can't."

"This is just dinner, Lark. No pressure, okay?"

She nodded, and the noise in her head began to settle. "You were sweet to make me feel welcome with you and your friends in Gruene. I enjoyed dancing with you that night, and it was sweet of you to invite me over." She swallowed. "But Wyatt, you're ten years younger than me."

"Eleven, but who's counting?"

"Fine. Eleven." She cracked a smile. "You've got your whole life in front of you."

"You talk like we're fifty years apart."

She began to move away from him.

He brushed her arm. "Hey, what's this all about?"

She made a fluttery gesture with her hands.

"Did I say something upsetting?"

"No." She pressed the heel of her hand to one eye.

"Lark, I'm not gonna lie. I've thought about you since Gruene. I get it. We don't really know each other, and you're still working through some things. Me too. I just enjoy your company. If it's just friends, I'll take it."

Now that the line was drawn, she had to jump on one side or the other. Friends was fine, but that's not what her heart wanted—even if her mind begged to differ.

"We don't have to be friends," she said.

His head jerked back and his face went white. "Okay."

"That's not what I meant. I mean . . . we don't have to be friends *only* . . . if you want to see what happens."

Wyatt cocked his head to one side like he hadn't heard her right. "You sure?"

"I'm sure."

He folded a paper towel in half and handed it to her. Their eyes met and she lifted her head slightly. His hand floated around her face like it was attached to a string, and her face dropped into it. He edged closer, thumbed a tear from her cheek, and lifted her chin.

"Okay," he breathed out.

And then he kissed her like it was his last mission on this earth.

"Wait." Lark gasped and pulled back from him.

"Weird kissing another guy?" Wyatt asked.

Lark nodded, impressed by his ability to read her.

"I know it's not the same, but I think I get where you're coming from. After I left the Army, I couldn't enjoy so much as a hamburger without feeling guilty. Everybody was like, 'Yay, you survived,' but there wasn't room in my head to celebrate anything. In the same moment that I lived, Vince Blazek lost his life, and he left a son without a father."

The words hit the pit of her stomach. *A son without a father? I've got two.* She could see how that widow might resent Wyatt—a man without a wife or a kid. That night in Gruene, TJ had asked him to call Blazek's widow. Now Lark got why Wyatt might be reluctant. He'd gotten the golden prize. His friend's wife had gotten the heartbreak.

Wyatt's eyes dropped to the floor, and guilt radiated from his face. Lark searched for the right words. "I'm sorry" wouldn't do. Finally, she set a hand on his chest.

"Not telling you this to make you feel bad—I'm telling you because I understand how you'd feel torn," Wyatt said. "One step forward, two steps back. When you come back from something like that, each good time comes with reminders of those who lost everything. You know?"

"Like we don't have the right to be happy again," she said. They stood in silence, and Belle's words seeped into Lark's consciousness. *James wants me to show the boys how to love again. I have to live in the present.*

Eighteen

Wyatt

....

That look on Lark's face said she understood. Wyatt went in for a deep, wanting kiss and her hands dropped, soft as snowflakes, over his shoulders.

After a long while, she pulled away and a startled expression overtook her face. "I might have burned our casserole."

"Yeah, I sort of forgot about cooking the steaks, too. Bet my grill's plenty hot by now." He cocked an eyebrow and gave her a devilish grin.

Lark bit back a smile. "Shall I put the rolls in?"

He flashed a thumbs up and returned to the backyard. Soon, the lush aroma of fresh bread wafted through the screen.

When the steaks were ready, he delivered them to the kitchen and covered them with foil. "Mmm." He sniffed at the casserole. "What's in it?"

"Mom's secret." Lark put a finger over her lips and gave a playful shrug.

"Is that right?" He pushed a curl from her eyes and went in for another kiss, one as intense as the last. It seemed as if dinner might never happen—but then a growl came from Lark's middle.

He laughed. "We better feed that monster. Give me a sec to wash up."

Lark filled their plates and set them on the table. Wyatt returned and pulled out her chair for her. No sooner did she sit than he rushed back into the kitchen.

He returned holding a wine bottle. "Guy at the liquor store suggested this one."

"A Napa Valley Silver Oak cab?" she said.

He nodded. "You've had this kind?"

"Not this vintage." She tapped the label and Wyatt's brow bent in confusion. "Vintage is the year it was created. In this case, 2012. Curious to try it."

They clinked glasses and sliced into their steaks.

WHEN THEIR PLATES WERE EMPTY, Wyatt took them to the kitchen. "Should I take that cobbler out of the oven?"

She appeared behind him. "Don't hate me." Her eyes went wide. "I forgot to cook it."

"We can toss it in my microwave."

"Cobbler needs to bake in an oven." She paused. "For forty-five minutes."

"If you have the time, I'll wait."

Lark placed a foil-covered pan in the oven while Wyatt leaned against a cabinet, arms crossed, pretty sure he had a goofy grin on his face. "This is cool, you being here." He walked closer. "You're something else, Lark. With your boys, how do you keep it all under control?"

"I don't have *anything* under control. You're the one who seems to have life cinched up."

A cynical laugh escaped his lips. "All due respect, but I'm gonna have to call bullshit on that one. Everything I had planned before— my career, and, Jesus . . . my body." He stretched his torso to one side like he had a side stitch.

"What?"

"Compared to who I was, I'm so much . . . less." *Less. Good job shooting all romance to hell with that comment.*

Her expression darkened and her head turned to the side. "You're smart and funny and . . . five scoops of handsome," she said, shocking Wyatt's senses.

He raked his putting turf–short hair. "You should've seen me before. I was a pretty good athlete in my day."

"There were pictures of you in your room in Gruene."

"Yeah." A smile bent his mouth when he thought about his old life, but reality killed it. "That explosion tore me apart."

"If you're trying to scare me off, try harder, soldier." Lark squeezed his arm and leaned into him. Her hair brushed his face and traces of fresh cucumber and mint tickled his nose. Her fingertip traced his chin and dropped along the base of his neck. His skin hummed as it trailed the hollow between his collarbones.

He stilled her hand. "Hey, I'm attracted to you, Lark—oh, God, am I ever. But you aren't seeing the scene under here." He tugged at his shirt collar. "It's downright gruesome."

"Stop it. I like you."

"I like you too, but you deserve to know. I come with some ugly scars. I'll understand if you just want to hang out as friends."

"Scars don't scare me. Listen . . ."

He dropped his head, but those true-blue eyes grabbed hold of him.

"I don't look like I did at twenty-seven." She gestured to her body. "Decades of life, not to mention having babies . . . they do a number on a body. They may not all show, but we've all got scars."

"I don't usually talk about this stuff . . ." He ran a hand over his chin.

"I want to know you better," she whispered. "You're safe. I'm not going to share what we talk about with anyone."

"It's not that."

"What, then?" Something changed in her face, something unreadable.

"You're not seeing the whole picture." He had to set her straight. Better to scare her off now than leave her regretting spending time with him later.

She turned away from him.

"You're leaving?" His head was like a slot machine with thoughts rolling in nonsensical combinations.

"Ahem." She cleared her throat from the hallway and a wicked smile rose on her face.

"What's going on?" he asked.

She opened her hand in invitation and, in a voice as gentle as a lullaby, said, "Come here."

His mind roiled at the prospect of Lark seeing his scars; he was certain she'd run, scream, or, worse, look at him with pity. But when he looked at her, he saw a woman who craved him like a dehydrated man craves water.

His eyes snapped closed and he let himself believe Lark saw him as he was . . . before.

Lark

....

SHE PULLED WYATT TOWARD THE dim lamplight at the end of the hall. The post-Army bachelor décor in his bedroom wasn't a surprise: no pictures except a framed snapshot of Zadie on the nightstand, a simple queen bed neatly made with a blue comforter and matching pillow shams, and a chest of drawers sat next to a mirrored closet.

She gave him a gentle push toward the edge of the bed, but he paused to rotate Zadie's photo toward the wall before turning back to her. His face was dreamy and scared at the same time.

"Shh." She put a finger to his lips, her eyes sweeping over him. "I've got you."

She soaked in his touch, selfishly intoxicated by his attention. Their eyes locked for a moment, exposing their vulnerabilities, the pain he kept from the rest of the world, a wound she longed to soothe. How could she make this beautiful man see himself through her eyes?

Wyatt bit her bottom lip in a seductive taunt, sending her hands into a frenzy, unbuttoning his shirt. He grabbed her wrists. "Lark? You sure?"

She answered with a no-going-back kiss and helped him remove his boots. Her body fell toward him. Her hands fidgeted with his belt until it broke free of the loops. It dropped to the floor and she unfastened his jeans.

"Here." He exhaled and lifted his hips, revealing navy plaid boxer shorts.

Her eyes drifted lower, confirming his interest in becoming better acquainted. She pushed the shirt over his shoulders, undistracted by the vicious scars covering his torso. Her hands followed his tight waistline, his hips to his thighs—the left one strong and sturdy, the right one misshapen, wrapped in bleached fabric, and connected to his prosthetic leg.

"Forgive me for asking—do we take it off, or does it stay on?" The question hung between them.

"Either . . . er . . . I haven't . . . you know . . . since it happened." His breath was ragged, his eyes hungry.

"What feels better to you?" she murmured.

"Let's leave it."

She dropped her black dress to the floor. His hand passed along the nape of her neck, and she arched her back. His gentle hands unfastened her bra and his lips traveled along her breasts, gracing her waist and the gray marks of childbirth. She clenched her toes when his fingertips hovered then hooked the lacy trim over her hip. His eyes flashed up at her, and the lace inched to the floor.

"Wyatt." She spoke his name like a mandate. She was a powder keg, seconds from detonation, and his mouth was finding all the tripwires.

Her fingers trailed over the puckered crescents scarring his chest. "Does my touch hurt you?"

He shook his head. "Look at me. Do you want to?"

"Yes." She gave a firm nod. "You?"

"I have some . . . eh . . . in the drawer," he whispered in her hair.

"I have a clean bill of health."

"Me too, but what about—"

"Can't get pregnant," she mumbled in between their kisses and closed her eyes.

"Shh." Wyatt placed a finger over her lips.

They clung to each other as if they'd waited a lifetime for their bodies to join together. A series of electrifying waves passed between them, and she held him tight as he moved inside her. Suspended in time, their bodies tightened. In their release, agony fell away, freeing them to experience joy again.

Afterward, weary and love-drunk, they curled up together beneath the white sheet. Lark wiped her brow and leaned over his shoulder, tracing the divots peppering Wyatt's body, until she fell asleep.

SHE WOKE TO HIS WHISPER.

"Hey beautiful, it's nine thirty. Don't rush on my account, but you said you couldn't stay late with Jamie's school tomorrow?"

"Eeeemmm," she moaned. "I'm okay here for a while." She was in no hurry to leave.

"Should I turn off the oven?" he asked.

Her eyes flew open. "How long have I been asleep?"

"Not long. Want me to check on it?"

"No, I'll get up. Can I use your bathroom?" she asked.

"The guest bathroom's nicer than mine." He gestured down the hall. "Think you'll be more comfortable in there."

Wrapped in the sheet, she retrieved her clothes from the floor and turned back to look at him. "Meet you in the kitchen?"

"You bet." His mouth pitched up on one side. "Be right there."

Nineteen

Wyatt

Even in the dim light, Lark saw everything—his fear, his excitement, the mutilated skin hidden beneath his clothes—and none of it scared her away. Her gentle touch grew more confident, like he was indestructible.

It was good to feel like a man again.

She didn't seem to notice his discomfort when he suggested she use the guest bath. Putting on clothes was neither simple nor smooth, and he preferred to do it in private.

Dressed in a T-shirt, jeans, and sneakers, he walked into the kitchen on a hope and a prayer.

"I was wondering where I'd put my shirt," he said.

"I was wondering where I'd put my date." She stopped scooping ice cream. Her bare feet flexed against the wood floor, and his button-down draped over her toned legs.

"Are you alright with . . . what happened?" he asked.

"More than alright." She leaned in for a kiss and he lifted her onto the counter. Warmth gathered in his belly, and he forgot all about the ice cream and the cobbler. Alarm bells went off in his head. *Are we going back for a second round?* If so, he was in.

"Still want that cobbler?" Her gaze wandered to the bowls.

"Sure." He lifted her and her feet found the floor. They took their bowls to the dining room.

"You're quite the cook."

"Not really. Mom made the casserole, and I bought the cobbler."

"So, your mom's a gourmet cook and your dad works at the brewery?"

"What made you think he's at a brewery?"

"You said he makes beer?"

"That's not his job." She laughed. "He and his buddies are in a contest. They're not very good. Dad manages the electrical co-op for rural areas."

"Who's your dad?"

"Frank Lovejoy."

"Frank? He's one of my clients—a great guy." With another look, the resemblance was obvious. "Can I tell him we met?"

"Sure," she said without hesitation, like she wasn't ashamed to say they were . . . What? Dating? It didn't matter what they called it. He knew how she made him feel.

The candles danced at the end of their wicks, throwing light and shadows over their faces.

"Should probably get home." Lark reached for her phone to check the time.

They stood, and Wyatt twirled a stray curl that had fallen over her eyes.

A self-conscious smile crossed her face. "My hair's a mess—there's no hope for it."

"I'll gladly take the blame for messing it up." He pulled her to him. As crazy as it might sound, he could've sworn their hearts were beatings in tandem. When she pulled away to get dressed, she took a part of him with her.

He held her hand as they walked to her car.

"Was a pretty great night, wasn't it?" she asked, and he answered with a kiss.

After her taillights faded into the darkness, he stepped into the house and found his shirt draped on a corner of the bed. Wyatt pressed it to his face and inhaled Lark's sweet scent. *May never wash this shirt again.*

♣

HE CRAVED HER FRAGRANCE THE next day as he sat at his desk, engaged in a losing fight with distraction, swaddled in memories of the previous night.

The coffee didn't help his nerves when her name popped up on his ringing phone. A bead of sweat raced down his back and he kicked his office door closed.

"Hey Lark." A judder in his voice hinted at his jumpiness and he slapped his forehead. *Should've stopped at one cup of coffee.*

"Last night's all I can think about."

"Me too. Are you doing okay?" *Jesus, Wyatt, that sounds like you forced her into it. Be cool, will ya?*

"Definitely." Her voice was a suggestive taunt. "Busy day?"

"Ah, I'm handling it." He'd like to handle *her*, but climbing through the phone wasn't an option.

"Haven't been able to wipe the smile from my face."

"Can't say I'm in any better shape. Last night, you made me feel—"

His door flew open. "Sorry, I didn't know you were in here," Barbara blurted after charging into his office.

"Um, yeah." Like a kid caught with his hand in the cookie jar, he wiped his forehead and sat straighter in his chair. His tone became all business. "After looking over the permit, I have to agree."

"Pardon?" Lark asked.

"Right. Um-hmm." He cleared his throat. "About your email."

"I didn't send—oh, someone's in your office?"

"Spot on. I'll consider what we talked about and circle back."

"Outstanding." She dropped her voice to impersonate a man. "I look forward to your report."

"Sounds good."

She laughed. "I'll let you go."

He set the phone on his desk and tended to Barbara's questions. When she left, he noticed two permits awaiting the runner, both marked with Frank Lovejoy's name. *Shouldn't trust these with just anyone. Best to handle these directly.*

TWENTY MINUTES LATER, WYATT ARRIVED at the Hill Country Electrical Cooperative office.

"Afternoon, Frank. Thought I'd bring these in person." He set the packets on Frank's desk. "Should cover everything for the Castell project." He waited a long moment for Frank's response.

A few seconds later, Frank's azure eyes lifted and he removed his half-glasses.

"Got a minute?" No longer staring at the papers on his desk, Frank rearranged his face and gestured for Wyatt to close the door.

"Sure." Wyatt landed in a chair facing the desk, unease socking his gut. "Everything alright, sir?"

"Yep." Frank's mouth turned up slightly on one side. "Since you told me about what happened to your leg, I've had you on my mind. How's civilian life treating you?"

So much for a casual conversation about Lark.

"No complaints."

"How long's it been since . . ." He waved a finger toward Wyatt's leg.

"Fourteen months." *Fourteen months, two weeks, three days, to be exact.*

"I was in Vietnam." He cocked his head to one side. "You may not want to talk about it. But, speaking from experience, talking to somebody who's been through that particular brand of hell helped me. If you ever need someone to listen, I'm here."

"I'll keep that in mind, sir."

Frank's eyes went to Wyatt's left hand. "Got any family around here?"

"Yes, sir." Wyatt told him about his sister in town, and his parents in Gruene.

"Families try to support us, but they don't really want to know what we've seen. Wouldn't understand that world." Frank steepled his hands.

"Agree. I'm doing alright, sir. Better than I've been in a long time."

"Better, huh?" Frank's words were drowned out by the mental gymnastics in Wyatt's mind. His eyes—those same, clear, see-through-you blue eyes as Lark's—disarmed Wyatt.

"Different for every soldier. Regardless, those places stick with us when we come home." Frank squinted and combed his beard with his fingertips.

"People see the physical damage, but don't have a clue what goes on up here." Wyatt tapped his head. "Or, worse, they assume they know."

"'Nam never left me. I can close my eyes and . . ." Frank snapped his fingers. "I'm back at the Ben Dinh tunnels by Ho Chi Minh City. Young mothers running for shelter with babies in their arms and kids toddling behind them. Hell, the mothers still kids themselves." He shook his head.

"Can't imagine." Wyatt wiped his forehead. "Nobody prepared me for seeing kids over there—really got to me."

"Uh-huh." Frank got a faraway look in his eyes.

After a long silence, Wyatt shifted in his chair. "Besides my leg being sore most of the time, I'm doing okay."

"Well, if the other stuff gets to you . . . just holler."

Frank sounded distracted. Wyatt suspected he had just found himself revisiting a place he didn't want to be.

"I appreciate your offer, sir. Say . . . I met your daughter last weekend when I went home to Gruene." He couldn't keep a hint of pride from his voice. "She hung out with us Friday night."

Frank thumbed an ear and worked his mouth. "That kid's had a time of it since losing her husband. Happy to see her get away for a few days."

"I enjoyed her company, sir. She's something else." A warm blush shot across Wyatt's skin. "We met the day she hit town, but that's a whole other story." He chuckled.

"Sounds like you plan to catch up with her?"

"Hope so." Wyatt gave a sheepish smile.

Frank's face changed. "I can spot bullshit a mile away." His gaze was intent.

Wyatt's head jerked back.

"Hanging out with my daughter doesn't mean she can pull strings for you around here." He stabbed a finger into the top of his desk.

"Uh, no, what?" Wyatt couldn't lock down the right words.

"Our decision about the turbines is firm." Frank's eyes crumpled around his words.

"Sir?"

"You're not going to hornswoggle the board by chasing after my daughter."

"That's the furthest thing from my mind." Swindling people wasn't in Wyatt's DNA. He pulled out the big guns. "Sir, Aggies do not lie, cheat, or steal—nor do we tolerate those who do." It was more than his college motto. It was the way he operated.

"Kid, you can recite that chant till the cows come home, but those are just words. I've met a few Aggies who weren't so virtuous."

"Sorry to hear that." A sweat droplet fell into Wyatt's vision. "Sir, my work is separate from my personal life. Lark falls into the latter category."

"As long as you don't expect her to work any magic here." He waved a hand overhead. "You got me?"

"Yes, sir." Wyatt had to admit his timing was convenient, even if Frank's suspicions were totally off kilter. "Sir, I understand your concerns, but I give you my word, I won't use your daughter or anyone else to bend the rules. That's not who I am."

While the words sank in, Frank's head bobbed for a minute. Finally, he let out his breath. "Guess I jumped the gun too quickly. Shouldn't have accused you like that. Might say I've had my hackles up since I heard about your company's changes."

"Sir?"

"Word is you're dropping services, cutting staff. Surely, you're privy to those sorts of things?"

"We've changed a few suppliers, but I haven't heard any talk about cutting services."

"Are they still pushing you to sell us on the wind turbines?"

Wyatt shrugged. "Doesn't matter. Your decision's made."

"Damn right it is. Here's the thing—drive through the middle of the state. See all those abandoned pump-jacks? Nobody's pulling them after the drilling's done. Imagine turbines rusting overhead when the next big idea comes along."

"Can't argue they produce clean energy, though," Wyatt said mildly. "They're efficient."

"At a cost." Frank took a sip from his coffee mug. "That firm running your show . . ." He shook his head. "Hate to burst your bubble, kid—I've had friends get caught in these acquisitions. They say they'll leave everything be, but soon enough the suits come in and scatter the employees to the wind. One buddy of mine moved three times in two years before they cut him loose."

"I understand."

"Do you? See, those French guys, or whoever's in charge over there . . . they don't have to answer to us." He fixed a steel-vise gaze on Wyatt. "You do. Remember that."

"I will, sir."

"And about Lark . . . well . . ." Frank drawled after what seemed like ten minutes. "Friends are good. She needs friends. But that's all. She's not in a place for any monkey business."

Monkey business? Who is this guy?

Wyatt glanced at his watch and then stood. "Call if you have questions about the permits. Sorry to rush off, but I have a conference call at the office."

He wished it was a lie, but it seemed he had one every damned day.

Lark

....

IN HER ENTIRE LIFE, LARK couldn't remember using the word *gaga* to describe anything, but as she took her boys to school and returned home, a glittery swirl of happiness surrounded her, and there was no doubt about it. She was gaga.

Her phone rang, and she fell into the overstuffed chair in the living room.

Bianca didn't give her a chance to speak before blurting out, "You've got some 'splainin' to do, Missy! Ran into your parents and your boys at the grocery store last night. Your mom mentioned you went out with friends. Said she was surprised I didn't come along."

"Remember the guy Charlie followed at the Mini Mart when I first hit town? With the leg?"

"GI Joe?"

"Yes."

"Oh say can you see and God bless America, he was hot."

"Still is." Lark swim-kicked her feet against the ottoman.

"Back up the truck and give me the scoop," Bianca said.

"Not polite to kiss and tell."

"Don't make me come over there and shake it out of you."

Lark spilled enough to satisfy Bianca's curiosity—Gruene and dinner at his house. "And . . ." she paused. "I stuck around after dinner."

"Did you, now?"

"Like I said, not polite—"

"Yeah, yeah, yeah. I get it."

"He's a great guy."

"You're a great gal. Birds of a feather, you know?"

"I do." Lark clutched the other details, keeping them tucked away in a hidden pocket like an exquisite secret.

As the afternoon progressed, Lark was surprised not to hear from Wyatt again. Finally, impatient, she punched out a text message: *How was your afternoon?*

WYATT: *Got slammed.*
LARK: *Sorry.*
WYATT: *NBD*

The brevity of his messages was disappointing.

LARK: *You sound busy. LMK if you can break free.*
WYATT: *K*

Did he just 'k' me? She stared at her phone, expecting more.

"Afternoon." Frank's voice startled her, and her phone spilled to the floor. "Here." He recovered it and set it in her hand. "What's wrong?"

"You scared me."

"Came in like always." Frank leaned on her chair. "Looks like we have a mutual friend. Wyatt Gifford? You bumped into each other in Gruene?"

"We sure did." She couldn't vanquish that smile.

"Maybe I'm jumping to conclusions, but I think that boy's sweet on you."

"What boy?"

"Wyatt Gifford. Poor kid. Don't worry, I nipped it in the bud." Frank lifted one of the boys' Matchbox cars from an end table. "He'll give you some space now. You should've seen him—the kid's got it bad for you. I told him you were working through . . . you know."

Her father couldn't have thrown her off more if he had pulled that cowhide rug out from under her feet.

"I'm fine."

"Don't need a college kid chasing you around." His words thwacked her across the head, and she felt her face harden with incredulity. Frank's gaze fell to the wheels of the tiny car. "You're edging toward forty, and the kid's barely left puberty."

The words sliced through her joy. She couldn't argue with her father's math, but why should she have to defend her relationship with Wyatt?

"What's that look supposed to mean?" Frank asked.

"It means I like him."

"From that face, you must hate me."

"Dad, I don't." She tried to clear her expression. "What did you tell him?"

"I told you already." He rubbed his beard thoughtfully. "What's the situation here, exactly?"

The man watches entirely too much television.

Both boys walked in, and Jamie tuned his antenna ears on his mother's conversation.

"Jamie, please take Charlie to the bathroom for me."

In a tag-team approach, Frank gestured at the toddler. "Charlie, go with Jamie."

"I'll take him." Jamie sighed. "But he's not gonna do anything but splash water in the sink."

"Try." Lark's words elicited a long harrumph, and Jamie pulled Charlie away.

"So? What *is* the situation?" Frank kept his eyes trained on the red toy car in his hand.

Lark bit back a swell of anger. "Stop saying 'situation.' It makes it sound like we're hooking up."

"What's that supposed to mean—hooking up?" Frank asked. Apparently, he hadn't seen the latest season of *The Bachelor*.

Lark peeked down the hallway. When she'd confirmed the boys were out of earshot, she said, "We're seeing each other." She couldn't control her mouth from curling into a grin.

"Dating?" Frank's wrinkled forehead rose with alarm.

"Yes."

"I don't want to see you hurt by this kid."

"He's not a kid, Dad."

"He's young." Frank's lips pressed into a serious line.

"Twenty-seven."

"Fine. Twenty-seven. He's just starting his life, and you're . . . in a different place. You just moved here and you're still settling in—career-wise, everything-wise." Frank set the toy on the end table. "He stopped by my office this afternoon and told me you met in Gruene. He didn't tell me about . . ." He waved a hand.

She took a long breath to let her anger thaw. "Dad, I can manage my romantic life."

"I'm worried for you." He reeled back. "Romantic?"

"Yes." There was a pause. "Wyatt's important to me. I care about him."

"Well, I care about *you*." They locked eyes, and he threw his hands up. "Fine. I'll keep my nose out of your business." He began flipping through her mother's *Redbook Magazine*.

"Well, at least I understand why he was too busy to text with me today."

Frank dropped the magazine to read Lark's expression. "You want me to call him?"

"Please. No. I get that you want to protect me. But I don't need protecting. Not from Wyatt."

"He's been through a lot, kid."

"Dad, I know. He saw his friend blown to bits. Losing his leg isn't the half of it. You should see what the shrapnel did to him—awful scars." She gestured over her chest. "He fought for his country and lost his career, his leg, and a good friend—and then, when he came back to the US, his girlfriend broke up with him."

"Lost everything but his truck and his dog." Frank chuckled. "Think I've heard this song."

"Dad."

His tone sobered. "He shared quite a bit more with you than he told me."

I'd hope so.

"It's like they took a melon baller to his body."

"Huh?" he said, puzzled.

"I saw the scars. He said he doesn't even remember how many surgeries they did to remove all the shrapnel before they could close the wounds."

"Oh . . ." He shot a sly glance at her. "Oh. I see."

"Moooooo-ooooommmm," Jamie called from the bathroom.

"Give your old man a break here. Go tend to your boys. You may be a grown woman, but there's only so much your father can take before dinner. Now git."

BEFORE SHE COULD GET VERY FAR, her phone rang. Spirits suddenly buoyed, she stepped outside to answer.

"Hi!"

"Lark?" a woman's voice said.

Not Wyatt.

"Yes?" She felt herself gathering inward.

"I'm Helen Rexrode with Klein, Morales, and Crow. Mr. Morales asked me to schedule a meeting to discuss a position with our firm. Are you available next Wednesday at 10:00 a.m.?"

"I am." She injected cheer into her voice but felt like a fraud. Her dad had pulled strings for her. How could she refuse an opportunity like this?

Then again, did she really want to dismiss parking tickets and proofread wills for the rest of her life?

Twenty

Wyatt

S hell-shocked and hunkered down in his recliner, Wyatt flipped channels. His mind couldn't digest what was playing before him, and he didn't want to digest the overcooked, room-temperature Marie Callender's roast beef dinner parked on the end table.

His phone pinged with a text from Lark, slapping more salt in his wounded heart.

A guy can only take so much rejection in a day. He dropped his phone next to his dinner. His patience only lasted a few seconds, though, and he soon picked it up again.

LARK: *Can you take a break?*

Yeah, I need a break all right. From women. He punched out a response: *Maybe later.*

LARK: *I really need to talk to you.*

The desperation in that one gave him reason to drop his firewall.

WYATT: *You OK?*
LARK: *No.*

Why do I do this to myself? He dialed her number, and she answered on the first ring.

"What's wrong?" he asked.

"I need to talk to you."

"I've still got a load of work to plow through. Like, ten different irons in the fire. Paperwork coming out of my ears." *Shameful alibis, maybe? But necessary.*

"Sorry to interrupt. It's important."

An ad for an upcoming *Full House* series reunion came on, and he fumbled with the remote to mute the television. "I guess I can take a quick break."

"My dad told me he saw you."

"Yeah."

"He told me what he said—how he discouraged you from spending time with me because I was grieving."

"About covers it," Wyatt said with an edge to his voice. "Hey, no big deal."

"Wyatt?"

"I'm here." His voice came out strangled and weak.

"It *is* a big deal."

"Don't worry about it. Hey, I'd better go back to my work."

"I could bring you dinner."

"I already ate." He scowled at the congealed gravy in its microwaveable plastic tray.

"Mom made more of that potato casserole. She's been practicing for this weekend."

"This weekend?"

"Oktoberfest. There's a preview party tomorrow night if you'd like to come. You could invite your sister and her family—"

"Her husband's out of town. Not sure about Kelli's schedule. Dad needs my help in Gruene, so I'm out, too."

"So, that's how it's going to be?" Her voice became terse.

"I told you. Work's keeping me busy."

"Really?" Lark asked. "I'm calling bull on that one."

"Aggies don't lie, cheat, or steal, or tolerate those that do." *They probably don't usually use the school motto twice in one day, either but desperate times call for extreme measures.*

"What the hell is your problem?" Accusation pierced her words.

"I don't just do . . . what we did . . . and go about my business like nothing happened."

"Make room on that high horse, mister. I didn't exactly go over there for a casual bounce around your bedroom. And I wasn't prepared for you to treat me like a stranger because you're overwhelmed at work."

"I'm not overwhelmed with work. I mean, I am, but—"

"Thought Aggies didn't lie?"

"They . . ." His throat caught. "They might exaggerate when they're embarrassed. Hey, give me a break. I've been on a roller coaster the past twenty-four hours."

"Me, too. Dad meant well, but he didn't speak for me—not accurately, anyway. I want to keep seeing you."

"What are you doing now?"

"Standing outside." *Like a little kid hiding from my parents.*

"Can we meet up tonight?"

She sighed. "I promised Mom I'd help her prep for that party. If you come tomorrow, you can see this crazy German beer-maid costume Mom made for me."

"Do I have to wear a costume?"

"No, although you'd look smashing in a pair of lederhosen."

"I think I'll pass on the . . . whatever-you-call-'em."

"Lederhosen? Those short German pants?"

"Yeah, I don't have any of those. I guess I could swing it if jeans are okay?"

"Jeans are perfect. I'll leave tickets at the gate—enough for your sister and Zadie, too."

"Lark?"

"Yeah?"

"Thanks for calling and clearing things up. After talking to your father, I didn't think I'd be hearing from you again."

"After talking to my father, I don't blame you."

Lark

WALTER'S RELENTLESS BARKING GREETED LARK when she stepped back into the house.

"You know me, dog," Lark scolded him. "Do you think I'm a masked robber?"

"Now, Walter, that's not how polite dogs behave," Millie chided him like he was one of her students, and he scratched his ear with his back foot in silence. "That's better." She began unloading the dishwasher.

"Mom, last night I had dinner . . .with a man," Lark said.

"I'm glad you're making friends, honey."

"We're not . . . *that* kind of friends."

"Beg your pardon?" Millie's voice rose in a tight question mark and she abandoned her sorting of knives, forks, and spoons.

Lark provided an expanded view of the previous weekend in Gruene, detailing her new friends, the dancing, the time she'd spent alone pondering her future, and enough about Wyatt to paint a rough sketch of their blossoming relationship.

"Awful soon, don't you think?" Millie sank her teeth in.

"Awful soon to . . . what? Feel good again? Come on, Mom. Will you trust me to make good choices?"

With a reluctant nod, Millie kissed Lark on her temple and didn't ask for more details, but she did have one request: "Will you *please* try on that dirndl?"

"I don't have the curves to fill out one of those costumes."

"Honey, will *you* trust *me*? I wouldn't ask you to wear a garment that didn't make you feel attractive. I've made . . ." Her eyes lowered to Lark's breasts. "Modifications."

THE FOLLOWING AFTERNOON, THE HOUSE practically vibrated to a Teutonic beat as the Lovejoys prepared for the kickoff party.

"It's beautiful, Mom." Lark stood in the mirror, admiring her mother's work.

Millie had delivered on her promise: she'd estimated Lark's lean measurements within a fraction of an inch, and added subtle padding in the blouse that provided welcome curves to boot.

Sitting on her mother's vanity stool, Lark watched in the mirror as her mother's freckled hands twisted her hair into braids.

"Might be hard for you, living with us again. Sometimes I have to remind myself you're an adult. I'm trying to do better. I really am." Millie ran a hand over the braids. "There. You're all set."

Lark turned around and took her hand. "Thanks Mom. Shall we?"

They walked into the living room and found Jamie wagging a finger at Charlie.

"He's not wearing his costume, Mom."

"Wuts a copstume?" Charlie wore a puzzled frown.

Lark and Millie joined forces to get Charlie sorted, and soon both boys were running around the house in their lederhosen like manic Keebler elves.

One look at Millie sent passion flickering in Frank's eyes. "Oh, my stars." He clasped her hands and pushed her back for a better view. Then he pulled her close and nuzzled her neck. "If we didn't have to take the kids . . ."

Millie giggled as they kissed.

Lark's heart warmed at the chemistry her parents shared. After giving them a long moment, she tapped her wrist. "Hate to cramp your style, but . . ."

At that, her mother reengaged her schoolteacher officiousness and herded the family into Frank's truck.

THOUGH THEY ARRIVED NEARLY TWO HOURS early, the venue was already crowded. All manner of German culture was present, including food trailers lining the sidewalks and polka bands warming up for what would be a night of continuous music. At the

Kinderpark area, a red, white, and blue bounce house drew small children like ants to waffle syrup, and Lark's boys weren't immune.

"Look at you, Der-Cutie." Bianca rushed to Lark's side and pecked her cheek. "Glad we can hang out together tonight since Dale's at that Arkansas game."

"Hi, Riley," Lark said, waving to Bianca's oldest.

"Hey." Riley lips parted into a smile. Wearing torn jeans and a "Hate is Baggage" T-shirt, her expression said she would prefer to be anywhere but Oktoberfest.

"She's too big to do the kid stuff and too young for the rest, so she'll watch the kids tonight—yours too—and I'll take her shopping in San Antonio this weekend."

"I'll pay you, Riley." Lark's offer widened the girl's grin.

"Shall we check out the Biergarten?" Bianca hooked Lark's elbow and they walked to the main tent, where an ongoing rotation of bands was set to play throughout the evening.

"Are you ready to polka?" the lead singer of Panic! At the Polka asked. He shared the stage with two singers, dueling accordions, a concertina, drums, and a mixed bag of strings. With the crowd's eager response, the tuba began its oom-pahs. A pair of twanging banjos jumped in while a drummer kept the beat.

The music played while adult attendees strolled past booths decorated by beer-making teams with entertaining gimmicks aimed to catch the judges' eyes and palates. A team of ministers proclaimed the healing powers of "Disciples Ale—so good that Jesus preferred it to wine," and a legal firm touted their "Barley Legal Ale" as being "one step ahead of the law."

Along the closed streets, the ladies took in the sights and sounds around the MarktPlatz venue.

They chicken-danced to the music of the Kraut-Ching-Tigers, a strolling polka trio. In no time, Lark's stomach ached from laughing—Bianca had a way of making that happen.

On the way back to the kids' area, a whistle caught Bianca's attention and she drawled, "That was directed at you, sugar."

Lark spun around with a smile intended for Wyatt.

"Lark Lovejoy, you never were one to disappoint," a man's voice bellowed over the crowd noise. "You don't remember me?"

Lark's smile sagged a little.

"Caleb Dietrich?" he said hopefully.

"Oh. Wow. Caleb. Wow. Dietrich. How . . . are . . . you?"

"Now that I'm laying eyes on you? Effing amazing." Caleb had stuck to the same Shaun Cassidy hairstyle that had waned in popularity when they were in middle school. The lean frame Lark remembered was now hidden beneath a profound beer gut.

"What have you been doing with yourself?" Lark asked.

"In the midst of a D-I-V-O-R-C-E." His rowdy eyebrows couldn't disguise the attention he was giving Lark's chest.

"Sorry to hear that."

"Ah, it's for the best. Heard you moved here. Wondered when you'd grace me with your presence."

Lark smiled and exchanged perplexed expressions with Bianca.

"We should go out and—"

Lark feigned distraction. "Do you remember Bianca?"

Caleb offered a glancing nod.

"I moved before junior high," Bianca added.

"Uh-huh," Caleb said before his eyes ricocheted back to Lark's curves.

"Well, honey, if you need anything—I mean *anything*—call me." He harvested a hamburger of a wallet from his back pocket, extracted a business card, shoved it at Lark, and leaned in for a hug.

She shifted to avoid his full-frontal hold. "Nice to see you, Caleb."

"Pleasure was 100 percent mine," he said.

Bianca clawed Lark's arm as they walked away. "Who was that?"

"Sissie Dietrich's husband."

"How'd she hook up with that creep?" Bianca rolled her eyes. "The way he stared right at your . . ." She looked at Lark's chest. "Girls."

A chill rose up Lark's neck and her hand covered her chest. "Mom added extra layers." She dropped her eyes to her counterfeit cleavage. "Might have been a mistake."

"Nah." Bianca put an arm around her. "Let's go see what our kids are up to."

When they reached the bouncer, Bianca's pulled her ringing phone from her pocket. "It's Dale. I'll catch up later." Speaking cheerfully, she wandered away.

Lark peered into the netted windows of the bounce house.

"Hi Mom!" Jamie mashed his face into the netting.

From the sidewalk, Wyatt's red-haired niece stuck out from the crowd as she skipped toward the children's area.

Lark waved to the woman following Zadie. "I'm Lark. Wyatt's friend?"

"Hi." She tossed a thumb behind her. "Wyatt's parking his truck."

Zadie pulled off her shoes and inserted herself into the bounce house.

"Sorry your husband couldn't come," Lark said.

"Gotta pay the bills," Kelli said with a shrug. "Wyatt told me our kids are in the same class."

"Jamie talks about Zadie all the time. Says she's his best friend, 'even though she's a girl.'" Lark chuckled.

"Yeah. She's mentioned your boy too. Said he's got a brother?"

"Charlie." Lark pointed inside the bouncer.

Kelli's eyes darted to her phone. "He's probably having trouble parking. Hope he doesn't have to walk too far. He's hurting. That leg's giving him fits today. You won't hear him complain."

"He's such a good guy."

"That good guy's been through three deployments and a grueling recovery, only to get trashed by a selfish girl who said she loved him."

"I heard—from his friend? TJ?"

Kelli eyed Lark without turning her head. "Good. So pardon me if I'm not quick to strap cans to the bumper the second he starts crushing on a woman."

Something told Lark Kelli wasn't asking *anyone* for a pardon. Especially not her.

Twenty-one

Wyatt

After dropping Zadie and Kelli off at the main entrance, Wyatt meandered through downtown Fredericksburg. Barricaded streets limited parking near the main thoroughfare, and he considered using that blue placard stashed in his glove compartment, but every handicapped spot contained a vehicle. He'd be lucky if he parked before the curtain closed on Oktoberfest.

Eventually, he gave up on street parking and pulled into his office's parking lot. Eight blocks later, his hip ached with every other footfall. *Damn, my leg hurts—maybe on account of my night with Lark? If so, it was worth it.*

Relief settled over him when he made it to the front gate, claimed his wristband, and located the children's area. Kelli and Lark were together, but neither seemed happy with their company. There was no telling what Kelli might've said.

So help me, Kelli, if you scare her away, I'll never forgive you.

Lark's face lit up when she saw him, and her outfit distracted him from thinking about anything else.

"*This* is what you were embarrassed to wear?" Between the braids and the whatever-you-called-it she was wearing, she was looking hot. "Remind me to send your mother a thank-you note and a dozen roses."

She laughed and gave him a frisky shove.

"Where's your dad?" he asked. "Gotta try his beer."

"Want to come along, Kelli?" Lark offered. "Bianca's daughter's keeping an eye on the kids for us."

"I'll just hang out here," Kelli said.

"Suit yourself." Wyatt shrugged. "Show me the way."

The walk across the park didn't do his stump any favors, and he tried not to wince, but damn, he could feel a blister coming on. The carnival atmosphere didn't distract as much as it annoyed him, like the polka band was stomping at the base of what was left of his leg.

When they reached the beer booths, Lark pointed to Barely Legal. "I'm interviewing for a position at their firm next week."

"Congratulations."

"Let's see if they want me first."

Two booths farther down, they reached Frank's booth. While Lark introduced Wyatt to her mother, Frank pushed a plastic cup into view. "Try my Lovejoy Ale."

Wyatt took it, and the tarry liquid hit his throat like cough medicine past its prime. He choked it down and wiped his mouth to hide his grimace.

"Like it?" Frank asked.

"Mmm," was all Wyatt could manage.

A man stepped up to the table beside him and smiled at Lark. "Lark, whatcha got here?"

"Dad's beer," Lark said, passing him a cup.

The guy gulped it like water and thumped the empty cup on the table.

"Have we met?" Wyatt asked.

"Prob'ly. It's a small town." He shrugged a meaty shoulder. "Caleb Dietrich." He didn't bother to respond to Wyatt's outstretched hand.

If this jerk doesn't stop looking at Lark like fresh meat, I might lose my mind.

"Woo-wee, Lark," Caleb bellowed through a cupped hand. Drunkenness was all over the guy—in his words, his appearance, and his smell.

Lark blushed at the unwelcome attention.

"How do you two know each other?" Wyatt asked.

Caleb exhaled his obnoxious breath in Wyatt's face. "That little lady and I go way back—don't we, Lark?" His question dangled, unanswered. "And just have a look at her now." He licked his lips like he was preparing to tear into a rack of ribs.

Wyatt leaned over the booth. "Need any help?" he asked in a low voice.

"I could use a trip to the ladies' room," she said, trading places with him. "Watch how much you give to him," she whispered.

Wyatt didn't need to be told. The guy was blasted.

Frank sidled up beside Wyatt as he filled glasses. "Listen up, I was out of line the other day. My kid set me straight." A bright smile shone under his mustache.

Wyatt put up a hand. "Don't worry about it."

"Wasn't my business. Sorry."

"You want the best for her." Wyatt offered an understanding nod.

Frank patted him on the back and returned to his conversation with the other men.

Caleb walked into the crowd behind Lark, and Wyatt took notice. *Something about that guy isn't right.*

"Can you keep an eye on this for a minute?" Wyatt tapped Frank on the sleeve and gestured to the beer he'd just set down on the table. "I need to . . ."

"Go see a man about your horse." Frank clapped him on the shoulder.

Following the signs directing attendees to the restrooms, Wyatt pushed past his pain to tear through the packed venue.

He found Caleb pinning Lark against a cinder block wall, his sausage fingers touching one of her braids, a smile on his face like *he* was the prize.

Why doesn't Lark kick him in the nuts and run?

Wyatt's mind went to a grave place. The polka band went silent. Energy whirled in his chest, and he took a cleansing breath. Like a leopard about to pick off an unobservant antelope, he contemplated his approach. *I'm gonna tear this jackass to shreds.*

"Wait," a voice said from out of nowhere, shifting his focus.

Use your good senses, dude. You're in Fredericksburg, not Afghanistan, and this joker is a drunk slob—probably someone's dad or husband, not the Taliban.

The voice returned. "I've got this." It was Lark's voice.

The heat from his chest cooled and Wyatt grasped for a slice of diplomacy. "Let's give the lady some space."

"What the . . ." Caleb squinted at him. "Stay out of it, boy." His hamster cheeks wobbled as he spoke.

"Step away from her, man," Wyatt said.

"I'm fine," Lark said, looking annoyed.

She's anything but fine.

"Seriously, Wyatt." Her see-through-you eyes begged him to contain his rage.

He took a long breath. "Why don't we let the lady get back to what she was doing?" He rolled his head toward the beer booths. "I'll walk you back."

"I don't need your help," Caleb seethed, stimulating the fire in Wyatt's belly. He took a wobbly step, and Wyatt reached out to steady him.

"Take your hands off me or I'll kick your skinny assss," Caleb hissed, sweat dripping off his forehead.

Throw down the gauntlet, asshole? I'm just the man to pick it up and shove it down your throat.

Wyatt's eyes met Caleb's. Recognizing a fight when he saw one, he pushed his chest forward and stiffened his shoulders.

Caleb formed a soggy fist.

Fist raised.

Fist moved.

Fist flew past Wyatt and dragged Caleb's body downward.

"C'mon, buddy." With a sarcastic chuckle, Wyatt bent to help.

"Not your buddy." Caleb slapped Wyatt's hand from his shoulder. "Piss off, cripple."

"Wyatt, I can handle this," Lark's parental tone wounded him.

"You heard her. Move on!" Caleb hollered.

"I'm not going to leave you with some drunken stranger."

"We're not strangers." Caleb crossed his fingers clumsily. "She and I are like thisss."

"Are you alright?" Lark studied Caleb for injuries.

"He's fine," Wyatt barked.

"I *said*, I can handle this!" Her angry whisper hit Wyatt with a smack. "Meet me at Dad's booth."

Her piercing words offered Wyatt one choice—to retreat.

Lark

SHE HOPED CALEB'S FAMILY WOULDN'T suffer for his misdeeds when he arrived home in the sheriff's car. In her experience, when a man was so quick to raise his fist, it spoke to his character.

Spent from all the drama, she trekked back to her father's booth.

"Hey." Frank waved.

"Are you alright?" Millie scooted toward her; she'd obviously heard about the dust-up.

"I'm fine." She looked at her father. "Have you seen Wyatt?"

He shrugged. "I think he left."

Millie's mouth twisted with concern. "Why don't you take the boys home? We'll catch a ride with one of the guys." She set the car keys in Lark's hand. "Put the boys to bed and take a bubble bath." She kissed her on the cheek and whispered in her hair, "Love you, baby girl."

Lark walked to the Kinderpark to collect her boys.

Suddenly, Wyatt's voice shot from the other side of the bounce house, "Zadie Claire, you heard your mom."

Lark traced it to the other side, where he was leaning into the netted windows and yelling, "Time to go."

"Hi, Wy-tat." Charlie waved feverishly. Jumping in his rumpled lederhosen, he was unfazed by Wyatt's foul mood.

"I thought you'd left." Lark touched his shoulder.

"Hey." Wyatt kept his eyes on the bouncer.

"I'm taking my boys home."

"Mmm." Wyatt nodded. "C'mon, Zadie."

"Can we talk about what happened?" Lark said.

"What's to talk about? You were fine letting a drunk maul you. You treated me like . . ." He bit his lower lip. "You pushed *me* away. Who is he to you?"

"Knew him in high school. Friends would be a generous description."

"So why am I in the wrong here?"

"You're sweet to defend me, but I can take care of myself."

"How'd you know he wouldn't hurt you?"

"How'd you know he would?"

"You shouldn't let him talk to you like that."

"I need you to trust me when I say, 'I've got it.'"

Kelli rounded the corner from the bathrooms and Wyatt put up a hand. She nodded begrudgingly, shooting a cautionary look at Lark.

Wyatt led Lark to a bench beneath a set of trees that must've been covered in five-thousand tiny lights. "You're mad at me for defending your honor?"

"My honor's just fine. Geez, Wyatt, I'm a grown woman. If I need help, I'll ask."

"That guy was a lot bigger than you. He could've—"

"I'm tougher than I look."

"When he touched your hair, I wanted to break his arm off right there and club him with it."

"Well, I'm glad you didn't." Lark half laughed. "That might have made next week's job interview with his father-in-law extremely awkward." Her face went serious.

With an embarrassed laugh, Wyatt gripped her hand. "I'm sorry."

"It's okay. Nice to know you're there for me if I need you."

With Oktoberfest behind her, Lark put her mind to preparing for her interview. Lawyering might never make her go tingly inside, but she wasn't about to blow off a prospective job, especially one her dad had called in favors to help her get.

The morning of her interview, she buzzed around rehearsing answers to anticipated questions as she tried to get Charlie ready for the day. It was no use. Charlie was in sloth mode, sinking into the carpet each time Lark tried to wrestle a shirt over his body.

"Miss Bianca's going to come for you, and she's bringing Garth," she finally said, switching to manipulation mode. "Let's get dressed so you can play."

Charlie nodded and immediately pulled on his clothes.

Ten minutes later, the doorbell rang. Walter Cronkite barked and spun in circles, following Charlie toward the door.

"Nakey jaybird!" Charlie announced, gesturing to his newly unclothed body.

"Charlie!" Lark tried not to smile as her boy patted his bare belly, dragging his shirt behind him.

"I'll take care of this nakey jaybird." Bianca drew Charlie to her. "Get yourself ready."

Lark did as she was told. A little later, she emerged from her bedroom with her hair in a tight bun.

"Wow." Bianca relaxed on the couch between Garth and a half-dressed Charlie.

"Are you guys still going to school?" Lark asked.

"They're not studying rocket propulsion at preschool today—they're fine," Bianca said. "Leave me a key to lock up."

Lark nodded and her brow line dropped. "My favorite suit's too tight. I found this one online." She twirled in a half-circle. "What do you think?

"Glad you're putting meat on those birdy-bones."

"DIRTY BONES," Charlie said, giggling.

Bianca cocked her head, "Mmm, honey, something's off with that one." She pointed to Lark's right shoe.

Lark stepped out of the shoe to inspect it. "Walter!" She shook the shoe and snarled at the dog. "This isn't a chew toy." Back in her closet, she retrieved a toe-squeezing, spiky version of the ruined heels.

"I'm off," she announced. She handed a key to Bianca, leaned down and kissed Charlie, and turned to leave.

"Go, get 'em, tiger," Bianca said.

LARK CHECKED IN WITH A DISTRACTED receptionist. A few minutes later, a woman in a navy skirt and a tweed jacket introduced herself as Helen Rexrode. A floral-patterned scarf fluttered around her neck as she shepherded Lark down a long hallway to a room swathed in dark wood, burnished metal, and hunting photos—a boardroom oozing masculinity, complete with a rolling brass cart and decanters of scotch. Two men stood on the opposite side of the table.

"Good morning," John Morales said.

Lark had met him at her father's sixtieth birthday party. John and Frank weren't bosom buddies, but they met for the occasional golf game, and John had been kind enough to arrange the interview.

"Thomas Klein." The other man offered a hand. Lizard-slitted eyes hid beneath shaggy eyebrows.

Surely his wife has told him how scary those things make him look?

John made small talk and asked about Lark's pro bono work, a topic she not only expected but looked forward to discussing.

"In college, I received an award for my work with domestic violence victims. After we moved to Houston, I assisted clients in a shelter."

John nodded but Thomas didn't look up; instead, he leaned back in his chair and removed his phone from his coat pocket.

"What would you say makes you unique?" John asked.

"According to your website, you have one female attorney. While I believe men and women are equally capable of managing legal matters, my pro bono work provided insight. Women tend to be reluctant with male attorneys after they experience physical or emotional abuse at the hand of a male partner."

"We aren't interested in building a practice representing domestic abuse victims," Thomas said, lifting his face from his phone.

Lark blinked, surprised the man had even heard her answer. Pausing to measure the energy of the room, her mind went to Sissie, Thomas's daughter and Caleb's wife.

"All due respect, Mr. Klein. Domestic abuse occurs at all socio-economic levels, and plenty of victims have adequate resources."

He grunted in response.

"I wish you'd been around during my divorce." Helen shot a look at John. "No offense, but the men who handled both sides of our case didn't want to talk about our dirty laundry no matter how many bruises were involved."

"I'm sorry that happened to you," Lark said. "This is the kind of situation I'm talking—"

"Offline, Helen." Thomas aimed his cold eyes at her, cleared his throat, and flattened his cuff.

Helen offered an apologetic nod and Thomas and John exchanged glances.

The picture didn't just come into focus; it flew off the wall and smacked Lark in the head. She wouldn't be happy here. This place was no different from the good ole boys' club she'd endured during her college internship.

She considered Sissie—raised by Thomas, and now scared of her own shadow. When that poor woman got married, it was like she'd climbed out of her father's misogynistic fire only to jump right into Caleb's misogynistic frying pan.

Like she was pulling the button on the red Viewmaster she'd carried around as a kid, memories flashed at Lark: Her male peers at the Calistoga internship teasing her about wasting her time to earn an "MRS" degree. *Click.* Her counting inventory in the tasting room while the men learned to operate the destemmers, crushers, and filtration systems. *Click.* The winery manager calling her "cute" for wanting to "play with the big boys." *Click.* Returning to school that fall filled with self-doubt, and ultimately jettisoning her wine-making dreams to pursue law school.

Then a more recent image clicked into place—not an image, really, but something she said: "I'm not that girl anymore." With a blink, she sat taller, like the woman she had become.

Across from her, John doodled on his notepad and Thomas Klein was as invested as the janitor rolling her cleaning cart in the hall.

"Can you think of anything?" John asked his partner.

Thomas coughed and tilted his eyes to the phone in his lap. Finally, he asked, "Lark, what brought you to Fredericksburg?"

He knows what brought me to Fredericksburg. This is a waste of time.

Lark let a heavy moment of silence sit between them while she checked in with her gut, and then she gave a slight shake of the head. "Mr. Klein . . ." She flattened her hands upon the table in an I-mean-business way.

"Call me Thomas." He stirred in his leather chair.

"Alright, Thomas . . ." Lark softened her voice. "I'm going to jump in here. When do you intend to fill this position?"

"Well . . . um . . ." He looked to his buddy for an answer. None came.

"Currently, we've got things pretty well manned," he admitted.

"Manned" is the operative word.

"That said, you are an attractive candidate."

"Thank you."

"Any other questions?" Thomas asked.

"As a matter of fact, yes. You guys bill . . . what? $450 an hour?"

Thomas tilted his head in interest. "$550."

"So you've sacrificed . . ." She made a show of looking at her watch. "Twenty-three minutes at that rate—plus whatever you're paying Helen—for this? And if we continue this charade, that number will double by the time she walks me to the door." Lark stood and gathered her purse and notebook and gave Helen a friendly smile. "Don't bother. I know my way. And I'm sure you have more important things to do."

Helen gave a satisfied smirk.

"I appreciate the opportunity, or whatever this was. You have business to conduct, as do I. I'll leave you to it."

There's no going back now.

Lark Lovejoy Mead was on her way. Where that was? She couldn't say.

Twenty-two

Lark

Dark skies growled, spitting rain on Lark's windshield. Within a few blocks, a gentle shower gave way to window-shaking, sky-emptying gusts that pelted her car as it splashed through intersections. She leaned over the steering wheel to wipe the fogged windows by hand until the defrosters caught up with the conditions. Her wipers fluttered and dragged, squealing in both directions.

"Here goes nothing." She flipped on her signal and turned into Hartmann-Haas Cellars. In front of the two-story event center, she checked her face in the mirror and gathered her purse and red leather notebook.

The rain slowed to a steady patter, and she paused to drop her notebook on the passenger seat. *If a job exists here, it won't be that kind of job. Unfortunately.*

Her heels cut into the ground and sunk below the gravelly layer to a muddy base. Each step was a fight to reclaim her shoes from the wet earth. She opened the door, and sheet rock dust filled her lungs.

She absorbed the proportions of the event space—larger than it looked from the outside—then called, "Hello?" pulling at her rain-soaked clothes.

"Somebody up there?" a man answered.

"Yes, sir."

"Can I help you?" He emerged holding a wrench.

"Is your manager here?"

"Eh, he's in the tank room. Next building." He gestured behind him. "South side. Looks like a barn."

Lark thanked him and ventured outside in time for another punishing downpour.

Walking from the event center to the tank room required fancy footwork. Gullies and potholes formed a gauntlet she'd have to cross. She attempted to hop over a pothole and landed inches from the high ground; her whole right foot disappeared into a puddle.

Where are my running shoes when I need them? I'd already be there by now. She considered going barefoot, but one look at the discarded construction materials littering the ground told her it wasn't a safe option. The storm was ruthless, but she spanned the dirty spillways, aiming for each gravelly plateau like she was playing hopscotch.

In heels.

In the rain.

If God is sending a message, I'm choosing not to open it.

The rain eased when she reached the crimson overhead door, which was just raised enough for her to pass beneath. She ducked under it and slipped inside—and the moment her heels hit the wet concrete she lost her balance and tipped backward. With nothing to grab, she bit it, ass-over-tea-kettle style. She shrieked as her hipbone slammed into the concrete floor.

She recovered quickly and pushed herself back to standing. She glanced down at the yard-wide muddy streak at her feet. If she had any pride, she'd go home and change clothes.

But once she saw the cavernous room filled with winemaking equipment, she couldn't walk away.

The building was cut into three sections—a glass-partitioned room held bottling machinery on her left, stacked crates on her right, and stainless-steel tanks perched on elevated platforms along the back of the building.

She recognized the nonfunctioning digital screens dangling from the front of the metal tanks, having read online about the hi-tech winery computers capable of tracking progress from first crush to final bottling.

A man coughed and she turned around.

"Hello?" she hollered against the sound of rain hammering the metal roof.

"Coming," a voice boomed and hazy light outlined his figure. "Lark?"

Her head jerked back. "Yes? Who are—"

A few more steps and Levi Gallaher appeared in his threadbare ballcap, jeans, short-sleeved polo shirt, and athletic shoes. A pleasantly baffled expression formed on his face as he repositioned his hat. "Um, are you . . . okay?" He pointed to her mud-caked shoes.

"I'm fine." She resisted patting the mud from her clothes, holding her arms away from her body. "Sorry about . . ." She toed at the sludgy mess she'd made on the floor.

He waved it off.

"You work here?" she asked.

He nodded, sharing a hint of a smile with her.

"I thought you had an irrigation business."

"Did, in Kerrville." He pursed his lips. "Now I work here. Anything I can do for you?"

"Afraid I'll lose my mind if I don't find a job. No one's looking to hire a lawyer around here, so . . . ." She pulled on a wide grin. "Are you hiring?"

"At Hartmann? Eh. Not for an attorney. Mostly dirty work here."

"I'm not opposed to getting dirty. Obviously." She waved at her clothes.

"Not sure we're talking about the same kind of dirt."

"I have experience pruning vines. I'm trainable, and I can be handy wherever you need me."

With doubt all over his face, he gave a birdlike tilt of the head. *Time to wave her winemaking freak flag.* "My undergraduate degree's in viticulture."

"*And* you're a lawyer?"

"One who's not opposed to dirty hands. Got anything?"

"We don't touch the vines. They're leased by another winemaker. You might talk to them. But we do need help painting and cleaning."

"I'm listening."

He squinted in disbelief. "You'd be unpacking supplies and whatever else comes up. Hourly. No benefits."

"I'll take it, assuming I can work while my boys are at school."

"Uh, okay." Levi's brows rose. "Care to know how much it pays?"

"You'll cover all that. When can I start?"

"Any time."

"Tomorrow after I drop my youngest at nursery school?"

"One more thing . . ." He dropped his head to stare at her shoes.

She blushed. "Oh. These were for a meeting I had earlier."

"Wear clothes you don't mind getting dirty."

"Got it."

"See you around nine." Levi smoothed the bill of his cap and returned to his work.

On the other side of the overhead door, the gullies had doubled in size, making high land scarce. Standing on a gravel plateau, Lark turned to look at the mechanical building. Her lungs filled with heavy air and she half expected a bolt of lightning to strike her in her tracks. She gave the elastic band in her hair a tug and unraveled her tight bun. Soggy curls framed her face as she looked at the sky. "Do what you're going to do with me—I'm done hiding from the rain."

The sun glittered against the wet pavement as Lark drove to Charlie's nursery school. She'd had just enough time to run home and change into dry clothes—thank goodness, since she'd looked like a drowned rat.

After retrieving her boy and amending his twice-weekly day care schedule to five days a week, Lark headed to Gillespie.

Bianca was waiting for her. "Are we employed?"

Lark placed a finger over her lips, inching closer. "Slight change in plans. I'm taking a job at Elke's winery," she said.

"I guess I was wrong about Elke."

"I'm not sure she knows. Actually, Levi Gallaher hired me."

"Who?"

"Cute Daddy? Ball cap?" Lark tapped her head.

"What about GI Joe?" Bianca's eyebrows rose.

"GI Joe? Oh, Wyatt's fine. We're fine. Working for Levi. That's all."

"Whew—you about gave me a coronary. If you were seeing GI Joe and Cute Daddy at the same time, it might just kill you dead." Her eyes grew ridiculously wide. "But what a way to go, right?"

Lark laughed.

"Incoming," Bianca warned.

Levi approached, tossing a nod to Bianca and holding out a pile of papers for Lark. "Bring these with you tomorrow, and we'll finish your paperwork." He waved and entered the school.

"I'd pay to watch that cutie-patootie all day." Bianca didn't miss a step. "I can't believe you figured out a way to make him pay you."

"Right, Bianca. I'm willing to do manual labor to look at a boy. You know me so well." Lark shook her head, but she was laughing.

⸎

AT HOME, LARK FILLED HER boys in on her new job while they enjoyed a snack, and then they curled up together in her room for a screening of *Moana*.

As the ending credits rolled, Millie called from the hall, "Dinner's almost ready."

"Be right there," Lark answered, nudging the boys to wash their hands before dinner.

"Here she comes," Millie sang as Lark entered the dining room table.

"How was your day?" Lark asked, helping a wiggling Charlie into his booster seat.

"No complaints." Frank took a sip of his iced tea.

"Do you have news?" Millie bit her lip.

"Mom's working for Kingsley's dad," Jamie said.

"At the law firm?" Millie asked.

"Law firm didn't work out."

Could've heard a pin drop.

"Hear me out."

Millie's face contorted as Lark provided the details.

"Oh, honey. You must've been so disappointed." Millie put a hand to her chin.

Lark took a sip of her water.

"I wanted this to work out for you." Millie face was pained.

"I know you did."

"I'm sorry, honey."

"Don't be. No use beating down the door if they don't want you."

"Do you think . . ." Millie covered her mouth. "What happened at Oktoberfest with Caleb hurt your chances with Thomas Klein?"

"No." Lark's face became fiercely serious. "And I'm not sure I care if it did."

"What happened, Mom?" Jamie's eyebrows rose. "Who's *Calerb*?"

"Caleb," Frank said.

"A man tripped at Oktoberfest and I helped him."

"That was nice. Why would that make it bad for you to get a job?"

At Grammy's confusion, Lark threw her a "here's-how-we're-gonna-do-this" look.

"Oh, it wouldn't." Millie tapped her forehead. "Grammy was just a little confused for a moment, that's all."

Seemingly satisfied with that explanation, Jamie took a bite of his fried chicken.

"I'm sure they wanted you," Millie pressed. "I'll bet they're having budget cuts or—"

"They don't need me." Lark's words came without emotion.

"Your Dad will call him, won't you, Frank?"

"No, he won't." Lark shot him a look.

Frank raised his hands in the air and froze.

"I'm handling this on my own," Lark said.

"What will you do?" Millie wrapped her hands protectively around her elbows, aiming her head toward the boys. "You can't just—"

"Hartmann-Haas will let me try out the wine business—prune vines, assist at their event center, wherever they need me. Plus, working there, I'll learn about the new technology everyone's using now; so much has changed since I went to Calistoga."

"Frank, don't just sit there." Millie reorganized the silverware on each side of her plate.

"Stop," Lark said. "I'm excited to work in an actual winery. Down the road, I'll decide if I want to go out on my own. Or I'll go in another direction."

"Lark, you're an adult. How long can you try out new careers like you're changing clothes?" Millie clenched her jaw. She cut her eyes toward Jamie and lowered her voice. "It's not like you need the money. Why do a job when you're grossly overqualified? You—"

"Let's finish dinner in peace," Frank said. "Come on, Mil."

"Well." Millie gave a hopeless sigh. "I just hope you're happy with your decision."

Twenty-three

Lark

....

If her eagerness to begin her new job was any indication, Lark was happy with her decision: she ran five miles around Fredericksburg and showered before her mother even woke the next day.

Once she dropped the boys at their respective schools, Lark drove to the mechanical building at Hartmann-Haas with purpose.

"Reporting for duty," she said, handing her paperwork to Levi.

"Halfway expected to get a call this morning saying you'd reconsidered."

Levi's words made her feel self-conscious, like she'd pushed him to hire her—which, when she thought about it, she kind of had.

"I know you said you studied wine in college, but this isn't that kind of job. You'll be doing—"

"Painting and cleaning, I heard you. Happy to be here. Put me to work."

"If you say so." He cocked a brow. "Let me show you around."

He unlocked the doors to the event center and gave her a quick tour. Ornate light fixtures dangled from the ceilings, out of place amidst the unfinished, unpainted surroundings. Cases of floor tile lined a wall of windows. Chairs and folding tables stuffed the deep storage closets, but the kitchen was without appliances.

Back at the mechanical barn, Levi pointed out the three offices upstairs. "Expect we'll see an operations center up there to oversee the crush, tanks, and bottling."

"Is Wolf's office up there?" Lark craned her neck like the man might be on site.

"S'pose he might use it someday." Levi lifted a shoulder dismissively. "Haven't seen much of him since he hired me."

"Where are the other workers?"

"Wolf cut 'em loose—even the contractors. Said they turned over shoddy work."

His voice faded to a near whisper. "Look, I don't understand how the guy runs his business, but he doesn't pay me to understand. Get me?"

"Sure. Elke told me they leased the grapevines to other wine-makers. I'd love to get my hands on them."

"Can't say what their plans are." He readjusted his cap and threw her a cautionary glance. "Except for making sure the main irrigation system delivers water to the trellis lines, I stay out of everybody's way. I'd urge you to do the same. Wolf's not the kind of guy who digs having extra noses in his business."

Disappointment settled in her bones. "Help me understand. You do irrigation, but you're supposed to install these tanks?"

"The tanks, the bottling devices, all the electronics." He waved his arms around.

"Don't you need a license for commercial construction?"

"That's where they have me over a barrel." He rolled those beautiful, fiery eyes and cracked a smile. "Pardon the pun. I'm licensed by the state to handle electrical and plumbing for farming or turf management."

"But this isn't—"

He put up a hand. "I'll admit, setting up a winery is about a dozen steps beyond my usual fare. Whatever, I'll figure it out. Have to. Not many jobs around here in my field that'll let me come and go whenever my kids need me." He licked his lips and walked to a table serving as a makeshift desk. "If I don't figure out this wiring and make these tanks work, I won't have this job for long."

"I'm dating an electrical engineer. I could ask him to look at it."

"I'll take any advice I'm offered. Meanwhile"—he handed her a notepad—"you can tackle these first. I warned you, it's not glamorous. Sure you want to do this?"

"I'm sure." She took the notepad and got to work.

IN THE FOLLOWING WEEKS, LARK wielded a caulking gun like a boss, closing gaps and sanding woodwork in preparation to paint. As expected, she saw neither hide nor hair of Wolf the whole time.

After prompting Wyatt to visit the winery for a good month, she couldn't believe her eyes when he appeared with a smile that could melt icebergs.

She wrapped him in her arms. "Did you meet Levi?"

He shook his head. "Didn't see him on the way in. But I brought three sandwiches in case he's around." He held up a bag of takeout.

"You're the sweetest. Let's find him."

Levi was crouched behind one of the tanks at the rear of the building. Despite the frustration painting his face, he managed to greet Wyatt warmly.

"Wyatt brought lunch for us," Lark told him.

"Just sandwiches," Wyatt said. "Heard you had questions about the electrical system."

Levi nodded. "Keep blowing the breakers."

"Can I look at the specs?"

"Over here," Levi said, gesturing.

While Levi dug through his files, Lark laid out the sandwiches on his table-slash-desk.

He retrieved a booklet and handed it over to Wyatt. "I'll be eager to hear your thoughts."

Neither man had much to say while they ate their sandwiches.

"Thanks for lunch, Wyatt." Levi wiped his hands on his jeans. "I'll give you some time to enjoy each other's company."

Before Wyatt left, Lark gave him the nickel tour and was surprised by his lack of enthusiasm. As she walked him back to his truck, she asked, "Are you okay?"

He stared at the event center over her shoulder. "I don't know about this place, Lark." He lifted the booklet. "He's crazy if he thinks he can run this equipment on lines installed eighty years ago. He'll black out the entire Hill Country."

"You serious?"

"Yeah, I'm serious." His smile fell lopsided. "Makes no sense— an irrigation contractor overseeing construction of a winery? Hiring an attorney to paint? Owner's nowhere in sight? This has bad news written all over it."

"Don't be like this."

"I hate to sound like your mother—"

"So don't."

"You're way overqualified."

"I like working here."

From Wyatt's frown, she could see he didn't understand.

LEVI WAS DIGGING THROUGH A box of pipe fittings when Lark came back. "What'd Wyatt think of the place?"

"He likes it."

"Doesn't talk much."

"Mr. Pot, I see you're acquainted with Mr. Kettle."

"Hmm?"

"Nothing. Most days, he's friendlier. Meeting you may have distracted him."

"Pardon?"

"I think he might be jealous. I mean—don't take this the wrong way, but you're not exactly an ogre."

"Thanks . . . I think?" He blushed. "He shouldn't worry. Anybody can see how you feel about the guy."

"I'm that obvious?"

"Um, yeah." He dropped his wrench. "Hope he can make sense out of those specs."

"He mentioned the old lines leading up to the place. Are you sure it can carry the voltage?"

"Damn." His lips turned inside. "I hope it's not that. Brought it up, and Wolf assured me he checked it out before he ordered the equipment. God, I hate talking to him. He has a way of making you feel stupid for asking questions."

Seeing the dread in his eyes, Lark mustered more enthusiasm than she felt to say, "I'll bet Wyatt will help us."

❦

THE NEXT DAY, LARK ENTERED the hardware store on the hunt for yet more blue masking tape.

"Lark?" Sissie Dietrich waved from a wall of paint samples. "Are you fixing up your house?"

"No house. Still living with Mom and Dad. I'm working at new winery off the highway."

"How cool. When's it going to open?"

"Wish I knew. Construction snags."

Construction snags. Electrical snags. Owner is AWOL. Next month? Next year?

"Sissie, I want to say again—I'm sorry about what happened before I came to town," Lark said in a confidential tone.

"I heard about Oktoberfest. You were sweet to help him."

"Wasn't a big deal."

"Heard the guy who attacked him has PTSD." Sissie's eyes grew wide.

Lark tried to contain herself, but anger pulsed in her chest and words flew from her mouth. "No one attacked Caleb, Sissie. He was overserved."

Sissie's gaze dropped to the linoleum. "Our daughter had a volleyball game that night, and he was sleeping it off on the couch afterward." She gave a small shrug. "Not really my business anymore." She raised her eyes. "We're officially separated."

"How's your daughter?"

"Sad, but . . ." She exhaled a hard breath. "Thankfully, she's involved in so many activities, neither of us have time to think about it. He's good to her, so, there's that."

Lark tilted her head to the side. "If I can do anything for you—"

"No, you've done enough. I mean that—helping him at Oktoberfest was kind. I suppose it could've been worse." Her posture slackened with resignation.

"Has he ever hurt you?"

Sissie's expression closed like a curtain. *Nothing to see here. Move along.*

"Would it help to talk to someone? I know some counselors. You wouldn't even have to go anywhere. They'd talk to you by phone." Lark removed a paint chip from the wall and jotted her number. "Call or text me. Any time."

Sissie took the paper and studied it like a puzzle she might solve.

"I mean that . . . any time."

"Thanks, Lark." Sissie slipped away.

BACK AT THE WINERY, LARK ran into Levi walking to his truck.

"Need another part," he said. "You wanna ride along?"

"Sure."

As they turned toward the highway, Levi glanced at her. "Do you remember Melissa?"

"Vaguely." She didn't want to be rude, but she would be hard-pressed to remember details about the younger sister of her high school boyfriend. "She was an athlete, right?"

"Volleyball and track," he said.

"And very pretty."

He nodded, and they sat in awkward silence.

"Want to talk?" she asked.

He worked his mouth. "Lark, I'm not alone. I have someone."

"Oh. I see. Do I know her?"

"Eh . . . no." He paused, looking like he was playing a mental game of rock-paper-scissors.

"Sorry. I'm asking too many questions."

"No, you're fine. Just . . ." His forehead puckered. "Haven't told my in-laws. They're struggling with losing her, and . . ."

"Your secret's safe with me."

His eyebrows moved like they were keeping time with his internal conversation. "Don't say anything, okay? They don't need to hear it through the school, or whatever."

She nodded.

He pulled into a parking spot at the parts warehouse and cut the engine. "Melissa and I . . . we thought we were in love, but it wasn't . . . well, probably not like you and your husband had."

"What was it like?"

"More like best friends." He dropped his chin. "Melissa and her friend Kara were more than friends."

For a man who never speaks, he sure is full of words today.

"They were happy. It took some time, but we worked it out." He slanted his head at a sharp angle. "Before the funeral, Kara told Mel's parents. It was more than they could handle."

"I'll bet."

"A part of me was relieved for them to know the truth. I hoped they'd, you know, embrace Kara. She loved Mel, and the accident destroyed her too." He shrugged. "But Mel's parents wouldn't believe her."

"I'd say you were most generous to stay in the marriage."

"I had . . . I *have* someone too."

"This person of yours . . . what's her name?"

"Travis."

White noise filled Lark's mind and she forced a blank expression onto her face. *Act cool, or he'll never share anything again. Be supportive.*

"If you're worried about coming out in Fredericksburg, you're not giving people around here enough credit. Love is love."

"Stopped worrying about what people thought years ago. I just haven't figured out how to tell Mel's parents. Hate to throw more on their fire."

"But it's been what? A couple years?"

"My kids have been through enough." He grimaced. "We're moving slow. Between my kids and their grandparents, someone's bound to get hurt."

Moving slow—not exactly how she and Wyatt had paced their relationship. *Was it a mistake?*

Twenty-four

Lark

Most evenings, Lark helped Jamie with homework, picked up the house, bathed the boys, and then read stories to them before tucking them into bed. Then, after wrapping up her mom responsibilities, she joined Wyatt for dinner or a movie at his place. Sometimes, he came over to her parents' place and they talked on the patio. The specifics weren't important, so long as they saw each other. After a few months, their end-of-the-day routine had become as welcome as sweet tea in August.

August, however, was ten months away, and the holiday season was right around the corner, introducing just enough chaos and interaction with extended family to knock Lark and Wyatt's finely oiled machine right into the ditch.

As if one turkey dinner wasn't enough, Gillespie Primary School kicked off the fowl-focused holiday with an annual Thanksgiving Luncheon where parents and grandparents outnumbered the student body, hair-netted women slapped rubbery turkey patties on melamine trays, PTO volunteers sponsored crafts, teachers hosted classroom tours, and high expectations provided fertile ground for disappointment.

While Lark unpacked googly eyes and glue bottles, Elke waved a wrist heavy with bangles and walked over.

"Long time, no see," Lark said. "I thought I might run into you at the winery."

Looking lost, Elke shook her head.

"You knew I took a job there, right?"

"What?" She laughed.

Lark didn't get the joke.

Her smile faded. "Since when?"

"A couple months ago."

Elke rolled her head to one side. "You're an attorney. What are you doing?"

"Whatever Levi needs me to do." At Elke's jaw drop, Lark added, "It makes me happy."

"How . . . great." Elke's voice was low and toneless.

"I'd love to help when y'all take over the vines," Lark said. The silence between them swelled like a blister. "I mean, if you guys decide to take them over?"

And, *pop.*

"Wolf tells me nothing." Elke chewed her bottom lip. "With all the travel, you know?"

"I thought I wanted a winery. Hearing how much Wolf travels, I couldn't pull it off as a single mom."

"Wolf doesn't travel for the winery." Elke huffed a sigh. "He manages that fund."

The fund she said he gave up because he couldn't work around all that toxicity?

"If you have time, you should stop by the event center," Lark said. "We've come a long way."

"Uh-huh." Elke looked as if Lark had asked her to inspect the toilets. "Happy Thanksgiving," she said and walked away.

Stung, Lark said, "You, too," and resumed her duties at the "Turkey Table," where she'd help students glue googly eyes, paper beaks, and fuzzy feet to pinecones to create table decorations they could share with their families.

"Twenty googly eyes and one glue bottle at each chair, will you, honey?" Bianca said.

"You bet," Lark said. "Is your mother coming?"

Bianca's shoulders trembled melodramatically. "She'd have to consult the man of the week for permission."

"Sorry."

"Don't be. Keep expectations low where she's concerned."

A few minutes later, Kelli coasted toward the table in a huff. "Got here as soon as I could pull away."

"Catch your breath," Bianca said. "We've got it."

"Zadie couldn't sleep last night—she was so excited Red was in town to attend one of her school activities for once."

"Looking forward to meeting him," Lark said, pleased with Kelli's growing warmth.

"Careful what you wish for." Kelli winked.

The bell sounded and teachers led lines of students into the cafeteria. Guests trickled in around them, forming directionless clusters.

"Can everybody hear me?" A serious-faced principal took the stage, tapping the microphone. The sound reverberated and children covered their ears. "On behalf of the teachers and students, welcome to our Thanksgiving Festival. Let's give a hand to our outstanding PTO for organizing this fun event."

At the back of the cafeteria, a man in still-darkened Transitions-style photochromatic lenses walked in beside a black-haired woman in a pink boucle suit.

"I'll be right back," Lark said to Bianca, abandoning her station to greet Jim and Nadine.

"I thought you weren't going to make it," Lark said.

"Since we were coming this afternoon anyway to get the boys, we shifted our plans. Thought we'd come early and surprise Jamie." Jim flashed a wide smile.

"Is that alright?" Nadine asked.

"Of course. Jamie's with Dad, over there." Lark pointed to the cafeteria line and her heart gave her ribcage a wallop: Frank was pushing a tray on Jamie's right—and Wyatt was pushing another on his left.

She resumed her spot and kept an eye on things from the Turkey Station.

"What's going on?" Bianca attached pipe-cleaners to a pinecone without missing a beat.

"James's parents are here. Surprise," Lark mumbled in mock amusement.

"Son of a biscuit. Do they know about . . ." She knocked her head to the left a few times.

"Not yet," Lark sang. "But the day is young."

"Wyatt'll be a gentleman," Bianca said. "Don't worry."

"What about Wyatt?" Kelli asked.

"My . . . former in-laws are here, and they don't know." It required no further explanation.

Wyatt

FRANK THREW A WINK WHEN Jamie's other grandparents joined them.

Wyatt got the message. Lie low.

He considered ducking out but couldn't disappoint Zadie, so he followed her to an arrangement that placed him, Owen and Suzie Gifford, and Red at the same table with Frank and the Meads. Frank was nice enough to make introductions and attempt to engage the other adults, but Lark's in-laws were stiff as two rusty lawn chairs.

"Your grandson is as sweet as he is sharp," Suzie said to Nadine.

"We agree," Nadine said.

"Me and Jamie play thoccer at retheth." Zadie tapped Jamie's arm. "We're the Gillethpie Gatorth."

"Jamie and I. Put Jamie first," Suzie instructed.

Nadine addressed Wyatt. "Zadie belongs to you?"

"No, ma'am. She's my niece." Wyatt kept his words brief to maintain a low profile.

Red raised his hand like he'd been called on in class. "That little darling's mine."

"And you are?" Nadine asked.

"Married to his sister." Red chucked a thumb at Wyatt.

"Wyatt's our friend, Grandma. Charlie found him when we moved here." Jamie snickered.

"Jamie, how about you work on that turkey?" Frank tapped Jamie's tray.

"Gueth what?" Zadie pushed up on her knees.

"Zadie, hon," Red mumbled.

"Lark'th coming to my Granny'th houth for Thankth-giving. Thee loveth Uncle Wyatt." She smacked her lips, making a *kiss-kiss* sound, which set Jamie to laughing and choking on his milk.

"Did she say Lark's going to your place for Thanksgiving?" Jim asked.

Suzie nodded. "We live in Gruene. Just a hop from your place to ours, sounds like."

"There's no reason Lark can't join *us* for dinner. All of you can." Nadine directed her words at Frank.

"Mighty kind of you to offer." Red waved with his fork. "But Kelli and Suzie are all set. Can't miss the green bean casserole—Suzie adds bacon."

"Red?" Wyatt put a finger to his mouth, but the gesture was too subtle for his big-hearted brother-in-law. "I think she meant to invite Frank, Jamie's granddad."

Zadie prattled on, "Drew wath thuppothed ta feed Goober, but he didn't. Then he thumped him . . . hard. And, Mrs. Rhodeth thaid, 'Drew, what are you . . .'"

Nadine just sat there, chin raised in judgment. Jim ate quickly and rose from his seat, stroking the waistband of his tan Sansabelt slacks. "Jamie, finish eating so you can show us your classroom."

"I'm all done." Jamie pushed away from the table. "Wanna meet Goober?" With Jim's nod, Jamie led the Meads away.

"I hope Lark doesn't take the brunt of this," Wyatt said.

"At some point, they'll have to accept that she has a life," Owen mumbled.

"I'm gonna check on her."

Wyatt walked over to the craft table.

"Hey," Kelli said. "Will you take my spot so I can go to Zadie's class with Red?"

As Wyatt was settling into his sister's seat, Bianca blew out a loud sigh and said, "Craptastic," under her breath.

Confused, Wyatt looked up as a sour-faced woman marched over and stopped in front of him. "I'm Francie Varga. The PTO president? You are?"

"Wyatt Gifford, ma'am. My niece is in kindergarten here."

"Where is . . ." She tapped the tabletop and looked at Bianca. "Where is the woman who was sitting here?"

"Ma'am, Kelli's my sister," Wyatt said.

"Bianca, I sent you an email about volunteer management."

"You sure did." Bianca glued on a beak without turning toward her.

"People can't just walk off the street and creep around our children. Volunteers have to be vetted. Forms completed. Background checks."

"Ma'am? I stepped over here to help out for a minute. I'm not—"

"Mr. . . . never mind." With a gesture, Francie summoned Bianca to follow her out of the cafeteria.

"What's her problem?" Wyatt asked.

"Chronic nastiness." Lark said it like it was a medical diagnosis. "Surprised the CDC doesn't require her to wear a warning label when she's out in public."

Twenty-five

Lark

Eight pinecone turkeys later, Bianca reappeared, clapping her hands together. "Okay, team, we can wrap it up. Turkey time's over."

"You alright?" Lark asked.

"Another day in paradise." Bianca fluttered her long lashes and changed the subject.

"I'm gonna run back to the office and wrap up a few things," Wyatt said, touching Lark's sleeve, as a flurry of volunteers bustled around them breaking down tables and chairs. "Talk later, okay?"

She replied with a nod, then packed up the supplies and carried them to the storage closet—the last place she expected to find drama, and yet . . .

"Lark, I'm sorry about Bianca and her friend," Francie said, pushing auburn strands over a shoulder. She scoffed and dropped her chin like she expected Lark to decode her expression.

"What friend?" Lark asked.

"That man who nearly assaulted Caleb. What was she thinking, letting him around our kids?" Francie's words were like a one-two punch.

Lark reared back. "Woman, you've got it all wrong. 'That man' is *my* friend, and he didn't so much as lift a finger against Caleb. The only thing he did was defend me."

237

"Oh." Francie gave Lark a calculated once-over. "Didn't realize you were the one who brought him here." Her perky little nose pulled up like an odor had offended her. "Sorry," she said unapologetically. "Please have him complete a background check before you invite him to participate in future Gillespie events."

"Fine, but while we're here, I'd like to have a word with you about Bianca."

"I'll handle Bianca."

"That's what I'm worried about." Lark breathed out. "Bianca is family, and I won't stand by and let you continue to treat her like dirt."

With a tinkling laugh, Francie took a step back. "I'm just saying she needs to follow the rules." She frowned. "Didn't know you were related. But I get it. We all have those people in our family."

"You're president of the PTO, not Miranda Priestly. Ease up. Some of us feel like we're crushing it just remembering to sign a permission slip before drop-off. Instead of shaming people when they can't give 100 percent, meet them where they live. Even if they only have time to send a check or help out at night, make room for them."

"No," Francie said. "Our children deserve more than"—she waved her arms overhead—"lazy, drive-thru parenting."

"Who are you calling a drive-thru parent?" Lark's face grew hot.

"Excuse me." The school principal's voice was deep and even, unlike his concerned face. He placed a box of paper on a worktable. "Mrs. Varga, can I have a word with you?"

Francie looked like her tongue had been cut out.

Before Lark turned to leave, she looked Francie dead in the eyes. "Happy Thanksgiving."

The cafeteria was empty but for a few lingering parents tossing debris into rolling trash barrels.

"Give you a hand?" A red-haired man asked.

"I'm done, but thanks. Are you—"

"Red, Wyatt's brother-in-law." He tipped his face and studied hers. "Now I see why my brother-in-law's always smiling these days."

"Thanks." Blushing, she pulled her keys from her bag. "I'm late picking up my youngest."

"Go get him. See you at the Giffords' tomorrow."

"Looking forward to it."

FORTY-FIVE MINUTES LATER, LARK pulled into her parents' driveway next to a shiny white Cadillac.

Wasting no time, Nadine approached with a fast-paced stride and pursed pink lips. Jamie scrambled out of the backseat and ran to Jim, who'd just emerged from the house behind Nadine.

"Your grandma's here, Charlie-man," Lark said, but Charlie merely groaned and rubbed his eyes. She looked at Nadine. "Don't worry, he'll perk up after a nap." She picked him up to carry him inside.

A disingenuous smile cracked Nadine's rigid expression and she followed them through the open garage door.

Walter yipped when they entered the mudroom.

"What the . . ." Nadine flinched and stepped back.

"Hush!" Lark snapped at him, and he dashed off. "Mom's latest rescue," she explained, shaking her head.

"Mom, I got my bag." Jamie appeared in the living room holding the overnight bag they'd packed the previous evening while Jim bent to give Walter a scratch behind the ears.

"Y'all were so sweet to surprise Jamie," Lark said.

"Big day for surprises." Jim rolled his gaze toward Nadine.

Lark deposited Charlie on the couch and walked into the kitchen to stuff Cheerios into Ziploc bags for the boys.

Nadine stalked in behind her. "Are you dating?" she whispered.

Lark swallowed and gave a quick nod.

"That man? At Jamie's lunch?" The question was thick with accusation.

Today's theme for the day: "That man."

"Yes." Lark stalled to measure further explanation.

"His family acts like you and the boys belong to them." Nadine shot her a look that could cut glass. "Like James never existed."

"I can assure you that James is still very much in our lives."

"I can't see how, if you're already—"

Abandoning the snacks, Lark met Nadine's eyes. "I will always love him, no matter who else comes into my life."

Nadine's hand flew to her chest. "You can't be with . . ." Tears swallowed her voice momentarily. "With someone else and still love him," she croaked out.

"He didn't want me to be alone. He told me."

"You're not alone. You have the boys and your parents. We're here too. You don't need—"

"Ahem." Jim stood at the edge of the room with Jamie. "Lark, if you'll give me your keys, I'll move car seats."

While Lark retrieved her keys, Nadine moved to the sofa and patted her lap. Charlie crawled over to her and laid his head on her thigh.

When Jim and Jamie stepped outside, Lark tried to make peace. "You raised a good man. I'll never let them forget him."

"No more talking," Nadine said. "Not around . . ." She nodded down at Charlie, ending their conversation.

Jim finished with the seats and Lark helped the boys into the Cadillac.

Minutes after the Meads' departure, Frank and Millie showed up. Frank delivered Walter to the kennel while Millie repacked her suitcase, adding a bag of spices she'd use to cook dinner for Harlan in Idaho, and then they were off.

By three o'clock, silence filled every corner of the Lovejoy house.

Wyatt

WYATT PACKED A GROCERY SACK with the makings for a steak dinner, tossing in a pint of Bluebell ice cream before he drove to the Lovejoy home to surprise Lark. He spotted Lark's car in the driveway. When she didn't answer the door, he walked around and found her sitting on the rear patio with a fleece blanket over her bare legs.

"Brought groceries to make you dinner," he said. "Your favorite ice cream, too."

"Sounds great." She slipped out of the chair, and a flowery scent drifted by as she passed him to enter the house through the patio door.

"You run today?" He gestured to her T-shirt and shorts.

"Should have, but it felt good just to sit and think for a while. Now that you're here, we could . . ."

"Uh-huh." Her words rushed over his skin and he pursed his lips like he was thinking about their options.

She shook her head. "What'd you say about ice cream?" "

"Oh, shit. Be right back." He high-tailed it to the front door to retrieve the goods and placed a grocery bag on the island. "Probably shouldn't have just shown up like this, huh?"

"Glad you did. I could use some company tonight." She gave him a devilish smile. Her head dipped to his neck. Her finger-tips crept under his long-sleeve T-shirt. She freed his belt with a snap. His belt buckle clanged against the tile floor, and her mouth warmed his neck. *I'd give her everything I own if she'd never stop doing this.*

His hands cupped her backside, lifting her. She leaned back and pulled off her shirt and her sports bra in one slick move.

The cool stone under her back produced a welcome perkiness, and her quivering moans tossed just enough fuel on the fire to make the both of them self-combust. He tugged the shorts from her hip and cocked one curious brow. "Commando, huh?"

"Running shorts have built-in undies," she said in a hot whisper.

"Learn something new every day." He studied her shorts for a moment, then shook his head and dropped them to the floor.

She pulled his hips to her, whispering, "I want you"—words that should've put him in gear. Instead, a flash of self-consciousness reminded him of his surroundings. He pulled away slightly. "What if . . ."

"Even Walter's gone."

"I know, but . . ." His mouth jerked to one side.

"Want to go to my room?" she taunted.

"Yeah," he said, and they raced to the bedroom, where she locked the door behind them.

$\text{\emph{\ss}}$

LATER, THEY REDRESSED AND ENJOYED a glass of chardonnay and a romantic playlist while Wyatt grilled steaks on the patio.

"This kind of life is what I'm talking about," Wyatt said. "You and me, making dinner together."

"Really? You'd be happy with a boring family life?" Lark asked, sending Wyatt's mind reeling.

"Heck, yeah." He cleared his throat. "Sure, it could get stressful—you know, one kid yelling at the other for destroying his LEGO spaceship?"

"I'm familiar."

"But no matter what, we'd be there together. One look across the room and, *BAM!*" Wyatt slapped his palms together. "All that craziness would fall away. We'd be side by side in that madness."

"Lovely . . ." She shrugged. "But . . ."

"I know what you're gonna say—marriage isn't so easy. Mom and Kelli have made me sit through my share of sappy movies."

"Movies show 'in health' but they don't show the 'in sickness' side. A lot happens after a young bride chooses her China pattern."

"I get it." Wyatt chose his words carefully. "Have you thought about . . . giving it another shot? I mean, later?"

"I'll be straight with you—I'll never forget James or what we shared. He didn't choose to leave me."

I know those words are as true as her eyes are blue, but did she have to say them out loud? Wyatt's throat caught and he forced a neutral face. He had stumbled onto a ragged fault line—one he couldn't escape.

"Your scenario, with your happy couple and kids climbing the walls, isn't something I aspire to," Lark said simply. "It's the relationship I *had* with James."

Jealousy shaded his emotions. "Sounds like an amazing guy," he managed.

"He was."

Ouch.

Searching for a detour, he segued to a story about the man's father, recounting Jim Mead's behavior at the luncheon. "Jim went on about his business like he was on the clock to eat his turkey. I almost said, 'Hey, buddy, will you turn around? Your wife is about to twist off—'"

Lark flashed a murderous glare.

Wyatt froze. "I didn't say it."

"James scratched his head wondering how he came from those two. To hear him tell it, Jim and Nadine parented like satellites—detached, like they weren't sure what to do with him."

"He was an only child?"

"Yep."

"Sounds awful lonesome."

"He got through it relatively unscathed. You'd never know they were his parents. He was a jokester, liked to talk, didn't keep his feelings wrapped up like them—although they seem to be undoing some of that packaging now." Lark sighed. "I feel bad for Nadine. Jamie and Charlie are all she has left."

Wyatt nodded while Lark talked about her in-laws. He couldn't sort out the jealousy pulsing through his system. Could Lark really let go of that kind of love and dedicate herself to another man?

Twenty-six

Lark

After dinner, Lark and Wyatt loaded the dishwasher like an old married couple and cuddled on the sofa, flipping between college football and old movies before landing on the ten o'clock news.

Footage of a Marine in combat gear caught their attention—after a thirteen-month deployment in Afghanistan, the guy had surprised his children at a school event. Three elementary school-age kids rushed to the middle of a gymnasium and wrapped their father in unambiguous love.

Wyatt wiped at his eyes.

Lark pressed pause on the remote. "Want to talk?"

He pointed to the still frame on the screen. "Daniel Blazek," he said in a weary voice. "His son must wonder why it wasn't me."

There were no words. All she could do was hold him tight. But snuggling didn't guarantee sleep.

WYATT RETURNED TO HIS HOUSE in the early morning.

A few hours later, Lark picked him up for their drive to New Braunfels.

As they pulled out of town, Wyatt angled his head and shot her a suspicious look. "Saw Levi at the lunch yesterday."

"What's that look for?"

"I'd like you working there better if the guy looked more like Kermit."

"You don't need to worry." She gave a small chuckle.

"But I do. He's probably just waiting for you to kick me to the curb so he can ask you out."

"Not happening." It wasn't right, making him worry. "Wyatt, you can't tell anybody, okay?"

"Okay."

"Levi's not into women."

"Bullshit," Wyatt said.

"True story. He made me promise not to say anything. His former in-laws don't know. They're super conservative, and . . . it's a long story. Did I tell you I met Red in the cafeteria?"

"You can't just switch gears like that."

"Just did. Tell me about Red."

"You tell me. What'd you think?"

"Interesting guy. What's his story?"

"Interesting's one way to describe him." He took a long breath. "When Kelli found him, he was this rough-around-the-edges oil-field brat."

"You say 'found him' like he was under a rock."

"Might've been." Wyatt shrugged. "Nah. He had a time of it— left A&M when the oil markets tanked. His parents couldn't cover tuition, so he worked at the Dixie Chicken. Planned to go back on his own dime. And then . . ." He paused. "Kelli got pregnant."

Lark tried to put Zadie in this story. The years didn't match up. "Zadie?"

Wyatt shook his head. "Pregnancy took a rough turn." He winced. "Wilder Bray came too soon—tiny as a baby bird."

"How sad."

He took a deep breath and exhaled. "Gotta give it to 'em—they kept it together. She graduated, and Red worked at the restaurant until Kelli landed her hospital job in Fredericksburg. He signed on with UniGlobal. A year later, Zadie Claire came. Been happier than ticks on a gorilla ever since."

"Kelli's not sure about me."

"Well, not gonna lie—her hovering can get on my last nerve. You haven't really seen her good side yet."

They exchanged looks. Wyatt chuckled.

"Yes, she has a good side. When I was stuck in the rehab unit, she called every day. When I got the job over here, she made sure I did my exercises at home. Never made me feel like less of a man. To this day, she still looks at me with respect, like I'm still the all-state quarterback of the loud-and-proud New Braunfels Unicorns."

"Unicorns?"

"Yep, Unicorns. We were tough enough to pull it off."

SHE DIDN'T SPOT ANY UNICORNS at Wyatt's parents' house, but it was clear there was a celebration going on there.

The front porch was covered in pumpkins, corn husks, and grapevine wreaths to commemorate the season. A grill large enough to smoke a pig on was parked between the barn and the house, emitting a cloud of deliciousness.

"What *is* that?" Lark sniffed the air like a search dog nailing down a scent.

"Dad's smoking the turkey over hickory chips. Does it every year."

Aromas of allspice and cinnamon greeted them when they stepped into the house.

"Back here," Suzie called from the kitchen.

Wyatt deposited the wine they brought on the counter, gave his mom a big squeeze, and aimed for the door. "Better check on Dad."

Lark peeked through the oven's hazy window at an onion-crusted green-bean casserole and sweet potatoes topped with a roasted marshmallow crust.

"Hope you came hungry," Suzie said.

"Starving."

"You're here!" Zadie ran into the kitchen.

"Hey, sweetheart," Lark said as the little girl stuck a finger in a bowl of whipping cream.

"Zadie Claire," her grandmother said, pinching her nose. "Get your finger out of there."

"I wathed my handth, Zuzu," she said, licking a finger.

As she ran off, Suzie asked, "Are you missing your boys?"

"Yes." Lark shrugged. "But James's parents need time with them."

"I can't imagine what they must be going through at the holidays." Suzie's face shifted quickly. "By the grace of God, there go I. We were so close to—"

"Well, thank God he made it home."

"Amen." Suzie's mouth bent into a smile. "We enjoyed visiting with your father at the lunch yesterday. One of these days, we'll get your parents out here and Owen can smoke some ribs for them."

"They'd love that," Lark said.

"Should we see how he's coming along with that turkey?"

"You bet."

Lark followed Suzie to the pad of concrete beside the barn, where Owen sat between Red and Wyatt in mesh-strapped folding chairs. All three stared at the smoker like it might get up and dance. A portable speaker was propped on an inverted plastic bucket and Pat Green was singing something to the tune of, "If it flies, it dies."

Makes sense, especially today.

Owen lifted the lid, releasing gray smoke.

"Don't lose your brows, Dad," Wyatt said.

Owen fiddled with a meat thermometer. "It's 165 degrees—bird's done," he said, closing the lid. "Let's get him inside and carve him up."

Red placed his beer on the ground, walked into the barn, and returned with tongs capable of assisting in the delivery of a breech calf. Wyatt held an empty foil pan at the ready. On the count of three, Red and Owen transferred a crisp-skinned, golden bird from the cooker.

Together, they all trooped back into the house. While Owen began carving and everyone else carried plates and bowls to the table, Lark opened the wine.

Once the food was on the table and the group was seated, Owen exchanged a glance with Zadie. "Zadie girl? Prayer's a big responsibility. You ready?"

"I practithed with Mom."

"Let's all bow our heads," Owen said.

Zadie waited for Kelli's reassuring wink, then began: "God ith good. God ith great. Let uth thank Him for our food. Amen." Zadie grinned while wiggling a loose front tooth with her tongue.

"Remind us where your parents went this weekend, Lark?" Owen asked.

"They flew to Idaho to see my brother. When James could no longer travel, they spent most of their holidays with us. Time for Harlan to enjoy them."

"Wyatt said your parents have supported you through thick and thin," Suzie said.

"Not sure how I could've done it without them."

"Is it weird living at home again?" Kelli asked.

"Some adjustments, but family is what we needed. Eventually, we'll find our own place."

"Sometimes, our kin is the only thing that can make things better. Right, Kel?" Red winked at his wife.

"Oh, right." Kelli nodded. "Guess what?"

"Zadie's going to have a little brother or sister!" The words burst from Red's mouth and Zadie jumped up and started dancing around the table.

"Congratulations," Lark said warmly, hoping she was chipping away at the icy ledge still clinging to Kelli's shoulders.

After dessert, Suzie shooed the men off to the living room to watch a college football game but Wyatt lingered in the kitchen near Lark.

"First time I've seen you skip the games to wash dishes," Suzie quipped.

"Put a pretty lady in the kitchen, and I'm there."

"There's always been a pretty lady in the kitchen, you dork." Kelli snapped him with a towel.

"Sorry," he said with a snicker.

Lark's phone swooshed with a text notification. "My hands are wet. Do you mind?" she nodded to her phone on the counter and Wyatt grabbed it.

"Your in-laws." He turned the phone toward her: *Sorry to interrupt. Boys are sick.*

"Great," she said with sarcasm, drying her hands. "They're probably just tired, but I'd better check in."

⋘

When Lark hung up, she shared the news: "Charlie treated his grandparents to an unhealthy dose of stomach troubles." She frowned. "Nadine's bathing Charlie, and now Jamie's complaining about his icky tummy. There goes my weekend."

"A bug's going around," Kelli said as Red walked into the kitchen to get another beer. "I told you to get your damn flu shot."

"Never got one. Never needed it," Red mumbled as he walked away.

"Should we get ready to go?" Wyatt touched Lark's back.

"You don't need to cut your time with family short."

"Yeah," Kelli chimed in. "We'll take you home tomorrow."

"See? You're covered. Enjoy your family." Lark's words had a collapsing effect on Wyatt's mood.

"You don't have to go alone," Wyatt said, sounding blue.

"Come on. You'll disappoint your mom and dad if you take off now. I'm not going to be any fun playing nurse." She slung her bag over a shoulder. Her eyes snagged on the frustration painting Wyatt's face. "I need to go. See you back in Fredericksburg?"

"I guess."

She thanked the Giffords, avoiding Wyatt's glum expression.

He offered a cool good-bye kiss and she made her way to New Braunfels to retrieve her clammy young men before turning west to Fredericksburg.

Wyatt

LARK'S ABSENCE LEFT A GAPING hole in Wyatt's spirit. Despite Zadie's efforts to entertain her uncle by covering him in plastic jewelry and pretend makeup, he couldn't be distracted.

Planted on the couch, he pretended to watch one of the NCAA football games. His lack of enthusiasm didn't go unnoticed by his sister.

"You look exhausted." Kelli ran a hand over his head. "Why don't you try out the new bed Mom and Dad bought for you?"

He dragged himself to the bedroom and crawled into bed. Tired as he was, he couldn't stop checking his phone.

At some point, he drifted to sleep, but it wasn't restful. Fantastic dreams mingled with desert memories. Metal wings flapped overhead. The wind spun wildly around explosive bursts. Voices shouted from every direction but his eyes were useless in the dusty air.

"Hump it!" a voice yelled.

Gunshots fired and Wyatt dropped to the hard ground. In the distance, a child wailed. Wyatt crawled toward the cries.

"Help," the child pleaded.

Wyatt's shoulder radio went off and Kermit's voice squawked, "MEDEVAC. MEDEVAC. GET A BIRD, NOW."

Wyatt crawled to find the child, who was screaming in pain. He wiped the dirt from his eyes. It was a girl, covered in dust and blood and tears. He hunched over her and metal shavings carved into his neck, back, and legs.

Over the girl's cries, a voice screamed at Wyatt, "GET OFF HER, LIEUTENANT!"

TJ's voice yelled from the radio, "YOU'RE KILLING HER."

"HELP ME," the girl screamed, and the ground quaked with a blinding flash.

Wyatt pressed the call button on his shoulder radio. "Romeo Viking, we need support."

Behind him, a voice hollered, "Too late. Romeo's gone. Radio's out."

Another soldier gripped Wyatt's shoulders. "OFF HER, GIFFORD. YOU'RE KILLING HER!"

Wyatt held his position, guarding the girl. "I'm here. Don't worry."

The child's cries became fainter.

Then everything went silent, and he lifted his head. A pink mist filled the air around him, like it had the day Blazek was killed.

Pushing the debris away, dusty red curls and full cheeks supplied a punishing sight. "Zadie! No, no, no. God, please not her," he pleaded.

She didn't move.

"I've got you." He held her tight and rolled toward a rocky outcropping. His shoulder hit a sharp edge, delivering pain to his core.

"WYATT," someone shouted overhead.

Not Gifford or Lieutenant. Wyatt.

"WYATT!" Kelli waved from the doorway. "Wake up."

He took a shuddering breath and pain shot across his shoulders. "Kelli?" He blinked rapidly, trying to adjust to the overhead light.

"Here." She helped him to a sitting position. "You fell out of bed and rolled on your prosthesis."

"What's happening in here?" Owen appeared in the doorway, yawning.

"Nightmare." That's all Kelli had to say for him to understand she meant "night terror."

"Sorry." Wyatt scanned the room. "Did I hurt anyone?"

"No," Kelli said.

"You're fine." Owen waved a hand. "We can handle a little noise. You okay?"

"Did I hit—"

"No." Kelli said. "Better talk to that doctor about it, though."

Wyatt gave a slow nod as consciousness took hold. What if Lark had been in bed beside him? She might've encountered the worst night of her life, and Wyatt might've destroyed everything they had together.

It's time to share my dirty little secret.

BACK IN FREDERICKSBURG, WYATT PICKED up a bouquet of yellow and pink daisies from the grocery store and drove to Lark's house.

When the door opened, he was met by Zombie Apocalypse Lark.

"You don't want to come in here," she cautioned.

"I do." He walked inside and handed her the flowers.

Illness floated like a bilious mist. The heater kicked on and pushed a mustiness through the vents—distinctive yet familiar, like the interior of a 1970s Volkswagen bug, that was a welcome addition to the air: it masked the aroma of vomit.

"Let me pick up groceries for you," he offered.

"We're okay." Her sluggish voice matched her form.

Jamie's eyebrows shot up. "I'm kinda hungry."

Wyatt took a seat. Feeling helpless, he knocked his thumbs together. "So . . ." He squinted at Jamie and Jamie threw a wink at him. "Jamie, you did it! You got your wink down. Alright, man. Give me one."

Jamie climbed out of his chair and the two exchanged fist-bumps.

"Better wash your hands," Lark said humorlessly.

"Ah, I'll be alright. I can handle a germy fist bump."

"Your call," she said with a frayed voice.

"So, buddy, have you built anything new with your LEGOs?"

"Wanna see?" Jamie's face lit with LEGO fever. He padded to his room, and Wyatt followed.

When it was just the two of them, he lowered his voice to say, "I want to help your mom, but she says she doesn't need anything. Got any ideas?"

"She always wants to do everything by herself." Jamie huffed. "We're all out of cereal and milk."

"You got it. Bring some paper and a pencil to the kitchen and we'll make a list." Wyatt put a finger to his lips.

"Our secret." Jamie giggled. Seconds later, he met Wyatt in the kitchen with a spiral notebook.

Wyatt flipped pages searching for a clean sheet. He landed on one with only a few words in Lark's looping handwriting, "Levi's house, Tuesday, Oct. 25."

Jealousy bit at him, but he stayed the course and made that grocery list—items a five-year-old would consider high priorities: fun fruit, goldfish crackers, cereal, milk, and juice boxes. He added paper towels, Lysol, and 7-Up for good measure before stashing the list in his pocket and returning to Lark's side. "Gonna run a few errands. Call if you think of anything."

He returned an hour later carrying two grocery sacks.

Jamie met him at the door and wasted no time digging through the sacks. Perched on a barstool, he lifted a cereal box over his head. "Look, Mom. Wyatt got us cereal."

"How'd he know we needed cereal?" she asked, narrowing her eyes at Jamie.

"Quarantine two growing boys in a house for a couple days, they're bound to run out of Rice Krispies," Wyatt said.

"Jamie, what do you say?"

"Thanks, Wyatt." Jamie peeled the box open and pulled out a handful of cereal.

After stashing the groceries wherever seemed to make sense, Wyatt revisited his truck and returned with an iced tea for Lark and two cherry Slurpees.

"Drink those in the kitchen. Grammy would not want red juice on her white furniture," Lark said.

"C'mon, Charlie," Jamie said. "You spill a lot. Let's go."

Lured by the radioactive-colored drink, Charlie obediently slithered off the couch.

"Walter still at the vet?" Wyatt asked.

"Didn't have the energy to go get him."

"Want me to?"

"No. My hands are full enough with these two." She gestured to her boys.

"You poor girl." Wyatt put an arm around her and she pulled away.

"I need a bath."

"Come here, Stinky." He pulled her close. "I've been thinking. I have a few appointments in San Antonio next week. Think you might be able to come keep me company?"

"What's wrong?"

"Nothing's wrong. Just my routine psych and leg checkup."

"I'll have to ask Levi for the time off."

"Didn't he say he'd be flexible?"

"Yeah, but I don't want to take advantage."

"I'd make it worth your while. Hotel. Dinner. You and me alone?"

"You make it sound pretty inviting." Lark wiggled her eyebrows.

"Let's get you well and make it happen," Wyatt said, dropping a kiss on her forehead.

Twenty-seven

Lark

....

In the next twenty-four hours, whatever parasitic monster had assaulted Lark's family retreated.

Before her parents returned, Lark gave the house a good scrubbing and retrieved Walter from the kennel; it was as if their little plague had never happened. And when Frank and Millie got back, they readily agreed to help Lark with the boys so she could accompany Wyatt to San Antonio.

Levi, meanwhile, was as accommodating as ever, encouraging her to go and have a good time.

On Monday morning, she stopped into Jamie's classroom to deliver a permission slip for that afternoon's trip to the library. An eggy odor of tempera paint socked her with queasiness, and she skated toward the back of the room—where, luck would have it, Mrs. Rhodes stood near open windows.

Jamie waved as she passed; Lark employed a fake-it-till-you-make-it strategy and smiled back, swallowing the warm acid skimming the back of her throat.

Handing off the signed paper, she explained, "I'll be out of town for the next two days."

She leaned toward the open windows. "Mom's around if you need anything."

"Have you seen Kingsley's mom?" Mrs. Rhodes asked.

"Not since last week," Lark said.

"Do you see her at work?"

Lark resisted laughing. "No. Her husband's the one who's . . ." *How to say it without sounding gossipy?* "When it comes to the winery, he's the more hands-on of the two." *That's a stretch.*

Mrs. Rhodes glanced at her students and spoke quietly. "I hope they're alright. Kingsley didn't come back after the holiday. We can't get a hold of them."

"They're always traveling. Maybe they forgot to call about him missing school?" The excuse tasted ridiculous in her mouth.

"Maybe so." Mrs. Rhodes gave an uncertain shrug.

Wyatt

....

THIS TRIP COULD BRING THEM closer or scare the love right out of her. How could he make Lark understand how an easy-going guy could become a monster in the night, or how much he feared putting her at risk?

On Tuesday morning, he picked her up, and they drove to San Antonio. They arrived too early for his appointments, so they grabbed some coffees and strolled into the Alamo.

Wyatt hadn't visited the shrine since he was a kid. The mud-brick walls weren't all that different from ones he'd seen during his service, and the place held a different meaning now.

They walked through the exhibits and read plaques detailing the battle. Finally, they stepped into the courtyard beside the old mission and sat on a bench in the shade.

"Pretty out here, isn't it?" Lark asked.

It was—especially the way the sun lit her hair. She was so beautiful . . . so everything, and Wyatt might lose her when she learned about his night terrors.

"Where were you on 9/11?" he asked.

"In college. What a crazy morning: I was late to a math class and was cutting through the student union when I saw people standing in front of this giant TV—remember the ones that took up a whole wall?"

"Oh, yeah."

"My instructor had no tolerance for latecomers, so I didn't stop to see what was happening. Made it to class, and everything was routine. Evidently, the largest terrorist attack on US soil hadn't crossed his radar."

"When'd you find out?"

"We didn't have all those computers and smartboards they have now, but there was a TV on a rolling cart in my next class. Our communications professor turned it on, and I swear, our class had never been so quiet. Our hearts broke."

"God, what an awful day."

"No kidding. All those voice mails from people saying good-bye. Made me rethink what I wanted to do. Realized I didn't want to be so far away from family." She shrugged. "What about you?"

"I was in fifth grade—they called us to the cafeteria. Our principal told us there had been an accident with some airplanes, but nothing specific. One kid who saw it on TV showed up to school late. Started talking about it like a Bruce Willis movie—you know? Rogue guys steal a plane? We thought he was full of crap. Throughout the day, kids were getting checked out early, but we didn't put two and two together."

"Checked out? Why?"

"Guess their parents thought they might be in danger. I don't know. Got home, and Mom switched on the news, and it stayed like that for weeks after. Man, we didn't turn the channel from Peter Jennings. That night, he showed pictures of those missing people like they might be wandering around the city."

"I talked to my parents and my brother throughout the day," Lark said, remembering. "My mom called me that night, fixated on the pregnant lady whose husband had helped divert one of the planes."

"In the cornfield, right?"

"Shanksville, Pennsylvania," Lark said. "Her last name was Beamer, and her husband was one of the guys who said—"

"Let's roll." Wyatt nodded and muttered it again softly: "Let's roll."

"He never saw their baby. Wasn't the only one. So many babies came along to the widows." Lark shook her head. "And about a dozen pregnant moms died that day."

Wyatt's brows pitched up. "Never heard that before." He stared ahead for a long time. "Changed us, too. Mom's always been a warm-fuzzy. Dad? Not so much. More like a man-up, be-tough kind of guy. 9/11 mellowed him out."

"We never said good-bye the same way afterward," she said. "I know it was a while before you went into the Army, but do you think it influenced your decision?"

"Damn right it did. World cracked right in two after that day— and not just for the people on the East Coast." He wiped a hand on his jeans. "This might sound crazy, and I was a kid back then, but I thought about it like this—remember all that ash that floated around New York?"

"Uh-huh."

"I imagined it like a cloud that drifted west, sharing the heartache with every state it passed.

"I can see that."

He shook his head. "Felt like the world was broken. Heck, just going to pick up your grandmother at the airport became an ordeal."

"Hard to remember a day when we didn't have to have a license to board a plane," she said.

He nodded. "I didn't understand the politics around it, but I was convinced I'd find my way overseas to fight whoever had caused so much pain." He rubbed a hand over his chest. "Didn't expect to see so many kids over there. The fight didn't make sense to them. Think about what would happen if foreign soldiers showed up in Gruene with their gear and weapons."

Lark blinked hard.

"Tell you how it would go down." Wyatt frowned. "Without a doubt, everyone would unlock their gun safes and pull out their

Browning Hog Stalkers and fight to the end." He tipped his head. "Then again, I'd hope Americans would've stopped those Taliban ass-holes before they hijacked a religion and terrorized innocent people."

"Any regrets about signing up?"

"No, but it was weird how at first people were running up to me and thanking me for my service, and then people started arguing about oil and conspiracy theories. It was like I left one country to fight over there and returned to a totally different place. Didn't matter what anybody said about it: We had a commitment to our operation and orders. We had to fight every damn day. Didn't matter who or what started the mess."

"I once saw a bumper sticker that said, 'America isn't at war. America is at the mall.'"

"Bingo." Wyatt met Lark's gaze. "One minute, they wanted us to avenge those attacks. 'Never forget' and all. Next, they looked at us like we were fools fighting a war nobody cared about."

"I've heard it was like that in Vietnam."

"Your dad fought over there, right?"

She looked surprised. "He did, but all he's ever said to me about it is, 'You can't understand war unless you've lived it.'"

"He's right. Damn right."

Lark's phone rang, and she winced. "Sorry. It's Levi. I should get this."

"Go ahead."

Lark

....

SHE STEPPED AROUND THE CORNER to take the call. Answering was the least she could do, considering he hadn't given her a bad time about taking off work.

"Hey Levi," she said brightly.

"Hey, Lark," Levi said. "I'm sorry to bother you."

"No bother. What's up?"

"Any chance you've seen or heard from Elke?"

"Funny you ask. I went up to the school yesterday to drop off a permission slip, and Mrs. Rhodes asked if I'd seen Elke because Kingsley had missed school and no one had been able to get a hold of them. I intended to check on her before I left the winery yesterday, but I forgot."

"Damn." Levi breathed out. "She's totally off the radar. Wolf, too. Bank examiners showed up this morning with a hell of a list of questions about the business—like I'd know what Wolf does with his money."

"Should I come back?" she offered.

"They're sniffing into Wolf's finances. Nothing for you to do. I'm sure there's just a misunderstanding somewhere."

"I hope so," Lark said.

"Don't think about this place. You guys have fun."

Levi ended the call but Lark kept staring at the screen. She wanted to believe there had been a misunderstanding—that Elke and Wolf had slipped up and forgotten to mail in a report to the banks—but her gut clenched with worry. On some level, their absence confirmed the suspicions she had dismissed since she took the job.

Wyatt walked toward her, angling his neck to see if she was still on the phone. "What did he want?"

"Bank examiners are at the winery, and Wolf and Elke are nowhere to be found."

"Hmmph." Wyatt jerked his chin to one side, looking unsurprised.

"I hope whatever's going on gets worked out quickly."

"Did Levi ever upgrade those power lines?" he asked.

"He emailed the information to Wolf, and Wolf said he'd take care of it."

"Sure he would," Wyatt said. "Have you seen anyone working on it?"

"No."

"Maybe the next owner'll finish the place."

"Huh?" she asked.

"Wineries can be like ski resorts—built by people who don't have the tools to manage them. Some sell a couple times before they break even. Wolf's probably holding out—trying not to put too much money into it before he sells to turn a profit."

"Maybe. I hope I still have a job when I get back."

THE MEDICAL CAMPUS WAS THE FIRST Lark had seen with armed guards at its gates. After she and Wyatt stopped at the visitor center to obtain a clearance pass for her, they presented their credentials to the guards and Wyatt drove them into the base—a conglomeration of hospitals, clinics, and dormitories that, together, formed the Brooke Army Medical Center, serving all branches of the military.

"First stop." Wyatt parked at a one-story brick building. "My psychiatrist's office. I want you to meet him."

Lark felt awkward. "Don't want to invade your privacy."

"Please come," he said. "It's important to me . . . to us," he said.

She followed him inside and took a seat in the waiting room while he checked in with the receptionist. He took the seat beside her a minute later.

"Had to sign a form so you could go back with me."

"You sure?" she asked.

"Yep. I'll go in first, talk to Doc Fisher for a while, and then he'll come let you in." He grabbed one of her hands and closed his eyes.

Twenty-eight

Wyatt

Dr. Fisher's receptionist, a middle-aged woman with spiky gray hair, peeked into the waiting room. "Gifford," she said, smiling, when she met Wyatt's eyes.

"See you in a little while," he told Lark before following the receptionist down the hall to Dr. Fisher's office. Inside, he planted himself in one of the two beige chairs opposite the desk where he'd logged plenty of hours excavating the emotional aftermath that had followed him from Afghanistan and Germany.

"Hello." Dr. Fisher walked in wearing a plaid shirt a few years out of style, khaki pants, and leather Rockport shoes with black rubber soles. He ran a hand over his head, unable to tame his flyaway gray hair.

Nice as the doc was, those first few seconds with him had a way of returning Wyatt to shaky ground. Reflexively, he braced himself as he prepared to have his head split open and examined—then, noticing his tension, deliberately relaxed his shoulders in preparation for the doc's introductory questions.

Once questions about leg pain and sleep disturbances were out of the way, the doctor always invited Wyatt to discuss new concerns. Most of the time, he didn't have any, so the doc took over. But today was different. Ever since his Thanksgiving nightmare, a riot had been rattling inside Wyatt's head—one he desperately wanted to quiet.

"How's your leg?" The doctor typed something on his computer. He was always typing—all the doctors were.

Ask a question, wait for your answer, then, tap, tap, tap it into your permanent record.

"Pain's always there, on some level. Ibuprofen helps."

"Need something stronger?"

"Heard too many stories about addiction. I've got enough troubles."

"We want you to be comfortable. When's your next appointment with your surgeon?"

"I'm hitting Intrepid this afternoon."

"Good deal." More tapping. He leaned back in his chair. "You brought your girlfriend with you?"

"Yes, sir."

"Alright. Before I meet . . . I'm sorry, I didn't catch her name?"

"Lark." Wyatt rubbed his chin.

"Anything you want me to keep off-limits around her?"

"Nothing, but I need your help. I had a nightmare at Thanksgiving. She wasn't there, but if she had been . . ." He closed his eyes. "I need her to understand, in case it happens around her, so she'll know how to handle them . . . er . . . me."

"Back up to Thanksgiving, Wyatt. Did you become physical?"

"Hurt myself, no one else. Fell out of bed." He tried to laugh, but he had business to cover. "I haven't told her—don't want to scare her. But if it had happened with her there and she'd tried to wake me, who knows what would've happened. She has to know what she's getting with me. Even if it means she bails, I have to be straight with her."

"Of course. Are you ready?"

"As I ever will be."

"Good enough." Dr. Fisher left to get Lark.

The next few minutes would change the way Lark saw him. Even if she said she wanted to stay with him, she'd always wonder if he might hurt her.

"Found a friend of yours," the doctor said, walking into the office with Lark.

"Friend? Not exactly, Doc. Lark's my . . . girlfriend?"

"I'm thirty-eight. Makes me kinda old to be called a 'girl.'" Lark patted Wyatt's knee. Her easy smile did little to stabilize his nerves.

"Age is relative," the doctor joked. "Wyatt, why don't you begin by telling Lark what you'd like to accomplish today?"

"I have PTSD, Lark."

She nodded. "Okay."

"Um . . . every so often I have these nightmares." He swallowed. "Night terrors," he corrected. "They can make for a scary scene. As we become closer . . ." The image of Lark's boys flashed in his mind. "If, at some point, say, the boys came around me more . . . at night? I'd want to prepare you and them."

Lark

....

ROBBED OF THE LIGHTNESS SHE'D carried only moments before, Lark read the doctor's solemn expression, not unlike the faces that had delivered bad news time and again to James. She thought she'd seen the last of pitying doctors and life-altering conversations.

Loving Wyatt is so easy, but why can't I love someone who's healthy? Why does everything have to get so serious when we've been having so much fun?

"Lark," Wyatt said. "Lark?" He touched her hand.

Her gaze floated toward him in slow motion.

"I don't have them often. When I do, I'm back in the Army, fighting . . ."

"Who?" she asked.

"Taliban." He scratched the back of his neck. "When I'm asleep, I don't know what I'm doing, and it seems real." He shifted in his chair. "Know how you can fly in your sleep but you don't actually get out of bed and go out on the roof? Well, my body doesn't know I'm asleep. I can, you know . . ." He lifted a hand and quickly dropped it. "Move and punch, er . . . not on purpose."

He bent to face her, but she couldn't hold his gaze.

"When I first moved to Fredericksburg and stayed with Red and Kelli, I'd wake up dripping in sweat, my heart beating out of my chest, but I didn't know what happened before I woke." He didn't say any more.

"That must have been terrible for you," Lark said, trying to mask her fear.

"For Kelli and Red, too."

"Is this common?" she asked the doctor.

"I think my spells are pretty minor compared to what I hear from other guys."

"It's important for you not to liken your experience to those of others," Dr. Fisher advised. "Everyone's different."

"Right." Wyatt nodded. "I finished the CPT program—"

"Wyatt's talking about cognitive processing therapy, where we revisited his most difficult memories, dissected them, and made sense of those haunting scenes."

"Isn't the worst part over?" she asked.

"Mostly." Wyatt faced her. "Here's the deal—I can't control what happens after I fall asleep. If you or the boys were around when it happened, I wouldn't want to scare or hurt anybody."

The mention of her boys pierced her chest, and she pulled her arms across her body. She found a single loose thread hanging from the upholstered chair and twisted it between her thumb and forefinger.

"Lark," Dr. Fisher said, and she lifted her eyes to a framed certificate on the wall. Unable to register the words on the certificate, she only saw images of Wyatt with her boys—reading stories in a gentle voice. But then she saw another image, too—one of Wyatt punching or shoving Jamie and Charlie—and the images twirled together. In a rush of fight or flight, her heart took a panicky leap.

"Lark," the doctor said. "Wyatt's taken the appropriate steps to mitigate—"

Mitigate. Lessening the damage wasn't acceptable, regardless of Wyatt's intentions.

"Even if you don't *mean* to hurt us . . ." She clenched her fists.

"Wyatt, can you give us a minute?" Dr. Fisher cocked his head toward the door.

While Wyatt stepped into the hall, the doctor took the vacant chair next to Lark.

"It's pretty obvious you weren't aware of any of this." Dr. Fisher's thoughtful expression was disarming.

"I read about PTSD, but I didn't picture . . ."

"I recognize your fear. As far as I understand, Wyatt hasn't hurt anyone during his night terror episodes, ever, because he's taken pains to prepare his loved ones, like he hoped to prepare you by bringing you here."

"He didn't tell me this was why he wanted me to come." Anger seeped into her words. "You should see the way my three-year-old looks at him, like he's a superhero. And, Jamie, my five-year-old, is reserved around people, but he'll hug Wyatt. I can't . . . I won't put my boys at risk."

"You have every right to feel this way."

"I worked in a domestic violence shelter in Houston, and I saw the terrible things people do to each other. It doesn't matter if it's on purpose or not, I can't let him—"

"Lark, I can't tell you what to do. You have to make decisions you feel are in the best interests of your family."

She gave a slight nod.

"You might consider keeping your boys away from him at night, giving him time to work through the night terrors? He needs time to heal, physically and emotionally."

"So, when he's awake, he won't hurt them, but there's no guarantee at night?" Her throat tightened.

"There are no guarantees, but he does understand why these episodes happen, and he's giving his all to get better."

"I know, and I love him—I really do—but I have to protect Jamie and Charlie. They've already lost their father. I can't put them through . . ."

Silence held the next uncomfortable seconds.

"We have support groups for families facing these challenges, if you're interested?"

"Do they ever completely move past it? The PTSD?"

"You're a widow. You've experienced grief—"

"Still do."

"To my point: grief wanes, but on some level it never completely goes away. A soldier doesn't wake up one day having forgotten his or her catastrophic memories. They can only work toward a day when those memories no longer disrupt their life."

"My dad was in Vietnam. Mom said it took a long time for him to come back to who he was before he left her. He's a caring man . . . wouldn't hurt anyone."

"Good thing she didn't give up on him." He paused.

She considered her father in Wyatt's position. Millie could've pushed Frank out of the house to protect Harlan, and no one would've blamed her. The idea jolted her with a confusing mix of shame and sympathy.

"Perhaps, your mother might share her experiences with you. The armed services didn't have resources like we have today after Vietnam. Soldiers had to work it out on their own, leaving their wives and children to suffer alongside them."

"Where's Wyatt?" She glanced at the closed door.

"Outside, probably having a seat in the hall."

"I don't want him stuck out there. He must feel awful. Can you bring him back?"

"Sure." The doctor stepped into the hall.

Wyatt returned, wearing an anxious expression. "You okay?"

"Yes. I'm okay. I'm sorry, Wyatt." She dragged the back of her hand across her cheek. "Geez, I hate ugly crying."

"Came to the right place." Dr. Fisher pushed a tissue box toward her. "This is the epicenter for ugly crying."

She laughed as tears tracked down her cheeks.

Wyatt leaned into her gaze. "I want to be the man you deserve, someone with a solid body and mind." He pushed his chair closer. "You're never gonna see me the same way again."

"Not so. Wyatt, I love you, and the boys love you too. I know you'd never hurt them on purpose. We have lots of time before we need to worry about us being at your place during the night." She snickered, and he winked at her.

"There are techniques we can teach you in case you're around during a night terror," Dr. Fisher said. "If you happen to be near Wyatt while he's asleep and you suspect he's having one, leave the bed right away. Keep your distance. Don't try to wake him. Once you're out of his reach, you can call out to him. Or you can go into the next room and leave him to ride it out."

"Is there medication he can take?" Lark asked.

"I take an antidepressant, and I think it helps," Wyatt said.

"When was your last night terror?" she asked.

Wyatt swallowed. "At Thanksgiving. I fell out of bed. Kelli and Dad called my name until I woke up."

"What was in your head during the nightmare?"

"It was like the day the IED went off, only we took fire, and this kid was in the middle of it. She kept crying and I crawled to her, you know? Trying to protect her. The shots kept coming, so I hunched over her." He shook his head. "She didn't make it." His voice crumbled, and his head dropped. "The kid . . . was Zadie."

Lark hurt in places she didn't know she had. "I'm so sorry." She leaned toward Wyatt, clutching his shoulder.

He lifted his head but stared at the wall to his right, avoiding Lark's gaze as he wiped his eyes.

"Wyatt, I'm sorry I freaked out," she said. "I didn't realize this was a thing for you."

"Wyatt has prioritized his recovery, and his work has paid off," Dr. Fisher said.

"Can the terrors get worse?"

"It would be unusual. Wyatt makes all his appointments and

takes his medications. He's doing the work. Might even be time to discuss reducing the frequency of our check-ins."

"Great," Wyatt said.

"Our time's almost up," the doctor said. "Without getting into the nitty-gritty of your relationship, I'll leave you with this: if you become a family or even just plan to keep steady company, we can provide resources for each of you. My nurse will pull reading materials for you to take. If something comes up in the meantime, just call us."

Wyatt made his next appointment while Lark stepped into the hallway. On each side were pictures of soldiers in dress uniforms who'd lost their lives in desert operations. It was all a bit too much.

AFTER LUNCH, LARK AND WYATT returned to the medical campus. This time, they meandered toward a building unlike the other structures. With its contemporary oval shape and palm tree–lined entry, the Center for the Intrepid was a premier rehabilitation center for wounded warriors involved in desert operations.

They walked inside, and Lark gestured to Intrepid's cutting-edge swimming facility and wave pool with a water track for surfing, like those advertised on cruise ships. "Have you tried surfing?" she asked.

"Nah. I'm more of a toes-in-the-sand, beer-in-my-hand kinda guy."

"I'd like to see that."

"Maybe you will," he said with a wink, and then he led her to the waiting area for the prosthetics clinic.

While Wyatt checked in with the receptionist, Lark took a seat. Across from her, a woman held a toddler in her lap, a girl about Charlie's age, who was watching a cartoon on her mother's phone. The child pigeon-toed her feet around her mother's knees. Beside them was a man whose hair grew in swirling patterns around scars on his scalp. He was tethered to a wheelchair, and was missing both arms and one leg.

Averting her eyes, Lark imagined who the man was before. Had he tickled his baby girl, encouraged by an intoxicating giggle like Charlie's? The child smiled at her father and, in return, the man's scarred lips clamped together in a pained expression of gladness.

Lark considered how the wife's existence had changed too. Did she have a career? Was she stressed about potty training their daughter or excited for an anniversary? Did she meet friends for lunch? What else did she lose when she became her husband's full-time caregiver?

"Hey." Wyatt returned and took the seat beside her. "Will you go in with me?"

"I don't want to make you uncomfortable." She steadied herself. If the last appointment was any indication, this wouldn't be a social call.

A middle-aged man with a megawatt smile and dark brown skin appeared at the door to the waiting area. "Gifford."

Wyatt waved and called out, "Hey, Trey!" He turned back to Lark. "Ready?"

Lark lifted her purse and followed.

Behind the door was a maze of exercise equipment and gymnasiums. Some contained the standard fare—treadmills and stair machines. Another held parallel bars. One contained three rectangles, each spanning the width of the gym, approximating sand, gravel, and turf. On the turf rectangle, a woman in her twenties worked to balance on a prosthetic leg with the support of two therapists.

They arrived at an exam room and Trey pushed the door closed. "How's it going?"

"No complaints," Wyatt said before introducing him to Lark. This time, Lark didn't flinch or laugh when he described her as his girlfriend.

"Good meeting you, ma'am." Trey's smile met his grayish-brown eyes before he shifted his attention back to Wyatt. "So, no complaints, huh?"

"Well, I guess I've got one." Wyatt touched his right leg.

"Alright." Trey pulled a pair of athletic shorts from a drawer and passed them to Wyatt. "You know the drill. I'll give you a few minutes." Once the door was closed, Wyatt wiggled his hips in a jerky motion to remove his jeans.

"Can I help?" Lark asked.

"Wouldn't refuse." He toggled his eyebrows. "I can take off these jeans, but it's more fun if we take them off together."

"Straighten up, soldier." She slapped his arm. "Let's do this." She helped him ease out of his jeans.

"I can handle the rest."

Lark sat and watched as he threaded his legs into the shorts. Then he balanced his healthy leg on the ground and hit a button on the side of his prosthetic. With a sucking sound, it broke away from his body and he laid it on the paper sheet. In a series of childlike hops, he scooted onto the table, then unfurled a plastic sleeve where cotton gauze wrapped part of his stump. The gauze clung to his skin as he rolled it away from his leg, and Wyatt winced when it stuck to an ulcerated spot. Like pulling off a Band-Aid, he yanked it away in one fluid stroke and dropped it beside his prosthesis.

A fiery round of acid hit Lark's stomach and she pushed back in her vinyl plus-one chair as her mind went a little fuzzy.

"You alright, babe? Your skin's green as the avocado they put on your tacos."

"Yep." She kept her answer brief and closed her mouth to prevent her lunch from making an unexpected escape.

Twenty-nine

Lark

S he'd seen and touched Wyatt's scars from the top of his shoulders to the bottom of his . . . well, bottom, but always under shock-minimizing mood lighting. She thought ALS had made her tough, but her reaction to the carnage hidden under that cotton fabric at the base of his right thigh had just proven her wrong.

Unlike a planned amputation, an IED made no effort to cut in straight lines or save adequate tissue to wrap the stump. Wyatt's surgeons had dealt with hundreds of splintered bone fragments and a jagged femur in his initial surgeries.

Under the exam room's cruel fluorescence, the ferocity of Wyatt's injuries screamed at her. Between his hip and his stump, a vicious purple seam bisected his thigh. Angled lines about a finger-width marked where staples had held the tissue together. The scars formed an ironic smiley face on a fleshy appendage that resembled an uncooked pork tenderloin.

Squirming in her chair, Lark looked past the tidier surgical scars to the more dramatic ones left by the metal shavings that had torn through his uniform to shred his flesh, leaving raised welts. Her skull felt heavy, and she lifted her gaze, finding the will to meet Wyatt's eyes in a moment of unbearable vulnerability.

Just when she thought she had processed the gravity of the situation, another awareness presented itself: the same force that sent Wyatt's leg, his body, his life on a jagged trajectory was what had brought them together.

He waved a hand to capture her attention and offered that sideways grin she loved. "What? Never seen a guy with one leg before?"

"None as handsome as you," she tried to joke while swallowing bile.

"Aw, thanks, little missy," he said in a John Wayne voice.

After a two-beat knock on the door, Trey entered the room accompanied by a bald man in tortoiseshell glasses.

"Lark, this is Dr. Calabrese. Dr. C, this is my girlfriend, Lark Mead."

The doctor nodded and turned to a wall-mounted sanitizer station.

"Trey said you've got a tender spot?" Dr. C asked as he rubbed his hands together. He rolled a stool to sit in front of Wyatt and touched the scarred incisions. "Is this tender?"

"No." Wyatt's cheeks were tense and his smile insincere, but he shifted his posture to provide better access.

"Here?" Dr. C asked, and Wyatt shook his head. The doctor moved to another spot. "Here?"

Wyatt jerked away. "Fu . . . yes."

"Hot spot." Dr. C shot a glance at Trey.

"Doesn't stop me from getting around," Wyatt said.

"Okay, I'm done torturing you." Dr. C. rolled back in his chair. "Trey, see what you can do." Returning to Wyatt, he wagged a finger. "Hurt or not, you get a spot like that one, you'd better call us. Infections can take you out of this world, my friend."

Lark closed her eyes. *Mother trucker. Can we get some good news around here, already?*

"I don't wear the leg if I get an infection," Wyatt said defensively.

"Any others, tough guy?" Dr. C asked.

Wyatt lifted his hip, and an angry welt came into view.

How did I not see that before?

Dr. C pointed out a spot on the prosthesis.

Trey nodded. "Give me a few minutes with this bad boy," he said, and both men left the room.

Wyatt gave a self-deprecating laugh. "Sucks to be so dependent on these guys. Bet you wish you'd stayed out in the waiting room?"

"I'm glad I came along." She was still feeling a bit lightheaded, but she managed to stand. "I hadn't seen your leg in the light before. Can't say how I'd handle it if I were in your place. You're brave."

He snorted. "When you don't have a choice, you might as well roll with it."

A few minutes later, Trey came back carrying Wyatt's prosthesis. "I smoothed this section, and"—he shot a finger at a chunk of foam—"added this. Let's see if it does the trick." He dipped his head forward, inviting Wyatt to try it out. It snapped into place, and Trey bent to fasten Wyatt's sneaker.

"Let's see it in action."

Trey led them to the gymnasium and threw a hand toward the simulated grass. Wyatt walked on the turf with relative ease.

"Think you can jog on it?"

"Treadmill's smoother." Wyatt said.

"We can do that. Let's go." Trey opened the door and they walked to an adjacent gym filled with a host of exercise equipment.

Wyatt mounted the treadmill and punched buttons until the belt whirled into motion. With a few more taps, walking turned into a jog.

"No problem," Wyatt said, holding his hands overhead.

"Don't try to show off for the pretty lady, cowboy. You fall and it makes us both look bad."

"Nobody's falling," Wyatt said.

Minutes later, they returned to the exam room so Dr. C could inspect Trey's handiwork.

"Other than the hot spot, the leg's in fine shape." Dr. C winked. "I know you're aching to run with it, but we need to get a little farther down the road. Assuming you can avoid infections, when the time comes, we'll talk about a carbon prosthetic."

"Awesome." Wyatt brightened. "I keep hearing about all these wounded warrior events—running and biking? Wouldn't mind trying them out. Plus, she's a runner"—he jutted his chin in Lark's direction—"so I'd like to see if I can keep up."

Dr. C. held up a hand. "Not so fast. You're still reintegrating. More healing to go." He turned to Lark. "Running increases perspiration and the potential for infections—not the best workout for someone with a prosthetic."

"Maybe you can try other forms of exercise?" Lark asked.

"Hmm." Wyatt bit his lip.

"I meant like swimming or riding a bike, you dope!" Lark narrowed her eyes at him.

Trey chuckled. "Doc, you and I might need to leave these guys alone to continue this conversation."

"We're all done here, so they can continue it elsewhere." Dr. C gave Wyatt a pat on the shoulder. "Call me if you need anything. Nice meeting you, Lark."

"You, too," she said. "Thanks for everything."

It really was miraculous what they had helped Wyatt achieve, although no amount of technology or equipment could've found success without his sheer determination. The guy didn't give up.

On the way to the hotel, his phone rang. "I've got to take this."

He grimaced as a voice spoke rapidly on the other end of the line.

"Today was marked off my schedule months ago. Tell Mrs. Chu . . . I know. I'll be there on Wednesday." He dropped the phone on his console.

"Wanna talk about it?" she asked.

"Nope." He grabbed their bags and they walked into the hotel.

He stopped beside a chair in the lobby and dropped the bags. "Hey, I need to apologize. Gotta tell you, work has me pretty rattled. They're talking about changes—eck, maybe layoffs. Shoot, I may have to find something different altogether. Maybe I can work on a rig like Red does?"

"Seriously?" she asked.

"Nah. They wouldn't hire me with this." He patted his leg.

"I can ask my dad if he's heard about any jobs."

"Please don't."

"Alright." She felt scolded. "But will you at least tell me what's happening?"

"Since the FU people took over, it's not enough to do the job they hired me to do. There are conference calls and so damn much busy work, not to mention the acronyms. Jesus." He sighed. "If this doesn't work out, I may have to find a job outside Fredericksburg. I don't want to, but—"

"You got a promotion, so they're obviously impressed with your work."

"Not a real promotion. They're just using my picture to make the jackasses look more American in their ads. Like they're supporting vets. No title or raise included."

"I'm sorry." She touched his forearm.

"Guessing how these people think is like playing darts with cooked spaghetti. Last week, we had a call where this new VP of . . . hell if I can tell you. Basket weaving? This French guy gets on the line with the same rah-rah pitch he throws at us every week. Like usual, he wasn't making any sense, so I muted the phone on my end. Figured I'd use the time to do something productive, but you can't work when that bullshit's playing in the background."

"Good lord."

"Nope. The big guy has nothing to do with this madness."

"Back up. Why are they taking you out of the field for conference calls?"

"No telling. Last week, Pepe Le Pew is all"—Wyatt waved a hand and affected a comical French accent—"'If we all put our meeends to eet, we can break rayycords. This will be eeempossible if we depend on shire luck.' He just won't give up." He barked out a sarcastic laugh. "Then, the joker says something like, 'Our strategies require us to place all our collective taleeents in one pot, and mainteeen laser fuckus.' *Fuckus!* Thank God I was muted. Wouldn't have a job if they'd heard what flew out of my mouth then."

"Bet whatever you said could be understood in any language." Lark let out a hearty laugh. "Sorry to laugh, but what else can you do?"

"What else can I do?" Wyatt lifted his palms.

Lark wrapped her arms around his waist. "Let's forget Mr. Laser Whatever and see what we can find to do around here, okay?"

Wyatt

WHILE LARK CALLED HOME TO check on her boys, Wyatt leaned over the hotel's check-in counter, but his appearance didn't break the clerk's death stare from his computer screen.

"Is the room for Gifford ready?" he asked.

The man tapped his keyboard. "I have a double queen ready."

"Didn't reserve a double queen. Look again, please." Wyatt dropped their bags to the floor and dug out his phone to retrieve the reservation.

When Lark had agreed to accompany him to San Antonio, she never could have known how many hours he'd spend planning one night—a night that had to be seamless, from the smallest details (packing his dressier jeans and a blue Polo shirt she'd once said she liked) to consulting Yelp and Zagat for restaurant recommendations. He'd left nothing to chance. He'd been determined that if, after Lark knew his secrets, she was still interested in him, he was going to deliver the night of her life.

Planning a romantic hotel getaway wasn't simple for a guy like him. In his limited experience, handicapped rooms, with their grab bars and accessible modifications, didn't lend themselves to passion. He'd already shared his biggest secrets, and he feared the small ones might pack a hefty punch when it came to his romantic evening with Lark. So he'd booked a room with an oversized bathtub and a separate shower with a low threshold he could cross easily.

"I have the confirmation," Wyatt shook his phone. "I paid up front for a specific room."

The guy didn't look up or answer.

"What's the problem?" Wyatt asked, growing more anxious.

"How's it going?" Lark's touched his back.

Caught. Crap. God, I don't want to explain why I require a certain room. Not in front of her.

"Just working out a snag on our room. They put us in a double."

"I don't care where we stay, so long as you're there."

That comment got the guy's attention. "You don't mind a queen?"

Before she could answer, Wyatt jumped in. "Already paid for the king deluxe suite with the separate tub and shower. That's what we're getting, right?" He shot a no-bull stare across the desk.

"Ah, here we go." The clerk's frown cleared. "Two keys?"

As the elevator climbed, Wyatt held his breath up, not ready to celebrate until he laid eyes on the room he'd booked.

At last, they arrived at their floor. With shaky hands, he slipped the keycard inside the slot in the door.

Once inside, Lark's smile told Wyatt he'd chosen well. She fawned over the view while he poked his head into the bathroom to conduct a thorough inspection.

Exactly as promised on the website. All systems go.

Thirty

Lark

....

Wyatt had to take another call from Pepe Le Pew, so Lark ran down to the Riverwalk to buy gifts for Jamie and Charlie.

From boutiques to restaurant patios, every curve offered a new view. In between, planters gushed with bright purples and yellows and reds.

Dr. Fisher had made Lark think about her father's post-Vietnam days. She hadn't even been born then, and she had so many questions. Not confident enough to bring it up with Frank, she parked on an empty bench outside a jewelry store and called her brother.

"Hey, Harlan, got a minute?"

"Sure."

"How much do you remember about when Dad came home from Vietnam?"

He cleared his throat. "Talking about Vietnam might take more than a minute."

"I'll take whatever you can give."

"Er, okay, well . . . Dad came home . . . must've been . . . end of '72? Not 100 percent on that. I couldn't have been much older than Charlie."

"Was Dad ever violent?"

"Damn, you're getting right to it. What's going on?"

"Learning about PTSD."

"Did Wyatt do something?"

"No. Just trying to understand. Keep talking."

"I don't remember him being violent. Moody? Yes. Coming home wasn't the whole 'Tie a Yellow Ribbon Round the Ole Oak Tree' picture."

"Isn't that song about a guy coming home from prison?"

"Depends. If your husband or dad was in the Hanoi Hilton, you had a yellow ribbon outside your house. It was an ugly time. People spat on vets coming back from Vietnam when they came home."

"What about Dad?"

He breathed into the phone. "Well, he'd get real quiet, and Mom would send me to my room or outside to play. Oh, and things got weird around the Fourth of July. Being a stupid kid, I wasn't too sensitive to how it affected him. I'd hear my friends talk about how their dads took them to that fireworks stand outside of Johnson City, so I would beg Mom and Dad to take me, too, and they did. Only, they wouldn't buy me the cool stuff. So, while my friends got roman candles and bottle rockets, we came home with sparklers and those worms that marked the concrete."

"Uh-huh." She started to get the picture.

"One year . . . think I was nine . . . I wasn't having it anymore, and I told 'em I wasn't a baby, right there while they were paying out at the fireworks stand. They wouldn't even let me get those tiny white bags that pop when you throw on the ground."

"They sound like gunshots."

"They're just bags of gunpowder, and, hell. I didn't understand. So I pushed harder. Dad stayed real quiet, but you should've seen Mom laying down the hammer on me."

"I'll bet."

"When she got me home, she took me to my room. Grabbed my arm so tight I thought it was going to fall off my body. She had that look when she bites her bottom lip and jerks her head to one side."

"I've seen it a few times."

"Well, you never saw it like that. She told me firecrackers

reminded Dad about some really bad things, like people getting shot, and if I pressed the issue, the only firecrackers I'd see would be the ones outside my bedroom window."

"Dang. What'd you do?"

"Kept my mouth shut and didn't bring it up again. Later, I learned about the war and felt like a jerk."

"You were a kid. Let it go."

"Yeah, well. Looking back, I can see he was pretty shaken."

"Went to the doctor with Wyatt today—sounds as if he's haunted by those same demons."

"You should ask Mom about it. Hell, enough time has passed, Dad might be okay with you asking him. Sorry to hear about Wyatt—sounds like he makes you real happy."

Wyatt

HIS CALL ENDED AND THERE he was, sitting all alone in this nice hotel room he had planned to share with Lark, so he tucked that damned phone in his back pocket and wandered down to the Riverwalk. Half a click away, Lark's blond waves caught his eye.

She was soaking up the sun on a bench while talking on the phone. She waved as soon as she saw him, giving him that beautiful smile.

He folded himself into the bench beside her, and she pointed to her phone and whispered, "Harlan." Didn't seem like anything too important, because she ended the call a few seconds later.

"Sorry, just catching up," she said. "How'd it go with the office?"

He threw his hands up in an "I give up" gesture. "How about we do something that doesn't relate to work?"

"Absolutely." She squeezed his hand as a gondola full of tourists floated toward them. "How about that?"

"The Riverwalk spans more than fifteen miles," a perky female voice bubbled from a speaker on the floating tour bus. Lark twisted her mouth to one side.

"Take it we can skip that tour?" Wyatt said.

She leaned into his shoulder. "Don't you just love this city?"

"I love being here with you, but . . ." He frowned like he'd just sat in something gross. "Sorry to bring her up, but—"

"Ashlen lives here."

Wyatt's head tilted back. "Yeah, so not a big fan of the city."

"Ashlen and millions of other people. Don't be like that."

Wyatt's hand went to his chest, making Lark question his readiness for their relationship.

"Do you need to tell me something?" Her stomach twisted as he took his sweet time to respond. "Wyatt?"

"You know the story. Talking won't change what she did to me."

"I'm sorry she hurt you, but . . ."

"But, what?" He finally turned to look at her.

"There's so much bitterness when her name comes up. It scares me. Maybe you're not ready to be with someone else." *Or, worse, maybe you're not over her?*

He stood and took a few steps toward the river. His lips moved, but no sound came out. Finally, he turned around. His face softened as their eyes met, and he walked toward her, flinching a bit with every other step. "Lark, my feelings for her are in the past. Sure, I get pissed when I think of her, but that's it." He returned to the bench. "She was a bitch to me, and I'm not gonna see her any other way."

"It's not a good sign that you can't enjoy San Antonio because she lives here." Her hair fluttered in the breeze, half-covering one side of her face, and he gently pushed it out of her eyes. "You're giving Ashlen miles of latitude over your happiness. I want to be with you, but it feels a little like she's here with us too."

"It's complicated."

"It's complicated?" She narrowed her eyes. "Believe me, I know complicated, buddy."

She threw him off balance.

After a few seconds, Lark touched his hand. "I had hoped your time with Ashlen . . . or whoever came before . . . would have made you ready for a relationship like ours."

He nodded, although he didn't seem entirely convinced. "I never should've brought up her name. I'm sorry."

"I'm more concerned about the bitterness I hear in your voice when you talk about her."

"I don't know." He got a faraway look in his eyes. "Sometimes, I think I should just go talk to her. Say the things I need to get off my chest and walk away."

"If you think it would help you gain closure, call her up and put this behind you," she bit out.

He blew out a big puff of air and gave a decisive nod. "Alright. I'll think about it—later. For tonight, let's put her and everything else behind us."

AFTER STROLLING THROUGH THE SHOPS and galleries, they returned to the hotel room to get ready for dinner.

"I'd love a nap." Lark plopped on the bed.

"I need a shower . . . unless you want to go first?"

"Can I just close my eyes for a few minutes? You're welcome to join me."

"You nap, I'll shower," he said, thankful for a cushion of privacy. With one of the hotel robes and his duffel bag, he closed the bathroom door behind him and removed his folding cane. It wasn't the sturdiest, but it'd work in a pinch, and it beat slipping and falling.

The room filled with steam soon after he turned on the water. He removed his leg and used the cane to steady himself as he moved under the spray.

"Rosemary-mint, hmm?" He poured the shampoo directly on his hair and propped the cane against the wall of the shower. The water pulsed against his midsection while he worked his hair into a lather. Eyes closed, he leaned into the stream.

Suddenly, a cool hand scrubbed his back. He jerked to reach for the cane as rosemary-mint suds stung his eyes.

"Mmm," Lark pushed a washcloth across his shoulders. "Too hard?" she purred.

"Oh, hey." Wyatt squinted past the foam. "You don't have to—"

"Hush." She took a step back and her gaze trailed over his body. "Riverwalk's pretty, but *this* view is exceptional."

Precisely what I wanted to hide.

Her lips brushed his shoulder, and he craned his neck to her. "View's better from where I'm standing." His eyes wandered down her body, but the swirl of panic and horniness flooding his system prevented him from enjoying what he saw.

"I'm sorry." He braced a hand against the shower wall.

"What's wrong? You're not happy." Her hands fell away from him.

He snickered and dropped his gaze to a rock-solid argument confirming that he was more than pleased by her company.

"Okay, so you're happy to see me. But something's off."

He ached to touch her. "It's not you." *Jesus, here it goes . . . the end of romance.* "I want to, but I can't relax in the shower. Balancing on one leg, I might fall."

"Oh, baby." Lark ran a fingertip up the back of his neck. "I'm sorry."

"For what?"

"The other day, when I asked if you wanted to take a shower together, you begged off and I razzed you. I get it now."

"Didn't think you'd find the cane or the old-man shower bench at my place sexy."

"Baby, I find everything about you sexy." Her words slipped down his back as gently as the soap she was running over his shoulders.

He turned around to kiss her. "Standing's harder than it might look."

"I see." Her mouth edged up on one side, and she shifted her weight, taking in the sights. "Well, then, you shower in private. We'll cover other matters later."

Lark

·············

THE LAST SUNLIGHT THREW A GOLD film on the Riverwalk as they strolled toward the patio of Bella on the River. The host directed them to a corner table, where candles flickered against the stone walls. They enjoyed tangy margaritas and dined on scallops, and after, they strolled below trees strung with millions of twinkly lights.

They returned to the hotel. The stress of the day seemed to evaporate, and they made love from dusk to dawn.

As they drove out of town the next morning, Wyatt said, "Next time we get away, it has to be longer."

"I like the sound of next time." Lark winked.

"We could take the long way home, check out the scenery, if you want?"

"I'm aching to see my boys." They weren't the only reason she wanted to get home. As much as she'd enjoyed her time with Wyatt, she needed time to consider Dr. Fisher's advice.

"Your dad's handling everything," Wyatt said.

"He is, but I don't want to abuse the poor guy. Plus, I need to check in on Levi, find out more about that stuff with Wolf's bankers coming around. I can tell there's something wrong, but he didn't want to burden me." She tried to play it cool, but fear had seeped into her bone marrow. Was she going to lose her job?

Wyatt took another call from his secretary. His politeness was overshadowed by the mounting irritation in his voice. To pretend she wasn't listening, Lark gazed out the window at a rolling pasture dotted with hay bales. A little farther, a N'OTIS CELLARS sign appeared and then disappeared behind them.

"Hang on, Barb. I need to pull over and write this down." Wyatt parked on the shoulder.

Lark googled "N'Otis." Pictures of the woman she'd met at the festival appeared.

Wyatt groaned. "I'll review it when I'm back in the office." He dropped the phone in his console and turned to Lark. "Please don't make me go back to Fredericksburg."

"How about taking a detour into Comfort?"

"Lady wants to go into Comfort? We'll go into Comfort. What's there?"

"A winery managed by a woman I met at the wine festival. She told me to stop by if I traveled out this way. I saw her sign a few miles ago."

"Okay, little lady. Happy for the digression. Put it into your app and be my navigator."

Fifteen minutes later, an electronic voice piped, "You have arrived at your destination."

"If you say so." Wyatt braked but there wasn't a winery in sight, only a tree-filled meadow. "Let's keep going."

A quarter mile farther down, the road curved around a belt of trees. On the other side, grapevines covered sprawling hills.

"Must be it," Wyatt said.

"Don't need to get out. I only wanted to drive by."

"We came all this way. Let's stretch our legs—or, in my case, leg."

Lark chuckled. "We've been on the road for a half-hour. You think we need a break?"

"A half-hour on the phone with Barbara is like three in dog years. C'mon, let's park up here and check out the crops."

Thirty-one

Lark

At nine thirty on a Wednesday morning, parking was a cinch in front N'Otis's tasting room.

"I just want to look at the grapevines, and then we can go." Lark left Wyatt's truck, her sneakers crunching on the gravel parking area.

A man stepped out from behind a building and lifted a hand over his forehead to shade his eyes from the blinding eastern sunlight.

"You open?" Wyatt asked.

"Always—except if the state tells us we're not." The man's chuckle revealed a charming gap between his front teeth and made his onyx eyes vanish into his full cheeks. He waved toward the road. "Tasha's on her way. Give her a few minutes."

"Natasha's the lady I met," Lark murmured.

"Mind if we walk out to your grapevines?" Wyatt said.

The man waved at the trellises. "Make yourselves at home."

Lark walked to the trellises, taking in the vivid reds and browns, and vestiges of faded greens.

"I'm gonna walk up there and check out that tractor," Wyatt said, pointing toward the end of the row.

What is the deal with men and tractors?

A few minutes later, Lark saw a trail of dust rise over the curtain of trees. A maroon Jeep soon rounded the hill and parked beside the tasting room. The driver climbed from her Jeep and called, "Zeke," patting her thigh, and a Labrador retriever with a coat like a wet black olive loped to her side, wagging his tail fiercely each time she repeated his name.

"Natasha?" Lark asked.

"Yes." The woman pushed her Wayfarers back over her long, silvery hair, revealing dewy skin and sapphire eyes.

"Lark Mead. We met in Gruene?"

"At the festival?"

"You probably meet thousands of people at those events."

"I do, but I think I remember you." She unlocked the door to the tasting room and gestured for Lark to follow.

Lark craned her neck to find Wyatt. "My friend's around here somewhere." Not seeing him, she walked into the building.

Clad in steel and glass, it had an industrial atmosphere. The combination tasting room and giftshop showcased N'Otis-branded wines, trivets, and wine glasses alongside jars of jams and gourmet spreads on rough sawn wood shelves.

Zeke dropped to the floor with an *oof* and Lark bent to pet him.

"Don't start, or he won't let you leave," Natasha joked.

"Awe, don't mind hanging out with you, sweet boy." Lark scratched his neck.

"Did you lose your friend?" Natasha asked.

"He's looking at your tractor." Lark waved a hand behind her.

Natasha tossed her purse below the counter. "Want a sample?"

"This early?"

"TABC makes me wait until ten." She gave a half shrug. "But I'm not charging you. So, how about some Chenin Blanc?"

"Sure."

Natasha cut the foil around the mouth of a bottle and jutted her chin forward. "Wait. You're the mom who worked in the wine business, right?" She squinted with a far-off gaze, like a fortune teller. "Which was it? Growing or selling?" She tossed the foil into an earthenware vase.

"I wish. Studied in undergrad."

"Right, viticulture—it's coming back to me. You studied to make wine and did something else." She huffed. "I tried *everything* else before I became a winemaker." She flashed a crooked grin.

"Pretty brave of you to go for it." Lark lifted a trivet made from locally sourced limestone.

"Brave or stupid, depends on the year." Natasha waved a finger 180 degrees. "This is what happens when your therapist tells you to find a hobby." Tasha pushed the glass forward. "Drink up."

The wine treated Lark's taste buds to grapefruit and sunshine. "This is superb."

"Thanks. You here to buy wine or learn?"

"Actually . . . I started working at Hartmann-Haas Cellars."

"I've heard about them." Tasha's smile fell away. "They ever gonna open?"

"Taking longer than expected."

"Are they paying you guys?"

"Pardon?"

"May come across as forward, but I recall you have children depending on you. And this came from someone I trust."

Lark nodded.

"There's talk the owners got in over their heads. If I were you, I'd keep my eyes open . . . wide open." Tasha's eyes mirrored her words.

"Will do. I'm checking out land, too. I might start my own winery." The words echoed Harlan's advice. *Had she just called her shot?*

Natasha rinsed a glass in the sink. "Winemaking's a hard bug to shake once it latches on to you. Wine's passion, from the ground to the bottle. Take your soul, entrust it to the vines. They absorb your love, pain, anger, happiness, and one day you realize you've cultivated a living, breathing piece of art."

"Hope I didn't wait too long to think about it?"

"Some folks think opening a winery's like that Kevin Costner movie—build it, and they will come. They throw money at it, make it attractive, and expect results. But it takes work to do it right—and science."

The bell clanged over the door and Wyatt walked in.

"There you are." Lark introduced him and, after a brief exchange of pleasantries, hooked his elbow. "Time to get on the road?"

"Ohhh-kay." Wyatt's face went blank.

"Have those kids to pick up." She threw him a wink.

"Alright." His eyes told her he detected an unexpected tension, and he hung back.

"Can I pay you for the sample?" Lark asked Natasha.

"It's on me. Let me know where you land on your winery."

"Will do. Thanks."

Wyatt wore a perplexed expression as they walked out. "What'd she mean, 'your winery'?"

"I mentioned I might open my own—someday."

"And?"

Lark laughed. "I don't have the bandwidth at the present."

"What was your hurry to leave?" he asked.

"She doesn't hold a favorable opinion about Hartmann-Haas. People can be catty about their competitors."

"Anything specific?"

"She said she heard the owners were 'in over their heads.'"

"Told you I had a bad feeling."

Lark didn't have enough information to defend Elke or her husband, so she deflected. "What's on your schedule this week?"

"The FU people are sending a marketing team or photographer or . . . I don't know. Someone's coming to town to take pictures. They want to show off my Army ties for their PR campaigns."

"Does that sound weird to you? I'm sure they're a good company. But these French guys, the . . ." She raised a palm.

"FU."

"Tell me FU isn't their real name."

"Foudre Unifie . . . FU. Means something about lightning."

"Means something else to me. Didn't anybody clue them in?"

"They wouldn't care. If they don't write it into a manual, it doesn't exist. Heck, they'll expect us to speak with a French accent before they're through." His laugh didn't hide his concern.

"Could get rocky."

"Tell me about it."

"And, they want you to be their spokesmodel? In your uniform?"

"Can't make this shit up. Sorry."

"Vent away."

"You don't need to hear my gripes."

"Sounds like they want to promote the 'red, white, and blue.'"

"Newsflash—those colors are in the French flag, too."

"Sneaky little bastards," Lark quipped. "Our collective occupational forecast might include a big FU . . . in the literal sense."

DREAD CHISELED AT LARK WHEN she arrived in front of Hartmann-Haas, and for good reason. A sturdy padlock on the gate prevented anyone from entering—at least, anyone with a vehicle. She parked on the unpaved shoulder of the highway and peered past the wrought iron gates.

Like a post-apocalyptic movie, the place was unnervingly still. She slithered between two iron posts. Her running shoes came in handy as she jogged along the gravel trail. A thin, panicky whistle laced each breath, and she didn't stop until she reached the mechanical barn. She bent to raise the overhead doors. They wouldn't budge.

She moved to the side of the building and stood on the tips of her toes to peek through the bottling room windows. The lights were turned off. The windows were littered with foreclosure notices.

With trembling fingers, she dialed Levi's number. It rolled to voice mail. "Dammit," she spat before shoving her phone into her pocket.

If this is how Wolf treats his business, how does he treat his family? Would he hurt Elke or Kingsley?

A rush of adrenaline fired through her body and she ran toward the house, kicking her feet harder and faster, sending dust flying.

Acid splashed Lark's throat, and a sickening lurch stopped her so abruptly she stumbled face-first into the gravel. She took a breath, found her feet, and didn't stop running until she landed on Elke's porch.

Rapping a fist on the door, she hollered, "Elke." Her breath frosted the glass windows, no longer framed with linen drapes. Even that grand piano was gone, leaving only piles trash scattered on the floor.

She moved to the side of the house and stopped at the window to the laundry room.

In the space where the washer and dryer had been, Lark recognized the unmistakable Calypso Blue, a color she knew well after painting the kitchen in the event center.

Details fell into place—the paint, the missing appliances in the event center, Elke's gourmet kitchen with stainless steel refrigerators and double freezers, a range befitting a professional chef, and that commercial ice machine. A picture of deception became complete.

Elke's indifference about the winery made sense now.

How was I so blind?

Frustrated by her lack of insight, Lark turned toward her car. With each step, the list of clues she'd ignored grew longer: Equipment arriving without the components needed for installation. Construction crews released for shoddy work.

She returned to the entrance and pressed her body between two posts. This pair was narrower than the ones she'd passed through earlier, and she became stuck. Pushing forward, she jammed her mid-section. As she broke free, one of the hinges scraped her hip. Blood streaked the light stone pillar.

Clutching her side, she climbed into her car. She could only think of one person who might have answers.

THE SIGHT OF LEVI'S TRUCK in front of his house offered a glimmer of hope. Lark punched the doorbell several times before the door cracked open.

"Why aren't you answering your phone?" Her voice came out sharp and accusatory.

"Well, hello to you, too." Wearing jeans, a Baylor University T-shirt, and a pair of Merrell work boots, Levi moved out of Lark's way as she barged into his house.

His easy-going expression had turned pensive, and something about him looked different. As his hair fell toward his face, she asked, "Where's your ball cap?"

He wiped his brow and guided her down a hallway to an empty bedroom. "I can't do this around my kids." He closed the door behind him. "My phone's in the barn, along with my jacket and my lucky Rangers cap."

"Not so lucky."

"Yeah, I guess."

"Who were they?" she asked.

"Bank people, police, a few guys in suits."

"I just left there. Everyone's gone now."

"How'd you get in?"

"I slid through the gates. Do you have a bandage?" She pointed to the bloody tissue over her hip. "Snagged on a metal hinge."

"Yeah. Wait here."

He returned a minute later with a handful of Hello Kitty Band-Aids, and she fastened two of them over the cut.

He frowned. "Might need a tetanus shot for that."

"I've got bigger problems."

"Bigger than lockjaw?"

She shook her head. "Where did they take them?"

"Nobody took them." Levi chided her. "Wolf moved them out before the cops came."

"Poor Elke."

"Poor Elke? If the bank's right, she knew. Better call your bank—my last paycheck bounced. Sounds like the equipment's being repoed. As I was leaving, a truck was taking the tables and chairs from the event center."

"What about Elke's family? And her grandfather?"

"That poor old man didn't see Wolf coming. The banker said Wolf leveraged the land and the buildings to cover his debts in Seattle."

Lark crossed her arms. "Funny. She said they left Seattle because his work life became so toxic."

"I wouldn't believe anything she told you." Levi scratched his chin, and his voice cracked. "If I don't find another job, I'm going to have to move back to Kerrville."

"We'll find you something." Even as she said it, she didn't have the first clue how to help him.

From his dismissive shrug, he wasn't convinced, either.

"What can we do?" she asked.

"We?" Levi's voice was laced with irritation. "I asked this banker friend of mine. He said the land'll probably get sold. If not, I thought I'd try to round up some investors. Maybe another winemaker wants to expand? One"—he blew out a long breath—"who'll give me a job so I can feed my kids."

"I have money."

Levi merely nodded. "Not the kind of money we'd need—"

"I have money," she repeated.

He patted her on the shoulder. "You can't fix this."

"Listen to me." She leveled a solemn face.

"Go ahead." He lifted a hand, inviting her to speak.

"I considered starting my own winery before I came to work here, and I looked at the costs. Let's not waste my work."

He studied her face.

"Before you go after other investors, give me a chance."

Thirty-two

Wyatt

Wyatt had lost focus. Restless anticipation had burned clean through any work he hoped to accomplish, what with the FU folks supposedly on their way to do God knew what with him. No doubt he'd be left to answer for the projects left incomplete because of FU's PR nonsense.

He glanced at his cell phone. Lark should've called by now.

"Knock knock." Kelli appeared in the doorway. "How's life?"

"Don't ask." He gave her an impatient eye roll.

"Stop or your eyes will get stuck that way."

"Hmm." He motioned for her to close the door.

"This place is off the rails, Kel," he whispered, shifting his gaze to the door behind her.

"The door's closed, Mr. Paranoid."

He inhaled sharply. "A couple of the guys mentioned there might be layoffs. Not sure I'll be able to stick around Fredericksburg if that happens."

"Can you take on more work or something?"

He blew out a breath. "I can barely finish the projects here on my desk. I'm doing everything I can—even agreed to let them take pictures of me to put up at the new corporate office. Apparently, they want to honor the vets in the company."

"That's cool."

"No. It's not cool. I think they're putting on a big show, making it look like they give a rip about what goes on in Texas so they won't get so much bad press if they start passing out pink slips."

"What's the big deal?" Kelli frowned. "Just smile for the pictures and stay out of their way."

"Big deal is they want me to convince the locals to put in those wind turbines, and it ain't happening."

"Don't get your panties in a wad. It's how big companies operate. Red deals with it all the time. Just do your job and let the fat cats think you're making progress with the turbines."

"When they hired me, I thought I could deliver. Didn't know this was an energy-neutral community. When they figure out it's a dead deal, they'll just hire someone else who thinks he can make it happen."

"Why would they can a guy they're honoring for his service? You gotta chill."

"I need to keep this job."

"Ah, I get it. The Lark Factor. Hey, I don't want you to move, either, but if you have to take a job somewhere else, Lark can follow you." She rolled her thumb over one of her keys. "Surely this isn't the only game in town. Can you ask Frank Lovejoy?"

"Anything he'd have wouldn't cover my truck payment."

"This thing with Lark's that serious?"

He gave a hard nod. "That serious."

"Then you're going to have be a big boy and figure out how to withstand this slow-motion catastrophe or move it on down the road. And, if you're that hot and heavy, you'd better tell Lark what's going on."

"I've told her some. But not everything. It's a bad time—she's stressed out."

"And you're not?"

"Something's going on at the winery. Bankers, and . . ." He stared at the ceiling. "Forget it."

"I have faith in you. You'll figure it out." Kelli sighed. "Zadie's got another birthday party this week for another kid we don't know.

Feel like I should turn over my paychecks to the people who make Elsa toys."

"Elsa?"

"*Frozen?*"

"Ah," he nodded, wishing he could disappear. Today wasn't the day for another one of Kelli's vent sessions.

"The kid's driving me nuts to get our tree up," Kelli said.

"Can I help?"

"No. She can wait till Red's home. She's going through another growth spurt. Don't ask how we'll afford to feed her when this guy arrives." Kelli donned a big smile and rubbed her belly.

Wyatt nodded—and then the meaning behind her words hit him and he rose from his chair. "You have a *guy* in there? How do you know?"

"After Wilder, we had to do an amniocentesis. Had one with Zadie too."

"Hmm . . . wow." He blinked hard and his mouth twisted into a smile.

"Red's thrilled. Then, again, he'd raise the roof if I delivered a litter of Pomeranians."

"I'm happy for you guys. Heck, I'm happy for me, too. Hope I get to stick around to meet him."

"You'll be around, one way or another."

"Hope so."

"Heard from Satan's spawn lately?" Kelli's mouth turned into a snarl.

"About the same."

"When is she going to get the message that you don't want to talk to her again?"

"Actually . . . I might just bite the bullet and talk to her soon." He was wading into shark-infested waters.

"Hell if you will."

"Hear me out. Lark's been on my case to make peace. Says offloading my baggage will help us have a healthier relationship."

"Healthier relationship? I'd tell Ashlen to get bent."

"Course you would."

"Who is Lark to tell you . . ." Kelli's cheeks burned red. "Doesn't make any more sense for you to let Ashlen back into your life than for Lark to be running all over town with Levi, Fredericksburg's Bachelor of the Year."

"She works for him."

"If you say so. Blame it on the pregnancy hormones, but that dude is smokin' hot."

Oh, Kel, if you only knew.

There was a knock. Before he had a chance to respond, Barbara poked her head in. "Meeting's canceled today due to a scheduling conflict."

Wyatt signaled to a stack of papers on his desk. "I'll work on this from home. You can get me on my cell." He dropped his pen. "Hang on, Kelli. I'll walk you out."

Lark
·············

IMAGES OF THE ABANDONED WINERY haunted Lark. She called Wyatt to fill him in, and he listened, wedging only an occasional word into the conversation.

"Tell you what—get your boys down and come over," he said when she paused for a breath. "We'll talk over beer-brined pork chops and a bottle of wine."

"Sounds like bliss."

Lark set down her phone and wandered into the kitchen. Word of Elke and Wolf's misadventures at Hartmann-Haas had circulated quickly in town—but to Lark's surprise, Millie didn't stir so much as a teaspoon of I-told-you-so into her pot of stew.

"Anything I can do?" Frank offered.

"Actually, yes. Can we go outside and talk? Just us?"

Compensating for the invitation she didn't receive, Millie said, "I'll stay here with the boys."

Lark slipped on a jacket and took her father's elbow.

"What's on your mind?" As gravel crunched beneath their steps, Frank eyed her curiously.

An unwelcome lump held Lark's words for a moment. "I don't want to upset you, but . . . can we talk about Vietnam?"

Frank stopped walking and pinned his gaze ahead.

I hit a nerve. A bad one.

"We don't have to," she wavered.

"It's okay, kid." With his head tipped down, he glanced at up her. "What? You worried about Wyatt?"

"How'd you guess?"

"He and I have talked about reentry," he said.

Considering the last time her father counseled Wyatt, she asked, "How'd that go?"

"When I came home, it helped me to know people who understood, so I told him I'd be there if he wanted to talk. He seems to be handling it okay . . . as well as anybody can, anyhow." Meeting Lark's eyes, he asked, "Maybe not?"

"I thought he was okay until I met his psychiatrist in San Antonio. He's dealing with more than I ever knew."

"Kid, you've heard the phrase, 'All gave some, some gave all,' haven't you?"

"Yeah."

"Every surviving soldier comes home dragging a suitcase of ghosts. Some of us carry more than others." His expression shifted to a fatherly, don't-lie-to-me stare. "Has he hurt you?"

"No. Never."

"Whew." His eyes flew heavenward.

"Violent nightmares seem to be his problem—he can hit and flail and never know he's doing it. He doesn't want to hurt me or the boys."

Frank bobbed his head as she spoke.

"Dad, I want to understand what he's going through. I was hoping we might talk about what it was like when you came home—I think it could give me some insight."

Frank ran a hand over his beard. "Okay, well . . . back then, nobody talked about PTSD. They called it adjustment disorder. Most everyone pretended not to notice us struggling—men don't cry, and all that."

"What happened over there?" Her question hung between them, and Lark saw images of Vietnam pass behind her father's eyes.

"Terrible things you can't just leave behind." He shook his head and seemed to refocus. "Kid, no one prepared us for reentry. Coming and going, it was absolute hell."

A rush of guilt ran through Lark; she reached for his hand.

"A bunch of eighteen-year-olds listening to The Stones, drinking beer, and chasing girls—suddenly, the government tosses us across the world. Next thing, we're standing in the middle of another family's domestic squabble holding M-16s with grenades in our pockets."

"Did you want to go?"

"I was scared shitless. But my dad fought in Iwo Jima, and his dad fought in the Great War. Figured it was my turn." Frank stared into the horizon, his mouth a thin line. "Didn't matter. Just shipped us to 'Nam. No questions asked."

"Can't imagine."

"Thought leaving your mom with a new baby was the worst of it. Besides all the . . ." He tapped his forehead. "People called us names and spat on us."

Lark squeezed his hand.

"Picture our house . . . normal and all that." He held out his arms. "In every room, a TV's playing . . . I don't know. *Apocalypse Now*? The volume's muted. Most people managed to ignore it. For us, that TV, those pictures followed us to work, to college, to bed."

Lark fought the impulse to cry. "You and Mom have always seemed so solid."

"Got married right out of school. Harlan arrived before I left." He winked. "Assumed you did the math on all that." A slow smile took his face. "Your mom's a good woman."

"Hard to picture her raising a baby alone."

"Your grandmother helped so she could go to school, but it

wasn't easy." He sighed. "Kid, she may drive you crazy, but she kept me going through . . . well . . . she saved my life."

"I love Wyatt, and I want to be there for him." She released a heavy sigh.

"So be there for him. No doubt he loves you the same—you can see his feelings written all over his face. Is it the age difference?"

Could you please stop with the reminders about my age? I have bigger issues. She shook her head. "I just . . . I can't let him hurt my boys."

"Ah, that." He wiped his forehead. "There's a million reasons they say war's hell on the home front. I had my moments—never got physical, but there were dark days."

"Was that why you didn't have more kids right away?"

He nodded. "Your mom wanted us in a good place before we brought another baby into the mix. You took your sweet time getting here, kid." His mouth curled into a shy smile. "Have to say, though, all that trying wasn't too bad."

"I'll bet." She gave him a playful punch on the arm.

"Listen, I can't tell you what to do. But I can't see you throwing away what you have with Wyatt without giving him a chance as a good thing. Talk to him. You'll find your fears aren't that different from his." Frank took her hand, and his silence concluded a painful glimpse into the past.

While they walked to the house, Lark mulled over this fresh understanding of her father and her lover—two good men thrown into hell, unable to scrape it from their souls.

BACK INSIDE THE HOUSE, MILLIE'S eyes flickered between Frank and Lark as she pulled a head of lettuce from the crisper drawer. "How was your walk?"

"Brisk." Frank moved to the living room.

Lark remained in the kitchen, letting Frank's words settle. Acknowledging his bravery was easy. But she'd overlooked her mother's strength—and hers had been the difference between a battered vet holding a cardboard sign by the highway and the loving man in the next room.

Lark sidled up to the war hero rinsing romaine at the kitchen sink. "I love you, Mom."

"Well, I love you, sweetheart."

"Mom?"

Millie turned off the water and cocked her head,

"For all you've done for me, the boys, and for Dad when he came home. We're lucky to have you."

⟆⟨

A FEW HOURS LATER, LARK arrived at Wyatt's house hungry for a warm embrace and a cozy dinner.

A blue truck was parked in front of the house, so she found a spot on the street.

She opened the front door and blinked several times, but the image wouldn't clear.

"Kermit?" she said.

Standing beside the human barnacle, Wyatt wore an apologetic expression.

Lark bit back a sigh. "What a surprise."

"Wyatt was surprised too," Kermit laughed to himself. "I was headed south for a fishing trip. He told me I was welcome any time, so here I am. In the flesh."

"In the flesh," Lark repeated.

Kermit gripped the padded armrests of one of Wyatt's recliners. "Love these babies. They are so . . ."

"Cookie Monster blue?" she supplied, summoning an approximation of cheer. "How long are you here?"

"You got me for the night."

She sniffed the air. "Wyatt, are we still cooking those pork chops?"

Kermit formed a finger-gun and his mouth clicked as he pulled the trigger. "Nobody's cooking. It's BBQ night."

"Oh, how nice," she mumbled. "Wyatt, can you help me with this clasp on my necklace?" She pointed to his bedroom, and he followed.

When they were safely out of earshot, she frowned at Wyatt. "I needed you tonight."

"He showed up, all 'surprise.'" Wyatt threw up his hands. "Couldn't turn him away."

"Hey, lovebirds," Kermit roared. "Eat first, canoodle later. This traveling man's about to eat his right arm."

"Let him," Lark deadpanned.

"Can I make it up to you?" He slid a hand over her neck, thumbed her chin.

"I guess," she said, and they returned to the living room.

"First, we've gotta give the lady the 4-1-1," Kermit clapped his hands. "Cracklin' Rosie's makes this big ole rib dinner. Better be hungry, cause there ain't any 'splitting an entrée' like ladies always want to do."

Wyatt leaned over and hit a button on the recliner, jerking Kermit upright. "Let's go."

ON THE WAY TO THE RESTAURANT, Kermit monopolized the conversation, detailing every punch, blow, and drop of blood witnessed at a mixed martial arts cage fight he'd recently attended.

The hostess seated them and delivered three water glasses.

"Make 'em pretty around here." Kermit waggled his brows.

A waitress appeared, snagging his attention. "What would you like?"

"Well . . ." Kermit's tiny eyes gaped at her nametag like she was an item on the menu. "Teena. Dee-lightful name, Teena."

"Kerm." Wyatt nudged him.

"Sure you won't help me down a bucket of beers?" Kerm asked like a hopeful child.

"I'm sure." Wyatt nodded.

"Since my buddy's out, two longneck Shiners, and the lady'll have . . . what would you like, Lark?"

"Dos Equis lager on tap in a glass with a salted rim, please."

"Picky, ain't she?" Kermit asked.

"Lark likes what she likes. And I like Lark." Wyatt touched her arm.

"Teena, why don't you bring us some jalapeño poppers?"

She walked away and Kermit's eyes grew wide. "That one there, now, she's a—"

"How's work?" Wyatt interrupted.

"They're keeping me busier than a Baghdad bricker."

"Remind me what you do?" Lark asked. *Besides showing up uninvited.*

"Manage roughnecks. They're tougher than tattooed cockroaches."

Lark didn't dare touch that comment.

When the jalapeño poppers hit the table, Kermit pulled the plate close and carefully evaluated and touched each jalapeño. After committing to one, he dunked it into ranch dressing and stuffed it inside his mouth.

Teena reappeared, pen in hand. "What would you like?" she asked Lark.

Walking out of Kermit's Redneck Dinner Theatre would be my first choice, but the show is in high gear—can't duck out now.

"I'll have the chicken special, salad with ranch, please," she said.

Wyatt ordered a half-order of ribs.

"I'll take the T-Rex Platter with mashed potatoes—extra cream gravy on those—por favor," Kermit said. "And . . ." He sighed. "Mac and cheese, okra, and beans."

"Healthy appetite," Lark said.

"Yup," Kerm said, beaming, like she'd just paid him a compliment.

The guys made the conversational rounds—family, other Army friends, and sports. In between, Kermit finished off those poppers just in time for the main event. He tore into his ribs the second the waitress put them down in front of him and, gesturing with a saucy bone, declared, "Mmm . . . so good you'll wanna slap your momma."

Oh, I'd like to slap someone, alright. She touched Wyatt's wrist under the table and, taking one for the team, attempted to find common ground with Kermit. "Wyatt said you met someone?"

"Yes, ma'am. Carlie's a hottie, and smart." Kerm shredded another rib. "The whole package. She's what they call an animal behaviorist, working on a PhD."

"Interesting." Lark contained her expression.

"She studies how gorillas and humans behave—comparing their everyday business, like peeing and eating. She hooks wires to their heads—both the people and gorillas, but not at the same time."

"Right." Lark shot a look at Wyatt.

"Told her I'd be her guinea pig so long as she doesn't 'lectrocute me on accident." He laughed and dropped the last of the ravaged bones on his plate.

KERMIT'S STREAM-OF-CONSCIOUSNESS PATTER continued until they arrived at Wyatt's house.

As soon as Wyatt parked, the car's back door flew open.

"Gotta hit the john," Kermit called as he scurried to the front door. He tried the handle. "You locked it?"

Wyatt tossed the keys out of his window, and Kermit unlocked the door and dashed inside.

"Who leaves their door unlocked?" Lark asked.

"Him, I guess? Hey, I'm sorry about this."

"He's tone deaf to basic manners. If you let him pop in whenever he gets a whim, he'll be at your door every time you turn around."

"He doesn't have anybody."

"He doesn't have anybody because he's a jackass," she said.

"He's not a jackass."

Her expression begged him to reconsider his answer.

"Okay, I'll admit, he's a bit of a jackass," Wyatt offered. "Please don't be angry."

"Why are you so protective of him?"

"Long story." Wyatt ran a finger over a leather seam of his steering wheel.

"Give me the short version." Her tone was sharp.

Wyatt took a deep breath. "Back in Kunar Province—"

"I know, foot patrol, yada yada." Her hand moved in a circle.

Wyatt turned to face her. No longer apologetic, his face was flushed and devoid of all levity. "Kermit busted his ass to get to me. He put the tourniquet on my leg. That jackass kept me from bleeding to death."

"Mother trucker," she breathed out, wishing she could suck back every bad word about Kermit she'd ever uttered.

"He can be a jerk, but the Army made us brothers. I owe him my life."

"I understand."

"Thank you. Remember our talk about how a couple can be in the midst of craziness and stay right in tune with each other?"

"I remember."

"Tonight, you knew I was stressing about Kermit running his mouth. You saw me. You saw my frustration. Even with all his . . ."

"Being a jackass?"

"Being a jackass," he said evenly. "It's not easy to keep your cool around Kerm, but you did it for me. Don't think I didn't notice." He kissed her.

"Hey lovebirds, you comin'?" Kermit called.

"Give us a minute," Wyatt said.

"Okay." Kerm lingered on the porch.

"Alone, Kerm."

Kermit raised one shoulder and scampered inside.

"If he wasn't here, I'd scoop you up and carry you straight to my bedroom." Wyatt planted another kiss on Lark—not just any kiss but a don't-forget-this-moment kiss.

"If he wasn't here, I'd let you."

"Damn it, Kermit, get the hell out of my house," he said into her hair.

"You'd better get in there before he breaks into your stash of good bourbon."

Thirty-three

Wyatt

At sunrise, Kermit took off for the coast and Wyatt reluctantly tossed his Army uniforms in his truck on the off chance the "Chicago team" showed up to take pictures for their employee feel-good campaign that day.

When he entered the TXEnergy office, Barbara looked up. "They're here," she announced. "One of them will take the photos. The other is a branding something-or-other—I suppose he'll tell you what he needs. Assuming they'll be done with you by lunch, I ordered a sandwich tray plus your standing order."

"Thanks."

Before he could break free, she covered her mouth with a hand and said quietly, "I offered them coffee and a cinnamon roll, but they weren't interested. Not all that friendly, either."

"Barbara, you're the best." His words put a big grin on her face.

Turning down the woodgrain-paneled hall leading to his office, a nauseatingly sweet patchouli mix entered his nostrils. The scent intensified until he reached the source.

"Howdy." He fashioned a friendly stance and introduced himself, offering his hand to the two men sitting outside his office. "You must be the men from Chicago."

"Daryl Dawson, I'm the photographer," said the fuller-figured man as he reached for Wyatt's hand. A scruffy brown beard hit his collar, and he wore sneakers, cargo pants, and a button-down shirt that was in need of a good ironing. "This is Lorenzo."

"Lorenzo Tyler," the guy corrected. He had enough product in his hair to ignite a refinery fire, was wearing one of those new too-small-for-a-real-man-to-wear suits, and remained seated, one arm over his black canvas, cross-body man-purse.

"This shouldn't take long," Daryl said. "Just need to get a few shots."

"How's this going to work?" Wyatt asked.

"We have some sites picked out." Lorenzo eyed the hangers draped over Wyatt's shoulder. "Bring those along. You may have to change in the car."

Lorenzo had clearly failed to consider the spatial challenges faced by an amputee.

"With my leg, it'd be best if I could change before we leave," Wyatt said.

"Fine," Lorenzo said. "We'll wait."

A FEW MINUTES LATER, WYATT followed the men to a field on the outskirts of Fredericksburg. Daryl took a few test shots; Lorenzo reviewed them, and then told him to take more. It didn't matter where they made Wyatt stand—the light wasn't right, or there were shadows, or there was too much of a breeze.

All that walking came at a price: Wyatt's leg was killing him. But he'd do just about anything to keep his job, so he painted a big smile on his face and played the game.

"Get one of him up there." Lorenzo waved to the forty-foot wooden pole behind Wyatt.

"Mind climbing up there?" Daryl asked.

They're kidding, right? Who the hell asks a guy with one leg to climb a power pole? The nerve of this jerk.

"I'm not built to do that," Wyatt said.

"You don't have to climb all the way," Lorenzo said. "Ten feet or so—just enough to make it look legit."

"Unless you're taking those pictures of me inside a cherry picker, we're gonna need another plan."

Visibly confused, Lorenzo turned to Daryl.

Daryl explained, and Lorenzo shook his head. "We don't have access to that type of gear."

"Then my response to your request is gonna be a hard no." Wyatt retreated to his tailgate.

After Lorenzo pulled Daryl in for a huddle, he hollered, "Mr. Gifford, let's go."

"I'm coming." Despite the magic Trey had worked on his prosthesis, pain was spiking from the edge of his stump to the core of his being. Every time his right foot touched the ground, he felt like an icepick was drilling through his flesh. It was all he could do not to pull the thing off and hop to the guy.

Lorenzo rolled his hand in a circle as if it might speed Wyatt's progress.

"Moving slow today," Wyatt said.

"We're on the clock, Mr. Gifford."

"I'm on one leg, motherfucker." His give-a-shit filter fell plumb off. Considering the lack of manners Lorenzo had shown him, Wyatt didn't see the use of bending over to pick the damn thing up.

"Excuse me," Lorenzo mumbled.

"Just ease up, buddy, alright?" Wyatt said.

Lorenzo gestured to the power pole. "Over there . . . please."

Wyatt walked toward the pole and waited for the instructions. His phone pinged with a text. Thinking it might concern actual work, he pulled out his phone. "Hang on."

ASHLEN: *Driving through Fredericksburg today. Any chance we could meet?*

This isn't the day, Ashlen. He shoved the phone back into his pocket and posed as he was told.

Lorenzo, clearly frustrated, wagged a hand and called to Daryl, "Get the block."

Daryl retrieved a wooden block and prompted Wyatt to prop a leg on it.

"Captain Morgan pose." Lorenzo clapped his hands. "C'mon. One foot on the block."

I have a better idea where I could put a foot. Wyatt angled his prosthesis at the knee and propped it upon the cube. When he was told to smile, he smiled, and when they told him not to smile, he frowned.

"Dave, can you 'shop the logo on his shirt?" Lorenzo asked.

"Easy."

"Whoa." Wyatt pointed to the gold star on his pocket. "This is logo enough."

"Hmm," Lorenzo said.

Corporate had told Barbara they'd use his picture for internal feel-good PR, but now Wyatt needed confirmation, straight from Lorenzo's pompous mouth. "What are you doing with these pictures?"

"Brochures, sales materials, can't say which segment," Lorenzo said, dismissing Wyatt's interest.

The words set off Wyatt's internal alarm system and he pushed his foot off the block. "Wait a cotton-picking minute. Nobody said anything about using them externally."

"These decisions are made at a level much higher than Po-dunk, Texas."

"Are you shitting me?"

"Daryl, what are you doing?" Lorenzo asked as Daryl retreated in a "my fingerprints aren't on this hot mess" way and began packing up his equipment. This obviously wasn't his first rodeo with Lorenzo.

Wyatt edged closer, performing a cost-benefit analysis of releasing his inner Hulk and popping Lorenzo back to Chi-Town. The way he saw it, it was a win-win.

"Mr. Gifford, it would be in your best interest to walk away and let us borrow the uniforms," Lorenzo said.

Wyatt tipped his head toward the rodent's face. "My uniforms don't belong to this company. They belong to the United States Army. You wouldn't know that, since your grubby little paws have never seen the inside a tactical boot."

"Settle down, soldier. The company will pay you for your time. Just zip your lip. We'll take care of the rest."

"Alright, slick. Let me help you get your jacked-up facts straight." He scratched his nose. "They told me these pictures would spotlight veterans who work for Foudre. Not for ads. These are for internal use only."

"Well, obviously, someone changed their mind since speaking to you."

"Obviously," Wyatt said, leaning into Lorenzo's patchouli stink.

"Can we just get back to work?" Lorenzo asked. "We're running out of time."

"Give me a second." Wyatt removed his phone and responded to a message. As he slid it into his pocket, his gaze met Lorenzo's impatient sneer. His thoughts scrambled to defuse the frustration swelling in his chest. *Keep it together. You're on home soil.*

"Mr. Gifford. Our flight leaves in a few hours, and we're way behind," Lorenzo complained.

Ashlen's text presented an opportunity Wyatt hadn't seen until just then.

"Ah, that stinks." He offered a rueful smile. "Unfortunately, I've got a family emergency."

Daryl began collecting his supplies, but Lorenzo wasn't going anywhere. "We have orders from corporate."

Wyatt stared through him. *I have a family emergency. Enough said.*

"Back to my original idea," Lorenzo said with renewed fervor. "We'll take your uniforms and arrange a stand-in. Daryl will Photoshop your face on a model's body."

"All due respect, sir, you're lost in the sauce if you think I'm letting you go anywhere with these uniforms."

"All due respect, you don't have a choice, Mr. Gifford." Lorenzo tossed him a scathing laugh.

Something wild took over. Wyatt pushed out his chest and drilled through Lorenzo with an icy stare. "You may call me *Lieutenant* Gifford, and unless you'd like me to introduce you to the Brazilian jiu-jitsu I learned in the Army, I suggest we call it a day and you get your ass to the airport."

Lorenzo jerked his shoulders in a shrug and stalked back to his car.

ALL THAT JACKASSERY MADE A MAN hungry. Wyatt drove straight to his office and walked into the break room to claim the ham and cheese sandwich, extra mayo, that Barbara had ordered for him—only to find that a herd of hyenas had ransacked the sandwich tray, Wyatt's special order included. He scrounged the remains of a picked-over turkey club and took it to his desk to catch up on the work he'd postponed while running all over town with FU's Mad Men team.

"How'd it go?" Barbara said from the door.

"It went." He didn't take his eyes off his desk.

"Song Chu just called." Barbara said. "I told her you were busy."

"If she calls again, please let her know I had a family emergency. Won't be available for the rest of the day."

"Anything I can do?"

"No, but you know how to find me if it's really important." He winked and took off toward the door.

Lark

....

LARK APPROACHED TWISTED SISTERS, THE cute coffee house on Washington Street where Levi had asked her to meet him. At the counter, she opted for green tea and a cupcake. Her nerves couldn't handle a jolt of coffee, but cupcakes were always a good idea.

"I called up some of my ag-banker friends," Levi said. "Wolf was in deeper than we thought."

"What about Kingsley?"

"Huh?"

"I haven't been able to get that poor kid off my mind. What happens to him in all of this?"

Levi's expression said he didn't care but compassion bled into his words. "Elke may not be ethical in her business dealings, but she seems like a good enough mother."

"Let's hope." She took a sip of her tea. "You think they knew they were about to get busted?"

"Definitely." Levi wiped his brow. "Can't help thinking about Elke's grandfather. Poor old man handed over his farm thinking he was passing along his legacy. Like Wolf would walk away from finance and become a farmer, live on the straight and narrow?" Levi stared at the ceiling.

"So much for leaving their toxic life behind. Sounds like they drag it wherever they go." She gave a wry laugh. "Can her grandfather can take it back?"

"Too late. Even if the old guy wanted it, Wolf leveraged it to the hilt. My ag-banker friend heard he took out these low-interest agricultural loans to build the winery and buy equipment. The winery was like a movie stage to convince his lenders he was legit. My friend said they think Wolf was laundering dirty money."

Angry steam began to build in Lark's chest. "Shit."

"I played right into his plan—willing to take on work I wasn't trained for, kept my mouth shut, didn't ask questions. I needed the job." Levi seethed.

"Did you ever suspect—"

"Not right away. Now? Looking back at how he canned the construction crews before they finished the buildings? How he never came around to check on us?" He sighed. "And even after I told him about the electrical issues Wyatt pointed out, he blew me off."

"Did someone tip off the authorities?"

"Wolf took the ag lenders as good old boys who conducted business on a handshake. He figured he'd just BS them like he did everyone else. But when they did their walk-throughs, they got the picture. Wolf had returned a bunch of the equipment he'd bought."

"Which explains why you didn't have all the parts."

"He fired contractors to keep a lid on expenses. Heck, he hadn't even applied for a liquor license."

"Did his bankers confront him?"

"Nope. They let the feds do that."

"Damn."

"Damn's right. The Farm Credit Administration doesn't screw around."

The bell clanged over the door and a man walked into the coffee shop.

"Granville." Levi waved to him.

"Who?"

"This is my ag-lender friend, Granville Mayer," he said, rising to his feet. "He can help us."

"Wait." Lark put her hands to her temples. "Are we doing this?"

"I thought we were. You said you had the money to make an offer."

"Levi." She hoped to stall him before the banker reached the table.

"Lark, this is—"

"Granville Mayer. Nice—and slightly terrifying—to meet you," Lark said.

"Thanks?" Granville wore a puzzled frown.

Both men sat simultaneously after Lark dropped into her chair.

"I didn't think I was going to be in the market for a winery quite this soon," Lark said.

"May have jumped the gun," Levi said to his friend.

"No, just . . . I need more information."

"That's why I'm here," Granville said. "There's an opportunity to purchase a winery at a bargain-basement price."

"Isn't everything getting repoed?"

"Not everything. The buildings and crops will remain."

"What about the leases?"

"Wolf didn't renew them, so the fruit will convey, assuming the plants survive," Granville said.

"If the vines are still healthy"—Levi seemed to be working it out in his head—"and I don't know why they wouldn't be . . . you could harvest in the fall."

Lark frowned. "Heard it can take forever to obtain a TABC liquor license."

"Until then, sell the fruit to another winemaker," Granville said.

Ideas began to take root. The mature vines could produce revenue. Levi could manage equipment and irrigation, and she'd hire a contractor to tackle the unfinished buildings. As a bonus, the house on the property would be more than adequate for her family.

"I already asked a friend to appraise it," Granville said. "If his numbers line up with mine, we're talking one point five, including any equipment not claimed by their creditors."

Less than I made on my house in Houston. How can I pass this up?

"Elke's grandfather valued it at $3 million before he signed it over. That was pre-construction." Granville brushed his brown hair away from his face. "Government will want to get rid of it. Peach of a deal."

While the men talked about Wolf's troubles, Lark stepped away from the table to use the restroom. On her way back, she passed a wall of merchandise—mostly T-shirts and gift items with cute sayings in bright colors. One mug read, "Call your shot."

Call your shot, Lark.

Queasiness bubbled from the pit of her stomach, but she wasn't going to scare so easily. She returned to the table, and before her butt hit the chair, she threw out the words, "Let's do it."

Wyatt had texted earlier saying he was working from home, and he'd mentioned a surprise. Doubtful he'd top what she was about to tell him.

The winery would anchor her to Fredericksburg. If she and Wyatt stayed together—and why wouldn't they?—it would anchor him, too.

"Great," she said out loud when she spotted the white Jeep in the drive. "More company." The heavy wood door was open, as it was most of the time when Wyatt was home on warm days.

With her nerves pinging like the tilt sensors of a pinball machine, she touched the screen door handle.

"You clean up good, Wyatt," a flirty woman's voice said from within.

Lark's hand fell, and she peeked through the screen door.

She made out a lanky blond in a peek-a-boo shouldered blouse standing in the kitchen. Her voice was soft and flirty even while complaining about a hectic travel schedule and demanding clients.

Conversational bits and indistinct chatter trickled into Lark's ears, muted by her bounding pulse.

"Glad you found a way to work it out," Wyatt said.

What. The. Holy. Hell.

"Always knew we could." She giggled and shifted toward the door.

"Ashlen, come back here," Wyatt said. "I need you—"

Lark rolled against the brick as the woman's heels clacked against the floor, marking the oak planks like she owned the place, and the two disappeared to the back of the house. She pressed her head to the screen. Silence sent another round of twists grinding through her belly, and she dragged herself away.

On the way back to her car, she passed the Jeep. Its vanity plate read "ASHLEN3."

And Lark 0.

Wyatt

He accepted Ashlen's apology, then caught up on stories about mutual friends. Once she collected the stuff he'd been keeping in a corner of his closet, his business with her would be over. *Have a nice life. Hope to never see you again. Finito.*

Had he known how she'd dawdle, he would have had her stuff waiting on the front porch when she arrived. She wanted to rummage through the boxes—said she was certain she couldn't have left so much in his old apartment before his last deployment. She examined every T-shirt and cosmetics container, even the ticket stub from a Rascal Flats concert they'd attended a few years earlier.

Standing there in his bedroom, she looked different. It wasn't the way she'd cut her hair or applied makeup, or how she was flashing the rock on her left hand. Ashlen wore the glow of a woman in love.

A tinge of irritation hit his senses at the reminder of her infidelity. *Let it go, man. Got a woman who loves me back now. No burning bridges, remember?* He took in a big breath and reminded himself to relax around her. Soon, he found himself talking to her like a friend and laughing with her when he carried a box to her car.

"Thanks for seeing me," Ashlen said, leaning into his chest. "I'm happy for you." She dotted his cheek with a kiss and drove away.

From his front porch, he typed out a message to Lark: *I've got news. Call me when you get a chance. Love you.*

He waited for the response bubble to appear, but his message went unanswered.

Close to an hour later, impatience got the best of him, and he dialed her number.

"You've reached Lark. Leave me a message."

"It's me. Please call me when you get this. Love you," he said on the voice mail recording.

Uneasiness grew into alarm as two hours turned to four. Finally, he dialed Frank's number.

"She came home sick this afternoon, hurried straight to bed. A virus or something," Frank said, unconcerned.

"Can I bring her anything?"

"No, she'll be alright."

Wyatt couldn't unwind knowing Lark was sick. Maybe it was his imagination, but as he replayed Ashlen's visit and reflected on that kiss she'd planted on his check—their meeting suddenly felt a hundred kinds of wrong.

Guilt chipped away at him, and the next twenty-four hours of radio silence from Lark compounded his remorse. Unable to eat or sleep, he couldn't stay away any longer. He grabbed his keys and headed for his truck.

WHEN FRANK ANSWERED THE DOOR, everything seemed to be as chaotic as usual—Millie was giving the boys their baths while Frank sorted through the day's mail.

"Had to check on her," Wyatt said. "Hope you don't mind."

"She's probably asleep." Frank chuckled. "If the boys aren't making too much noise. If it's any indication, she told us to keep them out of there."

"Maybe I should leave her alone, then?"

"Probably best," Frank said. "You're welcome to have a seat, though." He picked up the remote control and turned on the TV. "Should be a playoff game on somewhere."

"Try Fox," Wyatt suggested.

"There we go," Frank said, sliding back into his chair. "Baltimore and Dallas."

Through the next quarter, Frank commented on the refs' bad calls but Wyatt could do little more than toss out a few agreeable nods.

When halftime began, Millie joined them in the living room, slightly rumpled after bathing the boys and reading bedtime stories. "Ah," she said, as her bottom hit the chair. "I may be too old for this."

"Anything I can do to help?" Wyatt said.

"No thanks. They're all tucked in. Now it's my turn."

"How's Lark doing?" he asked her.

"I'm sure it's nothing pushing fluids won't cure. She asked us to leave her alone to sleep."

Hint taken. His eyes shifted to the darkened hallway leading to her room—so close to her, but not welcome. Finally, he stood. "I'm gonna take off."

"Oh, okay." Relief showed on Millie's face.

"You know what?" He hesitated. "I'm just gonna check in on her before I leave."

Millie gave a resigned shrug and exchanged a look with Frank. Wyatt frowned. What was he missing?

He tapped on the door, but she didn't respond. Silently, he turned the knob and opened the door. There was movement in the darkened room.

"*Grrr.*" Walter's profile appeared on the bed and his tail wagged urgently.

"Shh." Wyatt stepped toward the mutt. With a whine, a tail disappeared beneath the bed.

Wyatt's eyes adjusted to the darkness and he tiptoed to the edge of Lark's bed. He flipped the switch on her table lamp.

A moan came from the blanket covering her from head to toe.

"Hey, beautiful." He peeled the blanket from her shoulders with a gentle hand. "I've missed you."

"Mmm."

"Should we take you to the doctor?"

"Mmm-mm."

"Can I get anything for you?"

"I'm fine. Don't trouble yourself."

Wyatt couldn't ignore the brittle edge to her voice or black smudges on her rumpled pillowcase.

"It's no trouble. Hey, I have some news I think you'll like." His hand went to her shoulder and she jerked away.

"Give me some space, please."

"Babe, I understand you're sick."

She shoved the blanket off her body and sat bolt upright. "Wyatt, listen." She squinted against the light and waved crumpled tissues in her fists. "We are over."

The words hung in the air like clay pigeons that wouldn't fall to the earth.

"You heard me."

"What the hell, Lark?"

"Shh . . . my boys," she warned.

"They're fine."

"You need to leave." Her words turned their shared future to ash.

He froze, unable to walk away from her. His mind searched for her motivation.

My broken body? Unstable career? Night terrors? Meddlesome ex-girlfriend?

"If it's Ashlen, I talked to her like you wanted."

She shook her head violently. "Just go."

"Is it Levi? Did he put you up to this?"

"Go home, Wyatt." Her eyes twitched and she dragged a hand across them.

"We've worked through so much. Please, Lark."

"I *said*, give me some space."

The finality of her words carved Wyatt in two.

"At least, look at me, will you?" He stared at her, willing her to come back to him. "We can get past this . . ." He wiped his forehead and stood. "Whatever 'this' is? Lark?"

Without another word, she slid back under the blanket, leaving him helpless to argue.

His hands fell to his sides and he skulked toward the living room. "Is she awake?" Millie asked.

Wyatt shook his head and turned toward the TV.

"Jerry Jones is losing his mind up there in the booth," Frank gestured to the TV. "Shouldn't have spent so much on that running back."

"Yeah," Wyatt said numbly. "I'll let y'all have your evening back."

"You don't need to rush off," Frank said.

Millie cleared her throat.

Wyatt recognized his cue to leave. "I'll let myself out. Take care."

From his truck, he dialed Kelli's number. "Kelli, can I come over?"

"I'm tucking Zadie in for the night. Whatcha need?"

"I need to talk to someone."

"What's the matter?"

"I think Lark just broke up with me."

"That didn't last long." She paused. "Hate to say I told you so."

"You didn't tell me anything."

"Hello, McFly—told you she was fooling around with Mr. November."

"Don't make me do this on the phone. Can I come over?"

"Okay, but promise me you'll let me do the picking the next time you feel like dating someone."

Lark

....

AT MIDNIGHT, SHE WOKE to a curious warmth running the length of her spine. She moved, and it shifted and exhaled a gentle snore.

"Walter?" Lark whispered.

The dog crept to her face and snuffled at her nose, then swiped her cheek with a half-hearted lick.

"Not now, Walter."

At the mention of his name, his metronome tail swayed back and forth.

Lark flipped off the lamp, repositioned herself, and patted the space beside her. "Come here."

Walter tucked his head and curled into her embrace.

"You might be the only creature whose pity I can tolerate right now."

WALTER REMAINED BY HER SIDE in the following days, his dedication as appealing as his inability to vocalize judgment. He never talked back. He was happy to stay in his kennel when Lark deemed necessary. And the little guy had a way of knowing when she needed him most.

Unfortunately, not everyone in the Lovejoy house was as low maintenance. Jamie and Charlie had already suffered the loss of their father; she wasn't about to let them suffer more because of Wyatt. And that required the revival of her Happy Mommy Show: Obscure the pain. Stand taller. Perk up your voice. Grin like an idiot.

BIANCA TESTED THE HAPPY MOMMY Show when she appeared at the Lovejoy's a few days later.

Lark cracked the door open a smidge, enough for Bianca to press it open and saunter inside.

"Saw your dad picking up the boys after school. Said you're sick, but I knew you'd call *me* to pick them up if you were really sick." Bianca stepped into the living room, scrutinizing every corner like she expected to find Jimmy Hoffa's feet poking out beneath a chair.

The pair sat on the sofa and Walter scuttled up to join them, sniffing Bianca's hands.

Bianca addressed him, "How'd a mutt like you get so lucky to land here?"

"You know my Mom." Lark snickered. "Always on the hunt to rescue lost souls."

Bianca's face wilted like forgotten flowers, and her shoulders dropped. Then, with a sniff, she hitched up her posture. "Hope this mutt knows he won the lottery when he earned Millie's love." Her words hit Lark in the sternum.

"I didn't mean it like that." Lark tried to back-peddle, but tension separated them like bookends.

"I'm sorry for what I said about Mom taking in Walter. I've grown to love the pesky little mutt. Mom's got a heart for helping—"

"Little girls who needed a mom?" Bianca's chin trembled, and Lark scooted until they were hip to hip.

Both reached out to give Walter a pet, and Bianca patted Lark's hand. Bianca studied Lark. "Nasty bug, huh?"

"I guess." Lark offered a simpering smile.

"It's going around in Kelli's family, too." Bianca paused. "What do you suppose it could be? Malaria? Guinea Worm Disease? A GI bug?" She twirled a lock of her inky black hair.

"Probably." Lark placed a hand over her stomach.

"GI bug, my hiney." Bianca threw out a mocking laugh. "The only GI bug you got you picked up at the Mini Mart the day you came to town."

"Please."

"Well, your Army man's been under the weather too."

"He's not *my* anything." Ire pierced every word.

Bianca clucked her mouth. "Seemed like a match made in Mini Mart heaven." She gave Lark an annoying once-over. "You're looking puny, honey. How about I get you a cup of juice?"

"I don't need juice."

"Well, honey, what *do* you need?" Bianca asked, like Lark was a child.

"I need Wyatt to stop spreading our business around like the godforsaken flu."

"Let's not get too far ahead of ourselves." Bianca pursed her lips thoughtfully. "Wyatt hasn't let out a peep."

Lark threw a suspicious glance at her.

"Okay, maybe one itsy-bitsy peep, but Kelli's family, so she doesn't count."

"I'm listening."

"Ran into her at the grocery store, both of us waiting for that kid who works behind the meat counter—you know the one, with that one eye that doesn't track right. Kid's lucky he hasn't lost a finger cutting steaks. Sweet as he is, they've got to train him. Last time I asked for thick cut, he gave me—"

"Bianca." Lark splayed out her fingers.

"Thin enough for a Philly sub."

"No offense, but I don't care about the butcher at the HEB. What did Kelli say . . . exactly?"

"Right, right." Bianca tipped back in her seat and exhaled dramatically. "Well . . . as you might've noticed, Kelli doesn't mince words. Her exact words were, 'Wyatt's in such a tailspin, he doesn't know shit from bean dip.' Apparently, she believes your breakup put him in that condition."

"That's Kelli, always the poet." Lark said. "Did she say anything else?"

"You ended it and he's at a loss as to what set you off."

"*What . . . set . . . me . . . off?*" Lark punched each word. "He got back together with his ex. I saw them with my own eyes."

"In *salsa flagrante?*" Bianca waggled her brows.

"Didn't stick around for the gory details. No mystery where the whole thing was going."

"Well, I'll be. He told Kelli that the flu did a number on your head."

"My heart's broken but my head's just fine."

"Oh, honey. I'm so sorry." Bianca lifted a flattened palm. "Hand to God, Kelli didn't mention the little tramp."

"Kelli would kick Wyatt into next week if he told her he saw Ashlen." Lark gaped at the ceiling. "I should've read the signs. He got punchy whenever her name came up. I encouraged him to talk to her, get closure." Angry tears ran down her face. "Ha. He sure got *something*."

"I'll be."

"Dad tried to warn me. He said Wyatt was in a different place. He wants a family—his own kids. I was so stupid."

"You were in love, and love can make the best of us lose our minds. Some men have a knack for it—they can be thoughtless, horny pigs. I should know—my mother brought home some grade-A choice porkers."

Lark surprised herself with a snort.

"Woman knew how to pick 'em." Bianca closed her eyes, flattened her mouth, and dropped her voice to a whisper. "The worst ones couldn't keep their hands to themselves around me." Her expression lightened. "Some were alright. One let us swim at his house. Shit you not, he had three nipples and four chins." She flashed a red-lipped smile. "Another one flipped his false teeth in and out of his mouth. Before they had Match.com, my mother found men on *Ripley's Believe it or Not*."

Lark joined Bianca in a genuine belly laugh, and it felt so good.

Bianca squeezed Lark's knee. "Looking at you just now, it was like you were twelve again."

"A lifetime ago . . . before Lark Lovejoy took the crooked path."

"You haven't exactly returned to Fredericksburg as the town sinner. Your heart's as pure as when I first knew you. Now, the rest of you . . . who knows?"

Lark bumped her on the arm.

Bianca grabbed her chin and dropped a kiss on her forehead. "I just love you."

"I should've been a better friend to you after you left."

"We were twelve. Besides, your mom represented on your behalf. She kept up with us—even came to Austin a few times. Always hoped she'd bring you along."

"I wish she had."

"She wouldn't expose you to our dysfunction. When my brother died, Mom unraveled. After the funeral, your mom stayed the night with us. She might drive you crazy, but she's a good woman. They say you find out who your friends are when bad things happen—Millie was there for me."

"And here you are, even though I never did a thing for you."

"You did. You just didn't know it. When I was sad or confused, I used to say, 'What would Lark do?' And that gave me my answer."

"You didn't." Lark screwed up her face.

"Still do. I wanted to be you when I grew up. Heck, even after I grew up. Wanted to grow up into the kind of woman who had it together enough to offer a hand to kids who couldn't help themselves . . . like I was."

"You're doing that now, for me."

"Damn skippy." She patted Lark's thigh. "Sticking by your side like Aqua-Net on the bathroom mirror."

Thirty-five

Lark

The holiday season introduced fresh diversions. Millie and Frank unearthed the faded brown Rubbermaid tubs containing decorations and pulled out all the stops for the boys' first Christmas in Fredericksburg, with Harlan's old trains chugging at the base of a twelve-foot tree. Frank covered the house in a million twinkly lights and hung stockings over the fireplace. He built a life-size advent calendar shaped like a train, and Millie filled it with treats. They were in their grandparenting element as they gave the Lovejoy halls a meticulous decking.

Lark's new business provided a welcome distraction—evaluating equipment options and contractor bids, studying liquor laws, and meeting with vendors required a clear head. She referred often to a quote she'd written in her notebook: "Focus on the pieces surrounding you now and the people you have left. The rest only gets in your way." Ironic how advice she received from Wyatt's mother was helping her move forward after the breakup.

Opening a winery required a village. Without asking for help, Lark's family and friends stepped into high gear. Bianca picked up Jamie and Charlie from school when afternoon meetings interfered.

Frank helped Levi with the tanks and facilitated the electrical upgrades essential to power the grape-crushing and bottling systems. Harlan pitched in from Idaho, coaching Lark on websites and social media. Millie removed one of Lark's biggest obstacles when she officially abandoned her dream of sending Lark to work in an Ann Taylor suit and became Lark's biggest cheerleader.

Walter Cronkite joined the team, too. That irrepressible, snarling rat-dog developed a gentleman's spirit, accompanying Lark to the unfinished winery. Like Harry Potter and his elfin friend, Dobby, they were kindred spirits. When they ran together, his squat legs compelled Lark to take a slower pace and abbreviate her routes—he tuckered out after a mile or two—but she didn't mind. Starting the new business while raising two boys left little time for much else.

"Two cups of whole milk," Millie narrated her dinner preparation, squinting at the cookbook. "A teaspoon of paprika—"

"What are you making?" Lark asked.

"Egg noodle casserole. What are you wearing to your dad's open house tomorrow night?" Millie opened a cabinet.

"I'm not going."

"I arranged for Stacia Campbell to babysit," Millie said.

"No need. I'll be right here, at home, with them."

"They'll be in good hands. Stacia's a first-year teacher, fresh out of college."

"I'll pass."

"You'll break your father's heart. He has a surprise for you."

"Not interested in running into—"

"Where are you going tomorrow, Mom?" Jamie walked into the kitchen.

"Nowhere," Lark said.

"Doubt he'll be there," Millie said.

"Nowhere, Jamie," Lark reaffirmed.

"Lark, honey, your . . ."

"Mom."

". . . father's former colleague is unlikely to attend. They assigned another engineer in *that colleague's* place, although your dad's not too happy with the replacement. It's for the best, I suppose. Do you remember coming to your Dad's holiday parties when you were little?" Her voice became nostalgic. "You'd get all fancy in your Christmas dress and pretend to be the hostess, helping people with their coats and—"

"I was ten." Lark's nose crinkled.

"You were older than ten. Anyhow, you won't need to take coats, but I could use your help. And it would make your dad a happy man." Millie's eyes glistened with hope.

"He's already a happy man, but fine. I'll go."

Wyatt

IF NOT FOR THE TABLETOP Christmas tree Kelli and Zadie brought to his house, Wyatt wouldn't have even thought about the holidays. Each evening, over a bland TV dinner and a beer, with mindless television to counterbalance the silence, he pondered his dismal future. *Have I ever felt so broken or insecure?* Alone with his thoughts, he faced a certainty: his scars, nightmares, and baggage were too much for any woman.

But I don't want any *woman. I want Lark.*

FOUDRE UNIFIE WRAPPED UP A fresh batch of surprises for employees in time for the holidays—they called it Workforce Restructuring.

After Wyatt's photo shoot swerved into the ditch, he expected to be included in the first wave of layoffs in mid-December. He was spared—but as he'd learned in the Army, there's never just one land mine out there.

The week before Christmas, Barbara popped into his office. "Song Chu's on line one."

He could almost smell trouble burning from the flashing red light on his phone.

Might as well get it over with.

"Wyatt, it's Song. How are you?"

"I'm alright."

"Good news," she said with cheer.

We're sending you on your way with a Christmas ham and a severance check?

"The team selected you for a promotion. Operations Manager."

"What about Phil?"

"Phil's staying in Fredericksburg. We're offering you a position in our Lecompton, Kansas market."

"Another market?"

"It's about an hour west of Kansas City—the best of the city and the country."

Doubt you've ever crossed the Kansas state line, much less stepped foot in Lecompton.

Song described the goals, staffing module, and challenges of the Lecompton office, but her words short-circuited Wyatt's mind.

"Not sure Kansas is in my game plan," he said. "What if I decide to stay here in Fredericksburg?"

"That would be tricky."

"Please tell me you're not closing our office." Anxiety consumed every nerve in his body.

"Fredericksburg will remain open, but the ECC identified staffing redundancies."

"Pardon?"

"We're eliminating your position."

"Son of a—"

"Of necessity, the headcount must drop."

"Headcount? You mean layoffs?"

"We'll offer transfers and incentives."

"So, it's Kansas or the highway?"

"If you don't accept the promotion, we'll have a different conversation."

"How soon does this thing in Kansas go down?"

"As quickly as we can get you there. We'll provide a moving stipend for your family's relocation expenses."

"Don't have a wife or kids."

"Perfect. That should simplify the process."

Perfect.

"What about the holidays? I planned to spend them around here with my family."

"I suppose we can arrange for you to remain at the Fredericksburg site, at least part of the time, until after the new year."

The words buzzed in his ears; he clutched his chest.

"Are you still there?" Song asked.

"Sorry. It's a lot to digest." His life in Fredericksburg was already blurring and fading like a heat mirage.

"I'll email you the specifics. You'll need to acknowledge your acceptance electronically within seventy-two hours. If you go in another direction, email me."

As soon as Song ended the call, Wyatt picked up his cell phone and dialed Kelli's number. She took the news with more enthusiasm than he had. "Congratulations!"

"Thanks, but I like it here."

"Come on, Wyatt. After the crash with Lark, you could use a fresh start." From the sounds of it, Kelli had already packed his bags.

Wyatt ended the call when Barbara appeared.

"Just wanted to remind you about the CO-OP holiday party tomorrow night," she said. "RSVP'd to Frank Lovejoy and added the event to your Outlook calendar. You'll receive an alert to remind you thirty minutes prior. It's a come-and-go after work."

"Thanks, Barbara."

I'd thank her more if she could get me excused from the festivities altogether.

Thirty-six

Lark

A day later, the ladies entered the tasting room at Keenan Flannery Vineyards, Millie wearing a festive sweater and Lark in a winter white shift dress with a black Peter Pan collar. She had to admit, dressing up had given her an unexpected lift.

Guests trickled in for their obligatory pit stops on their way home from work. Bartenders juddered martini shakers and opened enough wine to serve at a Catholic wedding. Bow tie–wearing servers balanced trays filled with smoked salmon canapes and stuffed mushrooms.

Millie and Frank greeted guests, reintroducing Lark to people she hadn't seen since she was a teen.

While she made small talk, her mind remained on her boys. Despite her mother's endorsement, leaving them with a sitter she didn't know had threaded a tense energy through her body.

Barely an hour passed before she excused herself to call Stacia from the bathroom.

As Millie predicted, Stacia appeared to be providing exceptional care. Jamie and Charlie'd had healthy appetites at dinner and enjoyed a good scrub-a-dub-dub. If Lark hadn't called, Jamie told her, Stacia would still be reading *The Giving Tree* to them.

Lark couldn't complain. Her boys were happy and healthy. She was all dressed up. Why shouldn't she go back out there and enjoy the party?

She stepped into the hall just as the men's room squeaked open. She turned toward the noise.

"Lark?" Wyatt's mouth twisted into a confused smile, like he'd just seen a friendly ghost.

His voice poured over her skin, melting her composure.

"How are you?" he asked.

"Doing well. You?" She tried out a smile but it wouldn't stick.

"Good. Jamie and Charlie?"

"They're excited about Christmas." She chuckled, forgetting herself for a moment. "You should see Charlie—"

"I'd love to." His gaze locked on her face.

"To what?"

"To see Charlie." His expression teemed with hope. "Jamie, too."

Her smile flatlined. "No. Not a good idea."

"Oh." He stuck a hand in his pocket. "Are you all better now? Since you were sick?"

You mean, heartbroken?

"Oh, yeah," she said dismissively. "All better now."

"Lark, about what happened—"

"I'm helping Mom. Need to get back in there."

"Can I take you to lunch?"

"Thanks, but no. Mom's waiting on me." She edged away.

Wyatt's features crumpled and his gaze fell. "Have a good holiday. Please pass that along to Jamie and Charlie, too."

"Take care." Lark fled.

"There you are," Millie said when she spotted her, and she pulled her to the middle of the tasting room. "Dad brought a surprise for you." They stopped behind a man wearing dark jeans and a plaid oxford shirt. Millie gave the man's shoulder a soft tap, and he turned around.

Lark would recognize that knife-edge chin and crooked smile anywhere. "Harlan? What? How? You're here!"

He looked taller than she remembered, but his muscular arms and a lean figure were the same as always. He wore his wavy dark hair tightly shorn. A patch of gray framed his forehead. He laughed, and his clear blue eyes nearly disappeared.

"For two weeks, I'm all yours." He hugged her with such force, she rose from the ground. "Put me to work wherever you need me."

Wyatt

LARK WALKED AWAY, LEAVING WYATT to mull over their all-too-brief conversation. Her face had changed—her eyes twinkled brighter and her face was fuller than he remembered. When she walked away, she left him greedy for more time with her.

Since their break up, he'd spent countless hours rehearsing what he'd say when he got the chance. Now that opportunity had appeared and those words had vanished into the ether.

His heart kicked with hope and he gathered his thoughts. *Wish her a Merry Christmas. If . . . when . . . she warms up, get down to brass tacks.*

He pulled on a confident expression, marched around the corner . . . and found Lark in the middle of the tasting room with her arms fastened around a man's waist. The man lifted her and she threw back her head, curls dancing. That sparkle in her eyes said it all—she was in love.

All conversational bravery flushed itself from Wyatt's body.

The man said something to Lark and they laughed together. Their joy shot past the crowd and took aim at Wyatt, scoring his chest more deeply than any shrapnel ever had.

Clinging to Lark only made him a bigger fool. *Walk away. Take that job. Never look back.*

WITHIN THE HOUR, WYATT HAD emailed his acceptance to Song Chu. Much as it pained him, he tried to wrap his head around a fresh start, and he began planning his new life in the heartland. Soon, he learned that Lecompton had been the birthplace of the Civil War and was home to the largest indoor display of Christmas trees in the Midwest.

With a month-to-month lease, his life was as portable as a suitcase; there was nothing in Fredericksburg to chain him down.

A FEW WEEKS LATER, LECOMPTON'S Chamber of Commerce hosted a Mexican pile-on and margarita happy hour to welcome Wyatt to the area. Wyatt made a haul with company swag—a T-shirt from an insurance agent, pens galore, a parasol from Lecompton's Fancy Nail Day Spa, and four tickets to the pride of Lecompton—the largest indoor Christmas tree display in the United States.

At his side was Colleen, a blonder, feistier version of Barbara. She sewed her own clothes and delivered homemade sweets to the office every Monday morning.

The Lecompton community was friendly enough. Locals provided most of the entertainment—a bunch of nice people who worked hard and played harder when they gathered at their favorite 7th Street watering hole. On Saturday nights, downtown bars featured live music and entertaining people watching.

On that first Sunday after the holiday break, Wyatt dialed Kelli, eager to hear about Zadie's return to school. He hoped she might mention Jamie.

"What's shakin', baby bacon?" he asked when Kelli put Zadie on.

"Nuthin," Zadie said.

"How was your first week back?"

Zadie's face crumpled. "Uncle Wyatt, we lost Goober. He went to sleep in his cage and didn't wake up. It was so, so, so sad."

"Zadie, say that again."

"Listen." Zadie flattened her palms and closed her eyes, blowing out a dramatic breath. "This is important."

"I'm listening, Zade."

"We lost Goober, our ham-a-ster."

"Not that. The other part."

"It was so, so, so sad?"

"Zade? You said your S-words so well. Way to go!"

"Yeah, Mrs. Rhodes says two more weeks and I'm done with speech class."

"Awesome, Zade!"

"My daddy's home," she screamed. "Gotta go, Uncle Wyatt!" She darted away, leaving Wyatt to stare at an empty chair.

Kelli's ponytail swung into sight. "You still on?"

"Rest in peace, Goober," Wyatt said. "Congrats on speech therapy."

"She's worked so hard. How's Kansas?"

"So far, it's good. Good and cold. So damn cold."

"Have fun with that."

"People are great, though. Last week, the engineers brought all these contractors together at a barbecue joint to introduce me, and another guy treated me to beer and hot wings Friday night. Oh, and good news. I'm already moving out of the Super-8. Colleen found a duplex for me to rent."

"Yay, Colleen. What's it like?"

"Not on a tree-lined street, but it'll do."

"How long do you think they'll keep you in Kansas?"

"The way those bozos make changes? They'll probably transfer me to Timbuktu about the time I hang pictures on the wall."

"When you coming to visit?"

"Soon. Gotta get back to Fredericksburg to pack up what's left of my house for good."

For good.

"What's with that sad face?" Kelli said. "Be happy. You get a fresh start."

IN LATE JANUARY, WYATT RETURNED to Fredericksburg to pack up his place. There wasn't much to pack, which made cleaning up a snap. He'd made plans to meet Kelli for quick bite before he got on the road, so he sat on the front stoop and caught up on pre-game hype over the upcoming Super Bowl on his smartphone.

By late afternoon, though, all that sitting around started getting to him, so he climbed into his truck and explored Fredericksburg for old time's sake. He stopped at the Mini Mart for an iced tea and a bag of beef jerky before taking the main road to the edge of town.

The limestone tower in front of Hartmann-Haas Cellars sported a new sign with interlaced L's that announced LL CELLARS.

"*LL*? What the . . ." His mind roiled.

A few seconds later, the picture came into focus.

Lark and Levi. I never should've bought that story she fed me about him.

Thirty-seven

Lark

......

Having transitioned from resident handy woman at Hartmann-Haas to the owner and operator of a half-built winery, Lark discovered it would be a long while before she'd create wine.

She filled her days procuring equipment, licenses, and permits. When school resumed in January, Jamie and Charlie introduced the pandemonium of packing lunches, field trips, homework, special theme days, and birthday parties. Lark's single mom routine was anything but, as the family prepared for more changes.

A contractor began improvements on the house at the winery—adding a bathroom between the boys' rooms, repairing damage made during the last occupants' hurried departure, and clearing the lumber framing intended for Elke's addition. When the work was complete, Lark and the children would move from Frank and Millie's, and Double L Cellars would become Home Sweet Home.

Until she created her own wine, Lark planned to maximize her resources to generate revenue, renting the lion's share of the vineyard to other winemakers.

With the successful installation of systems in the mechanical barn, she copied a model used by mid-size wineries in California where winemakers outsourced the crushing and bottling processes in order to take advantage of state-of-the-art equipment. This revenue would fund Levi's position and present Lark with experience as she created her own label.

Her first taker was Natasha Otis.

Lark and Levi traveled a half-hour south to Comfort to sign the papers. To celebrate their collaboration, Natasha put out a spread of smoked brisket, potato salad, and green beans and opened a bottle of N'Otis's Chenin Blanc to go with a peach pie Lark had brought.

Resident gentleman and designated driver Levi opted for iced tea—and as luck would have it, he required every ounce of that sober concentration to navigate his truck through the torrential downpour that struck on their way home that afternoon.

Eventually, the rain abated to a drizzle, making conversation seem safe again.

"How's it going over there?" Levi asked.

"I should've said this earlier . . ." Lark looked at him. "You've been a good friend to me. With all my emotions flying around, it can't have been easy."

"What can I say? We've got a winery to finish. Talented painters are hard to find." He laughed.

"I'm thinking we should probably hire a professional one to fix my work."

Levi just smiled and kept his eyes on the road.

"Man, it seems like decades have passed since that day you hired me, but I haven't even been in Fredericksburg a year yet. Never thought I'd fall for someone so quickly." She shrugged. "Never thought it would blow up in my face, either."

"That last part surprised us all. When I saw you and Wyatt making those turkeys at the kids' Thanksgiving lunch, you looked happy. Guess things aren't always how they appear."

"All along, I guess I knew he wasn't serious. My dad tried to tell me. He's so young—in a different place. He doesn't want an old lady like me."

"Gave him too much credit. He was a fool."

"Both of us were. So, when are you gonna get Travis to move?"

"Nice subject change." He tossed a glance at her before focusing back to the road. The rain picked up again, and he adjusted the wipers' speed. "We're figuring it out. He needs a job, and I need to figure out how to make it work with Mel's parents." He squinted through the windshield. "The things you do for love."

"Oh, boy, are you singing my song, mister—the things we do for love."

No matter how the wipers tussled with the blinding rainstorm, the windshield remained murky as wax paper.

"The defoggers can't keep up." Levi glanced down and twisted a knob on the dash.

Lark peered forward at a brown blur in the intersection.

The truck shot sideways, and Levi gripped the wheel hard. "Haaang on!" he yelled.

Their vehicle fishtailed to the right. Then, in a microsecond pause, stillness folded around them, and Jamie and Charlie's faces flashed in Lark's mind. Her heart battered her chest and she inhaled sharply.

There was a *crash* along the truck's bed and Levi stomped on the brake pedal.

Lark dug her fingernails into the leather armrest of the passenger door. Her purse flew up and sprayed the cab with its contents. The windows cracked and folded like paper as airbags exploded from every angle.

They swayed to the right. The wheels juddered at the edge of the lane and the truck rolled. A guardrail stake hissed as it pierced the truck's roof and speared the center console, narrowly missing both occupants. Lark squeezed her eyes shut.

And then everything stopped.

She opened her eyes to Levi, held in place by his seatbelt and hanging upside down like a spider.

"You okay?" he asked, looking past the ten-inch piece of dark lumber anchoring the truck in place.

"I think so." Lark coughed on the sour airbag dust and her hand moved to a spot near her collarbone.

"Your head's bleeding." Levi pointed an unfocused hand,

She touched her head and drew back trembling, bloody fingertips. "Bad?"

"Don't think so. But don't try to move, just in case."

"We're okay." She glanced at the jumbled pickup. "We're okay." Subtle elation lined her words. "Where are we?"

"Maybe ten miles from home. Looked like a water buffalo."

"Say what?" she asked.

"Guys keep big game on their hunting ranches. Sometimes they get out." Levi unsnapped a pocket on his vest. His cell phone dropped into his hand, and he called 911.

Lark's mind returned to that day in Houston when she and Taffy Teagan met to discuss selling her house but ended up commiserating about widowhood, and Taffy mentioned that TED Talk about the people in Indonesia who grieved by living among their dead. When the time was right to say good-bye, Lark remembered now, mourners held a lavish funeral and sacrificed a water buffalo that carried their loved one to the afterlife.

Beneath the shadow of the airbags, wailing sirens drowned out thoughts of the afterlife. Soon, voices surrounded the truck.

"Who's there?" Levi called.

"EMS," a man said.

"Door's stuck," a woman said. "Folks, we're working on getting you out of there."

"Let's get the tool and pop this door," a man said.

"Hang tight," the woman said through the mangled door.

"Hang tight?" Lark repeated with a snicker. "What else would we do?"

"Don't move," a responder instructed.

"Again, where am I going?" she said.

A firefighter crawled through the back window. "Cover up against the glass and metal." He passed each of them a blanket. "I'm Terry." He explained what was happening outside the vehicle in the simplest terms possible, maintaining a composure that was unbelievably placid. Lark appreciated that; they'd had enough excitement for one day.

Terry placed plastic cervical collars on Lark and Levi while muted voices stirred outside the motionless truck.

Finally, the passenger door bent inward slightly and peeled away like the lid from a can of beans, and EMTs transferred Lark to a backboard and inched her away from the wreckage.

"I feel fine," Lark argued while a gurney rolled her toward an ambulance.

"Check that cut on her head," a man said.

"I'm all over it," the woman replied.

Lark glanced at Levi's truck—an unidentifiable heap of metal resting in a road covered in broken glass. Their survival was nothing short of a damned miracle.

The gurney rocked as its wheeled legs folded into the back of the ambulance. Beneath the glaring LED lights, a plump EMT with graying mouse-brown hair and kind, dark eyes squatted beside Lark. "I'm Sonia." She asked several questions and checked Lark's head.

"I'm fine." *I'd be finer without all this plastic around my face.*

"Until the doc says it's okay, we have to leave it on."

"Wait. Where's Levi? The guy who was with me?"

"They're taking him in a separate ambulance," Sonia said while she cleaned the cut on Lark's head.

"Did they find my phone?" she asked. "It was in my . . . purse." *My flying purse.*

A minute later, a patrolman passed Lark's phone and wallet into the ambulance and snapped the back door shut.

Once Sonia was satisfied with Lark's condition, she agreed to dial Frank's number and passed the phone to Lark.

"Yel-lo." Frank's voice sprang from the phone's tinny speaker.

"Dad? Don't freak out when I tell you this."

"I don't freak out."

"I'm calling from an ambulance."

A *bloop-bloop*, followed by an extended whine, announced the ambulance's movement.

"What?" Frank asked.

"I'm fine. It's a precaution. I cut my head, so they're checking me out—a precaution."

"You told me that already. What happened?"

"We got caught in the storm, and I guess an animal got loose from one of those big game ranches. The truck rolled. We landed on the guardrail, and they cut us out with the—"

"Jaws of life? Jesus, kid."

"It sounds bad, but I promise I'm fine."

"Thank God. What about Levi?"

"He was okay when I saw him. They said he's in another ambulance."

"Where are they taking you?" Frank's voice trembled.

"Where are you taking me?" Lark asked.

"Hill Country Memorial in Fredericksburg."

"Dad, we're going to Hill Country."

"Meet you there. Love you, kid."

❦

AT THE HOSPITAL, A PUTRID amalgam of humidity, antiseptics, and medicines hit Lark's senses, providing visceral reminders of the ALS clinic and the Houston hospital she'd hoped to forget.

EMTs rolled her past the nurses' station and into a cubicle, where a team of clinicians exchanged information about her vital signs.

"Ms. Mead, I'm Dr. Bennett. I'll be taking care of you." The doctor's skin was fresh-from-vacation dark and he wore pale blue scrubs with PROPERTY OF GILLESPIE HOSPITAL DISTRICT stitched on the pocket. "Are you in pain?"

"My back's sore like I stretched too much."

"You've got a good cut there." He pointed at her head. "Any wooziness or nausea?" He shot a flashlight into her eyes, touched her legs, and palpated her abdomen.

"My stomach's shaky, but that's nothing new—I recently started a business."

He nodded. "Stress can do it."

"Can I take this off?" Lark gestured to the plastic collar around her neck.

"Not yet. Hang tight until your lab work comes back. Then we'll send you for x-rays."

"Can I just get the x-rays first?"

"For a woman your age, we have to confirm you're not pregnant. Shouldn't be much longer."

Just after he made his exit, the curtain squealed open and a woman in checker-print scrubs said, "Ms. Mead, your father's here."

"Please let him in," Lark said.

Frank stepped past the woman. "Kid, I can't let you out of my sight for two seconds."

Wyatt

LOOKING TO KILL TIME, WYATT stopped in at the TXEnergy office. Recent layoffs had annihilated morale, as evidenced by the wringing of hands and muted voices.

Barbara's face brightened when he walked through the doors. She quizzed him about the ins and outs of the Lecompton branch until their conversation ran out of steam, at which point he excused himself to look over his old office—which, Barbara informed him, had been sitting empty since his move.

He pulled open a desk drawer, and a crayon drawing Zadie had made for him slid forward. He folded it and slid it into his pocket.

The Kansas office could use some color.

He glanced at his phone, confirming a later-than-planned start to his drive back to Kansas—no thanks to Kelli. He dialed her number.

"Are you still at the hospital?"

"Believe me, it's not for lack of trying. My day's going to hell. I was about to give my report." She gave an exasperated huff. "An emergency came in. I'll call you when I can clock out."

"Saying good-bye to the folks at the office. Keep me posted."

"Will do." Kelli ended the call.

"What's the deal, man? Can't break loose?" Brandon, a coworker with a year of seniority on Wyatt, showed up in the doorway. Brandon would stay on in a reduced capacity, and Wyatt didn't begrudge him the honor, considering a wife and kid were in the mix.

"About to take off," Wyatt said.

"Man, you missed all the excitement with Frank Lovejoy." Brandon's comment sent adrenaline pulsing through Wyatt's body. "He and Philip were back there looking over Phase 2 of the Castell project. Then he gets a call that his daughter was in a car accident. Should've seen the old guy bust a move. Didn't you go out with her?"

Wyatt's stomach dropped. "Yeah. Is she okay?"

Brandon shrugged. "They had her in an ambulance." His ringer chimed and he rushed a handshake. "Gotta take this call. Good luck in Kansas."

But Wyatt's mind was elsewhere.

Thirty-eight

Lark

....

Frank's forehead furrowed with worry; Lark thought of his heart and quickly said, "Dad? Are you okay?"

"Fine," he said, and stepped aside to make room for a nurse.

The woman peeled back the gauze over Lark's forehead. "The doctor might put some skin glue over it, but it doesn't look like you'll need stitches." She pulled out a plastic tray and ran a finger over the inside of Lark's arm. "I'm going to draw your blood." She dabbed Lark's arm with an alcohol wipe. "Tiny stick. There. Just relax."

The stick was quick, and Lark stared at her father while the nurse exchanged empty tubes for filled ones.

"All done," the woman said, and she disappeared from the room with the tubes in hand.

"Left my meeting when I heard you were in an ambulance," Frank said. "Your mom's on her way."

"Tell her not to rush. Doctor said it's all routine." Lark shifted her shoulders, trying to get comfortable. The thin mattress, vision-obscuring neck brace, and crunchy pillow didn't make it easy.

When Millie arrived, she quizzed the nurses on every detail, every monitor, and every test.

The curtain drew open and Levi appeared. Two plastic bracelets remained on his wrist—the orange one branding him as a "FALL RISK" caught Lark's eye.

"Fall risk?" she asked.

"You're wearing one too." He nodded toward her hand.

She lifted her arm. "Huh. How'd you get sprung so fast?"

"X-ray and bloodwork's normal." He gave a thumbs up.

"Good afternoon." Dr. Bennett returned and gave a courteous nod to Lark's entourage. Behind him, a nurse yanked the curtain closed—not just any nurse but Wyatt's sister, in all her pregnant glory. Lark had done a good job of avoiding her since the breakup, but there would be no such luck today.

"Hey Lark," Kelli said.

The doctor cleared his throat and tipped his head toward the curtain.

Kelli must have received his message, because she looked at everyone else in the room and said, "Might be a good time for y'all to get some air."

"They can stay," Lark said.

Kelli leaned over Lark and whispered, "You won't want an audience for this."

Lark gave her a resigned expression and Kelli ushered everyone out before stepping back inside the curtain.

"We got preliminary lab results and canceled your CT scan," the doctor said.

"Why?"

"As I mentioned earlier, we won't expose a woman of child-bearing age to radiation—"

"It's not an issue." She barked out a laugh.

"Your test was positive." Dr. Bennett's tone matched his no-nonsense demeanor.

Lark shot a look at Kelli. "Not funny." She tried to shake her head but that plastic collar limited her range of motion. "I haven't had a period in . . . I don't know how long it's been since they stopped. See, I'm a runner—"

"Your hCG fell within the higher limits." Dr. Bennett continued, "You're pregnant."

"Sorry, friend." Kelli offered a sideways smile.

Some friend.

"But I drank wine today."

"A glass or two of wine this early shouldn't affect the baby. We'll do a sonogram. Your age makes this a geriatric pregnancy, so talk to your OB about added testing."

Did he just call me geriatric?

"Dr. Bennett, Julie's waiting for you in room six if you want to let me take this?" Kelli pointed to Lark.

"I'll be back to check on you after the sonogram." He slipped out of the room.

"Lark, just so you know, I won't share your business with my brother."

"I would hope not. Assume you already know, I don't see him anymore, Kelli."

"Especially, now that he's living in Kansas."

Lark's eyes widened in surprise. "What's in Kansas?"

"FU transferred him."

"Dang. That must be hard on you and your family."

"We'll miss him, but it's for the best. Not sure how he'd take seeing you having a kid with Mr. Handsome back there."

"Levi and I are—"

"None of my business." Kelli waved her hands like she didn't want to hear another word.

"Kelli, we're *friends*."

"Told you, it's none of my business." She whacked the gel sanitizer pump on the wall like it had insulted her.

"Kelli, wait."

"Yeah?"

"Please wish them the best in Kansas."

"Them?" Kelli looked at her like she had three heads.

"He and Ashlen?"

"Ashlen's toast."

"Already?"

"Yeah. But, hey, she came around long enough to give you an excuse to break it off with him."

"Is that the story he told you?"

Kelli flashed her freshly sanitized hands.

"Right, none of your business. He probably didn't tell you because he knows you'd give him hell for getting back with her, but I saw them together. I saw her at his house, and I heard enough to know one of us didn't belong there."

Kelli's lip bent upward. "Wanted to shake that knucklehead for letting her come over. Told him to throw her crap away, but he never listens to me." She ran a hand over her burgeoning belly. "Is what it is, right? Anyway, someone will be by to take you to radiology. They'll put a lead apron over your abdomen to protect the baby."

The baby? Jesus, take the wheel.

Wyatt

HIS STOMACH PLUNGED TO THE ground and he visualized an unconscious Lark—her beautiful mouth connected to a ventilator, her sun-kissed skin obscured behind thick bandages. He had to tell her how he felt before it was too late.

He climbed into his truck and gunned the motor—pulse drumming, desperation ratcheting around his chest. Without giving it much thought, his truck landed at the hospital. He yanked the handicapped placard out of his glove compartment and threaded it over the rearview mirror.

Inside, he followed the signs directing him to the emergency room and knocked on the glass partition.

"Can I help you?" a man in scrubs asked.

"Lark Mead? Came in by ambulance," Wyatt managed between raspy breaths.

"Are you a relative?" the man asked.

"A friend. A close friend. I need to see her."

"Family only."

"Is Kelli Isbell here? She's a nurse."

"Who's asking?"

"Wyatt Gifford."

"Have a seat. We'll tell her you're here." He rolled his metal desk chair out of sight, and rolled back into view a moment later. "Kelli's not available. Can I help you with something?"

"She's my sister."

"Hang on."

Whooshing metal doors opened and Kelli appeared. "What are you doing here?"

"Lark got into an accident. She's here, somewhere. Can you find out about her?"

"Can't ask me about my patients, dumbass," she hissed.

"For Christ's sake, I need to know if she's okay."

Yanking him by his elbow, Kelli dragged him down a hall. "Bumped and bruised, but she'll live."

"Can I see her?"

"Are you trying to get me fired?"

"No, but—"

"Dammit," she mumbled under her breath. "Wait in there." She gestured to the waiting room. "I'll be off the clock in a few minutes."

Like it or not, Wyatt did as he was told. Across the room, he spotted Bianca wringing her hands and moved to sit beside her. "Hey. What have you heard?" he asked.

"They used the jaws of life to cut them from the truck." Bianca blurted.

"Them?"

"Lark? And Levi Gallaher?" she said.

"Together?"

"Yeah. They were at a winery in Comfort."

Wyatt's jaw tightened.

"Don't *even* go there." Her dark eyes drilled through him. "You don't have the right to say boo about where she goes."

"I'm worried about her. The hospital blew me off—I'm not anyone to her." He released a long sigh.

"That's on you for wasting her love like a popsicle on a hot day."

Wyatt's head snapped up.

"Don't look lost, soldier boy. 'Ashlen' ring a bell?"

"I haven't seen Ashlen since she came for her stuff."

"Her stuff?" Bianca faked a laugh. "You know damn skippy what you did."

"I didn't do . . ." Wyatt modulated his voice. "*That* . . . with Ashlen."

"Broke my friend's heart right in two." Bianca crossed her arms over her chest.

"Must've healed real fast if she was at a winery with Levi today." Wyatt flushed red. "I believed her when she said they were only friends—what a fool I was."

Bianca gestured to the door, where Lark's parents had just appeared. Not far behind, Levi Gallaher followed.

"Millie," Bianca said, rushing to her side.

Fury kindled in Wyatt's chest. He gulped back a swallow and pulled himself out of his chair. "What the hell did you do to her, Levi?"

Levi narrowed his eyes. "We had an accident."

"Didn't anybody ever tell you what happens when you drink and drive? Jesus, why aren't you in handcuffs?" Breath rushed from his mouth like air escaping a punctured tire.

"Hold up." Frank interrupted. "Levi wasn't drunk. It was work."

"Work? This guy's after a lot more than you think, Frank. If you want to protect her from anybody, it should be him."

Levi jerked away and challenged Wyatt with a glower.

"Piece of shit." Electric current shot through Wyatt's arm, and he gripped Levi's plaid shirt. "Bad enough for you to tell her you were gay. You could've killed her."

"Oh, my stars." Bianca blinked in surprise.

"How dare you? Drink and put her in your car? I'm gonna . . ." Wyatt's throat clamped shut, and he balled his right hand into a fist.

"Hit me if it makes you feel better," Levi said.

"Oh, you bet I will." Wyatt smashed his fist against Levi's orbital bone, and pain shot from his knuckles up to his shoulder.

Levi touched his forehead and pulled back a bloody fingertip, but his only response was to straighten his back and take a confident step toward his challenger. "No secret she caught you screwing around with your ex. You threw her away."

"Lucky for her, you were right there when it happened, all too ready to sweep her off her feet."

Levi's gaze didn't move. "Right. Keep telling yourself that if it makes you feel less guilty."

"Levi?" A man appeared behind him. "I got here as soon as I could."

Frustration and comfort swirled on Levi's face. "You shouldn't have come, Travis."

Travis squinted at the other men. "What's going on?"

"Nothing. We're good. Right?" Levi asked.

A spark of understanding flickered between them, and Wyatt's hands slackened. "I didn't . . ." Wyatt's gaze shifted to Millie, and they locked eyes. "I swear, Millie. I didn't."

"You love her?" Levi's question crossed a hard line, and Wyatt's expression contorted with frustration.

Before Wyatt could make sense of his question, Levi rammed both hands into Wyatt's shoulders. "Do you love her?"

"Yeah, I love her." Wyatt exhaled a quavering, angry breath.

"Then tell her," Levi commanded. "She's spent months beating herself up." He pointed to the metal doors. "Drag your ass back there and tell her."

An expectant stillness filled the waiting room, and Wyatt detected a string of nods between Bianca, Millie, and Frank.

His gaze locked on Millie. "How?"

She angled toward Wyatt and took his arm. "Levi's right. If you love her, you *must* tell her."

He thought of the holiday party, when she had her paws on some other guy. "Millie, I don't know if she feels the same."

"I think you do." She winked. "Let's go tell her." Millie waved at the nurse in the glass office and the doors hissed open.

Like a pirate walking the plank, Wyatt took wary steps forward. The tempo of his heartbeat threatened to blow his eardrums when they arrived outside Lark's room.

"Ready?" Millie asked.

With his nod, Millie retracted the curtain. Lark was gone.

"She was here a few minutes ago," Millie said.

"Wyatt." Kelli jumped into the room and shook a finger at him. "You're not supposed to be in here."

"He's with me," Millie said. "Where's Lark?"

"Radiology."

"We'll wait," Millie said.

"I hope you know what you're doing." Kelli gave a dismissive shrug and left the room.

"It'll be okay, son." Millie spoke in her patient teacher voice. "Just tell her the truth." She said it like she wanted him to be with Lark again.

"Here we are," a voice outside the curtain said, and the transporter rolled Lark into the vacant space and kicked the lock on the gurney's wheels before walking out.

"Welcome back," a nurse said as she reattached the cords tracking Lark's blood pressure and heart rate.

Wyatt had never seen such a beautiful image.

Thirty-nine

Lark

A fter learning she was pregnant, Lark wasn't surprised when she thought she saw Wyatt in her room. She blinked to shuffle the pixels, but he remained in the picture.

"Mom," she whispered. "What's he doing here?"

Millie bent to face her. "Honey, he needs to talk to you."

"No."

"It's important. Give him a minute, and then he'll be on his way."

"Mom?"

Millie parted the curtains and pulled them closed behind her as she left.

"Mom?"

Wyatt stepped toward Lark. "How are you?"

"I've had better days." She set her mouth in a straight line. "You?"

"Had better days myself." He gripped the cold side rail of her bed. "Sorry about the accident."

"I'll be alright." Lark closed her eyes.

Another nurse ripped the curtain open. "Need anything, Ms. Mead?"

"No thanks." She waited for the nurse to leave before saying, "Kelli said you moved to Kansas."

"Got transferred. A real promotion this time."

"Congratulations." Her smile landed a second too late.

He pointed to the plastic cervical collar around her neck. "Pretty . . . neck-whatever-that-is." His mouth turned up on one side, and she had to look away.

"All I need is a Bedazzler and bring on the bling."

"Before I leave town, I have to explain what happened."

"You don't."

"Please, hear me out."

Her eyes fell upon his face. "Wyatt, we had fun together."

Like an emotional Geiger counter, the overhead monitor sounded. *Blip, blip, blip.* The machine followed her heartbeats, tattling on her like a damned narc. The *blips* sped to a reckless *blip, blip, blip, blip, blip, blip.*

A nurse appeared. "Dizzy?"

"Nope."

"Your pulse is all over the place."

"Probably my nerves. Hospitals terrify me. My late husband passed away in a hospital."

"I'm sorry." The nurse checked the lines leading to Lark's body. "Blood pressure's spiking. I'll let the doctor know. Hit your button if you become dizzy."

"I'll keep an eye on her," Wyatt said.

The nurse gave him an unimpressed nod and walked out.

"I told Ashlen to stop by the house." Wyatt leaned over her. "But not for the reason you think."

"I'm old enough to know better." Lark swallowed down all the questions she longed to ask him, opting for, "Let's end on peaceful terms. I wish you and Ashlen a bright future."

"I'm not with her."

"Whoever. You're free to fall in love. Marry. Have babies."

"Listen, at your dad's Christmas party . . . you were with a guy?"

"Tall, dark, and handsome?" Lark jumped right to his weak spot. "That one?"

"Damn," Wyatt said.

Boom. A direct hit. Give him a little of his own medicine, Lark.

He cranked his head toward the ceiling. "You sure didn't waste time getting on with life."

"Wyatt, you saw me with my *brother*."

He sighed like he'd been holding the entire state of Texas in his lungs.

"What made you think—"

"I wasn't thinking." He ran a hand over his head. "I'm an idiot."

"Hmm."

"I saw you with . . . with your brother. You and he seemed so happy. Figured I was in the way, so I accepted the job in Kansas."

"You didn't—because of me?"

"You were moving on—or, at least it looked that way. Thought I'd best do the same."

Words swirled through Lark's mind, and she swallowed them. The sooner she got rid of him, the better.

"Ms. Mead." A nurse peeled back the curtain. "Good news."

I could use some of that right about now.

"Doctor said we can remove that C collar."

Wyatt shuffled aside, and the nurse unfastened the plastic collar.

"Awesome," Lark said. "When can I leave?"

"We'll see if we can break you out of here after your sonogram."

"They're putting you through the ringer," Wyatt said.

"You have no idea."

The nurse left and he returned to Lark's side. "Are you hurting?" he asked.

"I'm fine."

"Lark?" He touched her arm. "You know me. I never wanted Ashlen, or anybody else, since you. I only asked her over to make peace with her to make *you* happy."

"Wyatt, I want to believe you, but . . ."

He traced her skin from her elbow to the tip of her pinky.

Blip, blip, blip. The telltale monitor tracked her racing heart-beats as she spilled the words, "I heard you say you *needed* her."

Blip, blip, blip.

"I don't know if I said anything close to that, but I promise I didn't say anything to make her think I wanted to get back together with her. Heck, Lark. She's getting married. She never looked so happy when we were together. Just like she never made me feel as happy as I am with you."

Lark's stomach gurgled and she covered her mouth. "Why did you take her to your bedroom?"

"Her stuff was in my closet. Nothing happened." He put up a hand. "Okay, she kissed me on the cheek before leaving—but how you'd kiss your grandmother."

"My grandmother's dead."

He shook his head. "You didn't want to see burned bridges in the rearview mirror." His voice cracked. "That night I came over, when you told me to leave, I went over to Kelli's. She told me you were probably hurt because Ashlen came to my house."

Lark's face changed as the memory dislodged itself.

"I knew you wouldn't listen if I tried to explain."

"You're right," she said.

"But now, you know."

"I . . . I . . ."

"Yeah?" he asked.

"I'm gonna be sick."

Not a second too soon, Wyatt stretched an arm to the sink, grabbed the disposable plastic basin, and moved it under her mouth.

"There you go." He pulled her hair away from her face. "Gonna be alright."

She eyed him suspiciously. "You just watched me throw up, and you're still here?"

"Don't worry about it." He discarded the basin and wiped her mouth with a paper towel.

"Thanks."

"Feel better?" he asked.

"Kind of," she moaned.

"The timing's not great for this, but I have to tell you something."

"Am I too late?" A nurse ran into the room and removed the basin from the sink. She lingered for a yawning gap of time while Lark and Wyatt waited expectantly. "I'll be back to check on you. Hit your button if you need me sooner," she said, sliding out of the room.

"Lark, about us," Wyatt said. "I'm not ready to call us 'done.'"

"Not now. With all that's happened, and starting my new business—"

"What's the whole Double L thing?" he asked.

"The winery?"

"Yeah, is that about Levi?"

Lark gave a little laugh. "Levi's my friend, and he works for me. I named the winery after my parents. Lovejoy for Dad, of course, and Larkan is Mom's maiden name."

"Huh. I didn't know."

"Harlan inherited my grandfather's name, and I had the luxury of making my mother's alliterative child-naming dreams come true. Larkan Louise Lovejoy."

A nurse poked her head past the curtain. "Transporter's on his way."

"You poor thing. What are they doing to you now?" Wyatt said.

"Precautions."

"Knock, knock," Bianca said.

Without waiting for a response, Millie and Frank barged into the tiny room, Marx Brothers style, with Bianca right behind them.

Lark searched their faces. "Where's Levi?"

"Some guy showed up. Maybe a brother?" Bianca asked.

"Huh. Didn't know he had a brother." Lark bit her bottom lip.

"Travis?" Bianca said.

"Travis is . . . not his brother."

Bianca inched closer and flashed Lark the kind of expression cartoon characters get after they're smacked in the head with a skillet. "I have *so* many questions for you," Bianca half whispered.

"Not now," Lark said.

"They ever gonna let you get out of here?" Bianca asked.

"One more test," Lark said. "Say, could y'all give Wyatt and me a minute?"

At her daughter's request, Millie rallied the troops and cleared the room with a flourish.

Bianca's voice rose over the curtain as she left the room, "I still can't believe they hit a freaking water buffalo."

Those last two words reverberated through Lark's body like an earthquake. She closed her eyes. She'd never make sense of the ALS or James's death. It remained a sore spot between her and God. But in living each moment as fully as he could before he died, James had taught Lark how to live without him. Perhaps it was his turn to go gently into his good night.

Her eyes flew open and she gazed at the white, pebbly ceiling. "Godspeed, my love," she whispered.

"You alright?" Wyatt asked.

"Just need a minute to collect my thoughts," she said, letting peace wash over her and opening her mind to the poetic muddle that was her life.

In her efforts to appreciate Wyatt's pain, Lark had gained a new understanding of her father—not the man in the waiting room but an eighteen-year-old who got a girl pregnant and rushed into a marriage, a man who waged a war overseas and then fought a private war when he came home.

Before Wyatt, Lark had never known the pain her father carried, just as she hadn't known what a crucial role her mother had played in their family's stability. *Maybe it's time I assumed less and listened more?*

"Wyatt?" she said.

"What can I get you?" He jumped to her side.

"I want to believe you," she said.

"Listen." He put a hand to his chest. "My heart's two thumps away from smashing out of my chest and running out of here." He dropped to her side. "From the minute I saw you, I couldn't stop thinking about you. After that night in Gruene . . . well, I was ruined."

"I ruined you?"

"In the best way."

She couldn't help but laugh. When she met his eyes, everything was suddenly right in her world.

"Wyatt, we have so much to work through. My life is complicated."

"Oh, now your life's complicated?" He grinned.

"You have no idea."

He rearranged his face. "About my nightmares—I'm gonna keep seeing Dr. Fisher. If, *when* we get that far, I'll sleep in another room with a bolt on the door. You can lock me in at night."

She laughed. "You really think locking you away is the answer?"

"Whatever it takes."

"What about Kansas?"

"Kansas can't happen—not without you."

"I own a winery now," she said. "I can't leave."

"I love you." He leaned in close and dropped a kiss on her mouth, then made a face. "Pukey."

"Sorry. Get me a breath mint, and we could try that again?"

"I mean it." His voice quavered. "I can't leave you."

"What'll you do?"

He shrugged and raised a finger. "Heard about this new winery in town. Thought I'd call, see if the owner's hiring. Worked for you."

"Rumor says she's a real bitch to work for."

"I'll take my chances." He wrapped his arms around her.

"Hey, do you mind sticking around a while?" She pulled back. "Could use some company during the next test."

"Listen, I've traveled to the other side of the world, gotten blown up, and been put back together . . . all to find my way back to Texas . . . to fall for you. No way I'm leaving your side now."

The curtain glided back, and an orderly slid a wheelchair into the cubicle. "Ms. Mead, I'm here to take you to radiology. Ready?"

"Oh, yeah." Lark nodded with a satisfied grin. "I'm ready."

Epilogue

Fredericksburg, Texas
One year later

Jamie
....

Dear Dad,
Guess what? We got a new house, but it's not totally new.
It was my friend's old house.

After we moved in and got unpacked, Mom threw a party for my sixth birthday. Everybody came, even Grandpa Jim and Grandma Nadine. After the party, Grandpa Jim and I went to the park and he said he doesn't want me to forget you. He and I are gonna do stuff together—stuff you did when you were a kid, like soccer and playing with LEGOs.

One of these days, we're gonna make a ceremony and put pictures on a movie screen so everybody can see how cool you were. After the ceremony, we're gonna let your ashes fly away like birds. Grandpa Jim said we'd better wait until Charlie's old enough to help us. He's still a little kid and might not understand what it means.

Grandma Nadine said there's a lot of stuff she wanted to tell you before you died but she didn't get a chance. Mom said you can hear me from where you live in heaven, so I'm letting Grandma Nadine keep your ashes in a special jar at her house. Don't worry. She'll put 'em on a high shelf so no one knocks them over—like Charlie. Then, when she remembers the stuff she didn't get to tell you, you'll be right there to hear her.

Charlie was a baby when you left us, so I always tell him stories about you. I want him to know about all the fun stuff we did together and to know you were the best dad ever.

Mom bought a winery place where she grows grapes. I don't want to hurt her feelings, but I like the grapes we get at the grocery store better than ones she grows at the Double L. You used to say she was bossy. That's what Wyatt says, too. Every time I ask if I can do something, he says, "Ask your mom. She's the boss."

Mom and Wyatt got married. At first, I was afraid it might make you sad, but Mom told us you said she could get married if she found somebody who was good enough for Charlie and me.

Charlie and I walked next to Mom at the wedding. We wore ties and everything. It was kinda boring because we had to stand around forever while the minister made them married. The best part was the cake. Grammy got one that looked like the Double L. We got to eat as much as we wanted. People danced, and we jumped in a bouncy house, too. Everybody was happy—prob'ly because of all that cake.

Wyatt's really nice to Charlie and me. I think you can see us, even if you can't talk to us. I think you're glad that Wyatt's in our family.

Guess what? We got a new baby. She's a sister, and her name's Georgia Grace. She cries a lot, so it's noisy *at our house. We haven't had a sister before, but I think it'll be nice when she's bigger. I'm teaching Charlie how to be a good big brother like me.*

Mom said Georgia looks like Wyatt. That confused Charlie, 'cause Georgia doesn't have any shiny legs like Wyatt does. I'll explain it to him when he gets grown enough to understand.

Since we moved to Fredericksburg, Zadie's been my friend, but now that Mom and Wyatt are married, she's my cousin. It's noisy at her house, too. She got a baby brother. His name's Gifford Isbell. We call him Giff.

We miss you so, so, so much. I take care of Mom and Charlie, just like you told me to. Sometimes I let Mom take care of me, though, too, 'cause I'm still a kid.

Mom said it's okay to get sad when I miss you. She said it's okay to be glad for new people, too, like Wyatt and Georgia Grace. When I get sad, I close my eyes and remember you said, "You've got this, Jamie." Then, I'm not scared or sad anymore. I love you, Dad.
Your son, Jamie

Acknowledgments

Fifteen years ago, our oldest introduced us to Gruene, Texas. We ate lunch overlooking the Guadalupe River at The Grist Mill. Afterward, we walked next door to tour the historic dance hall. The floorboards bent beneath my feet and hinted of a story begging to be told. Years later, I revisited the gracious Hill Country communities and vintners along the Hill Country Wine Trail and Lark's story was born.

Bringing that story to the reader would've been impossible without the help of some amazing people who recognized something special in the roughest drafts. I'm deeply grateful to the Spark Press team for believing in me. Brooke Warner, Crystal Patriarche, Shannon Green, and Krissa Lagos made *Goodbye, Lark Lovejoy* come to life.

Others helped me nail down details. Colonel Patrick Seiber helped me understand a soldier's life. Thanks Pat, for your service to our country and your lifelong friendship. To the staff at the Center for the Intrepid and the Brook medical campus in San Antonio— you provide exceptional care for our desert war veterans and to the families who support them. Anthropologist Kelli Swazey helped me find a missing piece in Lark's journey in her TED Talk, "Life that doesn't end with death." Liz Krisanda, Executive Director of the ALS Association of Upstate New York, shared her experiences as an Army wife and mom and enabled me to tell Wyatt's story with authenticity. I found my elementary school classmate, Jana

Sandel-Walker at Lewis Wines along the Hill Country Wine Trail in Johnson City. Thanks, Jana for pouring the best Chenin Blanc we'd ever tasted. Cheers!

Writer friends can make all the difference in a day's work. Kristan Higgins reminded me to keep a "wicked pizzah" sense of humor. Fellow Texan, Amy Poeppel answered my endless questions. Leah DeCesare introduced me to Spark Press. Maggie and Jules made conferences *pop*! Audra, thanks for listening. Renita, we *can* do this. My RWA karaoke pals, WFWA patio writers, WTWA friends, Tall Poppy Writers, and Every Damn Day Writers reminded me I wasn't alone. Thanks to Kylee, Julie, Karen, Chelsy, Maris, Sharla, TOK, Doc Shari, Aunt Regina, Jen, and Debra for reading the earliest versions. Laura Ross edited with patience and shared a wealth of experience. Shannon Nisbet, you're my long-lost fairy godmother.

When I moved to a town where I knew no one, the Kansas Pickleball ladies made room for me. Thanks for reminding me to come out of the writing cave to play. You give me a thousand reasons to smile.

To my Summit Sisters for bracing me when I thought I'd fall. We'll always have Rick Clarke's tip from the top, "Who's your best friend?"

Thanks to our children for believing in their mom's/stepmom's dream, and to their father who pushed me to make it happen. I'm the luckiest girl in the world to have you all in my life.

To Yvonne Schmidt and Bobbie Wedgeworth, two remarkable women who inspired my love of reading and writing. You embraced a little girl who felt like "less" and showed her she could be "more." To this day, your voices remind me I can do this. Thank you.

Finally, thanks to you, the reader, for the gift of your time. I hope that you'll see a bit of yourself in these characters, enjoy a few laughs, and find inspiration in their journeys. It is my wish for each of you to discover your own brand of spectacular happiness.

About the Author

K ris Clink's relatable characters rely on humor and tenderness to navigate complicated relationships. Set in middle America, her novels are laced with romance, heartbreak, and just enough snarky humor to rock the boat. When not writing, Kris spends her time searching for an open karaoke mic and an understanding audience. Her great Dane, Sophieanne, runs the house Kris shares with her editor-in-training husband.

Author photo © Kacy Meineke

Selected Titles From SparkPress

SparkPress is an independent boutique publisher delivering high-quality, entertaining, and engaging content that enhances readers' lives, with a special focus on female-driven work. www.gosparkpress.com

That's Not a Thing: A Novel, Jacqueline Friedland. $16.95, 978-1-68463-030-1. When a recently engaged Manhattanite learns that her first great love has been diagnosed with ALS, she is faced with the impossible decision of whether a few final months with her ex might be worth risking her entire future. A fast-paced emotional journey that explores whether it's possible to be equally in love with two men at once.

Charming Falls Apart: A Novel, Angela Terry, $16.95, 978-1-68463-049-3. After losing her job and fiancé the day before her thirty-fifth birthday, people-pleaser and rule-follower Allison James decides she needs someone to give her some new life rules—and fast. But when she embarks on a self-help mission, she realizes that her old life wasn't as perfect as she thought—and that she needs to start writing her own rules.

And Now There's You: A Novel, Susan S. Etkin. $16.95, 978-1-68463-000-4. Though five years have passed since beautiful design consultant Leila Brandt's husband passed away, she's still grieving his loss. When she meets a terribly sexy and talented—if arrogant—architect, however, sparks fly, and neither of them can deny the chemistry between them.

The Sea of Japan: A Novel, Keita Nagano. $16.95, 978-1-684630-12-7. When thirty-year-old Lindsey, an English teacher from Boston who's been assigned to a tiny Japanese fishing town, is saved from drowning by a local young fisherman, she's drawn into a battle with a neighboring town that has high stakes for everyone—especially her.

Bedside Manners: A Novel, Heather Frimmer. $16.95, 978-1-943006-68-7. When Joyce Novak is diagnosed with breast cancer, she and her daughter, Marnie—a medical student who is on the cusp of both beginning a surgical internship and getting married—are forced to face Joyce's mortality together, a journey that changes both their lives in surprising and profound ways.

The Opposite of Never: A Novel, Kathy Mehuron. $16.95, 978-1-943006-50-2. Devastated by the loss of their spouses, Georgia and Kenny think that the best times of their lives are long over until they find each other; meanwhile Kenny's teenage stepdaughter, Zelda, and Georgia's friend's son, Spencer, fall in love at first sight—only to fall prey to and suffer opiate addiction together.